PENGUIN BOOKS

# FOR THE BRIDE

Becca Grischow is the author of *I'll Get Back to You* and a Chicago-based content creator, gossip, and ghostwriter for celebrity memoirs. She grew up in Geneva, Illinois, and the middle school rumors about her bisexuality were absolutely true. You can find her at your local coffee shop or sharing writing advice on TikTok and Instagram @BeeGriz.

## Praise for *For the Bride*

"*Bridesmaids* meets Emily Henry in this sparkling sapphic rom-com. Funny, sexy, and surprisingly tender, Grischow's sophomore novel sparkles with a captivating and unique voice. *For the Bride* manages a rare feat: It's a romance novel where the love story is as beautifully written and well earned as Alice's journey to self-love. I wanted to reach through the pages to hug these delightfully flawed and deserving characters."

—Alison Cochrun, author of *The Charm Offensive* and *Kiss Her Once for Me*

"*For the Bride* is an absolute master class in how to write a complex, meaningful romance. This book is a meditation on grief, a celebration of friendship, a laugh-out-loud good time, and a sparkling sapphic romance, all at once. You'll be smiling, swooning, crying, and maybe wanting to sing a show tune or two. I completely adored it."

—Bridget Morrissey, author of *That Summer Feeling*

"A razor-sharp and deeply emotional portrait of learning to love through grief, forgive through guilt, and laugh through pain—*For the Bride* is an enemies-to-lovers rom-com delight. Becca Grischow's writing is chock-full of grit and moxie and guided lovingly by sensitivity and heart. For the people who want to be better, for the people who think more bridesmaids should kiss, and for fans of romance everywhere—*For the Bride*."

—London Sperry, author of *Passion Project*

"*For the Bride* is a gritty queer firecracker by a rising force in romance. No one writes about love, friendship, and figuring out your damage like Becca Grischow. A resilient and sexy must read for 2026."

—Ella Dawson, author of *But How Are You, Really*

"Adorable and full of friction, but WOW, Grischow makes the tension worthwhile in this funny, sexy spin on enemies-to-lovers. Here comes the bride? More like here comes the book of the summer."

—Piper CJ, *New York Times* bestselling author of *The Night and Its Moon*

"*For the Bride* is a love letter to friendship with the tears still soaked into the paper. Grischow doesn't shy away from exploring the depths of all kinds of love in this beautiful novel, taking readers on an emotional and honest journey full of yearning and leaving them laughing through tears. An instant sapphic romance classic."

—Annie Mare, author of *Cosmic Love at the Multiverse Hair Salon*

## Praise for *I'll Get Back to You*

"Full of humor and tenderness, *I'll Get Back to You* inspires readers to embrace the surprises life tosses our way. A cozy, sexy romance."

—Ashley Herring Blake, author of *Delilah Green Doesn't Care*

"[A] delightful queer fake dating holiday romance."

—*Entertainment Weekly*

"Grischow's debut is as self-assured and charming as her protagonist desperately wishes she herself were . . . Grischow's take on fake dating is compulsively readable, funny, and full of heart. Readers will fall for this as fast as Murphy falls for Ellie."

—*Publishers Weekly* (starred review)

"Sweet and swift." —*Vulture*

"A festive and poignant romance about new adulthood, growing pains in friendships, and embracing your hometown. You'll be drawn in by the clever fake dating scheme, but Murphy's meaningful journey of finding herself in her early twenties is the real star. *I'll Get Back to You* is the Thanksgiving romance I've been waiting for."

—Susie Dumond, author of *Queerly Beloved*

"*I'll Get Back to You* is a completely charming sapphic romance set against a loving ode to the Midwest. From the Cubs mentions, to the anxieties about the future, to the very Illinoisan texture baked in all throughout, this book hit home for me in so many ways. I laughed just as much as I clutched my hand over my heart to swoon!"

—Bridget Morrissey, author of *That Summer Feeling*

"With compassion and heart, Grischow masterfully touches on the growing pains—emphasis on pain—and self-discovery associated with those early years of adulthood."

—Iman Hariri-Kia, author of *Female Fantasy*

ALSO BY THE AUTHOR

*I'll Get Back to You*

# For the Bride

BECCA GRISCHOW

PENGUIN BOOKS

PENGUIN BOOKS
An imprint of Penguin Random House LLC
1745 Broadway, New York, NY 10019
penguinrandomhouse.com



Set in Bell MT Pro
Designed by Cassandra Garruzzo Mueller

LIBRARY OF CONGRESS CATALOGING-IN-PUBLICATION DATA

Names: Grischow, Becca author
Title: For the bride : a novel / Becca Grischow.
Description: New York : Penguin Books, 2026.
Identifiers: LCCN 2025046740 (print) | LCCN 2025046741 (ebook) | ISBN 9780143138426 trade paperback | ISBN 9780593512487 ebook
Subjects: LCGFT: Fiction | Romance fiction | Lesbian fiction | Novels
Classification: LCC PS3607.R5688 F67 2026 (print) | LCC PS3607.R5688 (ebook)
LC record available at https://lccn.loc.gov/2025046740
LC ebook record available at https://lccn.loc.gov/2025046741

Printed in the United States of America
1st Printing

The authorized representative in the EU for product safety and compliance is Penguin Random House Ireland, Morrison Chambers, 32 Nassau Street, Dublin D02 YH68, Ireland, https://eu-contact.penguin.ie.

*For Laura and Lauren Skaar*

# For the Bride

# One

Of all the insufferable events straight people have invented, engagement parties must be the worst. Among the worst, at least, next to gender reveals and Dave Matthews Band concerts, neither of which I've been unlucky enough to attend. Prior to this evening, I hadn't been to an engagement party either, and it would've stayed that way, if not for Virginia Bennett.

So much of my life falls under that category: *if not for Virginia Bennett.* A decade ago, if Gin hadn't handed out cookies to our entire freshman dorm, I might have gone all four years at Dunlap College without making a single friend; if not for her soft red hair and freckles, I might have graduated still not knowing I was gay. As my friend, my girlfriend, my ex, and now my friend again, Gin has redirected my sails so many times, all of which led us here: to a roomful of unfamiliar faces ready to celebrate her engagement. And we will celebrate, of course.

Once we find her.

Imagine a Dave Matthews Band concert without Dave Matthews. Imagine a gender reveal without the looming threat of a forest fire. It all pales in comparison to an engagement party without the bride. We've checked the bathroom, the patio, the parking lot, even the dumpsters out back. Now, the groom and I have resorted to taking shifts: One of us takes a lap to look for our bride while the other guards the exit in case she returns or tries to escape.

Presently, I'm manning the post, harnessing my frenetic energy into shredding monogrammed cocktail napkins. Silver trays of champagne flutes rattle past, plucked up by members of the raucous but unbothered crowd. Maybe it's the heavy pours in the signature cocktails, but everyone seems too wrapped up in the wonderful time they're having to notice a missing bride.

"Alice, hey." Rishi rounds the corner, looking quite a bit worse for wear. The man is 90 percent stress, 10 percent pit stains, with two half moons soaking the armpits of his navy suit jacket. "Any luck on Gin?"

I shake my head. "Still just that one coworker who saw her at the bar earlier."

Rishi's lips flap with a sigh. He runs his fingers through his dark hair, wet with sweat. "Have we tried her phone?" he asks, sounding desperate.

"Are you talking about Virginia's phone?" Rishi's mother materializes beside me, her sari a flash of turquoise in my peripherals, but my attention sticks to the white clutch in her grip. "I think it's in this bag." She frowns and gives the purse a shake. "It's hardly stopped buzzing. The bride asked me to hold it while she ran to the bathroom."

"I can check the bathroom," I say. *Again. For the third time.*

There's a visible tick in Mrs. Bhat's jaw, and her plum-colored lipstick looks less flattering on a snarl. "Well, let's hope she's in there." Both her words and her glare are directed toward her son.

"There are two analysts here from the firm who have to leave before dinner. They drove in all the way from the city, so I need you to at least say hello."

I try not to bristle at this flagrant display of priorities. I was under the impression that the goal was to find Virginia so she could enjoy her own party, not take advantage of a networking opportunity, but maybe I misunderstood. Regardless, I choke down any commentary about how I, too, drove in from the city or that I, too, am supposed to leave early. It's not worth mentioning so long as we've got a bride on the loose.

"Why don't you go talk to the analysts." I guide Rishi a little closer to his mother. "I'll check the bathroom again and try to talk to the staff."

Mrs. Bhat seems pacified by the compromise, and Rishi is nothing if not a team player. "Thanks again for helping out," he says, so earnest that I can hardly stand it.

"Yes, thank you . . ." Rishi's mom trails off, but her mouth stays open and ready, like my name might appear on the tip of her tongue.

"Alice," I prompt.

"Alice," she echoes. "Alice, you're a good friend."

Maybe for her it's a throwaway compliment; for me, it's exactly what I needed to hear.

After a second unsuccessful check of the bathroom, I reroute to the bar, the site of tonight's only confirmed Gin sighting. It's possible that the bride had a few too many glasses of wine and wandered off, a classic Gin maneuver back in our college days. Not that I'm one to talk. You don't earn the nickname "Blackout Alice" by sitting at home drinking milk.

I'm dialing back into my role as gay Nancy Drew when someone behind me scoffs almost cartoonishly.

"Um, hello? Are you just gonna stand there without saying hi?"

I whirl around, following the bright, booming voice to its source: Chrissy, the final third of our college trio, balances a glass of wine in one hand, the other firmly planted on the waist of her pink satin dress. She's just as tall as I remember, but her hair—once long and box-dyed black in the bathroom of our college apartment—is much shorter now, a sleek coffee-brown bob.

"Oh, um, hi!" I clear my throat. "Chrissy! I almost didn't recognize you."

"Uh, duh. Maybe because it's been, I don't know, an eternity?" Chrissy pulls me into the kind of lung-crushing hug meant to make up for the last five years. She smells like citrus and cherry blossom, notes I can place only because I read them on her perfume bottle dozens of times back in our Dunlap days. Love Spell, I think the scent was called. I have never known sisterhood quite like living with Chrissy, a roommate who not only accepted me for wearing the same dirty leggings multiple days in a row but also willingly lent out her good perfume to help mask the smell of crotch sweat.

Chrissy guarantees there's no oxygen left in my lungs before releasing me to slowly reinflate. "Can you believe our Ginny girl is getting married? And oh my God, don't you just love Rishi?"

"Who wouldn't love Rishi?" I say. Truthfully, I've had more interactions with the groom in the last half hour than I have in the ten months that Gin and I have been back in touch, but I haven't heard a single bad word about the man. From what I can tell, Rishi treats Gin a whole lot better than I did.

"So what's new with you?" Chrissy asks eagerly. She does everything eagerly. Always has. "Are you still touring with that band?"

I fumble her gaze, falling into the rockslide feeling in my chest. Chrissy hasn't seen me since my early retirement from rock star life. "I left Cold Sweat a few years ago, actually."

She sticks out her bottom lip. "That's too bad! You guys were good."

*They probably still are*, I think. *I'm just not a part of it.*

I clear my throat and bravely lift my gaze to hers again. "I'm an assistant at Gentle Giant now. It's a pretty prestigious recording studio."

Chrissy hums around a sip of wine. "I think Gin mentioned you were doing some studio thing."

My nerves stand alert, a fast-piling stack of follow-up questions clogging my throat. *What else has Gin said? Did you know I would be here? Has she mentioned my dad?* I swallow twice and try a more relevant question. "Speaking of Gin, any chance you've seen her?"

"I was about to ask *you* the same thing," Chrissy says with an eye roll. "Like, hello? Virginia? You're literally the bride. Show up to your own party."

Before I can provide any context, a dark-haired waiter interrupts with a tray of champagne flutes. Chrissy plucks up a glass, officially double fisting, but not without giving the waiter an appraising up-down. "Thanks, cutie." She winks. "Love the tux."

The waiter pauses, considering Chrissy for another moment, then offers me the tray.

"No thanks," I say. "But any chance you've seen the bride?"

Oblivious, Chrissy adds, "She's the one in white."

The waiter tilts his head toward the hostesses' stand. "Bathroom up front," he says in a low, casual grumble, like he's not saving the day with this intel.

I'm gay Nancy Drew again, sparking to life at a much-needed clue. "I thought there was just the one bathroom in the back."

"There are two more single stalls," the waiter explains, still speaking directly to Chrissy.

I toss back a "Thank you!" as I speed off toward the front of the restaurant. "Chrissy, I'll catch you later, okay?"

"Sure thing!" she calls after me. "Let's grab a drink and catch up soon!"

But I know we never will. I'm sure she knows it, too. We'll see each other at the bridal shower and again at the wedding, where we'll likely have nearly identical conversations to this one, insisting that we *have* to hang out sometime, both of us knowing we don't really mean it.

I weave between clusters of well-dressed well-wishers, half in suits and cocktail dresses, half in tan tunics and jewel-toned saris. Rishi's dad emigrated from India, but his mom grew up here in the northern suburbs of Chicago in a less traditional Indian household; together, their friends and family make this mid-tier Italian restaurant look like the photo shoots Dunlap College used to do. We all know the type: They pick out one student per skin tone and pose them together so the brochure looks diverse. Plus they've got me in the mix, a visibly identifiable lesbian with a shag haircut and canary yellow pantsuit. All this *and* a gay person? Your liberal arts college marketing department could never.

The hostess points me down a short hallway, and as the waiter promised, there are two more bathrooms. I grab the handle of the ladies' door with the confidence of someone about to complete an escape room, but it barely gives.

A deep voice—decidedly not Gin's—barks from behind the door. "Locked means occupied!"

*Shit.* "Right, of course, sorry!"

I take a step back, then swivel around when a soft, familiar voice squeaks, "Alice? Is that you?"

I press my ear to the gents' door. "Gin?"

There's a full ten seconds of metallic clicks and switches as she futzes with the lock before pulling the door open an inch, just enough to catch a flash of her red hair and a hint of panic in her mossy hazel eyes.

"You okay in there?"

"Sorta." Gin's eyes bounce left to right. "Do you have your purse on you?"

"Have I ever carried a purse?"

She sighs. "Right . . . just get in here. I need help."

There's no time for questions; Gin grabs my wrist and yanks me inside with a swift tug, and once I can see more than an inch of her, I have my explanation as to why she's been MIA. The big red stain dribbling down her white slip dress has her looking more like a wounded World War II soldier than a bride.

"You're telling me we've been looking for you for almost an hour because you locked yourself in the bathroom over a *stain*?"

"It's not just a stain," Gin argues. "It's a huge stain on a white dress on a day where people are going to be taking a trillion pictures of me. I can't walk around my engagement party looking like I've been shot."

A giggle slips past my lips, which I instantly regret. "Sorry,

sorry," I mumble. "You just . . . you do kind of look like you've been shot."

Gin groans and rubs her temples. "I was hoping you'd have one of those stain-remover pens."

It's laughable that she thinks a Tide pen would help her case. She needs a bucket of bleach or, ideally, a whole new dress.

"So what do you want me to do?" I ask.

Gin's gaze ping-pongs from the mirror to me, from my shoulder pads to my shoes and back. "Could you switch with me?"

"Are you kidding?" I squint at the stain, then down at my yellow pantsuit. "I'm not wearing white."

"Neither am I." She motions to the big red blob on her chest. "I can't go out there like this, Alice. Please?"

A kick of guilt mixes with the obligation bubbling in my gut. It's that weird *anything for the bride* feeling that spreads like the flu leading up to a wedding. If Gin could let me back into her life after what a shitty girlfriend I was to her, the least I can do is let her look better than me at her own engagement party.

I paste on a smile. "You know what? Anything for you."

I turn around to undress, the sound of my zipper mixing with Gin's "Thankyouthankyouthankyou." I hand off my pants, blouse, and jacket behind my back, but despite plenty of sucking in and shimmying, I don't have a prayer of zipping into her dress.

"Can I have my blazer back? To cover the fact that this thing doesn't zip?"

Gin laughs, then drapes the jacket over my shoulders. "I look more bridal without it anyway." She pauses, then adds, "You can turn around, you know. It's really not a big deal."

"I'm trying to be respectful." It's been years since Gin and I were a thing, but this is her engagement party, after all. The least I can do is try not to look at her naked.

"You're funny," Gin says. "But most of these people don't even know we dated, and if Rishi or I cared, you and I wouldn't be here right now. And also, I'm clothed, so, really—turn around."

When I do, I'm face-to-face with a much more Zen Virginia Bennett, pulling off that shade of marigold even better than I did. It almost looks like something she might've worn intentionally. Meanwhile, I'm testing the limits of her rejected dress. It stretches tight like a drumhead over my boobs, drawing even more emphasis to the big red stain.

"I look like a bull's-eye," I mutter.

Gin smirks. "Sorry." But I know she's not really, and that's okay. It's her day. The first in a long chain of days that are hers, actually, but if anyone deserves that, it's Gin. She's earned the right to invent as many prewedding celebrations as she wants and make me wear whatever bullshit outfit at all of them.

We barely make it three steps out of the bathroom before Rishi rushes over like a skinny linebacker, nearly tackling his fiancée to the ground. I wince at the sweat marks he's probably getting on my blouse, but Gin remains unbothered. She smooths Rishi's wet hair off his forehead and kisses his cheek. That's true love, I guess—when someone is that gross and you want to kiss them anyway. I never quite got there with Gin . . . or with anyone, but the secondhand high I get watching them is unparalleled. It swells in my chest and prickles my feet. So I'm sure that it's real: true love, the kind that warrants multiple parties to properly celebrate.

The tinkling of silverware against glass slices through the din of the crowd. Mr. Bhat stands with his water glass aloft, directing us all toward our seats. "Dinner is about to begin."

*Shit,* I think. *Dinnertime already?* I feel around for my phone to check the time but come up empty-handed. I must have left it in the pocket of the pants currently being worn by the bride, who is blissfully unaware of my attempts at telepathic communication.

"Before we eat," Rishi's father goes on, "I'd like to say a few words about Rishi and Virginia."

A lump forms in my throat. I was hoping to be out of here before any of the dad stuff started, but I'm not going to pickpocket the bride during her future father-in-law's speech, so I steel myself instead.

"As many of you know," Mr. Bhat begins, "Rishi and I are quite close. So close, in fact, that he chose to come work at my firm. I'm not only his father but also his boss—and Rishi has not yet requested any PTO for the wedding, so, Virginia, make sure he gets on that, or I may not approve it!"

A low rumble of laughter moves through the crowd. I stare at the floor and try to pick out other sounds, the clatter of dishes in the kitchen and the gentle ambient music, anything besides this speech. Even so, when Rishi's dad speaks to how proud he is of his son, his voice splinters, and it chips at my composure. But I refuse to cry. I close my eyes and ride the sensation, imagining that I'm steering a boat over choppy waters when my insides rock up and down in waves. And this is only the engagement party. How the hell am I going to survive the wedding?

At last, Rishi's dad ends his speech with a toast, and a murmur of cheers trickles through the crowd. I turn to tap my invisible glass against Gin's, but she and Rishi have since wandered off, leaving nothing beside me but an empty space. The lump in my throat doubles in size. It's well past time to go.

When I relocate the bride, she's already wiggling my phone in front of her. "Looking for this?" She drops it in my palm, and the time lights up the screen. I'm *very* late, but when I start my goodbyes, Gin breaks out the puppy dog eyes.

"You're leaving already?"

"I have dinner plans with my mom," I remind her, and she backs off the guilt trip.

"Right. How is she doing?"

"She's all right," I say. It's been a while since I've seen her, so it's mostly an assumption. "It'll be good to check in on her and the house."

"And what about the Galena house?" Gin asks. "Any word yet?"

I shake my head. "Still trapped in legal purgatory."

Of all the unique miseries of losing a parent, the paperwork has been the most surprising punishment. The house jointly owned by Dad and his band is just one frustrating piece of the puzzle of settling his affairs.

"I miss it," I sigh, something I haven't even admitted to myself. "Not just the Outpost, but all of Galena."

"Ohmygod, GALENA!?"

I swear my skeleton jumps inside my skin. It's Chrissy, naturally. In college, Gin and I joked that Chrissy was our live-in noise complaint. It's nice to know some things don't change.

"Sorry, sorry. Didn't mean to sneak up on you," Chrissy says. "I just heard *Galena*, and I was like, hello? Spring break throwback."

"God, I miss those days." Gin looks momentarily wistful before fully frowning. "In retrospect, the band never should have trusted three college girls in the same house as their recording studio."

"Especially after we spilled all that boxed wine on the carpet freshman year," Chrissy admits. "The band should have banished us for that."

I laugh, my first honest laugh of the day. "You think The Handful never spilled booze in their recording studio? How do you think those records got made?"

"Wait. Hang on." Chrissy dives into her purse and pulls out her phone, then swipes until her eyes flicker. "There it is." She shows us a photo I both forgot existed and don't remember taking. There are a lot of those, unfortunately, but this one isn't so bad. In it, Gin, Chrissy, and I can't be more than twenty years old or less than ten drinks deep. We're three across on the porch swing at the Outpost, smiling like we'll be that young forever. It's a sweet picture, but my stomach begs to turn itself inside out, and I'm not sure if it's grief or the memory of vomiting coconut rum. What I'd give to be young, drunk, and stupid again, not yet wise to how bad things could get.

"This is gold." Gin laughs, and Chrissy swipes to another photo. This time, my stomach sours entirely. We're in the studio in the basement of the Outpost. A baby-faced Gin has two drumsticks stuck in her mouth, pretending to be a walrus, which could be adorable if not for my sad, lightless eyes beside her. It could pass as normal back then, just typical college stuff, the way I was drunk almost every night. Blacking out was an every-weekend type of thing, something to laugh about over hungover dining hall breakfasts.

Chrissy swipes one more time, and my stomach flops. This picture is the worst by far. She zooms in on a shot of me passed out with my head in a guitar case. "Pfft." She smirks. "Classic Alice."

Those two words echo through me—*Classic Alice*—and even though I'm standing completely upright, I feel like I'm tipping backward, falling through space until Gin catches me with a steadying smile. She knows what I know: Blackout Alice is a thing of the past.

"Such good memories in that house." Gin squeezes my shoulder. "And we have your dad to thank for all of them."

I like how often Gin brings Dad up. It almost feels like he's not gone, or at least it's proof he was ever here. I feel warm and rooted in place, at least until my phone buzzes with another text from Mom. I've lost track of time again, but Gin stops me before I can restart my goodbyes.

"I *know* you have to go, Alice. But can you please hang back for just five more minutes? For me? I have to give you something. Chrissy, you too."

I bite the inside of my cheek, wavering. There's that weird obligated feeling again. Mom will understand, I decide, so I smile and nod, and Gin leads us to the bar, where she produces three periwinkle gift boxes: one for me, one for Chrissy, and one for . . .

"You haven't seen Renee, have you?"

Dread drops into my stomach like an anvil onto a cartoon mouse.

Renee freaking Roberts. Maybe I should have expected to see her here, but it's been years since I've thought of her at all, much like you don't think about a stain once you've treated it. You just wear the dress again, forgetting there was ever a problem until, in the right light, you see that it was never really gone.

"I haven't seen her," Chrissy says.

Gin scans the room. "She had a work thing, so she might not have made it."

The nausea begins to subside. *She's not here, Alice. You got off easy. Time to leave and start preparing for how to avoid her at the next event.*

"Wait—isn't that her by the door?"

I look up, following the line of Chrissy's outstretched finger until I land on a flash of blond that makes my upset stomach throw a full-blown tantrum. And here she comes, seeping into our evening in a cherry red leather jacket, the clack of her high heels growing clearer and louder alongside my heartbeat, which thuds up my throat.

Gin squeals and scurries to meet Renee halfway, folding her into a hug. "You made it! Oh my God, I really didn't think you'd be here."

My gut kicks in protest. *Well, Virginia, we have that in common.*

The last time I saw Renee Roberts, she was the tooth fairy, and I was a piss-drunk Sonny Bono being tossed out of my own apartment. What sounds like a Mad Lib is actually about par for the course so far as interactions between me and Renee. At least one of us has been in costume every time our paths have crossed: Halloween bar crawls, themed parties, theater productions . . . even now, her black shift dress and red leather jacket could pass as her take on Cruella de Vil, and this wine-stained white dress makes me a literal target. Or perhaps a wounded dalmatian? I'd rather not stick around to find out.

One of Rishi's relatives intercepts Gin for a photo, so it's only Renee who joins us at the bar. She thumps her bag on the bar top, rattling every glass. "I'm so sorry I'm late, gals." Her voice is just how I remember it, a coarse mezzo-soprano. She gives me a bored once-over, down and up again, then pops her lips. "Alice."

A chill rolls down my spine. "Hi, Renee."

With that, she does a sharp quarter turn toward Chrissy, boxing me out, but I can still hear the smile in her voice as she says, "And *you.* It's been forever, hasn't it?"

"Two forevers, actually," Chrissy teases. "Last I saw you, I believe we were dueting . . . Lady Gaga?"

"Close," Renee says. "I was *dressed* as Lady Gaga. We were dueting songs from *Grease.*"

There's an ache in my chest like a dull saw pulling across my lungs. Gin's karaoke costume parties have been her birthday tradition since college, and given the damage I did at her twenty-fourth, I'm not surprised I wasn't invited to her twenty-ninth, but it does nothing to quiet my anxiety, which won't stop screaming at me that I don't belong here. *But you were invited,* my better sense argues. *You're supposed to be here.* So why do I feel like everything would be easier if I left?

"So Gin said you had a work thing today?" Chrissy asks, and Renee nods, her blond waves dipping down her back.

"Leave it to the Blomquist to need their events manager on a weekend."

"The Blomquist Theater?" I wonder aloud.

Renee's gaze shoots through the room, stopping just short of me. In a voice like artificial sweetener, she asks, "What other Blomquist is there?"

I swallow at least a dozen comebacks. I caused enough scenes in my day, and when Gin bounces her way back to us, I'm glad I kept my mouth shut.

"Sorry about that." Gin reclaims her wineglass. "Ready to do presents? Make sure you sit next to the one with your name." The three of us follow instructions, and Gin coyly adds, "You probably already know what these are."

I blink down at the box. It can't be what I think it is, can it? Chrissy and Renee seem to think it is, based on their matching smiles and jumpy eyebrows. I tug the bow loose and lift the lid to reveal a matte-black tumbler with my name printed on it in loopy iridescent letters. Beside it, a small cream notecard waits with a question that sucks the air from every corner of my lungs: *Will you be my bridesmaid?*

Chrissy is the first to her feet, her bracelets clanging like wind chimes as she dances toward the bride for a hug. "YES! A million times yes, duh!"

Renee's response is more subtle. She closes her box gingerly and looks up at Gin with a smile and a nod, quiet and doe eyed and almost as moved as I am by the ask.

When Gin's eyes land on mine, I slow my breaths, trying not to hurry this moment away. There's too much to feel and not enough time to feel it. Joy. Pride. Disbelief. My best friend and undoubtedly the greatest person I know is getting married, and she's chosen *me* of all people to stand by her side. I'm completely humbled and completely shocked, but I know my line, and I say it proudly.

"Of course, Gin. It'd be my honor."

That last word triggers something in Chrissy, who wags a pink manicured finger between me and Renee. "Wait. Who's the maid of honor?"

"I don't have a maid of honor." Gin straightens, a proud closed-lip smile lifting her cheeks till her freckles nearly kiss her eyelashes. "All three of you are so important to me, and you all have such specific skills and roles in my life, so I'm dividing up the duties."

Chrissy nods along intently, and Renee reaches into her purse, producing a small red notebook and a pen that she poises dutifully over a fresh page. I pinch my brows together, trying to look equally attentive.

"Chrissy, I was hoping you could work with Mrs. Bhat on the bridal shower since you're so connected throughout the city," Gin says, and Renee scribbles along with her, taking diligent notes. "Renee, you're the professional event planner, obviously, so I figured you could take the bachelorette party. And Alice." Gin turns to me last, a warm glow flickering in her eyes. "Would you want to give a speech at the reception?"

A buzz scurries from my chest to my fingertips, and for the second time tonight, I'm worried I might cry. "Of course," I choke out. "I would love to."

We all pose for a picture with our bridesmaid presents—Renee and Chrissy each got customized wineglasses, and my chest aches with gratitude that Gin thought to give me something I'll actually use. The four of us scrunch in for a selfie, and I strategically hold my cup in front of my chest to block some of the stain.

"Say Rishi!" Chrissy sings.

"Rishiiiiiiiii," we say in unison. It works just as well, if not better than, saying cheese.

"Oh-kay, sending this to everyone immediately." Chrissy's nails take off at a canter, clacking against her phone screen as she summons each of our contacts into a single text thread. She still has my number. That feels nice. "Oh my God, bridesmaid group chat!" Chrissy squeals. "Yay, it's starting!"

"Yay!" I echo. If it sounds a little forced, it's because it is. I'm excited to be Gin's bridesmaid. Shocked, yes, but also so far over the moon that my soul is in orbit. Prior to dating and living together and eventually going no contact, Gin was my closest friend, and it's such a privilege to be back in her life—not to mention her wedding. But even college Alice couldn't match Chrissy's energy without downing a few shots first. Now, sober and scooching toward thirty, trying to be young and fun feels like wearing a waterlogged sweatshirt.

Our bridesmaid selfie has a domino effect. Guests flock to the bride for photos, and Chrissy volunteers to play camerawoman, saddling me with Renee, who looks deeply annoyed that I'm here. Lucky for both of us, I'm about not to be.

"Well, I've gotta head out." I tip my head toward the door. "I'm already late for dinner with my mom."

The bow of Renee's top lip twitches in distaste. "How like you," she mutters, eyes somehow both icy and bored.

Just like that, I'm fuming. Were I not so desperate to eject myself from this conversation, I would point out that *she* was the one late to the engagement party. But that's not me anymore. I reach for my keys only to realize—again—that Gin has my pants and everything in the pockets.

"Gin?" I interrupt from a distance. "Do you have my keys?"

The bride steps away just long enough to hand off my key ring and hug me goodbye. We make a vague plan to grab dinner this week or next, and Chrissy squeezes me even tighter than she did earlier. Then she and Gin are back to their photo line, leaving me and Renee to exchange half-hearted waves.

What I try to say is *Good to see you!* But that's a lie. It hasn't been good. What comes out instead is just "See you," and even that earns me an eye roll.

"I guess so," Renee grumbles loud enough for only me to hear, but she traps me in her stare a second longer, freezing me in place with two vicious slivers of blue. "Quick tip for next time? Maybe don't wear white if you're not the bride."

A chill shoots up from my feet, but I'm not allowed the benefit of explaining myself before Renee boxes me out again. After all these years, she hasn't changed a bit.

I knew *of* Renee Roberts long before we ever met. Before Gin became a music teacher, she worked at an arts nonprofit, and Renee was her favorite coworker. They both studied theater in undergrad, and on top of her career in event management, Renee still hit the audition circuit and occasionally performed around the city. When Gin described the vision board hanging in Renee's cubicle—the clipped-out pictures of lit up theater marquees behind words like *ambition* and *goal-getter*—I knew for certain this person was not for me.

There has never been a shortage of things that are *not for me.* An office job like the one where Gin and Renee met, for example, is *not for me.* Neither is theater. Anything that could broadly be described as *woo-woo,* vision boards included, is definitely not for me, and neither was college, although I still snuck out of Dunlap with a diploma. Renee, on the other hand, earned her MBA from one of the country's most prestigious programs. She had a five-year plan to land a job at one of Chicago's major theaters, and I had an alt-country band and no real direction. By the time I finally met Renee Roberts in person, I already knew what to expect: my opposite. The sun to my moon, a grounded earth sign versus my flighty Gemini sensibilities. Gin always said that Renee was the best; from the moment we met, Renee acted like she *knew* it. Clearly she still does.

A different version of me—the version Renee used to know—wouldn't let her have the last word with that "don't wear white" comment. A different Alice would dig in her heels and order another round, throwing insults and drinks until she knew for certain that Renee had lost and she herself had won. But I'm not that Alice anymore. Not even close. Instead, I box up my tumbler, reminding myself that this stupid cup alone and the fact that it's not a wineglass are proof positive that I'm not who I used to be. If I stooped to the level of making a vision board, the only thing on it would be to prove Renee wrong.

# Two

A pickup truck isn't the most practical choice for a city driver, but it's easy to spot in the parking lot. The storm-blue double cab was one of Dad's last splurges, and his scent still clings to the leather interior—dive bars and Parliaments. I try to trap it in my lungs as I start up the truck, flinching at the time glowing back at me. Mom is likely stapling *LOST DAUGHTER* posters around the neighborhood by now, but our visit feels suddenly impossible given the emotional bullet train I've just stumbled off. I'm still deciding on my destination when another text from Mom sinks my stomach like an enemy ship. She's asking for my ETA. *Shit.*

I give myself until the first red light to make up my mind and give Mom a call. It goes to voicemail, and as instructed, I leave a message after the beep.

"Hey, Mom, it's me, I was jus—oh wait, hang on, you're calling me back, bye." I switch the line over. "Hello?"

"Hi, sorry, I was dealing with the pharmacy. They've been threatening me over your father's prescriptions."

My heart skips. "What? The pharmacy is threatening you?"

"Well, maybe that's an exaggeration," Mom admits, and my

nerves dial back. "The automated texts just keep getting more aggressive, and . . . these aren't the things they warn you about, Alice."

This has become Mom's catch phrase—not just since Dad died, but since his health took a turn. *These aren't the things they warn you about,* she's said again and again, from when Dad first stopped being able to brush his own teeth to when they asked us how many death certificates we wanted, and now, battling the autorefills of the deceased—Mom has always insisted that, when they teach you about death, they never mention these strange little miseries. If she weren't still mourning her dead husband, I might ask who "they" are and what "they" *did* teach her that prepared her for this mess.

A car horn blares, and I swerve back into the lane I didn't realize I'd drifted out of. A close call, compliments of my recurring daydream about a world where we all receive copies of *What to Expect When You're Expecting Your Dad to Die.*

"Are you driving?" Mom sounds worried but chirpier when she asks, "You're headed over then?"

My stomach feels wadded up, just like the last three or four times I've had to cancel on Mom. "I'm sorry," I sigh. "I know you don't want to hear excuses, but Gin went missing for an hour at this party, and it was a whole thing that kept me late, and I have work tomorrow, and—"

"I gotcha," Mom interrupts, and I can hear the effort she's putting into sounding unbothered, but the tremor in her voice gives her away. She's sad. Of course she's sad, and I feel like an asshole for being the reason.

"I'm sorry," I say again. Not that it means much anymore. We're well into May, and I haven't visited since Christmas.

Mom is quick to change topics, and it's a relief. She peppers me with questions about the engagement party, then about the wedding once I tell her I'm a bridesmaid. It's not long before what's left of my social battery flashes red.

"I should let you go," I tell her. "I'm just about home." It's as true as I need it to be.

"All right, well, text me when you get there so I know you're safe," Mom says. "And please come see us soon, okay?"

"For sure," I choke out, my voice as thin and flimsy as a wet party streamer. *Come see us*, she said. *Us.* As in her and Dad. There is no *us* anymore, but I don't correct her. It's not like she could ever forget.

I'm about to say goodbye when Mom tacks on, "And when you have a minute, we need to carve out some time to get out to Galena."

It takes all my self-control not to slam on the brakes. "So there's an update on the house?"

"Sort of." Mom coughs.

"Well?"

"Well, I was going to tell you this over dinner, but The Handful is planning a memorial concert at the Galena Playhouse for your father's Gone Day."

That's the term Mom and I went with for our new least favorite holiday. I personally liked *deathiversary*, and I think Dad would have, too. I can almost hear his gruff, booming voice, arguing, *I'm not just gone, you idiots! I'm dead!*

"A memorial concert," I echo.

In a cautious voice, Mom adds, "It's where they're kicking off their tour."

Their *tour.* Every molecule of oxygen disappears from my lungs.

"Alice? Are you there?" Mom asks, and I find a breath. Dive bars and Parliaments.

"So they, uh . . . they found a new lead singer?"

"Seems like it, yes," Mom says.

My fingernails dig into the steering wheel leather. I shouldn't be surprised. I knew it was inevitable. The band was—and is—far bigger than just my dad. So long as there are bills to pay and fans buying tickets, it's only logical that the show goes on. But logic can't fix a feeling, and when I picture The Handful taking the stage with a replacement Ricky Pierce, it feels like a bent nail is being hammered into my chest.

"We should go," Mom says after who knows how long of a silence. *We should go.* Not *I want us to go.* Not *Will you go? Should.* It's the right thing to do.

"Yup," I choke out. "We should go."

There's relief in Mom's voice. "I'm so glad to hear that."

*Glad.* I shiver. I want to be glad, too. I guess I am, deep beneath all the heartbreak. I'm glad that the band is honoring Dad in a place that meant so much to him. To all of us. Joy and grief are two thin gold chains running down my spine, tangled in an impossible knot right where my shoulder blades meet the driver's seat.

"Well, check your schedule when you get home," Mom says. "The show is the Thursday before Labor Day weekend. Maybe we could go up earlier that week to get the house in order before the band stays there."

*By which she means we need to make room for Dad's replacement.*

"Alice? You there?"

"Y-yeah," I stammer. "Sorry. I'll check the dates." I blow out a long, leveling breath. "But is there, like . . . is there an update on the house? The legal stuff?"

To my dismay, Mom feeds me the same old line. "The attorneys are still working on it."

I picture a group of strangers in suits huddled around a single sheet of paper for months, working it out like a word problem: If Richard Pierce is part owner of The Handful Group LLC, containing a half dozen subsidiary companies, one of which owns the Outpost, then what the hell happens when Richard Pierce no longer exists?

I pull off the highway, and Mom and I say our goodbyes, then swap *I love you*s before ending the call. The parks along the lakeshore are a peaceful stretch of green, breaking up the concrete with baseball fields and gardens, and I roll down the windows just enough to breathe in the spring breeze off the lake. I love Chicago, but some of my favorite places in this city are the ones that make me forget I'm in a city at all: the urban forests and parks and less touristy stretches of lakeshore, places where I can find a little quiet.

At home, I peel out of Gin's gunshot-wound dress and slip back into last night's pajamas, which wait in a heap on my bathroom floor. The sun hasn't even set, but I get ready for bed anyway, then crack a window, compromising the silence for a little fresh air. In spills the soundtrack of the neighborhood: The L rattles down its track. A woman yells her half of a phone call. In the distance, a car alarm has either just started or else has been blaring for hours. I don't often mind the noise of the city, but when I'm fresh off the suburbs, I feel stuck inside the sound.

While last night's pasta reheats, I cross-check my phone calendar with the paper calendar on my fridge, like I told Mom I would. August has a big empty stretch of days leading up to Dad's Gone Day, so I have no excuse. It looks like I'll be joining Mom to clean out the Outpost, and I'll be dreading it every second until then. I envisioned myself returning to Galena on my own terms, however felt right to me—but life has hardly ever played out the way I envision it.

I bring my pasta to the couch and browse the photos Gin has tagged me in from today. Among them is the bridesmaids' selfie: In it, three out of four of us rock big toothy grins—*say Rishi!*—but my gaze pulls toward Renee, whose soft closed-lipped smile bridges smug with seductive. My teeth lock together, grinding my first bite of rotini to a paste. Of course she just *had* to be different, didn't she? Or maybe I'm just a little raw on the subject of Renee Roberts.

I sigh and tap my thumb, summoning a dark-gray bubble over each of our faces, each with a tagged account: mine, Chrissy's, and Renee's. I'm surprised Renee hasn't blocked me or abandoned social media for a superior hobby like reading personal-development books to orphaned kittens. I thumb open her profile, which is public, thank God, and set my hardly touched plate on the coffee table, tucking my legs beneath me.

@TheReneeRob has a pretty bare-bones account. Her bio is plain, just two emojis: the comedy and tragedy masks and the red heart. Of the half dozen posts on her grid, the most recent is from her work holiday party with the caption "Merry, Bright, and Blomquist." I swipe through several group photos before I land on a solo shot, and it hits like a shot of good tequila, sending a hot, buzzy burn down my throat. Renee's bloodred satin dress hugs every delicious curve of her hips and the neckline dips to tease an irresistible shadow of cleavage. With her blond Hollywood waves and wintry blue eyes locked on the camera, she's a real-life siren. How could one person be so mean and so hot?

I swipe one last time, and in the final photo, Renee is joined by a living Ken doll in a charcoal suit. They're side by side, each with one arm tucked behind the other's back in a way that provides no hard evidence about the nature of their relationship. Not that I care. I tap the picture once, then again, hoping his account will solve the question of *Siblings or dating?* Instead, a pink heart bubbles up from the bottom of the photo.

"Shit!"

My pulse takes off like a rocket, matching the speed of my phone as I lob it across the room. It lands with a stuttering *th-thud* on the living room rug, the sound of me hammering the final nail into my own coffin. *Shit shit shit.* I just Liked Renee's photo from five months ago.

My brain blue screens, and when I scramble to retrieve my phone, I know there's only one reasonable thing to do: I hit the follow button, then close the app altogether, waiting for my heart rate to agree that this is totally fine and normal. It is normal, right? To follow someone and also like their most recent picture? I guess it'd probably be more normal had I done those two things in the reverse order, but maybe Renee won't notice. Or maybe she will. Maybe she's texting Gin separately right now, asking *What the hell is up with your ex?* And maybe I'm overthinking all of this.

I abandon my phone on the charger, cutting myself off from my screens and worst-case scenarios, apart from one final check before bed. My only new notification is an email from Renee, and I wheeze a disbelieving laugh at the subject line.

> **FROM:** Renee Roberts
> **TO:** Christina Amato, Alice Pierce
> **SUBJECT:** Bachelorette Party Survey—Please complete ASAP.
>
> Good evening, fellow bridesmaids! I've put together a questionnaire regarding Gin's bachelorette party. I've planned quite a few of these bachelorette trips, and the sooner you fill out the questionnaire, the sooner I can start planning!
>
> Thanks in advance.
> XO, Renee

"God, this girl is doing the most," I say to my audience of none. My throat squeezes tight. Would that I could text my dad. I swipe open our long-inactive text thread and treat myself to a few old messages, putting my heart on a spin cycle; then I open my Notes app and begin to type.

> *Hey Dad. Hope you're good, wherever you are. Quick question: What would you do if you* really *couldn't stand one of your bandmates?*

I know he won't respond, but the empty space feels like he just might. Sometimes it's nice to pretend.

# Three

This Monday begins the same as a dozen Mondays before it. Same eight o'clock alarm, same cup of coffee dressed the exact same way—one splash of oat milk and two packets of sweetener. Same as how Dad used to drink it, minus the bourbon.

*Routine* was a dirty word back in my Cold Sweat days. Any touring musician would tell you the same—it's all late nights and last-minute gigs, breakfast beers and gas station dinners between cities with names you forget. The Alice Pierce of Cold Sweat was a tornado of a person, touching down without warning, but the Alice Pierce of Gentle Giant Studios is a convert to the church of routines.

I pop in an earbud and file onto the bus, snagging my preferred seat near the middle. As usual, I check my email, but the same-old ends there: A surprise in my inbox earns an honest guffaw.

**FROM:** Renee Roberts

**TO:** Christina Amato, Alice Pierce

**SUBJECT:** following up :)

Good morning, ladies! Just making sure everyone received the bachelorette party survey I sent over last night! I've already received a few responses, and the sooner we have everyone's schedules and ideas, the sooner we can get this celebration on the calendar! Maybe we can have a wine night next week to iron out all the details? How's Thursday?

XO, Renee

I read through it twice, laughing both times, and my seatmate glares at me for expressing joy on the CTA. Joy is far from what I'm feeling, though. Disbelief, maybe? Shock? Highly concentrated irritation? It hasn't been twenty-four hours since Renee sent out the questionnaire. Did she really already need to "follow up :)"? And what does she mean she's received "a few responses" already? Aren't there only three of us?

My fingers leap to grab a screenshot of the offending email, but the bus lurches and my gut twists when reality catches up with my instincts. I have no one to send this to. Gin obviously isn't an option, and Mom would probably take Renee's side and compliment her on being organized.

If Dad were still around, though, he'd drag Renee through the mud with me. I take the screenshot, then drop it into my Notes app.

*Following up on an email you sent less than 24 hours ago? No law against that, I guess. XO, the bummer bridesmaid*

I smirk at my own joke and try to imagine what Dad might've said in response. Something witty and mean spirited, no doubt.

Whenever I had a bad word to say about anyone, Dad stood ready with three more. It didn't matter if he actually knew the person; anyone who so much as inconvenienced his daughter was fair game when our conversations devolved into roasts. In retrospect, I was often the one we should've been roasting, but had I been looking for accountability, I would've gone to Mom.

My next notification is a more welcome surprise: a text from Gin with her availability for dinner the next few weeks. I call dibs on her Friday night and, in a fleeting moment of overconfidence, offer to host. An incentive to clean the apartment, I decide.

Once I'm off the bus, it's a five-minute walk to the unassuming home of Gentle Giant Studios. If you blink, you might miss the only proof you're in the right place—a small gold plaque hangs on the door, engraved with two thin letters: *GG*. Apart from this one clue, this building could be any place that's no place in the city, an enormous brick fortress your eyes are meant to gloss over on their way to something more exciting. A few of us lucky ones know better; there is no place in Chicago more magical than the studio where platinum records are born.

Through the glass of studio A, I spot Aidan by the patch bay, looking sleepy in the same faded A Tribe Called Quest sweatshirt he wears on the daily. I rap on the glass, and he tips his cleft chin and waves with a cable in his fist, his silent request for another XLR.

Even after two years assisting at Gentle Giant, stepping into the storage closet makes me feel like a kid in Willy Wonka's chocolate factory. The wall-to-wall wire shelves house every mic, monitor, and synth under the sun, every piece of recording equipment you could dream up, plus a half dozen barely different alternatives to suit the pickiest musicians. I'm only here three days a week, but if I had it my way, I'd never go home.

I run Aidan his cable and lend a hand with the inputs; then the studio phone rumbles in my pocket, and I step out to buzz in our guests. Two flannel-wearing men, one tall and one short. In my head, I dub the tall one "Big" and the small, nervous-looking one "Rich."

"Welcome to Gentle Giant," I watch myself say in the reflection of Rich's aviators. "Can I grab you anything? Tea? Coffee?"

"Beer?" Rich's push broom mustache twitches with a hint of a smile. It's 11:00 a.m., not that he or any other rock star I know would give a shit. I swing by the fridge and tug one can free from a six-pack, and Aidan slouches out of the live room just as Rich pops the top.

"Whaddup," Aidan ribbits, and sticks out his hand.

"Aidan Davis, right?" Big straightens and claps his tattooed hand into Aidan's, pumping it twice. "It's an honor to meet you, man. Truly. Love your work."

Everyone loves Aidan's work. He's not just a local legend, either—the Grammys in his office speak for themselves—but I've always gotten a kick out of clients who are clearly a little starstruck. Yes, Aidan is a genius, but he's also worn that same raggedy sweatshirt every day since I started working here. Growing up in the industry, I've always seen my heroes as human, and humans make mistakes.

Like right now, when Aidan says, "You've already met my studio assistant, Alice Pierce."

*Shit.*

It's not that I never use my last name in professional settings, but I prefer not to with people I don't know, and Rich's response reminds me why. He tugs off his aviators and squints at me like I can be decoded. "Any relation to Ricky Pierce?"

My chest winds tight, but I can't bring myself to lie. "His daughter," I murmur.

Rich whistles over his beer. "Well, I'll be damned."

Big chimes in with "Your dad was a legend."

My smile is neither genuine nor convincing.

I hear this a lot: My dad was an icon, a hero, a legend. When people think of Chicago music, they think of Ricky Pierce, the man who all but invented the alt-country genre one sold-out show at a time. It wasn't just the gritty twang of his vocals or his masterful guitar playing, though. Dad was a real bottle rocket onstage, it's true, but he burned even brighter once he could step out of the spotlight and just be a person. Everyone loved Dad—not just industry folks but strangers, neighbors, cab drivers; my last name alone could've landed me a job at just about any studio in the city. But not Gentle Giant. Aidan vets his studio assistants more thoroughly than the FBI. If you don't know your shit, he'll happily replace you with someone who does, but most clients don't know that, and when Rich licks his teeth and says, "Betcha don't need talent with a last name like that," my skin crawls at the thought that he—or anyone else—assumes I'm only here because of my dad.

Our drunk country duo requests a closed session, so I won't be shadowing today, and it's just as well. Aidan gives me a quick apology and a two-finger salute, and I settle in at the desk, unfolding my laptop and booting up Pro Tools. On days like this one, I'm free to work on my own mixing and mastering projects, and I run out the clock mixing a folk EP between beer runs for the band in studio A.

My shift ends, and I step out into the sharp winds of early

evening. This morning's warm weather has given way to a wind advisory, but a lifetime in the Midwest has taught me plenty about dressing for the elements. Wear layers. Pack extra socks. Never get too attached to a sunny day. All the weather ever does is change. My hair whips across my face, and I unknot the flannel from my waist and turn against the wind, choosing the two-mile trek home over the bus. I feel almost pressurized, like a shaken-up can of beer that might burst if I don't walk it off. I wish I could blame it on sitting too long, but the dull ache expanding beneath my rib cage knows better. I miss Dad. I always miss Dad. More than that, I feel guilty for not wanting to be Alice Pierce all the time. I don't want to discuss my father with strangers. I don't want to put my feet up and lounge in his shadow. I used to take pride in being a mini Ricky Pierce, but some days I just want to be Alice, not the daughter of some dead legend.

I could choke on that word. *Legend.* It has one too many definitions for my taste. Dad *was* a legend back when he walked the earth and graced the stage, but now that he's gone, it's taken on a different meaning. He has more in common with Atlantis or the Loch Ness Monster. Legends. Myths. Subjects of discussion that don't actually exist. Every block closer to home draws me deeper into the ache. Dad doesn't exist—not anymore. Now, he's nothing but a story.

**FROM:** Christina Amato

**TO:** Renee Roberts, Alice Pierce

**SUBJECT:** RE: following up :)

Hi gals!! Loved the survey!!!! I'm literally so excited for this bachelorette trip. Thanks Renee!!!

Next Thursday works great for me, and I'm happy to host a wine night! Does 7:30 pm work??

**~*Never stop sparkling*~**

Christina Amato

---

**FROM:** Renee Roberts

**TO:** Christina Amato, Alice Pierce

**SUBJECT:** RE: following up :)

7:30 PM on Thursday works great! Thank you for volunteering to host, Chrissy. I'll bring the wine!

XO, Renee

---

**FROM:** Alice Pierce

**TO:** Renee Roberts, Christina Amato

**SUBJECT:** RE: following up :)

Hey guys! Sorry for the delay. Thursday works! I just tried opening the survey, but I think there's some kind of glitch—it's not supposed to be almost 50 questions, is it? Thanks!

---

**FROM:** Renee Roberts

**TO:** Christina Amato, Alice Pierce

**SUBJECT:** RE: following up :)

See you all Thursday at 7:30! Everyone please be sure to have *all 48 questions* of the survey filled out before we meet.

XO, Renee

*Hey Dad, quick question. Actually, 48 of 'em.*

*Love,*
*Your Dallas Alice*

# Four

My Thursdays and Fridays are routinely reserved for client work and practicing bass, but Gin's coming over, and it's been months since I've had company. Thus begins my two-day deep clean. I wipe down the baseboards. I degrease the cabinets. I scrub the floors with such aggression that even the former tenants must sense it. I won't let Gin be anything less than impressed.

Friday afternoon, I swing by the corner store so I can offer Gin something to drink besides water, and when I lug two cases of seltzer to the counter—one standard, one spiked—I feel a little like I'm getting away with something. Years have passed since I last bought booze.

"It's not for me," I assure the clerk as I slide him my ID. "It's for my friend." But he didn't ask, nor does he care.

At home, I load Gin's seltzers into the refrigerator, counting the weeks since we last hung out one-on-one. I went over to hers the day after Rishi proposed, but I don't think we've had a proper life catch-up since. I tick off the necessary updates in my head—Dad's replacement in The Handful and the memorial concert, plus Aidan's slipup at the studio and, in non-dead-dad-related news, the folk EP I just finished mixing. I pin each story to the squishy corkboard of my memory, hoping we'll have time for them all, then check my phone to see if there's any word on Gin's location. Instead, I'm greeted with a text from Mom.

**MOM**

Hey Alice. Any word about your availability to help clean out the Outpost before the memorial concert?

My stomach bottoms out. *Shit.* I distinctly remember checking my calendar, but I must've forgotten to text Mom about it.

**ALICE**

Sorry, yes! I'm available.

**MOM**

Great! What about rescheduling dinner?

Just then, my screen flashes to an incoming call from the front gate. I buzz Gin up, then pocket my phone. Mom can wait a little bit longer.

I slide open the dead bolt just in time to watch Gin trudge up the third and final flight of stairs. She's fresh from work, looking every bit the fun music teacher in jeans, a green-polka-dotted blouse, and dangly earrings shaped like the treble and bass clefs. They jostle and swing as she shoves a garment bag into my arms.

"Your clothes from the engagement dinner," Gin explains before I can ask. She breezes past me and toes off her ballet flats. "I got 'em dry cleaned."

"And here I was congratulating myself on pretreating that wine stain on your dress."

"That's perfect. You just . . . you know me."

It's universally known that no one spends more time at the end of the extra mile than Gin Bennett. Yes, she's liable to spill half a glass of wine on herself at the start of her engagement party, but she'd go to the ends of the earth if that's where your favorite dry cleaner was. How is it that I gave her the clothes off my back and I still feel like she's the one doing me a favor?

I stow the dry cleaning bag while Gin begins a self-guided tour of the concert posters framed down the hall. Most are vintage from the early days of The Handful, but a single Cold Sweat poster hangs in the center from my final headlining show. I listen for Gin's wind chime laugh when she lays eyes on my latest DIY effort: an entire living room wall collaged with vintage covers of *Rolling Stone* magazine.

"You're crazy for this." Gin twirls a finger toward my masterpiece. I track her gaze as it jumps from the old oak record cabinet to the leafy monstera plant I've proudly kept alive. "This place looks great," she says, then wonders aloud, "How long has it been since I've been over?"

"Since, uh." I swallow. "Not since right after the funeral."

For a too-long moment, it's dead air between us. Gin chews her lip, then softly asks, "Was that when I brought the lasagna?"

I have so few memories from those first few weeks without Dad, but the day Gin stopped by is one I won't forget. I can still hear the rustle of the trash bag as she walked laps around my apartment, deconstructing my depression nest one crumpled tissue and rotting takeout box at a time. It was humiliating, having my ex-girlfriend bring me dinner and clean up my mess, but it was also the first time in weeks I felt any way other than sad. It was the strangest swirl of shame and gratitude. At least someone other than my mom and The Handful gave a shit.

"Yeah," I sigh. "When you brought the lasagna."

It meant more to me than she'll ever know.

Our dinner arrives, and Gin and I unload the goods from a seemingly bottomless brown paper bag: tightly packed takeout boxes stuffed with white rice, plastic containers of curry with clear lids splashed in tomato reds and golden yellows. Just when I'm sure I've unpacked the last of it, I fish out one more piece of foil-wrapped naan.

"Did you order the whole menu?" Gin teases.

"I just got you everything that was marked dairy-free." I rip the receipt off the bag and read it aloud. "One chana masala, one chicken vindaloo, one aloo gobi, one yellow daal, two naan, and two orders of samosas."

"So there's a secret third person coming to dinner," Gin guesses.

"Cute," I say, "that you think I have a second friend."

The air thickens with the smell of garlic and turmeric, and we scoop up double servings of everything, then settle into the couch with a stack of napkins and a seltzer apiece—a boozy black cherry one for Gin and a regular lemon sparkling water for me.

"Why do you have these?" Gin asks, tapping the side of her hard seltzer.

"I just got 'em today," I say. "For you."

Her eyes narrow the tiniest bit, a flicker of worry shining through.

"I'm serious." I tuck my legs beneath me and hold a hand up in oath. "It was kind of weird, actually. My first time buying alcohol in . . . shit, three years?"

"Three years." Gin glances between me and her seltzer. "You swear?"

"On my original DVD copy of *The Princess Diaries*."

Satisfied, Gin nods and snaps the pop tab open. "Well, cheers to that." But it doesn't sit right, the way she's raising her alcoholic beverage to my sobriety.

"Cheers to . . . putting in the work," I try, and Gin accepts the revision with the tinny *clack* of her spiked seltzer against my sparkling water. I take a sip and, on the subject of sobriety, prepare to deliver the latest update on The Handful when Gin slams down her can with the conviction of a judge banging a gavel.

"So." She straightens. "I have news."

"You're pregnant," I blurt, and Gin looks terribly unamused.

"No, Alice," she sighs, and I roll my lips in, sealing my mouth shut as Gin tries again. She smiles and says, "We set a date."

"You set a date?!"

"We set a date," Gin repeats, "and picked a venue."

"And you're *not* pregnant?"

Gin rolls her eyes and shoots me a look that says *Shut up and stop interrupting*, so I scoot back on the couch, a perfect, silent listener. "So." She starts again. "We kind of took things in a different direction."

"You're eloping," I guess.

She swats my arm. "Alice! Stop!"

"Sorry, sorry!" I hold my hands up in surrender. "I'm just excited. I'll shut up. Just tell me."

Gin pulls her legs up onto the couch, folding herself into a perfect crisscross applesauce. "Things kind of changed after the engagement party," she explains. "It felt more like a party for Rishi's parents than for us."

"I can see that," I admit.

"Right? I hardly knew anyone there! So on the drive home,

Rishi and I talked about it. We don't want to spend our wedding day with strangers and pay for them to eat chicken or fish."

"Plus Indian weddings are supposed to be huge, right?"

"Huge," Gin echoes with a slow, knowing nod. "And the ceremony will still have plenty of Indian elements, but we don't want the big production. We want something small and intimate and fun with the people we love the most."

"Sounds perfect," I say. "So what's the venue?"

Gin pauses for a sip of seltzer, undeniably building dramatic effect before announcing the news. "The Bhats' backyard. We're gonna DIY it."

The size of her smile makes me want to apologize for how my stomach sinks like a body in a lake. I try to mimic Gin's expression, but I'm not the one with the theater degree. It feels like I'm wincing, so I can't imagine how pained I look.

Gin's face drops, her voice practically flattened. "You hate it."

"I don't hate it!" I say, laying the enthusiasm on thick. "I think it sounds amazing! It just . . . also sounds like a lot of work."

"I actually don't think it'll be that bad," Gin says brightly, then launches into an explanation she has absolutely rehearsed. "Most of the work is just going to be gardening and landscaping, which Rishi and I can help with since I have the summer off and he's already up in the northern suburbs for work. We're gonna invite maybe thirty people max, do flowers from the farmers' market, catering from this really good Mediterranean restaurant . . . super intimate, super simple. Then if Rishi's parents want to throw us a reception with all their friends and family, that's on them. What do you think?"

"I love it," I say as brightly as I can, not allowing a second of delay. "You're so right—that sounds totally doable."

Gin's smile comes back in full force. I guess I still can lie a little.

"So when's the big day?" I ask.

"Labor Day weekend."

My heart leaps halfway up my throat, but I maintain my poker face. "What day?"

"Saturday. It's the thirtieth."

*Two days after Dad's Gone Day.* I reach for my phone, eyeing my paper calendar on the fridge from a distance. "Is there gonna be a rehearsal?"

"Probably?" Gin lifts her plate from the coffee table and rests it in her lap. "We haven't nailed down all the details, but I promise the bridesmaids will be the first to know."

My heart lands back in my chest, but not without a little turbulence. It's not ideal, but it's not worth stressing out the bride over. I'll figure it out. It'll just be a really busy, really emotionally exhausting week for me that I'll somehow survive. Sober. No problem.

"What's the problem?" Gin asks. She can read me like a piece of sheet music.

"Nothing! I thought there might be something, but it's nothing." I set my phone down and keep my spirits up. "I'll be in Galena earlier that weekend, but I'll figure it out. Zero worries."

"Okay, good." Gin sighs, and her shoulders relax. I wait for her to ask about Galena; instead, she prods a samosa with her fork before picking it up and biting into it like a chicken nugget. "God, Alice. I'm so excited. *Virginia Bhat.* Doesn't that sound good?"

"You're taking his last name, then?"

She nods while she chews. "I'm more than happy to drop any affiliation with the Bennetts."

Gin doesn't discuss her parents much, but they've crossed my mind more than once recently. Last I heard, the Bennetts were still living in the same Memphis suburb that Gin has never returned to. Unless things have radically changed, Mr. and Mrs. Bennett are liable to interpret their daughter marrying a man as clear evidence you really can pray the gay away.

I try to sneak up on the question without ruining the mood. "Are your parents invited to the wedding?"

Gin scoffs. "No way. They don't even know I'm engaged."

Grief begs me to shake her by the shoulders and shout, *INVITE THEM! YOU COULD REGRET IT WHEN THEY'RE DEAD!* But I know better than to extend too much grace to the parents that called Gin "a lost soul" when she came out as bi.

"Let's talk about something else," she mutters, and I'm grateful for it. We have so much more ground to cover, but Gin beats me to our next topic. "Let's talk about the bachelorette party."

Not exactly what I had in mind, but I sweep up my minor frustration and stuff it away. I had plenty of months to vent about Dad. It's Gin's turn to talk through a life-changing event.

"Have you done the survey yet?" Gin asks. "Renee and I got drinks last night, and she wouldn't tell me what was on it."

"Did she tell you it was almost fifty questions?"

"Thorough," Gin remarks.

"Exhausting," I correct her. I reach for my phone. "I can show you, if you want."

Gin's smile tucks in at the corners. "I think Renee wants all those details to be a surprise." She swigs her seltzer, then adds, "She lives really close to here, you know."

My body reacts like I've just been told my building was constructed on top of a sinkhole. I assumed Renee Roberts lived in a high-rise downtown or at the top of a very, very tall ivory tower on the North Shore. "How far from here?"

"Like, three blocks? Closer to . . . what was that bar you used to love? Tweedy's?"

I force a small smile and a polite "Oh, no way," but my mind has been abruptly ejected from this conversation and into a map of my neighborhood, trying to determine the probability that Renee has been strategically avoiding me for as long as we've lived within walking distance. If she has, I hope she keeps it up.

"I wanted to talk to you about her." Gin shifts in her seat, less comfortable with this than she was about her parents. "I want things to be good between the two of you. I know at the engagement dinner Renee was a little . . . short with you."

*A little short.* What an interesting choice of words. Whatever Gin says next, I don't hear it over the blood pounding in my ears. *A little short.* The timeline between now and Gin and Rishi's Labor Day–weekend wedding could accurately be described as *a little short*, but the way Renee spoke to me—and just as bad, the way she *didn't*, how she turned her back and boxed me out. That wasn't *a little short.* That was pure mean-girl behavior, which is exactly what I've come to expect from Renee Roberts.

I tune back in for the tail end of Gin's impassioned speech. "You're both totally different people from when you first met."

I give a noncommittal shrug. She's right that I've changed, but it's tougher for me to believe that about Renee, given our last exchange. This is the same woman who used to show up to Gin's birthday parties early to redo my decorations, then insist on Gin opening her present during the party so we could ooh and aah over the best, most thoughtful gift of the evening. I wouldn't be shocked if present-day Renee pulled the same crap at Gin's bachelorette.

Gin sucks in a long breath through her nose, and it sputters back out through her lips. "Look. It would really mean a lot to me if you just tried," she says. "You can at least be nice and just *try* with Renee, right?"

She stares at me, eyes rimmed with hope. I can't extinguish that hope. That's bridal hope. Matrimonial hope. That would be a crime.

"Alice?" Gin presses. "I really think you guys might actually get along once you get to know each other."

"I'm sure we will," I say, but even to me it sounds hollow; two lies in one evening is more than I'm equipped for. The next part, though, is honest. "I'll try," I say. "I promise. I mean, hey. We have you in common, right? That's a good start."

"Right." Gin sighs with her entire body. "Thank God. Because you're both really, really important to me." She squeezes my shoulder, her eyes wide and glassy. "You guys are my family."

My stomach plummets to my kneecaps and rebounds to my throat. I, of all people, understand exactly how important family can be.

**MOM**

Did you see this?! They're making a musical about The Handful!!

http://www.musicalnewsyoucanuse.com/the-handful-comes-to-braodway

**ALICE**

I think that's fake, Mom.

**MOM**

Really? How can you tell?

**ALICE**

Look at the name of the website. Not legit. And they spelled broadway wrong.

**ALICE**

Also, look at Dad on the poster. His hands don't look right. I think he has six fingers.

**MOM**

Dang! You're good! My old eyes don't catch that stuff

**MOM**

I'm glad I sent it to you before I shared it! Do you have time for a quick phone call this week? Or maybe we could get lunch if you're not too busy. My treat!

# Five

Forty-eight questions on a bachelorette party questionnaire is, at minimum, forty too many. I haven't filled out anything this long since Gin made me take that damn enneagram quiz, but at least that was multiple choice and didn't require a reflection on my personal travel style. Do I have a personal travel style? And does Renee have a vendetta against multiple-choice questions? If the devil is in the details, Renee Roberts got her MBA in hell.

All attempts to fill out the questionnaire on my couch have ended in giving up or dozing off, so on Monday, I arrive an hour early for my shift at Gentle Giant, beating even Aidan to the studio for some deliberate survey time. At the desk, I speed through a series of questions regarding budget, dates, and dietary restrictions. When my fingers leap to key in a snarky response to a question about my "ideal bachelorette party vibe," I listen for Gin's voice in my head, calling us her family, and it smooths back my hackles. I'll fill out a thousand surveys without an ounce of snark if that's what it takes to keep this family intact.

I refill my coffee around the halfway point—question twenty-four—where I've gotten stumped every time. "Let's talk destination! Where do you think Gin would want to celebrate with her girls?" It's the wording that throws me off, mostly. Renee isn't asking where we'd like to go or how far we're willing to travel; she's asking us to read Gin's mind when she could instead ask the bride herself. But after many failed survey attempts and much consideration, I've landed on the right answer. Gin Bennett's perfect bachelorette destination. I type in "the Outpost," then key the backspace and replace it with "Galena."

Personal connections aside, Galena is a Midwestern mecca for a girls' trip—the wineries, the walking tours, the cute little boutiques with fancy candles and novelty tea towels with Dolly Parton puns printed on them? It's *darling*. Sprinkle on a little spring break nostalgia and I can't imagine a better place to host Gin's bachelorette.

The rest of the survey feels almost too specific to be useful, but I push through to number forty-eight, the final question and by far my favorite: "Any song suggestions for the bachelorette party playlist?" I mine my memory for the soundtrack of our Dunlap days, discarding all the musical theater that floats to the surface. "Girls Just Want to Have Fun" is an instant add, plus every Shania Twain track I can name. The memories are vivid—a rainy day crafting at the Outpost, thunder booming behind the stylings of Shania while Gin, Chrissy, and I sipped wine and played fast and loose with half-closed bottles of paint. It's a squarely happy memory from when my drinking was still fun and made me do silly things like finger paint pink hearts on Gin's thighs. It wasn't so cute later on when I drank for survival more than having a good time.

My fingers prickle, the memory as tangible as the coffee I wash it down with. I could create another soundtrack, a darker one, full of songs that stir up less flattering memories. "September" by Earth, Wind & Fire, which played at Gin and Renee's work holiday party while I drunkenly argued with their boss about who knows what. "You Oughta Know" by Alanis Morissette, Gin's go-to karaoke song at every one of her birthday parties, including the night we broke up. Worst of all, every Cold Sweat song, reminding me of everything I used to be, the mistakes I made and everything I missed while on the road—the birthdays and holidays, but also the lazy weekends with my then-girlfriend. I missed out on so much while lost in a boozy blur, chasing a dream that never even really felt like mine. I squash each memory like a bug, then add in a few more songs from our college pregame playlist, clicking submit once I hear Aidan buzz in.

"Whaddup, early bird," Aidan says en route to the kitchen, then pauses mid-step and scratches his stubbly chin. "I'm not booked until noon, right? Studio B?"

"Studio B," I confirm. "Noon to ten."

He checks his watch, pulls in a deep breath, then tips his head back. "*Fuuuuck.* Such a long session, dude." He slinks off toward the fridge and comes back with an energy drink. *Classic Aidan,* I think. Same sweatshirt, same vice as always.

Most shifts begin with Aidan handing me an input list, so that's what I'm expecting when he shows me his phone. Instead, I'm staring at a black-and-white photo of three rail-thin, tattooed white men leaning against a chain-link fence. Ahead of them, a massive and menacing pillar of a man blocks most of the shot. For a moment, I am not a person; I'm just a thudding pulse, beading with sweat. "That's my old band," I choke out, then take the phone from Aidan's hands, chewing my cheek. Why is he showing me this? And why can't I look away?

"I thought so." Aidan takes a long swig of his energy drink. I can smell it from here—peaches and batteries. "Cold Sweat, right?"

I nod, still staring at the photo. I've intentionally avoided Cold Sweat updates for the sake of my own sanity, so this is my first good look at the bassist who replaced me. He's a carbon copy of both the drummer and the rhythm guitarist. Gauged ears. Cropped, bleached mullet. Only the lead singer, Solas, stands out, the way I used to. It's his band now.

"Yo, earth to Alice."

I didn't realize Aidan had still been talking. "Sorry, what?"

"I said—it's crazy, dude," he says. "They just booked the studio."

My composure disintegrates. "Wait. Are you serious?"

Panic skitters through me like a rat down an alley, memories of missed lobby calls and arriving two hours late to studio sessions, still drunk from the night before, too wasted to lay down a bass line. Screaming at Solas. Getting screamed at right back. We both deserved it. We were assholes back then.

"Wh-when are they booked?"

"In a couple weeks," Aidan says. "They're cutting a few demos before . . ." He scratches his stubble, thinking. "They're touring with somebody later this summer. I don't remember."

But Google remembers. Cold Sweat is booked on a summer-long tour opening for a major pop-punk group, including a concert in Chicago this August being advertised as their hometown show. It has its own specific line of merch and everything, shirts and koozies that say *I broke a Cold Sweat in Chicago.* Jealousy scratches at the base of my skull, shredding my common sense. *That could have been me,* I think, but it's not really true. There is no alternate reality where I'm still playing in Cold Sweat. They're better off without me, and I'm better off, too. It stings, though, how their version of better looks so much more impressive.

"June thirtieth," Aidan reads from the studio schedule. "That's when they're coming in."

I swipe out of the Cold Sweat website and open my calendar. June 30. A Monday. "Can I go ahead and request that day off?"

Aidan gives me a thumbs-up and slurps his can of peach-flavored battery acid. "Just get your shift covered," he reminds me. And I need the reminder, considering the only other time I've taken off work was the month after Dad died. By the time Aidan's thoroughly caffeinated and ready for setup, I've already texted every other assistant about covering the shift. My loss is their gain. It should be a great session, so long as I'm not there.

Thursday night is the Great Bridesmaid Summit, as I've taken to calling it in my Notes-app texts to Dad. I haven't gone much of anywhere aside from the studio for the last year, and there's a nostalgia—albeit a grimy one—about taking the Red Line. The train shudders down the track like a rattlesnake with a belly full of commuters, and I get off just a few blocks from Chrissy's apartment, right where Chicago's gay nightlife butts up against Cubs baseball. This, I have often thought, is the true crossroads of America, and it somehow makes sense that it's where Chrissy lives. Her building is a classic greystone three-flat with an arched doorway tucked behind a wrought iron gate. It could very well be the same apartment she moved into out of college, but that was too many years and beers ago to be sure.

I'm scouring my email for the gate code when, behind me, someone clears their throat, and I'm instantly annoyed on a cellular level. Renee looks fresh from the office in a distractingly well-fitting pencil skirt and a red satin blouse tied in a bow around her neck. She tosses me a bored "Hello," then motions for me to step aside. I do, and she punches in the code with the ease of a regular visitor, letting the gate swing back to hit me square in the gut. A sound like a squeaky dog toy flies out of me.

"Sorry," Renee says, sounding very *not* sorry.

I grind my teeth and concentrate on Gin's voice in my head. *You can at least try. You guys are my family.* If Renee got the same speech, I've yet to see evidence.

Up a flight of carpeted stairs, Renee stops at the pink doormat that reads *Welcome home, babe.* The babe herself appears before we can knock, waving us into an apartment that feels every bit Chrissy. She's matured from the rhinestone-based decor of her college days—a little less sorority Barbie, a little more Lisa Frank's cool older sister. The faux-cheetah-skin rug beneath her fuchsia couch feels like an homage to eighteen-year-old Chrissy, but her kitchen is sleek, all white quartz with dashes of red and pink. On the counter, three stemmed wineglasses are already waiting, each one filled with—of course—pink wine.

"I hope you guys drink rosé," Chrissy says, teeing up my sobriety announcement nicely.

I clear my throat. "Thanks, but actually, I don't—"

"I love rosé," Renee interrupts, slicing me a quick prickly look. "But I believe I was in charge of wine." She pulls a bottle from her bag and presents it to Chrissy the way a waiter would tableside.

"No freaking way. This is my absolute favorite wine." Chrissy grips the bottle by the throat and holds it up like a trophy, smiling wide. "It's an omen," she announces. "This is going to be the best bridal party ever."

"Cheers to that." Renee claims a glass of rosé, and there's one in my hand before I can turn it down, but I set it right back on the counter.

"Should I give you the tour, Ali Pal?" Chrissy suggests, confirming that I have *not* been here before. Good to know.

I smile and sweep a hand through the air. "Lead the way."

We start in the kitchen, which Chrissy insists is "just, like, a boring kitchen," although there's nothing boring about the neon *CHRISSY'S KITCHEN* sign glowing purple on the back wall. Without asking, she grabs my wineglass for me, walking backward like she did in her days as a Dunlap College tour guide. She leads us to her office, where two things become immediately clear. The first is that the Chrissy I knew in college, the original-recipe Chrissy who glued rhinestones to wine bottles and bought everything in bright pink, hasn't entirely grown up. She's still here, just confined within the walls of her office.

Which brings us to the second realization: Chrissy has no idea what an office is. It certainly isn't this. There isn't even a desk, just two cushy pink velvet chairs and a matching sofa with lip-shaped throw pillows. There's a whiteboard, which feels office-adjacent, and the microphone-and-camera setup suggests some kind of content recording happens here, but the stack of Hula-Hoops and the bookshelf stocked with tarot-card decks don't call any specific type of content to mind. I make a mental note to google Chrissy later. For now, all I can think to say is "This is so you."

"I know, right?" Chrissy sets both wineglasses on the coffee table before plopping down on a pink beanbag chair.

"Lemme know if you need a refill," she says, nodding to my completely full glass, and I'm determined not to be interrupted this time, but once again, Renee is a little *more* determined to interrupt me.

"Go easy, gals. We've got a lot of ground to cover tonight." She turns over her shoulder, marker in hand and poised at the whiteboard, and pins me with a watchful look, like I'm a toddler wandering suspiciously close to the candy bowl, not a grown woman who isn't even touching her wine. Who wouldn't have touched it at all if I had been given a say, which I haven't. I can't get a word in. A white-hot spark of anger hits my rib cage like a battering ram. I'm speechless, and Renee whirls back to the whiteboard before I can change that.

"First things first." She refers to her phone, then writes out a set of dates in perfect print. "The last weekend in June is open for all of us, Gin included, so let's lock that in."

I pull up my calendar. It's the weekend right before Cold Sweat is in the studio. "That's awfully soon," I think aloud.

"So is the wedding," Renee parries. "And on that note, given the abbreviated timeline, I recommend that we pick a destination where I've already planned a bachelorette party. That way, we can tweak an existing itinerary. I suggest Scottsdale. I planned an amazing bachelorette trip there last summer, and my aunt owns a house that we could use for free."

"Scottsdale would be fun," Chrissy says.

"What are our other options?" I ask.

Renee frowns but obliges. She reads a list off her phone, writing each potential destination on the whiteboard. "Austin, Vegas, Nashville, Palm Springs, and . . ." Her frown deepens. "Galena?"

Chrissy lights up. "Oh my God! Your dad's house, right? Or . . ."

Her eyes shift from me to Renee as she scrunches back into her beanbag chair. "Sorry. I mean . . . is that okay to say?"

I feel instantly itchy from the inside out. Of all the ways Dad gets brought up, this is perhaps the worst: when people make him out to be Beetlejuice and if they say his name three times, they'll wake the dead or break the living.

"Yes, Chrissy," I sigh. "The house belongs . . . belonged . . . to Dad and the rest of his band. It's fine."

Chrissy brightens a little. "What did they call it? The Outhouse?"

I snort a much-needed laugh. "The Outpost," I correct her.

"I don't think we need to host Gin's bachelorette party at anyplace worthy of being misremembered as the Outhouse," Renee says, not at all amused. She lifts her hand to cross Galena off the list, and a spring-loaded protest flies out of me.

"It's not like that!"

Renee pauses, then turns with an icy glare and one barely arched brow. My insides twist. I wish I had practiced this pitch.

"Galena is like a mini Napa," I start, gaining confidence and momentum as I go. "There's a ton of wineries and a really cute downtown with lots of fun shops. There's plenty to do. Even if we just want to wander around like we did in college when we went for spring break and—"

"I know all about Galena," Renee cuts me off, knocking me off course, and my mind spins off in a thousand directions. *Which stories has Gin told you? I was never that bad in Galena, was I?* I can feel myself losing, so I play my best card.

"We can use the Outpost for free," I say. "And there'd be no plane tickets to pay for, which makes it even better and more affordable than Scottsdale."

Admittedly, I'm speaking a little bit out of my ass here. I haven't talked to anyone about using the house, but I don't see a world where The Handful would tell the daughter of their recently deceased lead singer that she can't have one last weekend with the place.

The beanbag chair rustles in the silence as Chrissy shifts. I don't love the look on her face—it's pinched but cautious, like she's worried a frown might offend. "So is the house like . . ." Her eyes flit around the room, refusing to stop anywhere for more than a beat. She delivers the rest of the thought just to Renee. "I'm worried that might be kind of a weird vibe."

Anger pulses behind my forehead. "Why would it be weird?" I ask a little too quickly. I want her to say it. I want her to prove she really has no shame.

"Because, like . . . your dad." Chrissy winces. Not apologetically but from the pure discomfort of the moment. *How cringe,* I think, *for my dad to die.*

I wish I could be honest. If I could, I would tell Chrissy and Renee that this year has sucked beyond belief, that it's so weird to be a bridesmaid right now, weirder than they can even imagine because neither of them has a history of dating the bride or is mourning a dead parent. I would tell them about the memorial concert, about Dad's replacement, how I have to go back to the Outpost to make room for a new lead singer—and how if there was another reason to go back, a trip like we used to take over spring break, maybe it wouldn't hurt so much. If we could go back to the Outpost, if we could sit by the firepit and spill secrets like wine on the living room carpet, maybe the four of us could get along the way Gin, Chrissy, and I did back then, before things got bad. Maybe we could make good memories, take pictures I remember taking. If I could, I would tell them this is bigger than a party; it could be the thing that makes my summer tolerable.

But it's not about me, so I can't say that. What I say instead is "It could be like old times."

"I don't think Gin would want to relive *old times*, do you?" Renee says, a little louder than seems necessary. "I think Gin would prefer something new."

And that's it. It's done. With a flick of her wrist, Renee crosses off Galena. No further discussion. No taking it to a vote. My heart wrings itself out like a wet towel, defeat seeping down to my toes. But it's not my party. I can't cry, even if I desperately want to.

I resign to the back seat of this meeting, apathetic about our remaining options. Nashville gets booted next. The bride isn't crazy about country music or clubbing, which rules out both Austin and Vegas, too. Three more lines, three more flicks of Renee's wrist.

"I guess that just leaves Scottsdale and Palm Springs." Renee twirls the marker between her fingers. It clacks against her stacked gold rings. "Just a reminder, I already have a completely free place for us to stay *and* an itinerary for a Scottsdale trip, so—"

"Didn't you say Gin would prefer something new?" The words tumble off my tongue before I consider whether it's wise to say them.

"Mmm," Chrissy hums. "That's true."

Renee's nostrils flare, and I can feel my pulse climbing up my throat. She's a dragon, and I just swiped at her hoard.

"It would be new to *her*," Renee argues. "And to you guys. It's just the same itinerary as th—"

"Nuh-uh." Chrissy wags a finger. "You said it, Renee. It's gotta be new."

Renee chews her lip and clicks the cap of the marker on and off again. Majority rules, and with a defeated sigh, she begrudgingly crosses out Scottsdale and draws a star next to the final remaining destination: Palm Springs.

Chrissy's high-pitched squeal sets off the dog upstairs. She throws her arms in the air, the pits of her elbows batting against her ears as she sways in time to the barking. "The springs, baby! Get pumped!"

I wouldn't call myself pumped but a bit smugly satisfied. If I don't get my way, neither does Renee, who frowns at the board like she's checking her work—or rather, how much work she has ahead of her. Chrissy raises a toast to our first major decision as bridesmaids, and I abstain, of course, but only Renee seems to notice. She eyes me as she sips, studying me through her wineglass. A pang of something hot runs through my veins; I turn away.

The rest of the evening is a series of more minor bachelorette-related decisions, such as *Themes: Yay or nay?* And *Are we doing the thing where all the bridesmaids wear black?* Chrissy and Renee speak a common language of bachelorette party traditions, and I try to keep up with what I'm voting against. We agree on no themes, no workout classes or major feats of physical exertion, and—much to Chrissy's chagrin—no penis-themed paraphernalia. By the end of the night, the whiteboard is a mess of ideas, and Renee snaps reference photos on our way out the door.

"How are you guys getting home?" Chrissy asks as we're slipping on our shoes.

"Red Line," Renee and I say in unison, and my worried glance collides with hers.

"Right, you guys are, like, practically neighbors!" Chrissy says, and my body registers the state of emergency before she even finishes the thought. "Y'know what? Why don't you just split an Uber? My treat. I charge rides to my work card, like, all the time."

Renee smiles weakly. "You really don't—"

"Already booked it." Chrissy flips her phone to show us her screen. It's as bright as her smile, glowing with an estimated pickup time of . . . now. She motions us both in for a group hug, and we reluctantly allow it.

"Thanks," I grumble. Renee can't even manage that much, but Chrissy beams like a pageant queen.

"You know I've gotta look out for my fellow bridesmaids."

Outside, a black sedan is already waiting, and when Renee climbs into the back seat, she doesn't scooch over, forcing me to go around. Clearly we have similar feelings about our surprise carpool. The car smells way too strongly of air freshener, and with no music playing, I tune in to the layers of traffic and whatever melodies leak from the open windows of passing cars. This, I hope, is how we will spend this entire drive: in silence, each of us staring out the window like two kids stuck in time-out.

Renee, it turns out, has other ideas. After a minute or two, she huffs, "I hope you're happy."

I dig my nails into my palms. "Why would I be happy, Renee?"

"Because you've made my life infinitely harder," she snaps.

This does, in fact, make me a little happy, but I don't admit that.

"This bachelorette party could've been simple and affordable," she goes on. "But no. You had to go and veto Scottsdale."

"And you vetoed Galena," I fire back, "which would have been the simplest and most affordable option. You're the one who said Gin would want something new."

"Forgive me for not wanting any of us to relive your college days," she says icily.

"And forgive *me* for thinking that Gin deserves better than you recycling your old work and passing it off as new."

"I have one month!" Renee wags a finger at me before putting up three more. "Four weeks! Do you know how difficult this is going to be? Can I take a *wild* guess and say you've never planned a bachelorette party?"

I slouch back, wishing I could slip between the seats. "I've never even been to a bachelorette party," I admit.

"Aha! Of course you haven't. If you had, you would know that I'm right."

"And you're *always* right, aren't you? Just *obsessed* with being right."

"I'm not obsessed with it," Renee hisses. "I just. Am. *Right.*"

Our driver switches on the radio and instantly turns up the volume, drowning us out with an early-aughts throwback, and not-so-subtly reminding us we're not alone. I'll send Chrissy money to tip this guy extra well and make up for tanking her Uber rating, but per the ETA glowing on the driver's phone screen, I have ten minutes before Renee Roberts is no longer my literal captive audience. And I made a promise to Gin. I need to *try.* So I sigh, crack my neck, and turn as much as my seat belt will allow, determined to look Renee square in the eye.

"Look. I'm sorry if I pissed you off tonight," I start. "You pissed me off too. We're probably going to piss each other off a lot in the next few months, but even if you hate my guts—"

"I don't hate your guts," Renee interrupts. "I don't hate anyone's guts."

"Fine. I'm just trying to say—you're completely valid in disliking me."

I wait for her to correct me again, but she doesn't. Instead, Renee shifts her weight and smooths her hands down her skirt without comment.

"I know I wasn't the best person when Gin and I were together," I go on. "But that was five years ago, Renee. A lot has happened since then. You probably weren't the best version of yourself in your early twenties either."

"In *my* early twenties, I was enrolled in one of the top MBA programs in the nation."

My laugh cracks through the car like a lightning strike. "Well, pardon me for forgetting I'm in the presence of the patron saint of having her shit together."

"I'm not a saint, *Alice*." Renee says my name like a swear. "I'm just not a mess. There's a difference."

I bark out a single disbelieving laugh. "Well!" I toss my hands. "There you have it! Gin asked me to *try*"—I make air quotes—"to get along with you, but if you're not playing along, then that's it. I have officially *tried*."

It's hard to get much of a read on Renee; the lights of the city cast oddly shaped shadows across her face, and just when I'm sure we've settled back into our mutual time-out silence, she blurts a question into the dark.

"Do you not drink anymore?"

Surprise zips up my spine—once, then again when Renee's eyes land on mine. They're the tiniest bit warmer and more curious than her standard icy stare. A muscle somewhere deep in my core unflexes.

"I'm sober," I finally say.

"Since when?"

"Since Dad's health took a turn. About three years."

"Right," Renee says softly, then after a short skin-crawling silence, "I'm sorry, by the way. About your dad. That must be tough."

*Tough* is exactly the word. Tough like a gristly piece of meat that you can't chew through, no matter how hard you try. Tough like a playground bully who's waiting for you in the same spot, rain or shine. For nearly a year, the grief has been consistent and unbreakable, something I can only wear through little by little but never all the way. "Yeah," I say. "It's been tough."

"Congrats on getting sober, though." Renee's tone is more even and earnest than it's ever been—at least when directed at me. Something stutters inside me at the sudden warmth, but Renee ices right back over. She straightens, lips pressed into a firm line, before muttering, "I never would've guessed Blackout Alice had it in her."

I scoff through my nose. "Yeah, well. I never would've guessed I'd be going to Palm Springs with Renee Roberts."

She rolls her eyes, but they don't meet mine again. Instead, Renee is back to gazing out the window, watching the lights blur into streaks. Without looking at me, she adds, "Anything for Gin."

"Anything and everything for Gin," I agree, and I swear I see the corners of Renee's lips twitch—not with a snarl but not quite a smile.

*Hey Dad,*

*Sorry it's been a while since I've written to you. It's been kind of a weird night, and I don't know that I really have anything good to say, but I just really miss you.*

*Planning Gin's bachelorette party has me thinking a lot about planning your funeral. They're not so different: just two parties planned in someone's honor, but without much of their input. When Mom and I had to pick out flowers and what type of wood your casket should be, I wished you were there to weigh in. We should've asked you what you wanted while you were still around.*

*What I'm saying is I'm sorry if your funeral wasn't exactly what you would have wanted. I'm not sure if you got to watch from wherever you are, but we had you buried in your Luccheses. I knew you would approve. I hope you approve of The Handful's new singer, too. I think I'm less upset about the band and more upset by the thought of some new guy using your room at the Outpost. I wish we could keep that house exactly how you left it, like a museum of you and The Handful with all your guitars and summer clothes. Sometimes I want everything to stop because you're gone. No one can take your place, Dad.*

*Love,*
*Your Dallas Alice*

# Six

The start of Chicago summer feels like the answer to a collective five-month prayer. Not that I pray, but if I did, a sunny forecast for Memorial Day weekend would be all the proof I needed that someone, somewhere, was looking out for me.

The studio is still open on holidays, but Aidan gave me the day off in exchange for picking up a shift this Friday night. For the first time in ages, I wake up without an alarm, blinking into the sun that falls in warm slats across my bedspread. I toss back my covers and muscle open a window, letting fresh air pour in, as thick and sweet as the yolk of a seven-minute egg. Warmth shimmers through me. It's finally summer.

I hurry through a truncated version of my morning routine, slipping on my favorite leather shorts and a plain white tank top. I don't bother looking in the mirror to futz with my hair; I'm too eager to get out in the sun and soak up the first truly nice day we've had since September. *Since Dad died*, I think, then type *Wish you were here* into my running note of texts I'll never get to send. Just then, an actual text appears from Gin, and the group chat pops off.

**GIN'S I DO CREW**

**GIN BENNETT**

Hey guys! Guess who booked a wedding dress shopping appointment!?! Mark your calendars: Saturday June 14th at Kilpatrick's Bridal Outlet. Appointment is at 9 A.M. and I figure we can do brunch after!

**CHRISSY AMATO**

YAAAAAAAAY!! OMG. It's HAPPENING!!! FYI, that's the day before Father's Day, so I'll have to head straight to my parents' place after brunch. Hope that's okay!!!!!

**RENEE ROBERTS**

Wouldn't miss it, Gin! Similar sentiments about Father's Day, but that morning, I'm all yours! Maybe we can get a carpool going, Chrissy? I'll need a ride.

**GIN BENNETT**

Omg, leave it to the girl who's no-contact with her parents to forget about Father's Day. But YAY!

**So glad you guys can come! I can't pick out a dress without you!**

**ALICE PIERCE**

**That Saturday works for me.**

**ALICE PIERCE**

**Yay!**

I blow out a breath, then turn my phone off and ditch it on the kitchen counter. I need a break from the constant correspondence, and lately, if I'm not texting the group chat, I'm barely resisting the urge to look up what Cold Sweat has been up to. What festivals have they played? What acts have they collaborated with? But the biggest question, the one I can't stop asking, would yield no search results: What would I say if I saw Solas again? I leave it all behind for this summer's inaugural iced coffee run.

Outside, the weather has transformed an ordinary day into something of a street festival. The sidewalks bustle with people, some debuting their shorts for the season, while others shed their top layers and knot them around their waists. Everyone I pass looks a little familiar, like I've seen them in a dream or in line at the grocery store, but I don't really *know* any of them. That's the beauty of living in a city so big that it could swallow the rest of the state in one gulp: I'm one in a metropolis of millions. I can be anyone or no one, Ricky Pierce's daughter or just another sleepy-eyed sucker walking into the coffee shop.

Or at least that's what I used to think, but one step into Grounds Crew and my heart skids to a stop. Near the door, a woman sits alone at a table, nose scrunched at her laptop as she toys with a strand of white-blond hair that's fallen loose from her claw clip. Renee Roberts, two feet away from me.

My immediate instinct—to bolt out the door and find a new favorite coffee shop—is thwarted by my own big mouth. I audibly gasp, drawing the attention of not only Renee but a half dozen other people, all blinking up at me with reasonable concern. Renee's head cocks as she plucks out an earbud, and my cheeks burn beneath her heavy-lidded stare. I try an awkward smile, but she doesn't match it. I wish to dissolve into coffee grounds. The next best option is to step into line.

I order my usual large cold brew, plus the last two chocolate croissants in the pastry case. A peace offering of sorts. The barista slips both croissants into one crinkly brown envelope, and I tip twice as much as usual. Good karma, I hope.

By the time I've swirled the perfect balance of oat milk and sweetener into my coffee, Renee's attention is back on her laptop, nose crinkled with focus. In a plain red square-neck tank and light-washed denim cutoffs, she's dressed more casually than I've ever seen her, although still in all her usual jewelry—hoop earrings, rings stacked on nearly every finger, and a single gold chain that rests just above her collarbones. The sun glints off it, and I feel the sparkle in the arches of my feet. Even dressed like the rest of us, she's striking. It's not fair.

"Special delivery." I rest my elbows on the chair across from hers and give the pastry bag a shake, but Renee's eyes don't budge. She holds up her index finger, one cherry-red nail pointing upward in a silent demand: *Wait.* I have half a mind to show her a different finger, but after two sharp slaps of the space bar—*clack clack*—Renee lifts her gaze to mine, unamused.

"Do you need something?" Her tone borders on offended, like I've barged into her office by patronizing a coffee shop.

"Well hello to you, too," I grumble.

Renee sets her jaw, pushes out a sigh, and tries again. "Hi, Alice." She says it like it's work. "Like I asked, do you need something?"

I shake the bag again. "I thought *you* might need a croissant."

"No thanks." Then she's back to her laptop, probably typing up a very long list of reasons I should leave her alone, which is precisely why I won't. It's a little fun, getting on Renee's nerves.

"Whatcha working on?"

Renee glances up at me, annoyed, then back to her screen. "Bachelorette stuff."

"Like what?"

She sighs again, then clicks her tongue. "Actually, since you're here, I could get your information for booking flights, if you have a sec."

"I have lots of secs," I rattle off. *Shit. No. NO!* "Seconds! I mean seconds! I have plenty of seconds! I have time!"

My cheeks are on fire, and a flicker of something combustible dances in Renee's eyes. She laughs, a bright, airy *ha* that pins me in place as I sink into the empty seat. I'd classify this squarely as laughing *at* me, not *with* me, but it's some consolation to know Renee is capable of laughter. As she types, her rounded red nails hit every stroke with the even precision of a trained pianist, and I catch myself staring. The spell only breaks when she spins her laptop and slides it across the table, presenting me with the usual airline forms so I can key in all the customary data: name, birthdate, TSA PreCheck info.

"These might have been better questions for the bachelorette questionnaire," I point out.

Renee is, as usual, unimpressed.

"That questionnaire is foolproof," she insists. "I've used it eight times."

"Did you say . . . *eight*?"

"Yes, eight."

"You've planned *eight* bachelorette parties?"

A small smile passes over Renee's lips, one that says *I'm guilty, but it's barely a misdemeanor.* "I'm an extraordinary event planner."

"Oh, I remember," I say. "You so *generously* replanned all of Gin's birthday parties."

"I wouldn't have had to replan them if you planned them well enough in the first place," she says matter-of-factly.

"What more did you want from me? It's a karaoke costume party. I wore a costume. I rented a karaoke machine."

"And you *broke* the karaoke machine on her twenty-third. If I recall, you drunkenly kicked it over when I tried to sing 'Seasons of Love.'"

"I would have done that sober."

"Oh *sure*." Renee props her chin on her fist, playing therapist. "And when Gin brought you to see me in a show and you snored through my entire solo, would you have done that sober, too?"

A cold burn of shame washes down my throat. "I was kind of counting on you forgetting about that," I admit. Or at least I was counting on her not bringing it up.

Considering how much of my early twenties is lost beneath a blanket of blackouts, it seems unfair of my brain to preserve all my worst memories. I can still feel the jostle of my shoulder as

Gin shook me awake, the blurred confusion of being sent home at intermission, but it's the look in Gin's eyes that I've tried and failed to forget. She was angry. Disappointed. But worst of all, not even a little bit surprised.

I squeeze my eyes shut and pull in a deep breath that morphs seamlessly into a sigh.

"I'm sorry I did that," I say. And I mean it. "I'm sure I apologized to you back then, too, it bears repeating. I really am sorry."

When I open my eyes, Renee's scowl has softened to a skeptical frown. "I'm not sure that you did apologize back then."

"Well, if I didn't, then I'm doubly sorry," I say. "Can I make it up to you? Do you want to sing something now? I promise I'll stay awake."

I catch the smallest tug of a smile on Renee's lips, but it's gone in an instant.

"Or how's this? You mentioned needing a ride to Gin's dress-shopping appointment. I could drive you. And I promise not to talk to you the entire drive. Consider it an extension of this belated apology."

Renee rubs her lips together, considering. She spins the gold band around her middle finger—once, twice. "All right," she says on the third spin. She tips her chin once. "You have a deal."

"Oh." I blink at her, feeling suddenly off kilter. I didn't think she'd take me up on that. I clear my throat and sit a little taller. "All right. Great. So I . . . can pick you up? Or we can meet at my place. Whatever's most convenient."

Renee's eyes narrow as she leans back in her seat, arms folded over her chest. "Trust me, Alice," she rasps. "*Nothing* about you is convenient."

## SATURDAY, JUNE 14

**RENEE ROBERTS**

Morning. Are you picking me up or should I meet you at your place?

**RENEE ROBERTS**

I'm walking over. Pick up your phone.

**RENEE ROBERTS**

I swear to God Alice if you don't pick up your damn phone

**RENEE ROBERTS**

I'm about to buzz your gate

**RENEE ROBERTS**

If you're still asleep I swear to God

**RENEE ROBERTS**

This Uber is like $200 Alice are you fucking kidding me right now?

**RENEE ROBERTS**

I CAN SEE YOUR CAR OUT HERE
I KNOW YOU HAVEN'T LEFT

**RENEE ROBERTS**

I'm getting an Uber.

# Seven

My morning is a high-speed race against the laws of time and traffic, and against all odds, I might be winning. Granted, I've broken many speed limits and possibly the sound barrier, but I squeal into the parking lot of Kilpatrick's Bridal Outlet just nine minutes past Gin's appointment time. Not great but also not technically possible by the GPS's projections. Had I known picking up a Friday night shift would keep me at the studio until 3:00 a.m., I never would've taken it, but it's too late now. I throw my truck in park, fling open the door, and take off at a sprint, then a jog, and finally a walk, huffing and puffing into the store.

"Are you okay?" the girl at the front desk asks, and I nod, too breathless to form a sentence. I scan the shop for a redheaded bride and startle back when I spot my own reflection instead. My sweaty pink face is embarrassing enough without the bed head or the crusty white ring of dried toothpaste around my lips, but maybe no one will notice my busted face thanks to my completely inappropriate attire: terry cloth pajama shorts, Nike slides, and a sweatshirt that has never before left the house. On it, a cartoon beaver balances a tower of martinis on his head above the words *BEAVER LIQUORS.*

"I'm . . . with them," I pant, gesturing vaguely with one hand and cleaning up my toothpaste mustache with the other. "The group that just came in. Gin? Virginia?"

Once the clerk has verified the bride's name and my sanity, she directs me past the racks of tulle toward our designated shopping station. There are rows of them, little shopping cubicles, each with its own changing room and three-way mirror. Around a raised wooden platform, four high-backed pink velvet chairs—practically thrones—are arranged in a crescent shape, and I finger comb my hair before slinking into the last available seat.

"Look who's here!" Chrissy reaches over to squeeze my forearm by way of hello.

Beside her, Gin's smile doesn't quite stick, but there's still excitement in her "Yay!"

On the opposite end of the crescent moon, Renee's upper lip curls like a fish snagged on a hook, and I swear I feel the ground tremble beneath me. She folds one long, tan leg over the other, glances down at her watch, then back up at me. Not with her usual icy stare but with a blank, flat expression—the face of a woman who was expecting the worst and got exactly that. Shame sinks like a lead weight into my stomach, and I begin a much-needed apology tour.

"Gin, I'm so sorry. And Renee—"

"Is this everyone?" a saleswoman interrupts, taking the platform like it's a stage.

"Yes, sorry about that," Gin says.

*Sorry about me,* I think.

Our saleswoman claps her hands and holds them clasped at her chest. It lands somewhere between a cult leader calling a meeting to order and the head cheerleader ready to kick off a routine. Either way, we're at attention. "Hi. I'm Rose. This, of course, is Kilpatrick's. Which one of us is the bride?"

Gin lifts a sheepish hand, but the light bouncing off her ring is less quiet about it.

"And who's the lucky guy?"

*Or girl,* I think. Gin just smiles and says, "Rishi."

Any unease in Gin's voice dissipates when she says her fiancé's name, like it's the password we've been trying to guess, the secret ingredient we couldn't quite identify. My heart stalls in my chest, and I miss the rest of what Rose has to say. I can only hear Gin's voice; those two little syllables of her fiancé's name and her whole demeanor changed. It's magic. It's love, and it makes my heart ache. I want that. Someone who makes everything better. I want to make everything better for someone else, too. It feels like all I ever do is make things worse.

Gin and Rose chat dress styles and price points, and I try to pick out scraps of vocab. *Mermaid. Trumpet. Tulle.* When Rose steps away to pull some options, I pounce back on the conversation.

"I am so, so sorry I was late, Gin. And that I look like . . ." I gesture to my whole messy self. "And Renee, I can't apologize enough. I swear I set a bunch of alarms, but I picked up a shift at the studio last night, and I usually don't get up until—"

"Hey." Gin holds up a hand like a crossing guard, but her voice is gentle, and there's a twinkle in her eye. "Slow down. Okay? You're fine. You made it. Renee made it, too. We're okay."

"Okay," I sigh, and Gin's lopsided smile gives me a little hope. Renee's dagger eyes do exactly the opposite.

She fixes her face, though, when Rose wheels in today's main event: a silver rolling rack holding six white dresses, each a little poofier than the one behind it. Rose leads our bride into her changing room and into the first choice, a dress that seems to match Gin's original vision: It's fitted from the beaded straps to the bottom of the lacy bodice. Maybe a little too fitted, though, considering the way her boobs spill out the top like biscuits from a tube.

Gin takes a few hesitant steps toward us, and when she turns to face the mirror, we get a view of all the industrial-looking clips and clamps fitting the dress to her frame. Business in the front, mechanic's shop in the back. I watch her eyes in the mirror as they follow the lines of her silhouette, her soft smile not clueing me in on what's happening inside her head.

"I really like this style." Gin swivels her hips, shifting the waterfall of fabric.

With the first word of approval, Renee snaps a picture. "For reference," she explains. "So we can keep track and refer to the photos later when the dresses blur together." She stands and untucks the tag, snapping a photo of that, too.

"That's so smart," Gin marvels. "Thank God for you."

A frustrated knot pulls tight in my belly. Why does it feel like Renee is competing with the rest of us, gunning for the title of Best and Most Beautiful Bridesmaid? Did she interpret Gin's lack of a maid of honor as a challenge for us to vie for the role? A second thought rustles in the bushes of my mind, one I don't want to look in the eye: Maybe it only feels like Renee is doing the most because I'm not doing nearly enough. I straighten up in my plush pink throne. I can step it up.

"How do we feel about the boob situation?" Gin studies her cleavage in the mirror. "I'm going for *on display but put away*."

"I wouldn't exactly call them put away," I offer thoughtfully. Chrissy giggles, but Renee shushes me, and my head snaps toward her with a look that asks *What the hell did I do wrong?* Her stare intensifies, underlining its message. *Everything, Alice. You're doing everything wrong.*

As the appointment goes on, every dress further establishes the pattern: Gin waddles out, silently assesses herself in the mirror, and makes a ruling on the dress that we're all supposed to agree with, actual opinions be damned. I mostly keep quiet, nodding and smiling whenever it feels appropriate, although I do blurt out a few comments I can't quite squash, feeling increasingly stupid each time I can't keep a thought inside.

"How many more do I have?" Gin whines from her changing room. After a resounding no on three dresses in a row, our bride's morale is dangerously low.

"Just one more," Rose says. "But it could be the one! It's the one with the sleeves."

"I love the one with the sleeves," I say to Chrissy, perhaps a bit louder than the whisper I intended.

Renee shushes me again, and not quickly either. She hangs on to the hiss for at least a count of three.

I cast a pleading look in Chrissy's direction, but she looks straight down at her lap, both hands up as if to say *Leave me out of this.*

"No opinions until the bride has already expressed her own," Renee scolds. "That's the first rule of wedding dress shopping."

"Sorry." Under my breath, I mutter, "How many rules are there? Forty-eight?"

"It's common sense," Renee whisper-shouts. "Kind of like showing up on time and dressing appropriately?"

"You know what else is common sense?" I hiss. "Not being a complete c—"

The rattle of the changing room curtain cuts me off, and Renee and I zip ourselves up, silent and attentive. Guilt hits my chest like a wrecking ball. *What's wrong with me?* I think. *Why can't I keep my stupid mouth shut?*

But when Virginia steps out in the last dress of the day, every thought evaporates from my brain except for one: *Wow.* She takes one cautious step forward, then another, and it's like I can see the aisle forming around her. Taylor Swift's "Wildest Dreams" plays faintly through the speakers, a violin over a heartbeat, and it occurs to me that, if Gin and Rishi's love had a soundtrack, it wouldn't be stacked with these emotional, romantic power ballads. It would sound like karaoke bars and dating-app notifications. Same goes for most of the couples I know. But seeing Gin in this dress, something clicks into place. I get it. She looks the way this song sounds—grand and dramatic and beautiful—and I wonder if that's what weddings are for. Are we trying to create something—an event, a party—that feels the way being in love does? Big, special, indulgent . . . there's something to be said about turning that feeling into an external reality. Dad's funeral was the same. The memorial concert will be, too. Maybe grief is just a long, lonely marriage to a person who no longer exists.

"Alice?"

I jolt in my seat and resettle into reality. Right. The bridal shop. Where Virginia Bennett has been transformed, veil and all, into a proper bride. And I've been . . . what? Staring into space and dissecting the role of ceremony in major life milestones? I'm genuinely afraid I'm going to open my mouth and what will come out is *Actually, Gin, when I saw you in this dress, I started thinking about my dad's funeral!*

"What do you think?" Gin's voice is dipped in hope.

She's a vision. She's a bride. "You look like a love song," I tell her softly.

Gin's hands fly up to her face, steepling over her nose as the sniffles begin, and my heart pinches. Renee digs a pack of tissues from her purse, but it's soon obvious that they'll be as much help as a single bucket bailing out the *Titanic.* Gin's shoulders begin to shake, and her crying evolves into full-body sobbing.

"Oh, honey." Chrissy jumps up to hug our bride, and Renee's blond hair whips back and forth as she searches for more tissues. I feel my pockets, including the pocket of my sweatshirt, and an idea smiles up at me in the form of a cartoon beaver. I peel off my sweatshirt, down to sleep shorts and a ribbed gray tank, but what's the damage at this point? I wad up the sweatshirt and pass it to Gin.

"Go nuts," I say. "Seriously. My clothes are your Kleenex."

Gin nods through sputtering breaths, then blows her nose into the sleeve, and I almost feel proud. Almost. Mostly, I'm glad that Gin's sobbing dies down, and Chrissy touches up her makeup so she's a photo-ready bride. There's a list of requisite pictures to capture: one of Gin in the dress and another back in her street clothes while holding the *I found the gown at Kilpatrick's!* sign. Rose insists upon a group photo, and my attempt to cover my bralessness with some clever arm positioning leaves me looking like a broken puppet.

It's an awful photo of me, and Chrissy immediately sets it as her lock screen. "I love this picture. It reminds me of the ones from Galena." She zooms in on me and my mess of bed head. "I mean, c'mon. Classic Alice, right?"

The words sear into my chest. *Classic Alice.* I could've sworn I left her in the past.

We celebrate the single most expensive purchase of Gin's adult life over brunch at a bar and grill down the street. It doesn't seem like the sort of venue to order a bottle of champagne, but Chrissy gets one anyway, and I put in two orders of mozzarella sticks, just for myself. "Sorry," I say to no one in particular. "I didn't have time to eat breakfast."

"You didn't have time for a lot of things this morning," Renee quips, and Gin shoots her a look she absolutely deserves. I probably deserve it more, though. What kind of adult woman can't properly set an alarm?

Once the champagne arrives and the waitress collects our orders, Gin proposes a toast.

"To the best family a girl could ask for." She lifts her glass high. "I couldn't do any of this without you." She proves that point when, after a sip of champagne, Gin begins conducting check-ins on each of our bridesmaid assignments.

Chrissy is first, promising "a bridal shower to end all bridal showers." A bold claim, but she's a bold gal.

"Same restaurant as the engagement dinner, right?" Gin confirms.

"Yes, but . . . remember that patio you loved so much?"

Gin frowns. "They told me they didn't rent it out for private parties."

"They don't." Chrissy lifts her champagne once more. "Unless the event manager is your boss's brother."

They clink glasses, laughs swirling together, and I file away the knowledge that Chrissy does, in fact, have a boss.

"What about the bachelorette party?" Gin turns to Renee, who straightens in her seat.

"Everything is just about booked," Renee promises. "I'll send out the itinerary by the end of next week."

Gin looks pleased. Bridal shower? Check. Bachelorette? Check. I tense when her mossy eyes land on me, but before I can decide whether or not to lie, she winks. "I'm not worried about your speech. You have plenty of time."

She's right, of course. So why do I still feel like I'm falling behind?

"Let's talk about the main event, though." Chrissy props her elbows on the table and rests her chin on both fists. "How is wedding planning going?"

"Great." Gin shrugs. "There's really not that much to do."

Renee's laugh is a two-toned ambulance siren. "That can't possibly be true."

"It is," Gin insists. She tilts to the side, feeling around for her purse. "Most of the work is going to be getting the Bhats' backyard ready. It overlooks this beautiful marsh with cattails and tall grass . . . I'll show you a picture, but Rishi and I are planting a ton of flowers so we don't have to decorate. Like, at all."

"Obsessed with that," Chrissy says.

"Well, if we can help with anything, let us know," I chime in, and Gin smiles.

"You guys were a huge help today. I really didn't want to try on any more dresses and then, boom. The very last dress." She holds both hands to her chest like she's pressing the moment there, stamping it onto her heart. "I wanna look at the picture again. Whose phone is it on?"

"Mine," Renee chirps, already scrolling. "One sec. I'll find it." But I can see her screen from here. If I squint, I can read the words in the search bar: "easy backyard wedding decor." I can't say that I'm surprised.

We split the check and say our goodbyes, each of us headed in separate directions for tomorrow's holiday. Renee has a train to catch to Iowa, Chrissy disappears in a cab to the western suburbs, and Gin is headed just down the road to celebrate Father's Day with her soon-to-be in-laws. When she hugs me goodbye, she holds on a few extra seconds.

"Call me tomorrow if you need me," she says.

It feels like my heart is developing a blister. Even after my shameful performance today, Gin is still as kind and supportive as if I had sewn her a wedding dress myself. I don't deserve it. I don't deserve her. And yet here I am anyway, trying my best. Only I'm worried my best isn't quite good enough.

"And hey." Gin squeezes my shoulder. "Happy early birthday, Alice."

Of course she would never forget.

That night, I stay up till midnight, as is my ritual for every big holiday since Dad's been gone—Christmas, his birthday, any day that makes his absence hurt a little extra, I stay up to face it, priming myself for the morning. When the clock on the stove rolls over to 12:00, it's officially Father's Day, and I'm officially twenty-nine.

I sleep like shit, but I wake up to a happy-birthday text from Gin and a phone call from Mom before I'm even out of bed.

"Morning, birthday girl! How's your day so far?" Every syllable is bouncy and exaggerated, like Mom is performing joy without knowing what joy feels like. I wonder which one of us she's trying to fool?

I yawn and throw back the covers. "Thanks, Mom. I just woke up, so . . . happy Father's Day, I guess."

It's quiet for a long time, Mom's uneven breathing the only evidence that she hasn't hung up. I'm halfway to the kitchen by the time she sheds the act. "I wasn't sure if I should even mention it," Mom says, sounding like my mother again. Tender and trampled.

"Yeah, well." I swallow. What else is there to say? I'm already workshopping excuses to hang up when Mom sighs—not a sad sigh, thankfully. More like a reset.

"Well. Since you mentioned it, I've been going through some old scrapbooks looking for Father's Day photos."

I tip my head, pinning Mom's voice between my cheek and my shoulder while I dig a clean mug out of the dishwasher.

"I didn't realize how long we had that porch swing out front at the Outpost," Mom goes on. There's a rustling behind her that crescendos to a staticky crackle, and I wince.

"What are you doing, Mom?"

"I'm trying to find these pictures . . . just . . . hold on."

I switch to speakerphone and dress up my coffee while listening to her dig through what sounds like a pile of dead leaves.

"Aha! Found it." Mom sounds victorious, then sighs again, wistful. "God, it's a cute one. You used to sleep anywhere as a kid—did I ever tell you that?"

"Mmm, I don't think so."

"Anywhere but your bed. I swear there are at least . . ." More rustling. "Three different pictures of you napping in a pizza box."

A smile sneaks up on me. I'm not always up for reminiscing, especially about Dad, but it's reassuring to know I was sleeping in odd places long before alcohol was part of the equation.

"But hey. Anyway. *Birthday girl.* Any plans for the day? I've got your present wrapped and ready, if you wanna swing by. I could get a cake or something."

This sinking, guilty feeling is getting a little too familiar. I never did reschedule that dinner with Mom. "Maybe sometime this week? Today's no good, but . . ." I check the calendar on my fridge, lifting up June to peek at July. "I've got a lot going on with Gin's wedding, but I should be able to find a good time."

The words stick to my tongue. *A good time.* I have time, but the thought of visiting Mom at that house just never feels good.

"Well, you're welcome anytime," Mom says. "Anytime at all. I'll rearrange plans if I have to. Just let me know."

"I will," I say, and I hope it's true.

Mom and I trade *I love you*s, then hang up without saying goodbye. Another ritual—this one I've insisted upon since I was a kid, back when Dad would leave for tour and I'd run out the side door in my pj's for one last hug. I didn't always know when I'd see Dad next, or if I did, it would be weeks or months away, miniature eternities to a kid like me. Just in case something happened, I made sure *I love you* was always the very last thing that we said.

It was, in the end, the last thing Dad and I said to one another. We didn't think we'd get two more weeks with him after his esophagus ruptured; instead, we got two more years of *I love you*s. Which might have felt okay if not for how many more Dad turned down. After the rupture, the doctor gave it to him straight: *You could live another twenty years if you just stop drinking.* But Dad gave it straight back. He told the doctor, *I won't.*

Not *I can't.* Not *I don't think it's possible. I won't.* As in *I refuse to try.* Not the twelve-step programs. Not psychiatry. Not rehab. We showed him brochures from facilities with cliffside cabins or breathtaking beachfront views, places made for people like Dad who could only be sold sobriety if it came in the shape of a ninety-day resort stay. We could afford it. We could send him. We were willing—and so was the band—to rearrange the pieces of our lives to make space for Dad to quit drinking. But he wouldn't. So I did. I needed to, or I'd end up just like him.

Some part of me thought if I quit, Dad would follow suit, but he didn't, and now Dad's gone and I'm left to feel it all, sober, the way he never could. Lonely, even though I don't have to be. Mom gave it to me straight. My present is waiting. So is she. All I have to do is go home, but I can't. I won't because it hurts too much. I rub my palms against my eyes and push the tears back inside. I really am just like my dad.

> *Hey Dad. Happy Father's Day! Or rather . . . SAD Father's Day! Sorry, I'm not feeling very funny. It doesn't feel like my birthday. It just feels like a bad, stupid day.*
>
> *I used to love when you told the story of how I was born the Saturday before Father's Day, how I showed up and made you a dad just in time to celebrate. It made me feel extra connected to you, but now it just feels unfair. My birthday really had to fall right on Father's Day the first year you're gone, huh? It's a sick joke, and I'm mad about it.*
>
> *I have to be honest—I'm mad at you, too, Dad. Because you should still be here. Getting sober has been harder than I ever imagined, and I know it would've been even harder for you. But I still can't believe that you weren't even willing*

*to try. You talked about seizing the moment and taking advantage of the opportunities I was afforded just by being Ricky Pierce's kid, but what about you? You turned down the opportunity to live, and I might not ever forgive you for that. You're not even here for me to yell at about it.*

*But I still love you, Dad. I always will. I wish you could come back.*

*Love,*
*Your Dallas Alice*

# Eight

The itinerary for Gin's bachelorette trip hits our inboxes first thing Friday morning, exactly one week before our flight to Palm Springs.

**FROM:** Renee Roberts

**TO:** Christina Amato, Alice Pierce, Virginia Bennett

**SUBJECT:** Palm Springs before the rings!

Hey ladies,

T minus 7 days until the big weekend! Well, not THE big weekend, but the biggest weekend before the couple of the century ties the knot! I've attached an agenda and packing list for your convenience, but let me know if any additional questions come to mind! **Please note that our flight leaves at 9:05 AM on Friday, so please set your alarms accordingly.**

Can't wait to celebrate our bride!

XO,

Renee

The message alone makes me grit my teeth, but when I click open the itinerary, it feels like my brain is on fire. Renee has provided a colorful twelve-page display of complete disregard for every group decision we made. The bridesmaids agreed on no workout classes or major physical exertion, but Renee has scheduled a six-mile hike. We voted no on themes, but Renee has assigned *three.* Neon pool party. Disco cowgirl. Dress like your favorite martini night.

I shove up from my desk, stomp out of my home studio, and yank my phone off its charger to text Renee, wtf I thought we said no themes???

Immediately, Renee switches on Do Not Disturb, and I seethe until I remember the time—Renee is likely at the office. Probably Chrissy, too, if she even has an office outside the playroom in her apartment. I text Chrissy, Have you read the itinerary yet?

Immediately, she calls.

"Sorry to buzz, but I figured it was faster!!" Chrissy's voice is even closer to a shout than usual. A gritty, mechanical growl rumbles and revs in the background. "SORRY IF IT'S LOUD!"

I wince away from the phone and thumb down the volume. "It's, uh. No problem. Where are you?"

"AT THE RACETRACK!"

"Like . . . for cars?"

"NO, SILLY!" Chrissy laughs. "FOR WORK!"

A million questions dogpile in my mind, but for the first time, Chrissy's job isn't the most confusing thing demanding discussion. She must step away from the racetrack; the engine noise dies down enough to hold a conversation.

"Anyway, the itinerary email," I prompt.

"So cute, right? The *Gin and Juice* T-shirts? Perf."

"Right. But did you see the themes?"

A pause, then skeptically, Chrissy says, "I thought we weren't doing themes."

"Exactly. Or anything too physically strenuous, but Renee's got us down for a six-mile hike."

There's a muffled shuffling on the other end of the line, followed by some distant engine revving and the *tip-tap* of Chrissy's nails on her screen. When she's back on the line, Chrissy says, "Huh. Weird." But that's it. No call to action or suggestion of accountability. Just *Huh. Weird.* My insides start to itch with a helpless rage I can't set free. Am I crazy? This is crazy.

"So what do you think we should do?" I press, and the line is silent far longer than I'd like. I've begun to pace the width of my bedroom when Chrissy clears her throat. Or maybe it's a car engine. Either way, the next part comes through loud and clear.

"I guess we should pack accordingly!" Chrissy says, and I stifle a groan. If I can't convince Chrissy that we should unionize, I'm out of options. Not unless I want to throw a tantrum, but I refuse to resort to the tactics of Classic Alice. When we end the call, I toss my phone onto the bed and flop down beside it in defeat. There's only one thing left to do: Shop for costumes.

The Palm Springs Airport looks less like an airport and more like the world's cutest outdoor mall, but it feels like it's built inside

Satan's sauna. After an ultra-early morning and a four-hour flight spent alternating sleep with *Diners, Drive-Ins and Dives,* I'm groggy at best, squinting into the too-bright sunshine as we deplane onto a tarmac that ripples with heat. It's an otherworldly type of heat, like we've touched down on a different planet a few thousand miles closer to the sun. I spot the group of neon-pink *Gin and Juice* shirts waiting for me in the shade, fanning themselves with their itineraries. Renee provided us all with physical copies, just in case we needed some not-so-light reading for the flight.

With everyone present and accounted for, an insultingly refreshed Renee leads us to the baggage claim with the authority of someone who has been here before, which she hasn't. Her cherry-red hard-shell is the first of our luggage to spit out onto the conveyor belt, followed by the same purple suitcase Gin has stayed loyal to since our Galena spring break days. Chrissy being Chrissy somehow sweet-talked the flight attendants into letting her carry on her oversize leather weekender bag, so I'm the last one standing at the carousel, watching bag after black tagless bag pass me by.

"Here comes the beast!" Gin shouts from behind me, and I turn, following her outstretched finger to the oversize luggage area, where my giant blue suitcase awaits. How the rest of them packed for every themed event in smaller-sized bags is beyond me. Big Blue here was an emergency purchase from Village Thrift, along with every neon swimsuit I could find and any article of clothing that might qualify as "disco cowgirl." Needless to say, I've already complained extensively in my Notes app to Dad.

I roll Big Blue back toward the group, feeling envious of everyone who chose to wear shorts. Moisture pools behind my knees and drips down my calves, soaking through my sweatpants. Thank God today is a pool day.

Renee leads us to the rideshare pickup zone, where she calls us a car. The plan is for her to put everything on her credit card this weekend, and we'll divvy up the costs after. According to Renee, this is standard practice for bachelorette parties. According to me, Renee is hogging all the credit card points.

"Ricardo will be here in four minutes," she says, then reads the license plate number aloud. "It's an SUV."

"So that should fit Alice's bag." Gin snickers. "Where are the rest of us going to sit?"

I sigh internally, then opt to lean in.

"Actually, I was planning on riding this baby all the way to the hotel." I smack my suitcase like it's a horse, throwing in a "Giddyup!" and earning a bright, bubbly laugh from the bride. *This is fun,* I think. *We're having fun. It's hot as hell, but so far, I'm doing okay.*

"God, you guys are the best," Gin says. "And this." She sweeps her hands all around. "This is the best. It's gorgeous here. Thank you so much for planning this, Renee."

"Anything for you," Renee says, and it feels like my rib cage has been laced up and pulled tight. Anything for Gin. It's the truth. All of us would bend over backward for this woman, and she would do the same for us. She *has* done the same for us, for *me,* when I least deserved it. If I can remember why I'm doing this—why I'm sweating in the desert wearing eye-bleeding neon pink, why I bought not only a new suitcase but an entire new wardrobe for this trip—if I can remember it's all for Gin, I can do it. There's so much I would never do for myself, but for her, I'd do it all twice.

Our SUV arrives, and once we've piled in both our luggage and ourselves, the driver changes the music to suit his audience. A greeting from Snoop Dogg kicks off Katy Perry's "California Gurls," and Chrissy swings her feet like a giddy toddler. "It's staaaarting!" she sings, just like she did at the airport this morning and again when the plane took off. I wonder when it will stop starting and start happening. Hopefully she'll alert us.

We get through "Man! I Feel Like a Woman!" and most of Whitney Houston's "I Wanna Dance with Somebody" before arriving at a hotel that looks like a collaboration between the makers of Barbie and Candy Land. The automatic doors part, and we're welcomed with a blast of air-conditioning into a lobby entirely sectioned out by color. All the neon-pink furniture is separated from the neon-yellow furniture and so on, and every square inch is positioned for a photo op. Renee files into line to check in, standing behind what looks to be another bachelorette party. The group is already dressed for the pool in little black bikinis and sheer black sarongs—all but one, of course, whose all-white getup includes a bedazzled captain's-style hat that labels her as the bride.

"I'm sooo glad we decided not to do the whole bridesmaids-wear-black thing," Chrissy whispers, and Gin nods in slow motion, eyes wide.

"It feels funeral coded," I add, and Gin traps a phlegmy laugh behind her lips.

"I usually think it's classy," Chrissy says, "but can you imagine wearing black in this heat? And it looks so stupid here of all places." She spreads her fingers and draws two circles in the air with her hands, encapsulating the Skittles bag we've been dropped into.

"I like our pink shirts." Gin pinches her own a few inches off her body to inspect the design: It's retro with loopy letters printed in a slightly darker shade of pink than the shirt itself. "They're cute but not like . . . Bride Tribe or Team Bride or whatever."

"I can't believe you left your bedazzled bride captain's hat at home, though," I mumble, and Gin laughs again, only this time, it doesn't stay behind closed lips, but ricochets off the color-coded walls. A man behind the front desk shoots her a scowl reminiscent of a cartoon villain.

"Ew, grumpy gills over here at the counter," Chrissy says with an eye roll. "How are you going to work *here* and be in a bad mood?"

"Imagine working somewhere where you're constantly interacting with party people," I offer. "Everyone is always having fun except for you. That might grate on the poor guy."

"Well, he should cheer up," Chrissy decides, "because Ginny is getting married and there are no bad vibes allowed." She grabs our bride by the shoulders and shakes her as if to rattle away any bad vibes she might've caught from being scowled at.

Renee rejoins the group with two sets of key cards and a clear agenda as to who will be rooming together. She pockets one pink plastic card, then holds out the other set to Chrissy and me, but Gin grabs them first.

"Chrissy, do you wanna be roomies again?" Gin bounces her brows. "Like freshman year?"

"Okay, love that!"

Chrissy snatches the key cards and passes one to Gin, knocking Renee's smile right off her lips. It's quick—just a fraction of a second that Renee's face goes slack before she swallows and pins a smile back in place, passing the single remaining card to me. My throat feels like it's closing up, but I only smile back, because that's what a good bridesmaid would do.

Per the instructions of the grump at the desk, we turn left at the neon cactus, twisting and weaving down a series of halls with dim overhead lighting that's almost yellow against the concrete floors. It's the opposite of the rainbow lobby, proof that this renovated motel used to be something dingier. We hang a left, a right, and then we're back to our regularly scheduled color scheme, plus a smell that's eerily familiar. I pinpoint it instantly: It smells like our freshman dorm, like old buildings and industrial cleaning products and mixed drinks. Unlike the dorms, each hotel door is painted a different candy-coated color, and Renee slows us all to a stop in front of two doors labeled 106 and 107—orange and pink, respectively. Lesbian colors. Nice.

"Should we meet up in twentyish minutes to go check out the pool?" Renee suggests.

I mush my lips together to keep from laughing. Renee is playing this off so casually, as if this twenty-minute break to unpack and refresh before pool time weren't already outlined in our itinerary.

"Sounds perfect," Gin says. "Just come knock when you're ready." She gives Chrissy a wink. "Our room can be the party room."

"Honey, wherever you are is always the party room," Chrissy gushes. "But sounds perf. See you guys soon."

With our *perf* plan decided, we file into our rooms. To match our pink door, we've got a pink dresser, pink mirror, and a long hot-pink curtain half covering a sliding glass door overlooking a patio. The carpet is Barney purple, and in the center of the room, a single queen-size bed with a pink headboard is dressed in the usual fluffy white hotel duvet. My stomach sours. *A queen? Really?*

Renee must be thinking the same thing. She marches straight to the room phone, punches a few numbers, and puts on her sweetest customer-service voice. "Hi, I was calling to see whether you have rolling cots available? I don't mind paying an extra fee." Based on her flattened expression, I'd guess it's not good news.

"Uh-huh." Renee sighs and rubs her temples. "Well, thanks anyway." She docks the phone and lets out a long, slow breath.

"I'm guessing there's no—"

She waves me off. "Take whichever side, I guess."

And I can't help it. I'm feeling petty. "So you mean I should just do whatever I want to do?"

She blinks at me. "Um, yeah?"

"Cool. So how about I ask you for your thoughts on which side of the bed I should take, but then I'll just go ahead and take whichever side I want."

Her stare is one part pissed, two parts confused.

"I could send you a survey," I go on. "Forty-eight questions about exactly how you think we should share this room for the next two days, and then I'll still just do whatever I want, even if we agreed not to do it."

Renee's nostrils flare. "Oh *come on.* This is about the themes?"

My laugh is more of a cry of disbelief. "Yes, it's about the themes, Renee. And the . . . oh, what is it?" I page through the massive printed itinerary. "Yes, right. 'We know our Gin is an early riser, so let's meet in the lobby at six so we can beat the heat before the sun rises! Please pack a canteen, CamelBak, or other bottled water.' Blah blah blah." I march across the room and thrust my itinerary right up to Renee's nose. "A SIX. MILE. HIKE."

Renee doesn't flinch. She speaks plainly. Sternly. Only in statements of fact. "Gin put me in charge of the bachelorette party. I collected input; then I planned the special weekend Gin deserves."

"Is this?" I tug on my T-shirt, holding it taut. "Not already special? We have matching T-shirts. We're in fucking *Palm Springs.*"

Renee rolls her eyes. "That's baseline."

"That's *absurd.*"

"No, actually, it's not," she says. "It's about what you'd *expect* for a bachelorette party, which you wouldn't *know* because you've never even been to one."

"Oh, right, Renee. You're right, as usual. I've never been to a bachelorette party, so tell me: Is it normal to share a room with an enormous tw—"

"HEY, BITCHESSSS. Where the fugggarrrryooou!?" The headboard rattles with the repeated thuds of someone—Chrissy—pounding on our shared wall. My breath stills in my lungs. Thin walls. I would have loved to have known that sooner.

More pounding. "It's been twenty minutes!" Chrissy shouts. "Let's gooooooo!"

"We're almost ready!" Renee hollers, a bald-faced lie, but the thudding gets wobbly and more hollow . . . and then it's coming from the sliding glass door. Renee draws open our hot-pink curtain to reveal a distant view of the pool and, up close and personal, both Chrissy's and Gin's asses smooshed up against the glass.

I'm not sure if what flies out of me is a laugh or a shout, but it's loud, and it startles Renee almost as much as the two surprise butts on display. She flips open the lock, and Gin and Chrissy squeal and sprint back toward their room, tugging up their bikini bottoms and splashing hard seltzer across the concrete.

"Slow down on the mini bar, party room!" Renee hollers, and when she slides the door shut again, it's like the air in the room has changed. We've been mooned; suddenly, nothing feels that serious. This is a party, after all. We're on vacation. Not my idea of a vacation but a vacation all the same. I snort a laugh at the four round ass-cheek prints left on the glass, and Renee rolls her eyes, but she cracks a smile. When she sashays off to the bathroom to change, I think, *Okay. Maybe we'll actually survive this.*

We put on our suits and meet our ass-print artists on their patio just ten minutes past schedule. The heat has gotten worse, but the view almost makes up for it. The sky is one seamless stretch of blue, interrupted only by mountains painted a shade of purple I've never seen outside a bruise. "So pretty," I mutter, ripping the tags off my new neon-green one-piece. This is the first and likely last time I'll ever wear it.

Past the sunny yellow gates, the Barbicide-blue water awaits, bookended by two amoeba-shaped hot tubs and bright-yellow umbrellas like daffodils springing up from the concrete. Color upon color, and that's without even acknowledging the hundred or so people milling and splashing about in a rainbow of suits. The only place for my eyes to rest is on Gin's all-white bikini. Her flip-flops are highlighter yellow, though, a small commitment to today's neon theme.

"Ready to hit it?" Gin asks.

"Maybe we should swing by the bar first," Chrissy suggests, sliding on her pink heart-shaped sunglasses—we all got a pair in the goody bags Renee handed out at the airport.

"No need for the bar," Renee says. "I had the hotel stock the cabana."

"Of course you did, you master event planner." Gin shimmies her shoulders while digging through her pool bag, fishing out her own sunglasses—they're the same heart-shaped ones, only white. When she slides them on, Chrissy snaps a selfie of the two of them, then motions us all in for a group shot.

"Say Rishi!" Gin cues.

"Rishiiiiiiiiiiii!"

Chrissy takes a few rapid-fire shots from different angles and continues to film as we walk in not-quite unison toward the pool, our flip-flops *th-thwack*ing like grace notes. Past the gate and the DJ spinning Madonna remixes, the bar is packed with girls ripping tequila shots, and gaggles of gay men in tiny trunks and fluorescent Speedos dance on any and every available surface, sipping from novelty cactus-shaped cups. Neon Pool Party, it seems, was not a theme mandated by Renee; it's the name of the event, printed on every highlighter-yellow koozie.

Ours is the only empty poolside tent, and we arrive just in time to stop a cabanaless freeloader from setting up in our spot. Who could blame him? Every pool chair and sun umbrella is spoken for. Five years ago, if I were in his shoes, I would have looted our mini fridge by now.

"No way! Hard kombucha?"

Gin wastes no time starting the party. I claim a seat on the hot-pink sectional and listen for the hiss and the snap of the can, bracing myself for the smell. Alcoholic or not, kombucha has always smelled like rotten wine to me.

"Ooh, grab me one!" Chrissy peels off her crocheted pool cover-up to reveal the teeniest neon-green bikini and a body likely built by some offshoot of Pilates. "This is, like, beyond cute, Renee. Thank you so much for booking this."

"Of course."

I turn just in time to watch Renee's fingers pinch open the last button of her white linen shirtdress. It falls open, parting around a black strappy bikini, its neon-pink boning tracing her soft curves at sharp angles. I can feel my pulse in the roof of my mouth. Of course she has the perfect swimsuit for the occasion, one that simultaneously adheres to the theme, stands out from the crowd, and activates a kick of something urgent and hot in my throat.

The black is stark against the neon, both high contrast against her skin. But that's not where my focus is.

It's not that I forgot Renee had great boobs. They're one—two—of her very few positive attributes. And she's always been hot. Anyone with functioning eyes would agree. But the gentle slope of soft skin sitting plush above each cup of her bikini . . . I mean, c'mon now. Who looks like that? That's just not fair.

"Um, Alice?" Gin says.

My attention snaps to the bride. "Huh?"

She's playing with the pop tab of her hard kombucha can. "You're staring."

"What? No." I meet Renee's sparkling eyes, and a tidal wave of heat crashes over me. She arches a brow, and I start to sputter. "Her—I mean your, uh . . ." I gesture to . . . I don't know what, but I keep waving broadly until I figure it out. "Your . . . your *shirt*." I motion to Gin beside me. "Isn't, uh. Isn't only the bride allowed to wear white?"

"Ooh, she's right, Renee," Chrissy hollers, and Renee's eyes drop to her shirt. She peels it off, eyes on me the entire time. It makes me sweat. Then again, it's a million degrees out. Everything is making me sweat.

Once there's a drink in every dominant hand—hard kombuchas all around and a bottle of water for me—we toast to what's sure to be a legendary weekend. The second round of hard kombuchas disappears as quickly as the first, and round three begins while we're all still taking turns with the SPF 50. When I offer Chrissy the sunscreen, she bats the bottle away.

"I don't burn." She smiles and tosses her blown-out bob. "I'm Italian. We just tan super well."

"At least put some on your face," Renee insists. "For wrinkles."

"Can filler melt?" I wonder out loud.

Gin swats my arm, stifling a tipsy giggle. A better reaction than I'd hoped given I'd meant to keep that as an inside thought. Chrissy is oblivious; she's fully wrapped up in her phone again, taking a selfie and smirking at a text seconds later. Gin sidles up to her on the sectional. "Who are you texting, Chriss?"

Chrissy presses her phone to her chest, looking faux guilty. "Oh my God, okay, don't make fun of me. Promise?"

Gin and Renee promise, but I keep quiet. I can make no such guarantees.

"Okay. So." Chrissy rolls her shoulders back. "Do you remember that waiter from the engagement party? The tall one with the super-white teeth?"

Gin gasps. "You're dating *him*?!"

"Stop, no!" Chrissy blushes. "We're just talking. But he was so cute, right? And I'm trying to stop dating people I work with."

I'm smearing my ears with sunscreen, but they still burn at the mention of Chrissy's job, which I still haven't figured out. "Who *are* the people you work with?"

"Coworkers. Duh." Chrissy shoots me a look like I'm the crazy one here. "Anyway, Gin, not to be annoying, but are we getting plus-ones for the wedding?"

Gin's laugh is practically carbonated. "Seriously? Would you really invite . . . wait, what's the guy's name?"

Chrissy's lips shrink down to a sour-lemon pucker, her eyes wide and darting left to right. "This is so bad." She winces. "I've just been calling him Waiter Boy."

"You don't know his name?!" Renee swigs her hard kombucha

before slamming it down on top of the mini fridge. "I watched you text this boy when the flight took off *and* when it landed and you don't even know his *name*?"

"I'm gonna figure it out!" Chrissy says.

I choke back a laugh. "Before or after they put *Waiter Boy* on the seating chart?"

Gin guffaws. Her cheeks are beginning to flush, but I'm not sure if it's the sun or the booze. "Wait," she says. "Waaaaaaaita-minute. Chrissy. Have you slept with him?"

"Oh my god, NO! Can you imagine?" Chrissy lazes back on the sectional and releases a loud, seductive moan. "Ohhh, Waiter Boy." She convulses for effect. "Don't STOP, don't STOP, Waiter Boy!"

Someone from a neighboring cabana whistles and yells back, "You tell him, girl!" Personally, this would send me into hiding. Not Chrissy. She jolts upright and takes a dramatic bow. The unison cackle that explodes out of our cabana could drown out two Madonna-spinning DJs and a crowd twice as loud.

"Oh my God." Gin doubles over, hanging on to her own knees for dear life. "Do we have to go into hiding the rest of the weekend?"

"I'll still associate with you in public." Renee shimmies her shoulders toward Chrissy. "That is, if Waiter Boy brings a friend."

The Waiter Boy jokes spill into the fourth round of drinks, and my only contribution—subbing *waiter* for *skater* in Avril Lavigne's "Sk8er Boi"—is an enormous hit. The girls shriek-sing the chorus repeatedly, and when the DJ finally puts it on, their victory howl is deafening, devolving into laughter and booty shaking and Chrissy filming every second of the fun. I sway my shoulders and smile when she turns the camera on me, but I can't match their energy. I'm weighed down by this sad, shrinking feeling in my belly that I wish would either go away or swallow me whole. I haven't been in a situation like this—me the sober one while everyone else is drunk—and I'd forgotten that I only started liking parties when I started drinking too much to remember them. I miss the person I could be when I drank. Not mean, aggressive Blackout Alice but the bubbly, brazen person I would become after the first two or three drinks. But I could never stop there. I've only ever been able to drink too much or not at all. Sober, I feel a little like I'm peering through the glass of an aquarium I can't jump into. When Avril gets to the bridge of "Sk8r Boi," Gin struts toward me, arms outstretched and a mischievous glint in her eyes. She takes my hands and tugs me up onto my feet for the last verse and chorus. I try to dance. I try to sing. I even lock eyes with Renee a few times and test out a watery smile. I'm still trying. With Renee. With everything. For Gin.

Somewhere between the sixth and seventh rounds of hard kombuchas, I turn into the annoying sober friend. It is sweltering, and Renee's minute-by-minute itinerary leaves no space for a trip to the emergency room.

"Plot twist of the century," Chrissy jokes while I pass out a third round of waters. "Blackout Alice making us hydrate? What's next? Is Willie Nelson gonna tell us to quit smoking weed?"

Gin laughs and shushes Chrissy, all in one breath. "She's Sober Alice now." Her head turns before her eyes do, lids weighed down over a clownish grin. "That's why you're *mothering* us. Right, Alice?"

Even through her drunken haze, Gin must see the hurt flicker in my eyes, because her smile slips and she chugs her water, apologizing by way of sobering up. Or so I think until she stands and clears her throat.

"Speaking of Willie Nelson," Gin says. "Did you know that Alice Pierce once performed with the man himself?"

My cheeks burn, and no SPF can save me. "Gin, please."

"No, no." She holds one finger aloft. "The people deserve to know one of the coolest stories of all time. The Handful was playing Willie's birthday party, right? In Texas? This *big* show, and we were right out of college. We got to be backstage, and Alice Marie Pierce." She burps. Grins. "Making *herstory*, slammed a beer and *joined* them. She *shared Willie's mic.* And Alice's dad had to be, like, *No no no, it's okay, security—that's my daughter.*"

Chrissy crackles with laughter, and Gin fumbles for her phone, insisting she can find a video. If it's possible for a person's soul to turn red, mine is blazing. I glance toward Renee, whose mouth hovers just above the lip of a spiked seltzer can. She's not laughing. She's not even smiling. A shadow passes through her eyes as they flick toward me, and then—

"Cannonball contest!"

It's a total Hail Mary, and for a split second, I'm not even sure I'm the one who said it, but I kick off my flip-flops and take off at a sprint. My feet scald on the concrete. My cheeks burn in embarrassment. I can't take another minute of this damn heat.

I jump, a clean cannonball breaking through the water, which isn't nearly as cold as I need it to be. I feel safe beneath the surface with the muffled bass beats, then even safer when a second cannonball splashes beside me, then a third and a fourth. We bob up to the surface one by one, their drunken laughs just as loud as the music. In this moment, even sober, I feel like a part of the group.

By the end of our pool day, Chrissy is the color of a boiled lobster, and three out of four of us are very drunk. Renee stumbles through the sliding glass door of our room, then flops down on the bed in her still-damp bikini, blond hair splayed out behind her like a mermaid.

"Sleepy?" I tease.

"Exhausted," Renee slurs. "I'm so . . . I don't even remember if tonight is Disco-Cowgirl night or Dress Like Your Favorite Martini."

"The martini one," I remind her.

She sits up, nose scrunched. "What are *you* gonna wear?"

"Blue," I tell her. "Because my favorite martini is water."

Renee snorts—adorable—then stabilizes herself on the edge of the bed, suddenly droopy eyed and serious. "I'm sorry about . . . the dress . . . themes," she fumbles out. "The dress . . . costumes. I just . . . it's just fun." She swallows hard, her soft blue eyes blinking in and out of focus. "I think I might need some . . . of your favorite martini."

A laugh fires out of me. Renee might be funnier than I thought. She topples back and starfishes across the bed, and in the time it takes me to fill a cup from the sink, she's asleep. I leave the cup on the bedside table and take the first shift in the shower. Tonight's look—and most of my clothes for the weekend—comes courtesy of Village Thrift. It's a cobalt-blue sheath dress that skims my shins, and with silver sneakers, I am . . . well, a tall drink of water.

When I come out, all dressed, Renee is awake again, holding a now-empty water cup and seemingly a bit more in control of herself. I, too, am looking for a bit of self-control. The longer Renee sits on that bed in her bikini, the tougher it gets not to stare at her boobs.

"Hey," Renee says, no longer slurring, but softer than usual. "Gin told me about the dress."

I pinch my collar. "This dress?"

"Her engagement-party dress. How she spilled wine on it and you switched with her." She bites her lip. "That was . . . really cool of you."

My heart loosens its grip. "It was her day. I was just trying to help." My gaze shifts to the empty cup. "Can I refill your water?"

Renee nods and hands off the cup. "Thanks." When I bring it back, she blows a raspberry. "You're being so nice to me," she complains.

"Do you want me to start being meaner?"

"Nooooo."

"Are you sure? I've stockpiled plenty of insults. You've given me a ton to work with."

She swats one limp hand like she's batting away a bug, spilling her entire cup of water in the process. I fill it up again, and Renee glugs it down, then pounds a fist against her chest, coughing twice. "I'm . . . sorry that I'm kinda drunk right now."

"It's a bachelorette party," I remind her. "You're supposed to be drunk."

"I know, I know. I just feel weird about it because you're not drunk. You won't be drunk. All weekend. I don't think." She squints at me. "Will you be?"

"I will not."

"That's what I thought, but . . . I didn't even . . . I didn't drink that much." Her head turns before her eyes do, and she peels a wet strand of hair out of her eyes. "It's just . . . *so* hot out there."

"Which is why we're drinking water," I remind her, but it comes out a bit infantilizing, and she rolls her eyes. I deserve that.

I refill Renee's water one last time, filling a cup for myself too.

I toss it back like a shot, and Renee makes a pinched sound, something adjacent to a laugh.

"You still got it in you," she says.

"Huh? Oh, you mean . . ." I mime taking a shot with my empty cup. "Only with water these days. Or espresso." I check the time on my phone. "You should shower. We've got dinner in thirty minutes."

Renee sits forward, holding my gaze for a moment longer than I expect. "You read the itinerary," she says in a light, airy voice that borders on impressed. It's likely just the booze, but I'll take what I can get.

"I read the itinerary," I confirm. "Now c'mon. Half hour. And you better not make me late."

# Nine

My alarm chimes at 5:00 a.m., launching me into pure panic.

*Where am I? Whose bed am I in? Did the tour van leave without me?*

My eyes shoot open, heart stepping on the gas. Some dormant neural pathway has sparked to life and thrust me back in time. I'm fresh off my breakup with Gin. On tour with Cold Sweat. In a stranger's bed. And another. New city. New stranger. I'm late. I'm still drunk, waking up beside a woman whose name I don't know.

*No.*

*Breathe.*

*You're fine, Alice.*

Gradually, my body unlocks, blood flowing back to my toes as I position myself within space and time. I know where I am. I know who I'm in bed with. Blackout Alice wasn't invited on this bachelorette trip, and the only drunk woman who got in this bed last night is snoring softly beside me, legs braided into mine.

Wait. Legs braided into mine?

Last night, Renee and I went straight back to the room after dinner at the hotel restaurant, where a gin, dirty, and espresso martini—Gin, Chrissy, and Renee, respectively—devoured chicken tacos alongside their water glass sidecar. Renee and I got ready for bed in total silence, then fell asleep with our backs to one another, each of us hugging our edge of the mattress. I'm positive. But she must've tossed, and I must've turned, and here we are, tangled in the center of the bed.

I hold my breath and keep as still as possible while I determine my next move. Should I wake her up? Shove her off? I could fall back asleep and let her deal with this later, but even with the AC on full blast, the pleasant heat of her body is growing less pleasant by the second. I draw in a breath, then gradually lift my leg and Renee's with it, the soft skin of her thigh slowly sliding off mine until she groans and rolls over, blond hair spilling on the pillow behind her.

I get dressed and ready, wearing my thinnest, most breathable tank top over a pair of swishy black athletic shorts. The high is 107. The sliding glass door is already hot to the touch, and when I open it, it's like opening an oven. I duck right back inside and triple-check the itinerary. We're scheduled to leave for our hike in half an hour.

I jostle Renee's shoulder. "Psssst."

No movement.

I shake her harder. "I think it's too hot to hike."

Renee groans—louder than before—then rolls onto her stomach and sandwiches her head between two pillows. Message received. I slip down the maze of hallways to the hotel restaurant, where I request "the largest cold brew you can legally sell me." The bartender brings me a very normal-size cup of iced coffee, so I order a second one, requesting that it come in one of the big novelty cactus cups I saw at the pool.

Gin wanders in just a few minutes later, dressed for a hike and looking a touch hungover. She joins me at the bar, her tired eyes darting to my coffee as she orders one of her own.

"Howdja sleep?" she asks through a yawn.

"Decent." I take a long sip of coffee. "Not enough. How long have you been up?"

"Not long. I thought I was running behind but . . ." Gin motions to the empty barstools surrounding us. "Where's Renee?"

My memory flashes back to the bed, to Renee's soft legs sliding over mine. I shake it off and grumble, "I tried to get her moving."

Gin nods, yawning again. "She's a heavy sleeper, but I think it's too hot to hike anyway. Are things going okay with you two?"

"Things are . . . okay."

The bartender slides Gin her iced coffee, and she pries the lid off and ditches the straw before tipping it back. "I thought maybe rooming together would help you two get closer."

The word pounds like a bass line through my head. *Closer. Closer. Closer.* I cough. "We're closer than ever."

Gin grins. "I knew you'd get along if you gave it a shot." She adjusts in her seat and takes another sip. "*Anyway.* What's new with you? I feel like I'm so out of the loop on your life."

"God, I don't even know where to begin." I try to sort through my most recent stories, but they all feel too depressing for a bachelorette trip. I'm trying to navigate how to bring up the memorial concert without being a total bummer, but then Gin's phone lights up on the bar top, and her attention dips. "Sorry, hang on just one sec." She opens the texts, all from her fiancé. "Did I tell you Rishi and I started a list of stuff we need for the wedding?"

"Like . . . a registry?"

"No, everything we need to *have* the wedding. Just, like, tables, chairs, and stuff. But I keep thinking of stuff we need to add to it, and we were talking this morning and . . ." She trails off as her thumbs fly across her phone. "Sorry." She sets it face down. "What were we talking about?"

"This concert," I start again, only to be interrupted by the arrival of my coffee cactus. Gin slaps a hand over her mouth to stifle a laugh, and she snatches up her phone to snap a picture just as Chrissy struts in dressed in a bright-blue sports bra and matching athletic shorts, a hot-pink baseball cap, plus full glam.

"If I don't get something caffeinated, I'm going to make a scene," Chrissy announces to anyone who might be listening, which apparently counts as placing an order when you're Chrissy. She has a coffee—no cactus—in her manicured hand by the time she sits down beside Gin.

"Are you drinking, Ali Pal?" Chrissy eyes the cactus cup.

"Coffee," I explain. "Just being festive."

"Chrissy, I was just catching Alice up on wedding planning." Gin swipes open her list again, and the conversation is once more pulled into the wedding vortex. I've sucked down half the contents of my coffee cactus by the time Renee races in, a frazzled mess of pajamas and outdoor wear. Her hiking boots squeak as she skids to a stop, wide eyed and panting, with a messy blond bun of hair wobbling on her head.

"Renee, yay! Thank God you're here." Gin motions to the empty barstool next to mine. "We're wedding planning, so we obviously need the insight of our professional event manager."

Renee is frozen in place, mouth parted. Her eyes—somehow both wild and sleepy—sweep down the line of us, getting a read on the situation.

"I'm . . . I'm so sorry I'm late?" she tries.

"You're fine." Gin waves her off. "You want a coffee? I'm serious about wanting your insight, if you wouldn't mind."

Renee slowly lowers herself onto the stool beside me. Her calf slides against mine, and she mumbles a "Sorry," but it reboots the memory of our legs tangled up in bed, and I flush. It was just a minute of my morning, nothing more than a side effect of us tossing and turning in our sleep, but it's a side effect I can still feel on my inner thigh, warm and tender. God, I need to think of *anything* else. I laser focus on my cactus cup.

"Why didn't you wake me up?" Renee hisses, leaning close enough that her breath tickles my ear. It absolutely doesn't help my case.

"I tried," I say, voice low. "You made a pillow sandwich out of your head."

Gin passes her phone down the bar, and I hand it to Renee. She only has to glance at the list before all concern regarding her lack of wake-up call is redirected. I watch as she swipes her red thumbnail only once, instantly hitting the bottom of Gin's wedding plan. She flinches, then swipes again. Certainly there must be more.

"Is this . . ." Renee clears her throat. Her voice is gentle, but I can hear the panic bubbling just below the surface. "What else are you using to wedding plan, Gin?"

"Just this right now," Gin says. "Should I be using something else? See, I knew I should ask the professional."

Renee's eyes are two blue windows into the battle waging inside her head, a tug-of-war between polite and honest.

"This is . . ." Renee sets down the phone and slaps on a smile.

"It's a good start. You know . . . *some* of what you need." She passes the phone back. "But let's set a time to discuss that more later. This is your bachelorette party, right? Shall we discuss our plans for the day?"

Per the itinerary, we should have left an hour ago for this hike. Per the temperature, we may never want to step outside again. Renee pitches a shortened route on the same trail, promising that we'll be back before the worst of the heat, but Chrissy's sunburn alone makes it a no go.

"That's fine. I have backup plans." Renee fumbles for her phone, reading from a document I don't recognize. Of *course* she has a separate page of contingency plans. "Option one." Renee holds a finger aloft, the bar lights bouncing off her rings. "There's a spa nearby with availability for massages at 11:00 and 12:00, so we couldn't all get them, but maybe Gin and—"

"I'd kinda prefer we do something together." Gin's face twists into an apology. "Is that okay?"

Renee swallows and nods, eyes set on her phone. "Sure, of course." But she sounds uncertain.

"I heard there's this aerial tramway thing that you can ride up to a restaurant," I suggest, and Gin instantly brightens.

"That would be cool!"

"Maybe if we bought tickets a month ago." Renee's eyes snap to mine, a sharp, scolding blue. "It sells out, Alice. Everything does."

"Sorry," I grumble. "I was just brainstorming."

"We don't need to brainstorm. I've already done all the work. For example, there's a paint-and-sip place with same-day availability and a karaoke bar that opens at two o'clock . . ."

"Or we could just wander around downtown," I suggest. "See what we find? It could be fun to explore."

"It could be *more* fun to pick something we already know we'll enjoy," Renee argues.

"But half the fun is finding something together," I point out.

"Is the other half getting sunburned and lost and blowing a bunch of money?"

"I'm sure there's plenty of shade."

"And I'm sure there's—"

"Can I say something crazy?" Chrissy interrupts, flashing a saleswoman's smile. "Would you guys just wanna go back to the pool?"

Gin slaps the bar with both hands, visibly relieved. "Oh my God, thank you. That's exactly what I was thinking."

Based on Renee's eye twitch, I'd guess we're not all on the same page. "Are . . . are you sure?" Her lips tug around a smile she can't quite commit to. "We have pools back home."

"But we had so much fun there yesterday," Gin says, eyes twinkling at the memory. "And I know we won't have a cabana today, but so long as we can get umbrellas . . . and frozen drinks? And SPF?"

I chew my cheek, thinking before I speak. I'm not in love with the idea of risking sun poisoning, but the soft, hopeful smile playing on Gin's lips is tough to argue with.

"I did have fun at the pool," I admit.

"I packed three other bikinis, and I need to send Waiter Boy a pic of me in at least one of them," Chrissy adds.

Our bride turns toward our undecided voter. "Is that okay, Renee? I don't mean to suggest that your ideas aren't great. I just don't want to be zapped before we go out tonight."

Renee gives a wan smile, folds her hands, and says, "The pool sounds perfect." For an actor, she's not very convincing.

Back in our room, I expect Renee to give me the third degree about this morning's alarms, but she seems to have dropped that grievance and moved on to a larger one—today's change of plans.

"We flew all the way here, and for what? To sit by the pool? You just *had* to push the pool, didn't you?"

I rip the tags off a highlighter-yellow tankini and sigh. "Renee, has it occurred to you that maybe we're on the same team?"

She stomps around the room, still in her hiking boots, her full lips pressed into the smallest, grumpiest pout. The thought drifts by like a pool floaty in the deep end of my brain: *Renee is pretty cute when she's mad.* I shove the thought back to wherever the hell it came from. I am absolutely *not* going there.

The I Do Crew regroups on the patio: Gin in her same white suit from yesterday, Chrissy in an orange string bikini, and Renee in a plunging red one-piece that feels less like a bathing suit than a trap. Ever since this morning in bed, it's like my brain has recalibrated. It's impossible to keep my eyes off her tan lines, the soft pale skin of her breasts against the honey-bronzed parts of her that have already seen the sun. I slip on my heart-shaped sunglasses to block my wandering gaze, but for the rest of the day, it's like the universe is playing pranks on me. Somehow, I'm the one who ends up rubbing sunscreen into Renee's back. Not long after, Gin orders a frozen piña colada and Renee ties the cherry stem into a knot with her dexterous tongue. It makes me pulse. Whatever activated this morning when we woke up intertwined, I can't shut it off. It's like an alarm, ringing in the background every time our eyes catch from across the pool.

"This heat is starting to get to me," Renee mutters. The water whirls around her as she turns and wades back to the shade of the shallow end. I watch the sun tattoo between her shoulder blades dip in and out of the water, undecided on whether to rise or set.

Maybe the heat is starting to get to me, too.

# Ten

The disco-cowgirl dress code allowed plenty of room for interpretation. Chrissy struts into the hotel lobby in a pink sequin dress, black knee-high stiletto boots, and a rhinestone-studded cowboy hat. She is a *moment*, and I am . . . feeling some regret. Not about the bell-bottoms or the red bandanna tied around my neck. But maybe I shouldn't have committed to this stick-on handlebar mustache.

I knew the mustache was a risk, but in my head, it was also an enormous hit. Hilarious pictures. A well-crafted memory, compliments of exemplary bridesmaid Alice Pierce.

Instead, Chrissy looks momentarily confused before adjusting the bandanna around my neck and resticking my mustache where the heat has caused it to peel up. "The mustache is . . . such a fun choice!" she says, underwhelmed, if not a little confused.

Gin's reaction is better; when she stumbles into the lobby in a cow-print vest over a sparkly, strappy white dress, she staggers back, points, and shouts, "MUSTACHE!" with an explosive laugh. I'm extremely pleased with myself but a little concerned about the lag in Gin's eyes.

"She was loving that mini bar," Chrissy murmurs.

"Should we grab you some water before we go?" I suggest.

Gin grips my shoulder for stability, adjusting the strap of her silver kitten heels. "I'll drink water at . . . What's the restaurant? The Blue Lagoon?"

"Lagoon 42," a voice behind us says, and we turn to face Renee, by far the chicest disco cowgirl among us. Her blond hair cascades in loose waves from beneath a black cowgirl hat, and she has the boots to match, plus heaps of rhinestone jewelry that hang like fringe around her neck and wrists. Of course, she's dressed in her signature red, a vest with matching trouser shorts that graze her knees. The outfit is a knockout, and it registers in my throat. Because it's also very . . . well . . . gay. I have no clear read on Renee's sexuality, and her *Siblings or dating?* picture remains a mystery. But this outfit? That's a Kinsey six, and Renee herself is a perfect ten.

Our Uber arrives, and we give Gin the front seat, squeezing three bridesmaids across in the back. I'm stuck in the middle, battling for space with Chrissy's extra-long supermodel limbs. A thought zips past.

"Chrissy. Weird question. Are you a model? Like, for your job?"

She revs up her Weedwacker laugh and swats a hand. "Oh, you're way too nice to me, Ali Pal."

Another dead end in my pursuit of what this woman does for work.

Lagoon 42 is a big wooden building surrounded by both real and artificial palm trees. Inside, the lights are dim and blue (like lagoon water, I suppose?), and Gin stumbles twice on the way to our reserved table . . . or rather, our reserved bar top.

"Sorry, gals," the hostess says. "We overbooked. Lotta bachelorette parties tonight."

There's no sympathy in the tick of Renee's jaw, but Gin is

unfazed. She claims a barstool and unfolds a menu, perfectly tipsy and content, and hey, if the bride's happy, we're all happy. We fill in the surrounding seats: Chrissy on Gin's left, Renee on her right, and me on the far end, shouting to be heard over the thudding club beats.

"Should we all do a round of water first?!?" I yell. Gin's eyelids look droopy, and if she doesn't slow down, we'll be carrying her out of Lagoon 42 in approximately 42 minutes.

"A round of water," Renee repeats to the bartender, who nods and hands the first glass to Gin. The bride pouts and flicks her straw, but the protest ends there.

"I get it, I geeeeeet it," Gin drawls. "Safety first."

"Safety first," Chrissy repeats, then frowns, thinks, and asks, "What's second?"

Without missing a beat, Gin says, "Teamwork."

"Teamwork!" I agree. "It's a good thing you've got a good team, huh?!"

Gin can't hear me. She leans all the way forward and captures her straw in her lips like a snapping turtle, and I don't mean to laugh, but I do. This she somehow hears.

"Don't laugh at me." Gin frowns around her straw.

"No, no, I'm not laughing at you," I lie. "I just . . . I saw another bride go into the bathroom, and she looked like she was gonna throw up."

Gin's gaze swings from Chrissy to Renee. "What did she say? I can't hear her."

The bartender returns, and everyone orders their first round of fruity cocktails, plus a heinously overpriced mocktail for me. Anyone charging more than seven dollars for grenadine and seltzer is running a scam, and the owner of Lagoon 42 must be a Nigerian prince with an overactive email. I toss a few appetizers onto our order. If I learned anything in college, it was not to let Virginia Bennett drink on an empty stomach. The bartender knows a drunk bride when he sees one; he makes Gin's drink last, serving it just as our calamari and brie bites arrive. *Safety first,* I think. *Then teamwork.*

"Cheers!" Gin sings, splashing at least a quarter of her coconut martini onto the bar. Chrissy's pink drink matches both her dress and her sunburn, and she drains it in one solid swig.

"Daa-ha-haaaam." Gin laughs, then follows suit, tipping her head back and emptying her glass down her throat.

"Chug, chug, chug!" Chrissy pounds on the bar as she chants. "Renee, you too, girl!"

Renee twists her gold thumb ring, then mutters, "Ah, what the hell," plucks the straw from her copper mug, and goes bottoms up on her cherry mule. She breaks to cough halfway through, but on the second go, I hear the crush of ice against her teeth, and Chrissy and Gin let out a victory cry. I contribute a "Woo!" for good measure, triggering a domino effect throughout the dining room. On the far end of the bar, a bride in a white *WIFE LIFE* crop top climbs onto her stool and swings a costume-store veil overhead like a lasso while her friends echo my "Woo!" and shake their asses from the safety of the floor.

Chrissy's jaw drops. "Are they trying to . . . out-fun us?"

The answer, of course, is yes. Knowingly or not, every bachelorette party in this restaurant has opted in to a competition to see who can have the best time. As the *woo*s die down from the far end of the bar, a cluster of women in matching black bodycon dresses pound their fists on their table. Among them, a leader in all white emerges, taking a knee and thereby flashing the bar as she gulps down something shimmery and pink. Not to be outdone, a group of women in neon wigs kicks off a sing-along of Journey's "Don't Stop Believin'," which is, notably, not the song that's currently playing. I have a hard time believing I would enjoy this even if I were drunk, but Gin is having the time of her life.

"Another coconut martini, puh-lease." The bride nudges her glass toward our bartender, and her eyes droop down to his silver name tag. "Thankyous'much, *Shawn*."

"You're very welcome . . ." Shawn stretches his eyebrows and leans in toward Gin, waiting for her to fill in the blank with her own name, but she doesn't catch his drift. Instead, she blinks back at him, her heavy eyelids never fully lifting.

"These are so good." Gin taps one opalescent fingernail against the rim of the glass. "Actually, *Shawn*." She pauses, clearly satisfied with herself. "Shawn the *bartender*. Can you make me *two*?"

Shawn laughs before whisking her empty martini glass away, but he doesn't bother with her question. Gin doesn't mind; in fact, she forgets about Shawn and her coconut martinis altogether when she spies the big purple flower decorating the calamari plate. She tucks it behind her ear, a single splash of color against her all-white ensemble.

"Gorgina!" Chrissy laughs, snapping photos from all angles as Gin rotates through six or seven poses, pursing her lips then framing her face with her hands. Chrissy's jaw drops again when she swipes through her options. "Um, hello? I'm sending these to Rishi immediately."

"Tell him I looooove him," Gin slurs. "Oh, and send him the

one from the pool, too! The one where my boobs look soooo good." She grabs her boobs through her dress and smooshes them together just as Shawn the bartender sets a single coconut martini in front of her. Instead of blushing and slouching away like sober Gin would do, our bride howls in laughter, still holding her own rack. Shawn slinks away without a word, and we all burst into laughter, even me.

"Oh my God." Chrissy smacks Gin's thigh. "I haven't seen you this drunk since . . ." She pauses, then giggles to herself. "Well, not since your ho phase after you and Alice broke up."

My eyes go wide. "What's this about a ho phase?"

"Oh my God," Gin squeals and kicks her legs. "We are noooot talking about this. Not on my bachelorette!" She pauses and feigns sobriety quite unconvincingly as she announces, "I was never a ho. I was always a perfect angelic bride." She makes a little halo with her fingers and holds it over her head, smiling up at the ceiling.

"Great impression," I deadpan. "Now tell me about the ho phase."

"I was not a ho!" Gin insists.

"You were kind of a ho," Renee mutters into her drink. "You were with a different girl every week."

"Nuh-uh," Gin whines, then bites her bottom lip and shyly adds, "Some of them were guys."

"Virginia Angelie Bennett." I click my tongue against the roof of my mouth, tutting and shaking my head. "I can't believe you kept this from me. You said Rishi was the only guy you'd been with."

"I meant, like, *been* with." Gin makes a circle with one hand and jabs her pointer finger in and out of it, a fourth-grade representation of how hetero sex works.

"Ew, stop that." Renee swats away Gin's demonstration. "I don't want to think about Rishi's penis."

A devilish spark flashes through Gin's eyes as she reaches for her phone. "Do you wanna see it?"

In unison, all three of us bark, "No!"

Thankfully, another round of cocktails appears before Gin can push the point. "I loooove our bartender," she slurs. "Don't you just loooove our bartender?" She walks two wobbly fingers toward poor Shawn. "We should get a picture together," Gin insists, wide eyed and extremely serious.

"I'm happy to," Shawn obliges.

"Can you take it, Alice?" Gin asks, and I set up the shot. "But wait. Not like this." She plants her palms against the bar and pushes back, the stool stuttering beneath her. "I'm gonna . . . I think I should . . ." Without finishing the thought, Gin acts on it, hoisting herself up on the bar and very nearly sitting on the calamari. I can feel the eyes of the other bachelorette parties on us, hot with envy that they didn't think of sitting on the bar to increase the visibility of the fun they're having. "Okay, so my fiancé's name is Rishi," Gin explains, leaning in so Shawn can hear her over the music. "So instead of saying cheese," Gin goes on, "we say . . . OH MY GOD."

I smell it first. The singed smell of too many middle school mornings with a straightening iron in hand. I'd recognize it anywhere: the smell of burning hair.

I hear it next. The loud, piercing shriek of a bride whose perfectly styled ends have dipped a little too close to the candle on the bar top. When I see it, it's in fragments. The lick of a flame. The stretch of Gin's eyes. The horror on the face of poor Shawn the bartender. And my thumb, steady and eager on the big red button, getting the shot.

Then, in one swift, desperate motion, I grab my mocktail and toss its contents directly at Gin's head. It all happens so quickly, yet simultaneously in slow motion, but in the blink of an eye, I'm looking at a partially drenched, entirely shell-shocked Virginia Bennett, looking like she might topple off the bar at any second.

"Okay, maybe we come down now." I grab both of Gin's hands, and she slides off the bar but not out of her daze. The restaurant murmurs and stirs, the other bachelorette parties trying not to stare.

"Are you okay?" Shawn, the now-bewildered bartender, asks. Gin doesn't respond. She's too busy raking her trembling fingers through her hair, her lower lip wobbling as she turns sheet-ghost pale.

"She'll be fine," I answer on her behalf. "Can we close out?" I smack down my credit card, and Shawn sweeps it away.

"No, no," Renee insists. "We're putting it all on mine, remember?"

"It's fine," I say. "We'll figure it out later."

Or maybe we won't. Maybe I'll put this enormous bill on my credit card and never see a dime of it ever again. Right now, I don't care. I just want to get us out of here. I take my eyes off Gin just long enough to call us a ride.

"Is it really bad?" she asks, but it comes off as more of a plea. "Tell me the truth, Alice. Is it bad?"

It doesn't look awful, exactly, but no one would call it good. Against her sleek shoulder-length tresses, the burnt chunk is noticeably shorter, fraying like old shoelaces in some places and dead tree branches in others. She'll certainly be losing a few inches, and her curtain bangs might become a little more like venetian blinds.

"It'll be fine," I say, pocketing my phone. "We're gonna go

back to the hotel and order room service, and when you get home, your stylist will just cut off an inch or two." *Or three. Or four.*

Either Gin knows I'm downplaying it or she really hates room service. Her wail carries throughout the restaurant, turning heads at several tables. We are definitely no longer a front-runner for the bachelorette party having the most fun, but the competition has come to a halt out of respect for a fallen player. As I guide Gin toward the exit, three separate brides try to step in, pulled by some white-veiled bond to offer up encouragement. Unfortunately, it falls on deaf ears—or damaged ears, at least, thanks to Lagoon 42's bold decision to handle the situation by cranking the music and drowning it out.

Our ride arrives, and we pour Gin into the back seat. Renee slides in after her, quick to be the one to sit beside our bride in need, but I'm not far behind, so Chrissy takes the front. Halfway back to the hotel, Alicia Keys's "Girl on Fire" plays through the radio, and Gin bursts into big snotty sobs, and the driver turns the radio off. The only words out of his mouth are "Have a good night!" as we spill out into the hotel parking lot. As if a good night were even still on the menu. The best we can aim for is a safe landing for our bride back in her hotel room.

It's hardly ten o'clock, but we're all turning in, and as the only sober one in the group, I don't particularly mind. Unlike the boozy, musty scent of the hotel hallways and the burnt-hair smell of Lagoon 42, our room smells like clean cotton sheets and eucalyptus. It's comforting. And quiet. I peel off my handlebar mustache and tie up my sweaty hair while Renee stands still as a column holding up the ceiling, silent until she catches me unpacking my pajamas.

"What are you doing?"

I arch a brow. "I'm . . . getting comfortable?"

She twitches. "Why?"

"Because we're done for the night?"

"But we can't be," Renee insists. "I already paid for bottle service at Bar Sol. Three bottles of champagne. Do you know how much money that is?" She's perfectly still, but the thoughts keep spilling out, faster and faster, like they're chasing her down. "I messaged the DJ. I paid him to play 'Gin and Juice.' I told him what table we're at so he can spotlight—"

"Hey. Renee?" I interrupt. "The bride's hair caught on fire, okay? That's kind of a night-ender."

"But . . . but there was a plan!" she cries out either to me or herself, or perhaps some higher power who seems to have forgotten that Renee is in charge. I give her a sorry smile, and her head hangs low. She says it again, weakly this time. "There . . . there was a plan."

"And it was a good plan," I assure her. "It just went off the rails."

At this, Renee flinches, then eyes me skeptically. "Did I just hear you say it was a good plan?"

"All things considered."

Her lip curls, eyes two suspicious slits of blue. "But what about all that mean stuff you said about the itinerary?"

"I have my complaints," I confess, as if I haven't already made that clear. "But I'll save my full review for tomorrow. As for tonight . . ." I pluck up the room service menu. "We're getting tacos."

Renee grumbles in stubborn defeat, then yanks off her boots

and joins me on the edge of the bed. We order the same chicken tacos we had last night, the closest we can get to a routine amid the madness.

"See? This works out great." I try out an eager, Chrissy-style smile, but Renee seems wary. "I mean it. Those tacos were way better than the food at Lagoon 42, anyway. I think the calamari was made out of the same stuff they make Crocs out of."

"Great. So I screwed up the restaurant choice too." Renee blows out a breath and lies back, propped up on her elbows, while I finish placing our order.

"I'm too hungry to entertain your moping right now," I say, "but I'm getting you a churro, so maybe things are looking up."

Our dinner arrives in a brown paper bag dropped unceremoniously at our door. Not really room service, but it is food that's been served to our room, and I'm starving. Renee and I have each had a turn in the shower and changed into our pajamas—red silk shorts and a matching sleep shirt for her, running shorts and an old Willie Nelson shirt for me. From his birthday show in Texas. Go figure.

Our room has no table, so we eat our tacos in bed, but not before laying out towels on the duvet. Renee insists.

"Always doing the most," I mutter, smoothing a towel flat.

"What was that?" Renee cups her ear. "*Thank you for not letting me sleep in crumbs, Renee?* Oh, you're so welcome."

We swipe at each other on and off throughout the evening, but it's different than before. More playful, often unnecessarily dramatic for entertainment value. When she mentions a musical and I don't get the reference, Renee calls me "culturally bereft." When Renee can't name a single Willie Nelson song, I call her "the dumbest thing to ever come out of Iowa." There's an air of appreciation around every insult and overdramatic diss. Just after midnight, I'm loudly booing Renee for admitting that she flosses *three times a day* when Chrissy texts us from next door to request we keep it down.

"A first time for everything. The human noise complaint thinks we're too loud." I show Renee the text, and she snorts while still actively flossing her teeth. Getting ready for bed feels less awkward tonight, almost familiar, like we've had a hundred sleepovers before. But we haven't. Renee and I have never, ever been friends, and I'm still not sure that we are, but we're certainly . . . something. Whatever it is, it wasn't on the itinerary.

# Eleven

For the second morning in a row, my alarm propels me into panic.

*Where am I? Whose bed am I in? Did the tour van leave without me?*

I draw in a long, stabilizing breath. *I'm in Palm Springs. I'm safe. I'm fine.*

I am also, once again, entangled in Renee Roberts.

It's not just absurd; it feels nearly impossible. I slept on top of the covers as a precaution against this, and still, we're in the same tangled mess as yesterday: Renee's bare thigh rests on top of mine, one arm slung over my stomach in a half hug. Her warm exhales flutter against my neck, sending a prickle of want across all my nerve endings. I feel her breath hitch as she starts to stir, wincing at the sound of my alarm, then jolting awake when she realizes who she's snuggled up with.

We both startle back to our respective sides of the bed, and Renee's eyes flash around the room, rightfully confused. We don't discuss it, though; when I shut off my alarm, I'm greeted by a text from Gin that pulls all my focus.

**GIN'S I DO CREW**

**GIN BENNETT**

Good morning!! Hope everyone slept well! I had the craziest dream where my hair caught on fire at a bar . . . that qualifies as a nightmare, right? Thank you guys for all of your help last night. I literally have the best friends on the planet.

SO. That said. I'm so, so sorry to do this, but Chrissy (my literal hero) has a client who owns a chain of hair salons, and they have a location in Palm Springs! Long story short, she pulled some strings and they're fitting me in to fix my hair. Thank GOD. Only problem is they can only take me right when they open at 10, which means we'll probably have to skip drag brunch. I'm so sorry again, but I hope you guys understand. I know I'll feel so much better once it's fixed, and that way I won't be a nightmare the whole flight home! Text me when you wake up just so I know you saw this. Love you!!!

Upon reading the text, Renee lets out a whimpering groan. I look up just as she threads her fingers into her messy blond hair and stares at her phone like she's trying to explode it with her mind.

"Classic Chrissy," I say, trying to lighten the mood. "She always knows the right people."

"Guess so."

"Have you heard the story about her dating a guy for an entire summer just for free VIP tickets to Lollapalooza?"

Renee throws back the duvet and sulks off to the bathroom, somehow not hooked by the Lollapalooza story. I listen for the dull hiss of the shower as it flips on, then the hum of the plumbing as I craft a text to Gin that's equally silly and supportive. So long as we're managing schedule changes, I check on our flight home—it's on time, same gate, same everything. At least some things are going according to plan.

I'm still in bed when Renee emerges, showered and ready, wet hair dappling the shoulders of her red T-shirt dress. I kick off the covers and jump to my feet.

"I can be ready to leave in about ten?"

She flinches. "Leave for where?"

"For drag brunch." I make a beeline for Big Blue, digging through my innumerable options. "No dress code for this, right?"

Silence. When I turn to Renee, she's fiddling with her rings, brow creased.

"I don't think it's right to go without Gin and Chrissy," she says.

"What else are we supposed to do? Sit around?"

Renee lifts a shoulder. "We could pack."

"According to the itinerary, we have a late checkout. And were you not just complaining that we came all this way only to sit by the pool?"

Renee's mouth closes and opens, a Venus flytrap hoping to catch a valid argument, but there isn't one. I'm dressed and ready before Renee has decided between a strappy pair of wedges and sensible white sneakers.

"Go with the wedges," I advise. "It's a drag show."

She frowns toward my feet. "You're wearing sneakers."

"Well, yeah. Because look at me. And look at you."

"What about me?"

A tiny fire blazes down the backs of my ears as I fumble for an answer that's not completely humiliating. "You're . . . well, you're *you*," I manage. "I mean, look at you. That's not what normal people look like."

Renee's mouth twists into a smile, but her brow stays furrowed, not quite sure what to make of that . . . or me. "Thanks," she says cautiously. "I think."

We arrive at the restaurant at ten on the dot, as does every other bachelorette party in town. I recognize the wig-wearing group from Lagoon 42—mostly by the singular bridesmaid who remains committed to the bright-blue bob—and the women in the matching bandage dresses are back with a brand-new coordinated group look: pajamas. Based on their demeanor, I'd guess it was less of a choice and more of a desperate hungover decision. When a queen in a '50s-diner-girl dress escorts us to our seats, Renee still seems a half-step off, nervously checking her phone for updates from the bride. But when the lights dim and a queen waddles out in a semirealistic palm tree costume, I watch the sparkle ignite behind Renee's eyes. Every performance further confirms we made the right call by not missing this. A black queen with a knee-length wig dances on tables, stilettos stepping between cocktails and plates of scrambled eggs. A queen by the name of Maybe Gaga performs "Born This Way" with original choreography, and Bloody Mary and Mimi Mosa show down in a comedy battle for America's Next Top Cocktail, snatching up dollar bills from the crowd to determine a winner. My favorite performer by far, though, remains the palm tree. She stands statue still in the center of the restaurant until the grand finale, a Mariah Carey group number that ends with the palm tree setting off a glitter bomb.

"You were right," Renee admits when the show ends. She brushes glitter into a neat pile in the lap of her dress. "That was excellent. I'm glad we came to that."

I gasp through my nose. "Say that again. The part about me being right."

She considers me for a moment, then scoops up the glitter from her lap and drizzles it into my hair. It falls into my eyelashes, and I pin her with a joyless stare.

"I hate you," I say flatly.

Renee grins. "I don't think you do, actually."

The restaurant has to reset for the next sold-out brunch in an hour, and since we haven't heard from Gin or Chrissy, Renee and I wander toward a diner down the street. We leave a trail of glitter on the sidewalk behind us; I'll be washing tiny sparkly flecks out of my hair for at least a week.

"We're like gay Hansel and Gretel," I joke, motioning to the sparkles breadcrumbed behind us, which sparks a heated discussion about the assumed sexual orientation of fairy-tale characters. Renee and I butt heads on the Big Bad Wolf and Cinderella's stepsisters, all of whom I insist are gay, but Renee wholeheartedly disagrees.

"What about Jack?" I throw out. "You have to agree that Jack is gay."

"Jack?"

"Of beanstalk fame."

Renee scrunches her nose, considering. "A straight man wouldn't trade a cow for magic beans, would he?"

"Or risk his life for a harp," I add.

"But the giants are straight," she decides. "I'm fairly sure they're married, and giants in general have a conservative energy to them."

I kick a pebble across the sidewalk, and it bounces off the platform of Renee's wedges. "You're a lot goofier than I thought you could be."

"I'm not being goofy," she deadpans. "I'm having an intellectual conversation about the assumed sexuality of storybook characters."

"You're right," I agree. "This is *very* serious business."

We carry this very serious, very sophisticated conversation into the diner with us. Rapunzel is straight. Goldilocks is straight. Little Miss Muffet is a certified bisexual. After our waitress comes around to top off our coffees for a second time, I'm caffeinated and courageous enough to ask, "What about you?"

"Me?" Confusion darts through Renee's eyes, but she blinks it away. "Oh. Me."

"You don't have to answer," I rush to say. "I was just wondering since me and Gin are . . . but then Chrissy is . . ."

"The straightest person alive," Renee supplies.

Her laugh bounces off mine, a crackling whir against my one loud *ha*. The sound is perfectly percussive and surprisingly well balanced. After another sip of coffee, Renee shrugs.

"I'm bi," she says. "I thought you already knew."

"Why would I know that?"

"My resemblance to Little Miss Muffet."

A small laugh catches in my throat. "I guess I could've assumed," I admit. "Can't say I know any actor living in Chicago who's completely straight."

At this, the playful energy between us simmers away. Renee's eyes sweep the table, voice shrinking down to almost nothing when she says, "Well, I'm not an actor anymore."

"What?"

I lean in, certain I misheard. When her gaze lifts to mine, she looks a little less like herself.

"I'm not an actor anymore," she repeats.

"I mean, I know you manage events at the Blomquist, but on the side . . ."

Renee shakes her head. "Not anymore."

"Why?"

"I just don't have the time. Between auditions and self-tapes and the late-night rehearsals . . . it was too much."

My chest tightens around a bundle of memories from my Cold Sweat days, the relentless gigging, how fried I was by the constant *go go go.* "I think I get that. From being in a band. It's a lot of hustle."

"Exactly. And I can't be at rehearsals until eleven at night, get home after midnight, and be up for work the next day. It's not sustainable." Renee's delivery is a bit rehearsed; it's clear she's had this conversation many times before, possibly with herself in the mirror, but no amount of reasoning can erase the hint of regret that clings to her voice.

So I have to ask. "Don't you miss being up onstage?"

"Don't *you* miss being up onstage?" Renee parries. She folds her arms and leans back against the vinyl booth cushions. "There comes a point when you have to ask yourself: Am I willing to let this kill me? Am I willing to push and struggle and starve if that's what it takes to do what I love to do? Or do I want to live a comfortable, normal life with a normal job that still gets me through the front door of a theater every single day?" Something quick and painful darts through her eyes, and she squeezes them shut. "Sorry," she whispers. "I don't mean to assume, but I'm guessing that's what you did, too."

"I don't know what you mean," I admit.

Renee opens her eyes again, arching a brow. "You quit performing in favor of something more practical, right?"

"I quit performing because I needed help," I correct her. "Cold Sweat used to cancel a show a month because I was too drunk to play. Then Dad's esophagus ruptured, and I blacked out for, like, a week straight. We had to cancel the rest of that tour, and then Dad got his diagnosis and . . . I didn't want to end up like that. I couldn't get sober on the road. And I had to get sober, or I'd end up like my dad."

I dip my gaze into my coffee, feeling a little like I've split open a vein. And in front of Renee, of all people. When I drag my eyes back up to hers, there's not a drop of judgment waiting there. Just compassion. Curiosity. I keep going.

"I needed to try something new, meet new people. My only network in Chicago was through The Handful or Cold Sweat, which was tough. I didn't want to be Ricky Pierce Jr., but I had a pretty rough reputation from my Cold Sweat days. I knew a little about recording and audio engineering just from being around the Outpost since I was a kid, watching the band write and record albums every summer. So I taught myself a lot, then started hitting people up, meeting and shadowing engineers. And yeah." I shrug. "Now I'm assisting at the best recording studio in the city. Pretty cool."

"And it pays better than touring, I assume," Renee says.

I rub a knot from my neck. "The assistant job is unpaid, actually."

It's silent between us, just the clatter of stacked plates and the burble of coffee warming up a mug. Diner noise, until Renee finally lets out an "Oh."

"I have some money from my dad," I explain. "Less than I was expecting. I, uh. I think he blew a lot of it on booze, which is tough. So it's not enough to coast forever, but for now . . ."

Renee nods curtly. "Sure."

"And I'm meeting so many people at Gentle Giant. It's a great way to build up my freelance portfolio," I prattle on. "Which, hopefully, I can fill up with session work so I don't have to go back to the live-music scene."

"Or you could just go work in an office like the rest of us," she points out.

I rap a knuckle against my mug. "See, that's where you're wrong."

Renee draws back, puzzled. "Oh?"

"I am actually incapable of that kind of thing." I take a long sip of weak diner coffee, and Renee tips her chin, intrigued. "Maybe it's that I grew up seeing my dad do what he loved for a living, but I've never been able to hold down a normal job. I can't make myself care about anything the way I care about music, so I have to find a way to make music work in some capacity. It's what I'm meant to do."

"Do you *really* think that?" Renee grips the edge of the table, leaning in close enough to get a read on me. "You think there's one specific thing that you were created to do?"

"Yeah," I say. "I do. Is that stupid?"

Her eyebrows answer on her behalf.

"So you don't feel like you're meant to do theater? To perform?"

"I'm meant to pay rent," Renee says flatly. "I didn't dream of coordinating fundraising events for a living, but I wanted to work in theater, so I made a five-year plan to achieve that. And I'm a good event planner." She pauses, almost a stumble, like she tripped on her own words. "Well. I'm *usually* a good event planner." Her gaze hangs low. "Current evidence aside."

I roll my eyes. "Oh, c'mon. We had fun on this trip." I'm surprised by how much I mean it. Maybe my expectations were low, but I had a far better time than I expected.

Still, Renee doesn't look up.

"I'm serious." I nudge her foot beneath the table, demanding her attention. It works. She drags her icy-blue eyes up to mine, but they're dim. Disappointed, but not in me. In herself.

"Look. Pretend this weekend is a recording session, okay? You hired the right musicians. You mic'd everything up correctly. But you can't completely control the take, right? You can only create the environment that allows the moment to happen."

Renee pauses to consider, drumming her nails on the laminate tabletop. "But if this were theater," she says, "we had an airtight script, an amazing cast and crew, and"—she motions to herself—"an amazing director, if I may be so bold. So it doesn't make sense that things went so off the rails."

"So you're saying nothing ever goes off the rails in theater?" I challenge. "I'm fairly certain you had an audience member snore through your solo once."

She pins her bottom lip beneath her teeth, but it doesn't quite block her hint of a smile.

"And also, this isn't theater," I go on, "and it's not music either. It's just . . . life. And life isn't a series of executed plans."

Renee looks at me a little longer than I expect her to, like she's searching for something in my eyes. "I guess you're right," she acquiesces. "But none of the other bachelorette trips I've planned have ever gone so . . . so . . ." She circles her hands, searching for the right word.

"Up in flames?"

Renee snorts a laugh, gripping her mug with both hands. She's still a little stiff, but less so, her arms resting on the table so that I can see every phase of the moon tattooed on her outer wrist. I look at the tattoo, and suddenly, it's beneath my fingertips, my hand sliding over hers to press my thumb into the waning crescent. She tenses for a moment, then relaxes beneath my touch.

"It was a good trip, Renee," I say, "even if it didn't go according to plan."

We have the pictures to prove it. Renee and I drink mug after mug of watery diner coffee while swiping through photos from the weekend. I show her the shot I got of Gin's hair catching fire, and neither of us can stifle our laughs. Tragedy plus time equals comedy, I suppose, although we won't be showing this to Gin anytime soon. As she compiles photos into a post, Renee follows me back on Instagram, and it feels like a milestone. We're trying, like Gin asked, and I think it might be working. I've just begun to ask about Renee's tattoos—the moon phases on her wrist and the sun between her shoulder blades—when the other half of the I Do Crew arrives in a waft of expensive hair products. Chrissy's salon connection did not disappoint—Gin's burnt curtain bangs have been trimmed down to eyebrow-length ones that cover her forehead, and while she's lost a significant amount of length, she's gained plenty of layers. It's cute. Flirty.

"I think Rishi is gonna freak out," Gin says, tugging on her bangs.

"He'll love it," Renee assures her. "It really brings out your curls."

"It's *Little Orphan Annie* chic," I blurt, and Renee shoots me a *Watch it* look, but Gin isn't offended. In fact, she looks downright impressed.

"Look at you with the musical references." She elbows me in the ribs, and I shrug, not beating the charges.

"I guess I've been hanging around you theater kids too much."

"Hey, I'm not a theater kid!" Chrissy protests. "I'm just loud."

And self-aware, God bless her. The four of us laugh until the booth shakes, but Chrissy's Weedwacker cackle flies high above the rest, proving her point and escalating our laughter to a roar. A warm certainty settles over me. Today, there's no theme, no sequins, no tequila shots, but it's the most fun I've had all weekend. If only the other bachelorette parties could see us now.

It's just past noon when we call a car to the hotel, our final destination before it's back to the airport. Renee and I play the bachelorette playlist softly from my phone as we gather up errant accessories from around the room. I'm stuffing my cowgirl boots into Big Blue when the light hits just right through the sliding glass door, and I can distinctly see the butt-cheek prints still perfectly preserved there. My laugh is a soft breath through my nose, but inspiration strikes.

"Hey, Renee," I call out, working with some effort to zip my suitcase all the way.

Renee steps out of the bathroom with a mouthful of electric toothbrush. "Urtsurp?" she garbles, then holds out a finger and disappears back into the bathroom. "What's up?" She tries again, raising her voice over the running faucet.

"I had a thought."

"That's . . . ominous."

"It'll be fun, I promise."

It only takes a minute or two for us to hatch our plan, and Renee's eyes flicker with mischief as she volunteers to make the phone call. She switches to speakerphone as we shuffle out onto the patio.

"Hello?" Gin picks up on the very first ring. "Everything okay?"

"Um, not really." Renee's theater degree is out in full effect. Even I sort of believe the rough edge of worry in her voice. She follows me to the patio of the party room next door, our steps stealthy and soft on the concrete. "Have you looked out at your patio?" Renee asks.

"No, why?" Gin's voice has an edge now, too. "Is everyone okay? What's go—"

"NOW!"

On my cue, Renee hangs up, and we both tug our shorts down. The rattle of Gin drawing open her curtain is followed by a piercing shriek. Even in the desert heat, the glass feels a tiny bit cold against my butt, and I wiggle it against the door, leaving the best ass print I can. Beside me, Renee does the same until we both hear the click of Gin unlocking the door. "GO GO GO!" I yell, pulling up my shorts, but Renee has already taken off at a sprint, crossing back into the safety of our hotel room a few steps before I come barreling in.

"YOU BITCHES!" Gin scream-laughs from behind us, but I've already locked our door and pulled the curtains tight, barring any chance of retribution. Renee has collapsed on the bed in a fit of heavy breaths and victorious laughter. She pumps her fists while Chrissy and Gin pound on our shared wall, rattling our bed frame and the lamp on the table. Renee doesn't even acknowledge it. She's too busy laughing, fingers splayed across her chest as she tips her head back in a raucous cackle that gets me laughing just as hard. Just looking at her makes my smile bigger, my laugh louder. She can deny it all she wants, but Renee Roberts isn't as straitlaced as I thought, and when our gazes catch, I swear her icy-blue stare is beginning to thaw.

**MOM**

**Hi Alice! Do you know when you might be free for dinner? Love you!**

**MOM**

**When do you leave for Palm Springs?? I still have your birthday present! You might want it for the trip!**

**MOM**

**Hey sweetie! Hope you're having fun in Palm Springs! Let me know if you need a pick up from the airport or anything! Love you!**

# Twelve

We touch down in Chicago in the purple of dusk, and a heavy melancholy settles over me. It's that end-of-vacation feeling that hangs like a wet velvet cape over my shoulders—I felt it at the end of every summer growing up when it came time to trade crackling bonfire nights at the Outpost for the weight of real life and responsibilities. Back then, it was school, homework, and bass lessons; now it's studio shifts and dishes—and actually texting my mother back.

Between Chrissy's pink, peeling skin and Gin's emergency haircut, it's clear we've been changed by our two nights in Palm Springs; the I Do Crew is a ragged bunch, plodding through the airport without saying much. Even Renee seems a little sick of her own logistics when, at baggage claim, she asks me about expenses, yammering about whether I want to submit a receipt for the Ubers and Lagoon 42 and . . . I short-circuit. Nothing but static between my ears. I don't have the brain waves to direct toward this.

"I'll cover those." I wave Renee off. "Consider it a gift."

Her lips twitch. "But you said your studio job is unpaid and that—"

"Renee," I warn. "It's a gift. And if you make me think about numbers right now, I'm going to explode."

We can already hear Rishi idling outside in the pickup lane, paying homage to our weekend by blaring Snoop Dogg's "Gin and Juice" at max volume. Tired as she is, it gets a laugh out of his fiancée, who distributes hugs goodbye. Chrissy follows her out to catch an Uber, and Renee turns to me with a hopeful half-smile. "Any chance of me getting a ride?"

There would be, if there weren't a prickly and persistent tug in my chest that needed addressing. I don't want to feel all the hard feelings that I know come with going back to Mom's house, but I don't want to feel this guilt either. It has to be one or the other. I adjust my grip on the handle of my suitcase, scanning the sterile airport for a sign to point me in the right direction.

"I'm sorry," I sigh out, deciding.

"Sure, I get it." Renee nods and takes one gratuitous step back. She's not offended; it's more of an apologetic understanding, an actor taking a note.

"No, no. It's not . . ." I shake my head. "I would, but I think I need to stop by my mom's."

"Oh." The tiny crease between Renee's brows smooths out, and her eyes soften. Behind her, the sliding glass doors open and close, letting in the screech of city buses and trunks slamming shut, a thousand little distractions, but I can only look at Renee, who looks right back at me. It's like our eyes are magnetized, and it's an effort to pry our gazes apart. It's strange—just a few weeks ago, sharing an Uber with Renee Roberts was a punishment; now, I really wish I could offer her shotgun.

In the parking garage, I load Big Blue into the back of my

truck, the weight of a half dozen unused disco-cowgirl outfits working against me. At least no one can doubt my commitment to being a good bridesmaid, but it's past time I stepped up to be a good daughter, too. I route to Mom's house, queuing up the only song that feels right: "Willin'" by Little Feat. Dad's favorite, buzzing through the speakers of his truck as I steer it back to where it came from, the tree-lined streets of the suburb where I grew up. Every emotion shuffles like a deck of cards in my chest. I missed it, but also I didn't. I'm happy, but I'm also haunted.

I spent three quarters of my childhood at this house, but less than a quarter of my memories are set here. Mostly, I remember our summers at the Outpost, and of the few scattered memories I do have from here in Oak Park, Dad is in so few of them. Mostly, it was Mom and me, with Dad popping by between tours. I worry sometimes that I have more memories in this house *without* Dad than with him. When I stayed with Mom after the funeral, it almost felt normal, like he'd be home any day and we'd all go back to the Outpost. That was a shade of grief I couldn't reconcile—feeling like nothing had changed while knowing it would never be the same.

I close out of the maps app and let Little Feat sing me the rest of the way. I pull up the driveway, and the emotional card deck in my chest slows its shuffling when I spot an unfamiliar car in Mom's driveway—a generic silver Lexus that could belong to anyone. Maybe one of Mom's book club friends? I loop around past the hydrangeas to the side door, the one Mom never locks. It swings open, like always, and I step inside, down the wood-paneled hall and into the kitchen.

And . . . there's a man in my mother's kitchen. At least I assume it's a man. A reasonable assumption based on the stature of the person seated with their back to me. Their red-and-white Hawaiian shirt stirs up some vague recognition, but I can't place the silver slicked-back hair of the person wearing it. They're knuckle deep in a bowl of trail mix, touching all the other snacks while digging out a cashew.

"Um, hello?"

The man startles enough to knock the trail mix on its side. When he whips around to face me, it still takes a second for me to place him out of context. He looks like any number of white guys in his early sixties: ruddy cheeks and wire-frame glasses, like Santa's slimmer younger brother. But then it clicks. I know that face: It belongs to Kurt Stanley, the drummer for The Handful.

"Alice, hey!" Kurt's smile crinkles his cheeks up to his eyes. A perfect thumbprint of a dimple appears in the center of his stubbly chin. "Jeez, let me tell ya, you could've given me a heart attack."

"I could say the same for you." I shake off the shock and give Kurt a hug. He smells like unfiltered cigarettes, a smell I recognized as Kurt's signature scent long before I even knew what a cigarette was. Dad always loved the story of when we stopped for a burger at a bar in Indiana and six-year-old Alice proclaimed, "It smells like Uncle Kurt in here."

"How've you been, kid?" Kurt digs out another cashew and pops it in his mouth. "Still at Gentle Giant?"

"Sure am." My gaze flicks from him to the car out front. Gay Nancy Drew is back for a hot new case: What the hell is Kurt doing at my mother's house?

"Great, that's great." Kurt offers up a lopsided smile but still no explanation for his presence.

"Is . . . is the band here?" I ask.

Kurt's mouth shrinks behind his mustache, shaky cashew-dusted fingers nudging his glasses up his nose. "I, uh. Well, no." He clears his throat just as Mom's voice rings through the house.

"Kurt? Is someone here?" She appears on the stairs a moment later, and a smile breaks over her face. "Alice! What a surprise!"

"A nice surprise," Kurt amends. He clears his throat into his fist, and Mom joins us in the kitchen. The two of them stand shoulder to shoulder, facing me as a united front, and a chill zips down my spine. *No. It can't be that.* I run my tongue over the ridges of my teeth, trying to conceive of any possibility, any scenario where this isn't what it looks like, but then Mom snakes an arm around Kurt's waist, and I freeze.

"What the hell is going on here?" My voice comes out strained, but it's nothing compared to the tightness in my chest.

Mom's lips press into a firm line. She glances nervously up at Kurt, then back to me. "Kurt and I . . ." Her lips wobble a little. "Well, you know Kurt."

I do know Kurt. Or I thought I did. Now I'm not sure I even know my own mother. I grit my teeth, biting down on every rude, honest thought that tries to slip out.

Mom keeps going. "Kurt was the one who originally suggested the memorial concert in Galena." Her hand hasn't budged from its resting place on his hip. "We've always stayed in touch since we lost your father. The whole band has, but Kurt is . . . well, Kurt has shown me a lot of kindness through all of this."

"Kindness, huh?" I can feel my pulse in my jaw. "What else did he show you?"

"Alice Marie," Mom snaps. "Show some respect."

"Show some respect for Dad!" I fire back. "The man has been dead less than a year, and you're already dating his drummer?"

"We're just getting to know each other," Mom argues.

"Bullshit." I cough out a bitter laugh. "You've known each other for years. Don't sugarcoat it. Just say that you're fucking."

"That's enough." Mom's voice cracks like thunder through the room. Every trace of humor has disappeared from her face; what's left is red-hot anger and exhaustion and that deep, haunted sadness we've both been carrying all year.

I shouldn't have come here tonight.

"She's been trying to get you out here, kid," Kurt offers. As if that's supposed to help, knowing that Mom was just *dying* to give me the news. Bile rises in my throat with a vision of the not-so-distant future—Mom cheering for her boyfriend at the one-year anniversary of my father's death.

"I should go," I choke out.

"You should stay." The desperation in Mom's voice makes my stomach churn. "There's a storm coming in, honey. It's not safe, and we should talk about this."

"I should go," I repeat, colder and more detached this time. "I'm sorry." And I really am, because I know I won't be back anytime soon. There's a look in Mom's eyes that I'm sure I'm reflecting right back to her. The look of someone who knows better than to cry right now but really, really wishes she could.

I'm almost to the door when panic cements me in place, the ache of knowing in my gut that I'm forgetting something. My wallet? My keys? When it hits, it's like a pool cue scratching against the billiards table of my belly. I turn back to catch Mom's gaze, and my voice breaks. "I love you, Mom."

"I love you, too," she croaks out, and only then can I finally leave.

In the truck, my headlights flip on just as the first raindrop splashes against the windshield. It's like a permission slip for my nervous system—the sky and I both split open, and the rain comes down in sheets. I stare myself down in the rearview, pitying every stupid tear racing the others down my cheeks as the storm turns my truck into a snare drum. It beats down like it's been saving up for this moment, waiting for right now. Over the rattle, I can still hear my dad whistling at the rain, saying, "It's been dry lately. We really needed this." And maybe I needed this, too.

The tears stop before the rain does, and I'm back on the road, feeling like I'd rather feel nothing at all. I want to opt out of this moment, skip the hurt and heartache and escape from my head. The urge is almost primal. Strong as ever, even after three years sober. I could drain a fifth of liquor or a double bottle of wine. Any old mind eraser would do. I remember the leftover hard seltzers I bought for Gin, all huddled together in the back corner of my fridge, and just the impulse, the thought of it, relaxes me. I know it shouldn't, but it does. There are only five hard seltzers. They have to go somewhere. No one would have to know but me. My phone chirps at me to turn down my street. *Then the destination is on your left: home.* I watch my hands on the steering wheel. They don't budge. My phone starts rerouting, but I'm not following my directions. Something else is steering, and it knows where we need to be.

It's a quick drive, and my eyes are set straight ahead, ignoring the voice chirping *At the next light, make a U-turn.* There's an empty parking spot right out front of Tweedy's, my favorite bar. Like they knew I was coming. Like a warm welcome back.

I don't go inside, but I don't drive away. I just idle in the spot, stalling in the in-between. In the window of the bar, the neon lights smudge like watercolors behind the diagonal rain. God, there's so much rain. Just when I'm sure we've made it through the worst of it and summer has carried us into the clear, the storm comes again, reminding me I'll never get too far. Real life isn't a Palm Springs vacation with 350 days of sunshine a year; it's a Midwestern summer—rain one minute, sun the next. The highs and lows happen all at once, and somehow, we're meant to feel it all.

A tap on my driver's side glass breaks the spell. Through the water droplets, I spot a cherry red raincoat. Two worried blue eyes. I don't roll down the window; I unlock the truck, and Renee sidesteps through the gap between my front bumper and the car parked ahead. She slips into the passenger side, a plastic bag from a nearby drugstore crinkling in her lap. I've caught her on the way back from a snack run—or, I guess, she's the one who caught me.

"Hey," Renee says, gently. That's all she says. It's silent aside from the rain on the roof of the truck, then the swish and crinkle as she tears into a bag of barbecue chips. Wordlessly, she offers them to me, and we stay like this for a long while, snacking in silence, staring at the lights of the bar. When we're down to the crumbs, Renee claps the orangey-brown powder off her fingers and pushes back the hood of her raincoat, splashing a few raindrops onto the center console.

"So," Renee says. The second syllable out of her in . . . how long? Ten minutes? An hour? It feels like a lifetime has passed while we've been sitting here, idling in the rain. Her eyes find mine, cool and blue, then shift back to Tweedy's.

"I'm not going in," I say, defensive.

She nods. "Okay."

More unnerving silence. "So . . . I should probably go home, huh?"

"Is there booze at home?"

*Yes*, I think. "No," I say.

"Are you sure?"

Silence again. Too much of it. My kick-drum heart pounds a heavy rhythm.

"Okay," Renee whispers. "You're staying with me."

*Hey Dad. Remember when I asked you about whether you see everything that's happening here on Earth? Right now I have to assume you do and that you already know about this because I can't be the one to tell you about this. Because it really fucking sucks.*

*I probably told you this when I was little or drunk, but Kurt used to be my favorite member of The Handful (other than you, of course). It was probably just that he was always single and would play rock star with me while the rest of the guys were busy with whatever wife or girlfriend they had at the time. Kurt was fun and weird and patient and he could make a fart sound on like nine different parts of his body. Did he ever show you that? Anyway, I don't know how that guy could be dating my mom. Not that Mom isn't fun and patient, too, but she's your wife. Or she was. I guess "till death do us part" means that at death . . . it's splitsville, baby!*

*Sorry to joke, but I have to. I know you understand that more than anyone. If I don't I'm worried that I'll burst into tears on Renee's couch and then she'll come out here and I'll have to talk about it.*

*I don't know, Dad. I wish you could come back, even if just for a second. I'm not sure if you would've had the right things to say about Renee or Mom and Kurt, but I know you'd have a good joke that would make me feel better. But I think the real reason I wanted to write to you tonight was because I was thinking about you when I was parked outside of Tweedy's. I kept thinking how good it would feel to not have to feel this way, if I could have a few drinks to sand down the edges of the hurt. It's the first time it really clicked for me that you probably felt that way too. I can't imagine how awful it would feel to find out that you're dying, but I wish you would've felt it. Maybe then you would've done something about it and tried to stick around.*

*I miss you so much, Dad. I'm angry with Mom. It's so much harder to be angry—really, REALLY angry—at someone you love. Are you mad at Mom and Kurt, too? Can you even get mad after you die? Maybe feelings are reserved for the living because we're still invested.*

*Love,*
*Your Dallas Alice*

# Thirteen

I've crashed on more than my fair share of couches. Actually, in my glory days, a couch was a luxury. Cold Sweat might have had the Bank of Ricky Pierce backing our tours, but accommodations still ranged from crinkly beanbag chairs to deflating air mattresses on a distant cousin's basement floor. Needless to say, I logged a great night's sleep last night beneath a fuzzy red blanket on a deep chenille couch. Renee's couch. A month ago, I would've mistaken this for a nightmare.

God knows what time it is when I stir awake, squinting into the light pouring in through the floor-to-ceiling windows.

I shift to sit up beneath the fleece blanket—*the good blanket,* Renee called it last night when she set me up in her living room with sleepy tea and more pillows than any one person could need. She showed me how to work her TV, asked me one last time if I had everything I needed, then gave me plenty of space to cry. She didn't hover or supervise, but she kept me safe from myself, and in the light of a new day, that's a larger gift than I know how to unwrap.

I fold up the blanket and find my phone on its charger. I didn't see much of the apartment in the dark, but its industrial feel, the high ceilings and exposed ductwork, reminds me a little of Gentle Giant. I would have imagined Renee living inside a modern-art museum, all stark-white lines and hard angles and color-coded everything. Instead, her buttercream walls boast a mismatched gallery of art prints and pictures that hang seemingly at random, although it's too visually balanced to be accidental. I imagine her plotting and measuring each frame, her nose scrunched up in concentration.

Plenty of familiar faces smile back at me from the photo wall. There's a picture of Gin and Renee at a Cubs game and another with Gin, Renee, and Chrissy kneeling on the back of a boat with windblown hair and tipsy smiles. In the center of the wall, a gaudy gold leaf frame surrounds a photo I have memorized: Renee posed with that blond Ken doll at her office holiday party. *Merry, Bright, and Blomquist,* I recite in my head, wondering why I committed her caption to memory.

At eight o'clock on the dot, the coffeepot gurgles to life. Cars hiss down the wet pavement, off to their Monday-morning meetings, and it occurs to me that Renee should be doing the same. She hasn't made a peep, and I won't be making the mistake of letting her sleep in again. Down a hall lined with framed playbills, I rap a knuckle against her bedroom door.

"Renee? Are you up?"

No response. Cautiously, I push the door open, revealing a tidy, feminine bedroom with a four-poster bed in the center. Renee sits up beneath a lavender quilt, wincing into the daylight with her blonde hair falling every which way. My pulse flutters, and in my mind's eye, I'm in bed beside her, Renee's smooth, sculpted legs tangled with mine. I cough, shoving the thought away.

"Shouldn't you be getting up for work?" I ask.

Renee blinks at me, confused, as she finger combs her bed head back. An enormous gray T-shirt hangs loose and lazy off her shoulder, and panic stretches her sleepy eyes as she paws for her phone on the end table, checking the time. "Sorry." She coughs. "Had to remember what day it was." Her voice is a low, sleepy rasp. "Monday, right? I, uh. I took today off."

"Oh. Sorry to wake you."

"It's fine." Renee rubs her eyes, then reaches for her nightstand again and slides on a pair of round wire-frame glasses. "You want coffee?"

"More than anything on this earth."

In the kitchen, Renee digs two mismatched mugs out of the cabinet—one big bellied and teal with a chip in the lip and another with a twirly-lettered roastery logo on the side. She fills both to the brim and gives me my pick of the two. I choose the teal one, worrying my thumb against the chipped porcelain. It feels lucky somehow—or maybe it's just the grand luck of the last twelve hours, that Renee happened to be passing by right when I needed to be found.

I follow her back to the couch, still collecting details of the apartment like souvenirs. Renee's home is so much more normal than I expected—the basket of unfolded laundry, the brown-spotted bananas in the fruit bowl, the abandoned stack of mail cluttering the small oak desk in the corner.

"Great apartment, by the way."

"Thanks." Renee brushes her fingers along the giant waxy leaf of a thriving elephant ear plant. "Enjoy it while you can. They're raising the rent, so . . . we'll see."

"Well, it's a great space." The next thought is meant to stay inside, but it flies out anyway. "Not at all what I was expecting."

She squints at me over her shoulder. "What were you expecting?"

"I don't know. You're just so organized and clean cut, but your apartment is . . . eclectic?"

Renee lifts a brow. "Am I allowed to contain multitudes, Alice?"

We settle on the couch, backs against the khaki armrests, toes almost touching on the center cushion. We're a set of matching bookends, each holding our mug steady in both hands.

"So," Renee starts. "Last night."

*Right.* I fight through a swallow, then a deep inhale that pours out as a wavering sigh. "Yeah. Last night. Thank you for letting me stay with you."

"Of course." Renee's voice is slow and measured, like she's trying to suss out exactly what drove me toward a late-night staring contest with my old favorite bar. She sips her coffee cautiously, eyeing me from behind her mug until the steam fogs her glasses. When her lenses clear, Renee's eyes lock on mine.

"So what's going on?" she asks outright.

"I was . . . a little shaken up." An understatement but not a lie. "It was a hard night. I'm glad you found me."

Renee's lips tick up on one side. "I did sacrifice the good blanket for you. That was very big of me."

I grunt a laugh. "At least you're honest."

"Yes, well. You can be, too, you know."

"I can be what?"

"Honest," she says.

My stomach folds itself in half.

"You don't have to," Renee amends. "But know that you can if you want to talk about it. Whatever it is."

It feels like I have mosquito bites on my stomach lining. I'm not sure whether it's safe—or even possible—to scratch. *Do* I want to talk about it? With *her*? Probably not. She doesn't know my family. She never knew my dad. But I know I can't feel this way anymore. All bottled up. My texts to Dad are devastatingly one sided, and based on my interactions with Gin as of late, I'm not sure she has space to discuss anything besides the wedding. I close my eyes and try to smooth my nerves like a blanket over my lap.

"So you know how my dad was in a band?"

"The Handful," Renee softly supplies. She remembers. That feels nice.

"Right. So. Last night . . ." Immediately, the words jam in my throat. I lift my mug for a sip of the only liquid courage I'm allowed these days. "My mom is dating the drummer."

A wave of nausea rolls through me, and I ride it out with my eyes squeezed shut. When I open them, Renee is studying me closely. It's like she's holding me up to the light, seeing me from every angle. I shiver.

"How are you feeling?" she finally asks.

A puff of air escapes my lips. "Shocked, I guess? I swung by my mom's to surprise her last night, and Kurt . . . well, he was just . . . there."

"Wait." Renee blinks. "This *just* happened?"

"Yeah."

Another long, trembling silence. I run my thumb back and forth along the chip in the lip of my mug. When I'm brave enough to lift my gaze, Renee's eyes catch mine so gently, the way my pillow catches my head at night. She's never looked at me like this before, soft and warm. The good blanket can't hold a candle to this.

"Thanks for telling me," she finally says, and by the low, even timbre of her voice, she may actually mean it. "Do you . . . know him well? The drummer?"

"Yes. Kurt."

"Kurt," she repeats with the exact right amount of disdain in her voice. A warm prickle of solidarity.

"I haven't seen much of him in the last few years," I admit, "but we spent every summer together in Galena. He was one of Dad's best friends, and . . ." My head begins to spin. "I don't know. He's Uncle Kurt, you know? He's not literally my uncle, obviously."

Renee nods. "I get it." She blows a breath over her coffee, and the steam momentarily fogs her glasses again. It's impossibly cute.

"So you're close, then?" Renee asks, and my throat goes dry. *What were we talking about?*

"Kurt?" Renee prompts, reading my expression. Hopefully not too well.

"Right. We were close, yeah. Especially when I was little. He was like . . . the human embodiment of flip-flops."

Renee's lips curl up.

"He's funny, too," I go on. "He used to recycle jokes from old stand-up comedians, but I didn't recognize it as George Carlin or John Cleese or whatever. I just thought he and my dad were comedic geniuses. And Kurt was sort of permanently single, so . . ." A chill zips through me. Warning lights, flashing red in my mind. "Do you think there was something going on with him and Mom before my dad died?"

Renee's face twists up. Maybe that thought should've stayed inside.

"I . . . I don't know your mom," she says.

"Right. Of course. Sorry. I didn't mean to—"

"Hey." Renee extends a leg to brush her fuzzy sock against the arch of my foot. Just a poke. A tap. An acknowledgment that I'm not alone. "I don't know your mom," she repeats, eyes steady on mine, "but I do know that I've assumed the worst before and been . . . a little wrong."

In spite of myself, I laugh. "Renee Roberts, willfully admitting to being wrong? Well, now I've heard everything."

"A *little* wrong," she doubles down. "Don't let it get to your head." She brushes her foot against mine again, and my chest floods with heat. Renee's cool blue gaze is the softest it's ever been, and I fumble beneath it. My eyes leap around her apartment for a safe spot to land. Somewhere comfortable. Somewhere familiar. I find a stopping point at the fruit bowl, and an idea clicks into place.

"Do you have plans today?"

"I . . . don't think so." She sets down her coffee and tugs an elastic off her wrist, then piles her hair into a loose knot. "Don't *you* work today?"

"Nope." Today is Cold Sweat day at Gentle Giant, and I'd rather not think about it. Or about Kurt and Mom. "Are you hungry?"

"I could be."

I swing my legs off the couch. "Good. Because your bananas are about to go bad."

Renee's kitchen is as eclectic as the rest of her apartment—every utensil I could ever need hangs off a pegboard beside the fridge, but none of them match. Enormous industrial tongs—the kind I'd imagine they use at a pig roast—hang beside rubber spatulas in primary colors reminiscent of an Easy-Bake Oven set. When Renee catches me inspecting her duckling-print oven mitts, she shrugs and says, "It's all from Village Thrift."

"Ah. Love that place. Really came in handy for my disco-cowgirl getup."

Renee's nose twitches. "I wouldn't have taken you as a secondhand gal," she admits. I have to bite my cheek to fight off a wicked grin.

"Am I allowed to contain multitudes, Renee?"

The bachelorette playlist makes great cooking music—"Girls Just Want to Have Fun" is up first—and when I start to sing along, Renee joins in. Softly at first while she slices bananas no thicker than a page in a book, but by the chorus, our performance has grown loud and impassioned. We sing into rubber spatulas, whipping our hair for an invisible crowd. Around the second chorus, I drop out, and even Renee's kitchen-karaoke voice blows me away—she has the perfect mix of grit and growl, but the sound is sweet and open, gliding butter smooth over the high notes. When she catches my eyes on her, she stops, and my cheeks sizzle alongside the pancake batter that I dollop onto the griddle. *I wish Dad were here*, I think. I wish he knew that I still make his pancakes. That sometimes, I'm okay.

Once I've flipped the last pancake and switched off the stovetop, Renee and I convene at the breakfast bar with freshly topped-off coffees and golden-brown short stacks.

"Heavenly," she says, just from the sweet, buttery smell.

"It's Dad's recipe." I slice off a bite with the side of my fork. "He used to make me banana pancakes every time he came home from a tour."

Renee gives me a small smile. "Was he gone a lot?"

"Kind of. A little over half of the year. We went along with him on tours when I was really little, but it was harder once I started school. I had orchestra concerts and stuff we had to be around for."

"I didn't know you were in the orchestra."

"As a kid, yeah. I got started on the upright bass, actually." I lick syrup from my lips. "Anyway. That's why I loved summers in Galena. Everybody all in one place for three months."

Renee hums in recognition. "The . . . what was it called? The Outpost?"

I bite down on a smile. "Yep. The whole band, plus me and Mom, like a big ole band summer camp. Except the one year in middle school when my parents sent me to an actual band camp, which . . . was awful, so I never went back. The Outpost was way better. The Handful would write and record an album every summer and tour it the following year. So I got a lot of time with Dad then." *And Kurt,* I think, then swig my coffee, trying to forget.

Renee swirls her fork through the syrup pooled on her plate, tracing loops and patterns before she asks, "Do you have pictures?"

"Of Dad?"

"Yeah, and the house in Galena."

A petty, protective part of me kicks in protest deep in my chest. *Now* Renee wants to see the Outpost? After she shut it down as a bachelorette party destination? I scan her eyes for signs that she's just being polite or, worse yet, trying to tease me. Instead, a flicker of genuine curiosity catches me off balance. I dig up a few spring break photos on my phone: Chrissy, Gin, and I are skiing in one, slapping bags of wine in the snow in the next. *Classic Alice,* I think, and my gut twists, but my college memories in Galena are mostly good. Senior year, our spring break overlapped with the tail end of The Handful's spring tour, and on the band's way home, worlds collided for one glorious, drunken night. Those photos are by far my favorite.

"Here's Dad doing shots of tequila with Gin. And here's Chrissy doing shots of gin with Kurt."

Renee leans in for a closer inspection. Her chin hovers over my shoulder, casually close in a way that leaves me floaty. "So Chrissy and Gin know Kurt."

"Yeah." I swipe the photo away, but Kurt is in the next one, too—I'm real little, sitting on Dad's shoulders with Kurt juggling guitar pedals to get a smile out of me. I set my phone face down beside my syrupy plate and search for a fresh distraction, something to talk about that doesn't trigger my Kurt-related acid reflux. I find it, wrapped in gold, in the center of the gallery wall. "I want to ask about *your* pictures."

"Oh?" Renee swivels in her seat, tracking me across the room. "Which ones?"

"Well, I know this one." I brush my fingers over the photo from the Cubs game. "And this one." The picture on the boat. I'm aiming for casual, like I'm only now noticing the photo in the gold frame when I trace it with my index finger. "What about this one? Who's the guy?"

Renee breathes a laugh and crosses to join me, looking up at her own smiling face. "That's my ex, actually."

My gut reaction is relief, then confusion as to what I'm so relieved about. "Your ex," I echo.

"Brian," she says.

"Brian is such a classic ex-boyfriend name."

"We actually broke up, like, a week after this was taken." Renee turns to me sheepishly and adds, "I should have done it way sooner."

"Sounds like a story."

She shrugs. "Not really. He was a good guy. We lived together and everything, but I . . ." Renee trails off, and I watch her eyes shift in and out of focus, like she's deciding how much of the picture to show me. "We met while working on a show together," she finally says. "The very first rehearsal, there was this spark, and we were inseparable. But then, six months later, when we wrapped the show . . . we didn't have anything in common anymore."

"So you . . . moved in together?"

"Brilliant, right? But he had a gorgeous condo by the lake, and I thought maybe we were just going through a phase, so when he gave me a key at our one-year anniversary dinner . . ." She shakes her head. "Not my best decision."

"And yet he still made the wall," I point out.

She nods and takes a long sip from her mug. "He's a good guy," she says. "Just not my person. We're still friends. At least friendly. I'm hoping we'll be like you and Gin someday."

With that, Renee wanders back toward the kitchen, her hips swaying with every step. Tiny flashes of her red shorts peek out and disappear again beneath the hem of her oversize shirt. It's hypnotic, and even when I pull my eyes away, they're pulled right back by the words—

"You've gotta be kidding me."

Renee smacks her phone on the counter, tossing her hands like a disgruntled sports fan. "The maang tikka doesn't work with the bangs."

"Come again?"

She groans into her hands and grumbles, "Check the group chat."

When I do, I find two new texts from Gin—two pictures of her trying on the wedding jewelry that's been passed through generations of Bhat women. She models two variations with her new haircut, neither of which are great. The gold pendant that's meant to rest on her forehead either disappears behind her bangs or completely disrupts them in a way that looks, for lack of a better word, stupid.

I laugh through my nose, but Renee isn't amused. Her face scrunches as she pulls her phone close, fingers swiping diligently for solutions. "It's okay," she mutters. "We can fix this."

"What is there to fix?"

Her swiping is audible now, almost aggressive, as though pressing harder will equate to searching harder. "There has to be a better way to style these bangs, right?"

"She could pin them back," I suggest. "But the wedding is two months away. Her bangs will grow."

Renee rips her gaze from her phone and pins it to me. "What if they don't grow enough?"

"Then we'll cancel the wedding," I say.

"What?!"

"I'm kidding! Shit, Renee. It's not that deep. Gin's not even asking for solutions, is she?" I swipe up in the text thread and flip my phone to show the evidence. "Look. She's just asking which option we liked better. She's not asking for help."

Renee mushes her lips, slowly shaking her head. "I don't know, Alice. I'm just worried." Her tongue wets her bottom lip, and it's like windshield wipers for my brain. *What were we talking about again?*

"Did you see that list on Gin's phone?" Renee asks, and I resettle into the conversation.

"I did."

"It's a mess," Renee says. "That's not how you plan a wedding, Alice. They need help."

I draw in a breath, and my shoulders come with it, but my lips stay pressed in a firm, unwavering line. I, too, have my concerns about Gin's lack of a proper wedding plan, but this is Gin Bennett we're talking about. Bringer of lasagnas. Forgiver of dumb, drunk mistakes. Maybe I'm giving her too much grace, but it's only because she's done the same for me.

"She's trying her best," I finally say. "And correct me if I'm wrong—you know I'm a rookie—but it's not our job as bridesmaids to plan the wedding for her, is it? Aren't we just supposed to support her and do whatever she asks us to do?"

Renee frowns, considering. She taps out a rhythm on the counter, her rings clanging against the granite. "Well, Gin did ask for my help on that list."

"She did," I agree. "And maybe you can encourage her to be a little more specific with her asks so we know exactly how to help."

Renee nods and returns to her phone, visibly calmer. "I think I'll send her that checklist from Kyra's wedding. And Aubrey had that amazing spreadsheet."

"And I'm sure you have a ton of resources from work," I tack on.

"Yeah, yeah." Her eyes stay glued to her screen until my phone buzzes with eight new texts—links to spreadsheets titled "WEDDING MASTER SHEET" and "Seating Chart 3.0" filled with names and information from eight separate weddings. Aubrey, Kyra, two different Katies . . .

"God, you have a lot of friends," I mumble.

"Two of them are my sisters." Renee sets her phone down, mission complete, then scrubs her hands over her face, blocking a sound like a groan crossed with a whine. "She's just so bad at this. I know I'm being a bitch, but it's ridiculous. I've been in eight other weddings, and not one of those brides has been this disorganized. It makes no sense."

But it's perfectly clear to me. "Did those other brides have their parents in the picture?"

Renee's face goes blank, lips parting with a breath of protest. "But the Bhats—"

"Are Gin's in-laws," I finish. "You know that's not the same. They're already hosting in their yard, and it's not the big wedding they would've wanted . . . I'm sure it's complicated. It's always complicated with family."

Renee twists one of her rings, brows pinched in thought. "But . . . but Gin said *we're* her family, right?"

"Well, yes, but—"

"And she doesn't have a maid of honor. It's all of us."

"I . . . that's true," I concede.

Gin's voice is in my head. She's told us more than once that she couldn't do any of this without us. And what have we told her? *Anything for you.*

"Then we're not just bridesmaids, are we?" Renee concludes.

"You're right." I give a firm nod. "We're all she's got."

## GIN'S I DO CREW

**GIN BENNETT**

Hey ladies! Thanks to Renee and her amazing wedding planning templates, Rishi and I are finally feeling organized and have a specific vision for this wedding. Thank you again, Renee, for all your help and advice!

We finished compiling the list of items we'll need for the wedding, and we've decided to divide it up between the bridesmaids, the groomsmen, the Bhats, and of course, me and Rishi. My hope is that the three of you can work together and hit up Chicago's secondhand stores to find these things. Per Renee's suggestion, I've tried to be as specific as possible!

Rishi and I request that the bridesmaids thrift/provide the following items:

- 20 folding chairs (we're looking for a specific style, I'll send pics. We already have 10, and we LOVE the look, so we just need 20 more that match)

- 5 round foldable dining tables (60 in.)

- 30 plates (ceramic, 12 in.)

- 30 forks, spoons, and knives

- 30 dessert plates (ceramic, 8 in.)

- 30 water glasses (green glass, no clear, 8 oz.)

- 2+ large coolers (one pale green, one coral pink)

- 2+ large trash cans (metal, matching please!)

- 2+ recycling bins (not the blue ones—black or tan preferred)

- 2 long tablecloths for bar and buffet (ivory or eggshell, scalloped edges)

- 5 round tablecloths for dining tables (ivory or eggshell, scalloped edges)

- 8 vintage rugs (4x6 feet to create an aisle)

- sound system (Alice's work???)

- 2 handheld microphones (Alice's work???)

- speakers (Alice's work???)

- 30 cloth napkins (pale green)

- 30 place cards (Renee, you have the best handwriting—would you mind?)

- 7 terrarium centerpieces (I'll send the link to the DIY instructions)

Let me know if you have any questions. Thanks in advance you guys <3

# Fourteen

I read Gin's text on the bus home from work—my second shift back since the Cold Sweat session. Aidan has yet to mention how things went with my former band, which is fine. Preferable, actually. As is, I'm slapped with reminders of their upcoming Chicago show at every turn—the posters, the targeted ads. But I have enough to worry about without agonizing over a band I'm no longer a part of. For example: this massive, ultraspecific list of wedding requests. I fear that our bride may have overcorrected, but Renee asked for specifics, and she certainly won't be disappointed.

As promised, Gin sends links and reference pictures to guide us, then instructions for the terrarium project, which looks doable, albeit messy. It'll take up most of a Saturday, and . . . how many Saturdays do we even have left? I swipe open my calendar and count off the weeks—six, seven . . . eight. Eight weeks until Gin and Rishi walk down the aisle, and we have zero of the required vintage rugs to create said aisle. On my second read of the list, I feel myself sinking into it, like I'm being lowered into a hot, bubbling cauldron of *the feeling*—that *anything for the bride* feeling I've been afflicted with since the engagement dinner. But it's different now. I'm more determined. Beneath the obligation, there's a thrilling undercurrent, a scavenger hunt–adjacent rush. It can only mean one thing: I've being sucked into the wedding vortex, where everything else is irrelevant.

I don't realize I've missed my bus stop until we've passed it, and it feels like divine timing that I look up just as we lurch to a stop at Village Thrift. It's like the list is in charge now, directing my steps off the bus and through the automatic doors into a cloud of thrift-store smell—a distant whiff of a musty basement shaded with ammonia. I reach for a basket, then stagger back when I spot a familiar profile near the used books—a gently upsloped nose and full lips, blond hair twisted back with loose tendrils framing her face. Renee leans against a bookshelf, eyes skating over the pages of a worn hardcover. When I'm close enough to read the title of the book, a laugh fires out of me like a shot from a cannon.

Renee startles, eyes wide and wild at first, then softer when our gazes catch. She tucks *Controlling the Controllables: A Guide to Inner Peace* beneath her arm and smooths her sleeveless linen blouse in her signature red. A second laugh flies out of me when she glances down at her slingback kitten heels and, more notably, the shopping basket beside them piled high with green cloth napkins.

"Is something funny, Alice?" Renee arches a brow.

"Oh, nothing." I nudge her basket with the toe of my sneaker. "Nice napkins. Are there thirty of them?"

I watch for Renee's signature eye roll. Instead, a smirk toys with the corner of her lips, and a pleasant shiver rolls through me. I grab a basket of my own and try to match her pace as Renee patrols the fluorescent aisles of secondhand housewares.

"So the list," I say.

"The list," she echoes, then clicks her tongue once. "I told Gin to be specific, but who knew she'd take it so far?"

No sooner has she said it than Renee snaps her mouth shut in resignation. Because this is Gin we're talking about. Going above and beyond is all that she knows. Now it's on us to do the same.

With an hour until Village Thrift closes, Renee and I narrow our focus. Tablecloths. Tonight, we are only looking for tablecloths. We scour the racks of linens, discussing the subtle difference between eggshell and ivory. Village Thrift has neither. In fact, they have no tablecloths at all, only bedsheets that fool us again and again.

"This store has given me a stick-on handlebar mustache, cowgirl boots, and a dozen neon swimsuits," I list off. "But tablecloths? That's where they're drawing the line?"

"We could come back on Tuesday when they restock," Renee suggests.

"Controlling the controllables. Did your book teach you that?"

This earns me that eye roll I was looking for, but she pairs it with a smile. "The joke will be on you," she insists, "when I achieve inner peace. Just you wait."

She certainly has a long way to go, though. When we file into the checkout line, Renee is visibly anxious about leaving with only the napkins. She spins her rings while perusing the list, which she's already pasted into a note on her phone.

"We're gonna be fine." My hand instinctually floats to the space between her shoulder blades, but I pull it away. "This was just the first, super-spontaneous shopping trip. We'll plan better for the next one."

"We just don't have a lot of time," Renee mutters, and she's right, but she's forgetting something critical. Our secret weapon of connections.

"We have something better than time," I remind her. "We have Chrissy."

Renee's laugh is like the shake of a tambourine, and it shimmers through me, spilling goose bumps down my arms. It's *such* a good laugh. Hard to earn, which makes it that much sweeter.

When the line shifts forward, she sidesteps closer to me, and I breathe in her clean scent. Eucalyptus, I think? It's a delicious disruption from the musty thrift-store smell.

"I always thought you were funny, you know." Renee bumps my thigh with the shopping basket. "I just didn't know you could also be . . ." Her eyes slit as she searches for the word, and my brain butts in with a hundred dangerous suggestions. *Sexy. Irresistible.* "Thoughtful?" she says.

I clear my throat. "Interesting. I always thought you were both a total bitch *and* deeply unfunny."

Renee snorts. "And now?"

"Now?"

"Yeah. What do you think now?" Her mouth quirks up, and there's a glimmer in the crinkled corners of her cool blue eyes. The longer I look at her, the higher the tide inside me rises. What do I think now? I can't tell her that. I'm not even sure—it's just an inkling. The early stages of a feeling I think I recognize, but it's been so long.

Renee tucks back a stray blond tendril, and I follow her fingers, the way they brush against the shell of her ear. Gently. Intentionally. Something pulses inside me.

Finally, I say, "I'm still deciding."

Outside, the dark has settled on a truly perfect Chicago summer night, the warm, breezy kind that should serve as a blueprint for the entire season. The rain has washed away so much of early summer; I can hardly believe it's already July.

"I can take these." Renee nods to the grocery bag of napkins in my grip. Her apartment is just down the block, but she goes out of her way to walk me to the bus stop: A small gesture but it swells inside me, fueling the fire every time her arm brushes against mine. It makes me wonder if I'm not the only one with an inkling. I'm fighting for my life to combat the urge to say something like—*hey, Renee, you're walking pretty close to me. Want to tell me what that's about?* But if I speak up, I'm sure she'll stop, like this was all an accident she'll take care to avoid from now on.

"So Tuesday," Renee says, snapping me back to the world of logistics.

"Tuesday," I repeat. "What time are you off work?"

Her stride breaks for half a pace. "It . . . kinda depends."

"Oh . . . okay?" I look at her sideways. "Is it safe to plan for six o'clock?"

"Yeah, but . . ." Her face twists up. "I'll just text you when I'm on the way home, okay?"

Renee finds her pace again, but I can't get a read on her. She pins her focus across the street, toward home, and something spins inside me, a reversal. This is all backward. Shouldn't Renee be trying to hammer down the details while I'm the one dodging specifics?

"You know, for such a planner, you don't know your own schedule very well," I tease, but Renee just rolls her eyes.

And then she hugs me goodbye.

Renee and I have *never* hugged. I'm not sure what moves her to do it now, but her arms fold around my neck, the bag of napkins rustling between my shoulder blades. It's a soft breeze compared to the thunder of my pulse. My cheek presses to Renee's soft shoulder, and I breathe her in—eucalyptus and clean cotton sheets, exactly the smell of our room in Palm Springs. I had attributed it to the hotel, but I guess it was her. That gentle, comforting scent was Renee all along.

By the end of the week, Chrissy has secured ten terrariums from a client, because of course she has. I have to pick them up, though, along with the four rugs she gets from "her rug guy." As the only bridesmaid who doesn't work nine to five, I spend my days off from Gentle Giant zipping around the city in my truck-turned-mobile-storage-unit. There's no time to practice bass or work on my own projects or anything else these days—the wedding pulls every second of my free time. At least that's what I tell myself every time I swipe away a text from Mom like it's a spam email. I don't have the energy to work through those feelings right now.

As planned, Renee and I return to Village Thrift to shop the restock—she texts me when she's on her way, but she doesn't arrive in work clothes. Her wine-red sports bra peeks out from beneath a half-zipped black hoodie, her bike shorts tight as a second skin.

"Gym?" I guess.

"What? Oh." She toys with the zipper on her sweatshirt. "Sort of." She tips her head toward the store. "Shall we?"

"Yes, and *shall we* discuss where you came from, or are you being vague for a reason?"

I don't mean to come right out with it, and when Renee's eyes dart away, I feel the blood drain from my face.

"Sorry. Ignore that. That was an inside thought that just flew out."

Inside, Renee bends to grab a shopping basket, then turns to me, visibly perplexed. "What do you mean *flew out*?"

"Just what it sounds like. I'm not always making a conscious decision to say something. Sometimes it's . . . sort of like a sneeze? It has to come out."

Her nose scrunches. "That sounds . . . made up," she admits.

"I know. I wish it was. Instead, I get to feel bad about this shit forever. Like in Palm Springs when I made that comment to Chrissy about her filler melting in the heat? That was mean."

"That was . . . funny," Renee admits.

"And that's the problem," I say. "Because sometimes, people laugh. It's funny—*ha ha, Alice says what everyone else is thinking.* And then other times, I'm annoying or I'm rude. Like when we were dress shopping and I kept blurting stuff out and pissing you off."

Renee purses her lips and opens them with a pop. "I . . . may have been a bit hard on you," she admits. "I was mad that you had offered me a ride and then slept through my calls and—"

"And I still feel awful," I interrupt.

"But," Renee cuts back in. "I slept through my alarms in Palm Springs, so I suppose it happens to the best of us."

"I'd still be happy to pay you back for that Uber," I remind her.

"And I'd still be happy to pay you back for the expenses you covered in Palm Springs," she counters. "Also the napkins. Maybe we should work out a system for who's paying for what on this shopping list?"

"Maybe," I murmur, but I know once we get to the counter, I'll be quick on the draw to put my credit card down. Dad's drinking budget might have put a sizable dent in my inheritance, but Renee worries about money in a way I never have, and it's worth the expense just to keep that worrying to a minimum. For her and for me.

On the hunt for water glasses, Renee and I sort through shelf after freshly cluttered shelf, but it's a minefield of vases—some tall, some squat, all plain and likely left over from gifted floral arrangements. I must've donated a dozen just like these after Dad passed. I turn over a squat square vase in my hands, wondering if it could somehow be one of mine—if we shared an apartment at one point, this vase and I. My chest hollows and slowly refills with pressure, familiar and unwelcome. That's the funny thing about grief. You run into her everywhere, even in thrift-store aisles. I'm mentally slipping into inky black quicksand when whatever tune is playing through the store speakers fades into the start of a new song. A guitar strums its bright, twangy opening chords, and my chest lifts. It feels like a welcome visitor.

"Do you know this song?" I tilt my chin toward the sound.

Renee shakes her head. "I didn't even realize there was music playing."

We're quiet for a few bars, and my insides tense as the first verse sets in. "Willin'" by Little Feat.

"I was named after this song," I whisper. I press a finger to my lips, then point up toward the speakers on the lyric about "Dallas Alice." Renee hears it, and her eyes crinkle, but she doesn't say anything. She just listens—both to me and the music. "Dad always called me that," I tell her. "Dallas Alice. Even though neither of us had any connection to Texas. But this was his lullaby for me. Well, this and all the songs off *Songs for Alice*."

A small smile plays across Renee's lips. "I love that."

"It's also like . . ." I scratch my neck. "Maybe it's not the best lullaby. It's a song about long-haul truck drivers doing drugs to make it through a shift."

She shrugs. "That's what most music is about, though. Right?"

"Drugs?" I ask skeptically.

"Making it through."

Renee holds my gaze with a gentle intensity, and I feel like I might fall if she drops it, like the floor will split open and swallow us both. As the second chorus kicks in, Renee hooks her pinkie around mine, like a link in a chain, and I feel rooted by something larger and stronger than I've felt in a very long time. A sense of belonging. We stand, interlocked, just as still as any two dusty figurines on the shelf, until the last chord rings out and my eyes well up with tears. Not happy tears but not sad ones either. I don't really know what this feeling is, but Renee doesn't let me feel it alone. She doesn't let go, not even when the next song starts. Not even when an employee swings by to ask if we need any help.

"We're okay, thanks," Renee says in a voice so sweet I could crumble. But I think she's right. We're okay. With her, I'm okay.

*Dad—how did you know you were falling for Mom?*

*Love,*
*Your Dallas Alice*

# Fifteen

Chicago starts to shrink as we inch toward the Cold Sweat concert, the posters slowly closing in on my block. They spread through the city like a rash, plastered on the old brick building near my bus stop, and when I board the bus, the ads are on there, too. Texts trickle in from old acquaintances, asking if I'm playing the show or if I'm planning to attend or, more commonly, if I can score them free tickets. I wonder why I ever gave out my phone number. I wonder where these messages were when my dad died.

On a particularly hot Monday morning, Aidan requests my help for setup in studio B. He posts up in the control room, instructing via intercom while I scuttle around the studio testing mics and swapping cables. I've learned so much as a studio assistant, but I look forward to when I'm in Aidan's shoes, the one with the vision. When he comes on the intercom with a "Hey, Alice," I turn to make sure I haven't crossed any literal wires. Instead, Aidan's brows are raised behind the glass, sincerity written into the grooves of his forehead.

"I think you should go to the Cold Sweat show."

It's like my spine has been surgically replaced with an icicle.

Two weeks have passed since Cold Sweat's studio session, and he'd yet to mention it, so I'd thought I was in the clear. "What?"

The look on Aidan's face is so careful and earnest, I would hardly recognize him if not for that damn sweatshirt. He holds down the intercom and addresses me through the speakers on high.

"I've been thinking about it a lot," Aidan starts. "You're damn good at this, Alice. You're going places as an engineer. But your old band is going places, too. The lead singer . . . Solas, right?"

I nod, my pulse thudding just at the sound of his name. Solas Callaghan, an enormous redheaded gargoyle of a man, once co-captain of Cold Sweat, now front and center without me. We weren't cut out to share the spotlight—I was drunk and unpredictable. Solas was domineering and constantly cheating on his girlfriend. It wasn't a good look for any of us—but more sustainable in the long run for him, apparently.

"Well, Solas is a star, dude," Aidan goes on. "He's the real deal. The shit we worked on is really shaping up. I dunno what happened with y'all, but I'm just saying that if you patch things up . . . they'll be cutting an album soon, and if you could sweet-talk your way into production credit on that . . . that could be career-making for you."

My grip tightens around the cable in my fist. He's probably right, but I don't want to hear it.

"Just something to consider," Aidan says. "A little career advice."

"I'll think about it," I say, even if thinking about Cold Sweat is the one thing I've been trying not to do.

That night before bed, I dive into the black hole I've dodged for so long. Band interviews, singles, video clips, every publicly accessible memory I've missed from the last three years of Cold

Sweat. I scroll until my eyes go dry, searching high and low for a quote or a photo, a song I could twist and twist beyond recognition till I'm convinced it's a diss track about me. But there's nothing. Solas does not talk about me. Interviewers have stopped asking. There are a few mentions of me on the band Subreddit, but aside from that, it's been largely forgotten that Cold Sweat ever had a different bassist. It's a little heartbreaking—but a little peaceful, too. It's enough to trick myself into a few hours of sleep before I'm back in the studio for another shift.

Work keeps me busy, but it keeps Renee busier. She hasn't said much about what's happening at the Blomquist, but then again, the wedding monopolizes most of our conversations, and work steals most of our time. Coordinating schedules between the bridesmaids is a nightmare, but we finally land on a Saturday morning, six weeks before the big day, when all three of us are free to build centerpieces. Chrissy arrives right on time, albeit with a yoga mat slung over her shoulder.

"I'll have to dip out a little early," she warns, and I'm marginally annoyed but more concerned that we're one bridesmaid short.

Renee arrives not long thereafter, but while a ten-minute delay might be negligible for someone else, it's awfully suspicious when it's Renee. At a glance, all is well; she's put-together, as usual, in a red-and-white ringer tee and denim shorts, hair in a low ponytail with a few loose pieces intentionally framing her cheekbones. Nothing about her is visibly off, but when she apologizes for running late, there's something clunky about her delivery. It's like she's talking to us about one thing but her mind is somewhere else entirely.

I mouth "You okay?" to her when Chrissy is otherwise distracted, but Renee doesn't offer much—just a quick glance toward

Chrissy and the promise of "later" through gritted teeth. "When it's just us," she whispers, and, despite my worry, I love the sound of it. *Just us.*

We schlep the centerpiece supplies up to my apartment—cardboard trays of succulents, slouchy bags of potting soil, and the terrariums. Our gardening project has nothing on Gin and Rishi's landscaping work, though. The group chat has been inundated with progress pictures of the Bhats' backyard, transformed by hours of manual labor. Limestone pavers and lush butterfly bushes, plus the existing cattails and prairie grass of the marsh, create a near-finished picture of a ceremony site fit for a fairy tale.

I lay out a tarp in my living room, and for an hour or two, we're a three-woman assembly line: Chrissy fills the terrariums with dirt and rocks while I shimmy succulents out of their plastic pots, and Renee does the planting. We're not quite finished when Chrissy has to split for her hot-yoga class, but only after capturing dozens of pictures of us with our centerpieces.

"Don't get up! I know how a door works!" she calls on her way out, blowing two kisses behind her. "Love ya!"

"Love ya back," I call, and I can tell how much I mean it. I didn't realize how much I'd missed her all these years—that wild, wonderful enigma of a woman. The door clicks shut, and then it's just me and Renee. *Just us.* I wait a while to see if she brings it up, whatever it is that's weighing on her. But she doesn't, and a thought burns in the back of my mind: Maybe it's me.

I have to close my eyes to ask. "Did I do something wrong?"

"What?"

I suck in a breath and ask again. "Did I do something—"

"You did nothing wrong," Renee interrupts, and only then am I brave enough to open my eyes. Hers are dim; they drop down to her hands, and she pinches her knuckle. With her rings stowed on the coffee table, safe from the dirt, she has nothing to fidget with.

"Is it . . . Chrissy?" I guess.

Renee shakes her head. The tarp crinkles as she pulls her legs farther beneath her. "It's . . ." She cycles a deep breath. "It's work."

"The Blomquist?"

She nods once, then her gaze flits around the room, resting anywhere except on me. Her eyes are steady on the ceiling when she finally confesses. "I lost my job."

Silence. For a few seconds, my brain is entirely blank. Then it actually registers what she said, and I don't understand; all I can hear is the blood pounding in my ears. Even straight from the source, my gut insists that this has to be a joke. But the sorry, solemn look on Renee's face, how she combs her hair back with shaky, dirty fingers, speckling her blond strands with soil . . . she's really not herself. My chest feels like it's pressed inside a trash compactor. I have so many questions, but for once, I don't talk. I just listen.

"The Blomquist lost an enormous chunk of funding," Renee starts. Her voice is flat. Detached. "Our federal grant was completely eliminated, so the board decided to restructure and . . . six of us got laid off. It wasn't just me."

"I'm so, so sorry, Renee."

Still, she won't look at me. She's stiff and withdrawn, like there's something else she's not telling me.

"When did this happen?"

Renee hesitates. "A while ago."

"Can you be more specific?"

Her eyes track toward the window, as far away from me as possible. "I don't know if I want to tell you."

"Renee."

She huffs a small, sad laugh. Not a *ha ha, that's so funny* laugh, but a *ha ha, my life is pitiful* laugh. Her voice stalls between a whisper and a whimper when she says, "Remember how I was late to the engagement party?"

*No.*

"I had to go in to clean out my desk."

*No no no.*

We're both silent as I try to strong-arm the truth into making sense. This is Renee Roberts. Renowned overachiever and vision board manifester. Executor of the five-year plan. From the moment I met her, I understood Renee as a woman who tied a leash around her life and taught it to heel. And it did. It worked. She has become what she said she would become, done exactly what she set out to do.

And still had it all fall apart.

I pinch the spiky leaf of an aloe plant, trying to sort out the scramble of emotions in my chest. I'm sad for her. Confused for me. And I'm angry. She's been lying for weeks.

"Why didn't you tell us?"

Whatever Renee is choking back doesn't go down easy. Her eyes pinch at the corners, damming back tears. I see how much this confession is costing her, and my anger ebbs back a bit. When Renee finally speaks, her voice is frail, each word limping out after the next.

"What was I supposed to do? Waltz into my friend's engagement dinner and say, *Hi, hello, I'd love to be a bridesmaid, but by the way, I just got laid off*?" Renee shoves to her feet and begins to pace, and my eyes track with her, back and forth, the tarp crunching beneath her feet. "I couldn't make it about me like that. And then *you*." She swivels toward me, and my throat burns. "Gin told me you were going to be there, and I thought, *Oh, here's this drunk asshole that weaseled her way back into my friend's life—*"

*Ouch.* But fair. And it's not like I was thrilled to see her, either.

"—but then you're not," Renee goes on. "You're not that person at all. You're working for this prestigious recording studio—"

"For free," I remind her. "Unpaid."

"And here I am, a failed actor and now a failed event planner, too—"

"You haven't failed at either of those things. You're just not doing them anymore."

"Then what am I doing?" Renee spreads her arms wide like a pterodactyl flapping its wings. "I'm a planner. I plan things. I planned my whole stupid life, and I did exactly what I said I was going to do. I got an MBA. I got the dream job, and I still ended up flat on my ass. Meanwhile, you get to do the musician thing and barely even worry about money."

And the anger's back, surging through me like an electrical charge. "Because my dad died?" I cry out. "Sorry, do you wanna trade?"

"No, that's—" Renee slows to a halt. Her blue eyes flash with regret, and she draws in a shaky breath. "I'm sorry. That's not what I meant. Let me just . . ." She lowers herself back to the tarp, kneeling in front of me and sitting back on her heels.

"I know you didn't get as much money from your dad as you expected," she says. "But you've always had money from your parents. Even before you lost your dad. Right?"

I bite my cheek. "Sort of."

"They paid your half of the rent when you lived with Gin, right?"

"Well, yeah."

"And your groceries? And utilities? Did you ever have to pay for your own—"

"Okay, I get your point. I had an enormous safety net while I was touring with Cold Sweat."

Renee prods gently, but she prods all the same. "And how did you pay for those tours when you were just getting started? For the van rentals and the gas?"

A fresh shot of anger seeps through me, but she's not wrong. Cold Sweat wouldn't have taken off if not for the money Dad put into it. "That's true," I admit. "You're right."

Renee's lips tug into a sad sliver of a smile as she presses both her palms to my knees, making my skin buzz.

"It was so easy to hate you," Renee says, "when you were Gin's mean, drunk girlfriend living her dream on her parents' dime. It was so easy to resent you. And I'll be honest." Her grip tightens, heat shooting up my thighs. "I'm still jealous of you. I wish that I wasn't, but I am. You can afford to pick up the check on a bachelorette trip. You park at the airport even though it's literally so expensive. You can do what you love for no money and still afford to live in the neighborhood I'm getting priced out of. But you . . . it's different now." She blinks, and a soft sparkle returns to her eyes. "You're different. You're sober. You're . . . I like you. I didn't expect it. You—" She pauses, then adds, "You've become such a good friend."

It takes every ounce of concentration not to flinch away. A good friend. Right. That's what I am.

"My heart breaks for you and everything you've been through," Renee says, "and I wouldn't trade places with you in a million years. But I'm still jealous of you, Alice. I wish I could pursue my dreams the way you get to."

My memory whirls back to our conversation at the diner, how Renee assumed my shift to studio work had been a financial decision. I know it's a privilege to do what I love, but I've hardly considered how the alternative might feel. Had I been born into a different family with average finances, I'd be just like Renee—putting my passions second to survival, and even then, it's all come undone for her. The thought rots in the pit of my stomach. It can't feel like living so much as staying alive.

My hand moves without my permission, brushing back an errant blond strand, my touch lingering on her neck. "It's not fair," I breathe out.

"Nothing is fair," Renee says. "It's not fair that I lost my job or that you were born into money and I wasn't. It's not fair that your dad died so young. None of it's fair. But I'm still trying." A hint of a smile twitches on her lips. "That's actually why I had to tell you now. That's why I was late. I just got an email from the Philharmonic that I'm in the final round for a job on their events team. I was so excited, and right away I thought, *I can't wait to tell Alice.*"

A floaty feeling rises in me. "Really?"

"Yes." Her eyes sparkle like sapphires, and I wish she'd always look at me this way. Like I'm made of pure gold. There are goose bumps on my soul. "But then I knew I had to come clean about my last job and . . . I'm so sorry, Alice. I should have told you sooner, but I haven't really told anybody. You've shared so much with me about your dad and The Handful and what's happening with your mom . . . I couldn't lie to you anymore. I want to be honest with you the way you're honest with me."

"Always," I whisper, laying my hands over hers. "I will always be honest with you, Renee."

But not with myself. I will lie to myself for as long as I have to, just to keep things exactly like this. When my routine bends around thrift store trips with Renee and late nights at my place lettering place cards, I tell myself Renee and I are just getting closer, like Gin hoped. We're *trying*. This, I tell myself, is what good bridesmaids do. They cuddle up beneath the good blanket while practicing job interview questions or workshopping wedding speech ideas. They're in constant communication, like one long conversation interrupted only by sleep and studio shifts. They're together nearly every day—for wedding prep purposes at first, but with time, it becomes an assumption. Cooking for two and mornings at Grounds Crew. It all becomes part of my routine. Because we're friends. Renee said it herself, so I have no choice but to believe it.

# Sixteen

With the number of hours Renee and I put into prepping for the Philharmonic interview, I'm not surprised to hear it was a rousing success. She calls me the moment she steps out of the office, and I can hear in her voice how wide she's smiling. There's no offer on the table yet, but the hiring team adored her. They all but told her she had the job. That alone is cause for a celebratory dinner.

It's a Friday night in late July, and Renee sits on the edge of my kitchen counter, swinging her feet and filling me in on interview details while I slice red peppers for fajitas. I planned the meal around her favorite color, complete with bright-red fruit punch and a cherry pie for dessert.

"The Philharmonic said I'll hear back early next week," Renee says, but there's mischief in the slant of her smile. She reaches for her phone, and something flashes behind her eyes. "But there's *also* a job at a theater in the suburbs, and I'm extremely qualified."

The peppers hiss and sizzle as I slide them into the cast iron, and I adjust the heat while Renee reads the job listing aloud. I've almost forgotten what it was like to cook without Renee keeping me company like this. Moments like these feel so natural, so correct.

Renee doesn't linger on the details of the administrative job; instead, she skips ahead to what really interests her: the theater's lineup of shows for the season.

"We've got *Come from Away, White Christmas* . . ." She gasps through her nose. "They're doing *Grease* this fall! That's certainly a sign."

"A sign of what?"

"That I'm meant to have this job," she says plainly. Like it's obvious.

I don't do the woo-woo stuff, but the certainty in Renee's voice, the hope turned tangible by the appearance of a very common musical in this theater's season, almost makes me believe it, too. I nudge the peppers around the pan and ask, "So what's the deal with *Grease*?"

"*Grease* was the show that got me hooked on theater," she explains. "Dad showed me the movie as a kid, and I just never let it go."

"Is your dad a theater guy?"

"He's a welding engineer for a heavy-machinery company back in Iowa," Renee says. "So . . . no. But I was hooked, so Dad pulled out the park district catalog and let me pick out all the dance classes and theater camps I wanted to take."

"I'm not sure that I've seen *Grease*," I admit, and when Renee insists we watch it tonight, my groan of dissent is no match for the persuasive powers of her smile.

"You owe me." I shake my kitchen spoon at her. "We're watching *The Princess Diaries* next time."

"Only if you promise not to say all the lines."

Both times we've tried to watch it, Renee devolved into a twitchy mess when I said every line several seconds before the actor did.

"If I'm not allowed to say the lines, then you're not allowed to sing along to *Grease*."

"Fine." Renee folds her arms. "Say the lines. But don't get mad if I don't laugh at every joke when you've already spoiled it."

"You're a tyrant," I tell her.

"You're a menace," she fires back, but the way she says it—the way we bicker now compared to the start of the summer—is wholly different. It feels less like a fight and more like we're building to something.

"I think you'll like Rizzo," Renee decides as we settle into the couch, each of us cross-legged with a plate of fajitas in our lap. "You kind of remind me of Rizzo, actually," she says.

"And who is Rizzo?"

"My bi awakening."

Heat swells in my chest, but I tamp it down and grab the remote. For the first time in my life, I am willingly searching for where to stream a movie musical. "Okay, but who is Rizzo in the movie?"

"One of the Pink Ladies."

I blink at her. "O . . . kay?"

"The girls with the matching pink jackets? You have to know the jackets."

My apology comes in the form of willingly paying $3.99 to rent this movie.

"I obsessed over those jackets as a kid," Renee goes on, digging into her fajitas just as the opening credits begin. "Dad had a red bomber jacket that was kind of similar. It was enormous on me, but I'd wear it around the house. And then he got me a real Pink Ladies jacket for my birthday, just like theirs, but I cried, because I wanted a red one. Just like Dad's."

Grief rises in my throat, sharp and hot, but I gulp it down. "So you just stuck with red from then on, huh?"

Renee lifts a shoulder, nodding until she's swallowed her first bite. "Red goes well with blue. It makes my eyes pop." She opens her hand on the word *pop*, making a firework with her fingers that bursts inside me, too, sparkling in my chest as Renee rambles on. Now that she's talking about theater, she can't stop. Her face glows as she reminisces on productions past and the hyperintense professors in her BFA program. I pause the movie—not because I don't want to miss anything, but because I'd rather watch this: The undiluted excitement that shines like a spotlight behind Renee's eyes. She stops only when our phones both buzz on the coffee table at once—a text from Chrissy about tomorrow's bridal shower.

"I assume I'm driving you to that?"

Renee bats her eyelashes and rests her chin on the backs of her hands, framing her face in a look of sheer innocence. "Sorry to always be that friend," she says.

There's a kick in my stomach. Right. Because we're *friends.*

I roll my eyes just to pull myself away from the adorable face she's making. "I really don't know how you live here without a car."

"Here?" Renee points toward the floor. "We are talking about Chicago, Illinois, right? The city with arguably the best public transportation in the country?"

"Sounds like maybe you'd prefer to take the train."

"Never mind." Renee straightens. "I take it back. Chicago is a driving city. Thank God I have you, Alice." Every word drips with sarcasm, but my body can't take a joke. I swallow the hot pulse in my throat and hit play on a movie that I would detest under any other circumstances, but it's different with Renee. Everything is. She works up a sweat dancing in her seat, and when she lifts her hair up off her shoulders, I catch a flash of the sun tattoo between her shoulder blades.

"You never finished telling me about your tattoos," I point out.

"I didn't, did I?" This time, she's the one to pause the movie, freezing Danny Zuko in the middle of "Greased Lightnin'." She turns her wrist over, showing off the phases of the moon.

"This one." Her finger lands on the waxing gibbous. "Is a reminder that if the moon is meant to change, so are we."

"Beautiful."

"And the sun." She motions to her back, then pauses, scrunches her face up tight, and shuts her eyes so she doesn't have to look at me when she says, "So I was in a production of *Annie*."

My eyes go wide. All I can whisper is "No."

"I saw the sun on this tattoo flash sheet and thought—"

"Please. I hate where this is going."

". . . Oh, the sun will come out tomorrow."

"No," I repeat. "Take it back."

Renee shakes her head, and when her eyes open, they're filled with not a small amount of glee. "I can't take it back. It's tattooed on my body forever."

"I wish I'd never asked."

"Too late." A coy smile tugs her lips into a perfect open parenthesis. "At least now I don't have to carry my most embarrassing secret alone."

"Is that really your most embarrassing secret?" I challenge. "That you have an *Annie* tattoo?"

Renee rakes her teeth over her bottom lip as she thinks. "I

think my most embarrassing secret is that I *love* my *Annie* tattoo." She rests her elbow on the back of the couch, chin in her hand as she turns the question back on me. "What about you? What's your most embarrassing secret?"

"What is this, an eighth-grade slumber party?"

But Renee looks at me expectantly, so I lie. I pick some drunken story from my early twenties, something innocuous that barely earns a reaction. I'm breaking my promise to be honest, but I can't tell her the truth: My most embarrassing secret by a landslide is that I have a raging crush on my fellow bridesmaid.

**GIN'S I DO CREW**

**CHRISSY AMATO**

Hey girlie pops! It's almost bridal shower time!!!!! Not to brag, but Rishi's mom and I are practically BFFs now. My girl Asha and I have patio setup totally under control, so all you lovely ladies need to do is show up and shower our girl Gin with all the love and attention she obviously deserves! Oh, and presents too. Duh. Lots of presents.

**GIN BENNETT**

You're the best Chriss. <3 And omg, of course you and my future mother-in-law are friends now, ha ha.

**CHRISSY AMATO**

ALSO . . . you're gonna laugh. But. Waiter Boy is allegedly working the day of the shower.

**GIN BENNETT**

OMG

**CHRISSY AMATO**

But we're gonna be busy as fuuuuuck. So can you guys keep an eye out for him for me? Sending you a pic so you know which hottie we're looking for.

**RENEE ROBERTS**

CHRISSY WHY

**GIN BENNETT**

OMG NO CHRISS

**RENEE ROBERTS**

OF ALL PICTURES TO SEND

**GIN BENNETT**

I'm SCREAMING

**ALICE PIERCE**

What the hell is going on why did I just open my phone to a full nude of Waiter Boy

**CHRISSY AMATO**

It's the only full body pic I have!!!!

**ALICE PIERCE**

You're unhinged

**GIN BENNETT**

I'm crying this is so funny

**RENEE ROBERTS**

He is pretty hot though . . .

**CHRISSY AMATO**

Right?!?!?!?! The abs?! THE BICEPS?!?! BYE.

# Seventeen

The unofficial theme of Gin's bridal shower is *The Chrissy Amato Show.* That much is evident from the moment we arrive; when Renee and I step onto the patio, we're given hot-pink feather boas, bestowed upon us by Chrissy and Asha. They're wearing matching pale-pink custom tees that say *Virginia is for lovers,* only *lovers* is crossed out and *Rishi* is printed over it.

"Welcome, welcome!" Asha greets us with a wide smile and enormous hugs. Gone is the snarling woman from the engagement dinner; Mrs. Bhat has been fully Chrissy-fied. She sweeps her arms, motioning with her feather boa to the patio as a whole—the photo backdrop made entirely out of paper hearts, the big inflatable engagement ring, the pink sequin tablecloths and silver cushions on every seat. "Isn't this just . . ." Asha glances at Chrissy. *"Perf?"*

I barely contain my snort; Renee nudges me, a smile plastered on her face. "Yeah," she says. "Totally perf."

Gin is easy to spot from across the patio; her sparkly white feather boa flutters behind her as she scampers toward us, gathering me and Renee in one giddy group hug.

"Yay, all the bridesmaids are here!" Gin says, then softly, still holding us close, "Do you think Chrissy brainwashed my mother-in-law?"

We turn toward Asha, who, mid-conversation with an auntie, tips her head back with a Weedwacker cackle.

"Yes," I say.

"Definitely," Renee agrees.

"Cool." Gin smiles. "I'll thank her later."

After a trip through the buffet line, Renee and I carry our bruschetta-packed plates to a table at the far end of the patio. Chrissy appears almost instantly, sliding into an empty seat beside me.

"Any eyes on Waiter Boy?" For days, she's regaled us with the details of every text, voice memo, and lewd photo exchanged between her and this man whose name she still does not know. I am deeply invested; Renee, less so. Now, Chrissy is halfway through describing what she envisions for her and Waiter Boy's perfect first date when Renee's phone buzzes, and she disappears into it, frowning and scrolling until Chrissy pauses to whine.

"Hell-ooooo? Renee? Are you even listening?"

Renee sets her phone face down beside her plate. "Sorry. Just work stuff."

My body reacts the way it would to a misplayed note. *Work stuff? What could that mean?*

"Just closing out a few things before we start . . ." Renee's eyes flick to one of the card stock programs scattered across the table. *"The shoe game."*

Chrissy lights up. "I love the shoe game."

"I hate the shoe game," Renee says in near unison.

I'm intrigued. My eyes bounce between them as I prepare to pick a side. "Am I supposed to know what that is?"

"Essentially, the bride and groom each take off their shoes, and they hold one of each," Chrissy explains. "So like, one heel and one men's dress shoe. They sit back to back, and someone asks a question. Like, who is the messy one in the relationship? They hold up Gin's shoe if they think Gin is messy . . ." Chrissy lifts one hand in demonstration, keeping the other at her side. "And vice versa."

"So they can't see how the other one answers," Renee interrupts. "It's to see if they agree on things."

I nod, only sort of getting it. "Sounds . . . fine?"

"It's pointless," Renee says flatly.

"It does sound like something straight people would like."

Chrissy, representing straight people, pouts. She flips her feather boa over her shoulder, smacking Renee in the face in the process. "It's funny," she says while Renee spits out a feather. "And I'm the one who wanted to play it, so be nice."

Not five minutes later, Asha taps a fork against her water glass, calling everyone on the patio to attention. Except for me. My attention is still entirely caught up in what *work stuff* might mean. Based on Renee's less-than-convincing smile, I'm guessing it's nothing good, but she seems determined to keep her eyes off mine, like I might see something she's not willing to share.

The game begins just as Chrissy explained: Gin and Rishi pull up their black vinyl banquet chairs so they're back to back, each of them barefoot and holding a high heel and a dress shoe. Asha stands ready with the microphone and a prepared list of questions.

"Who's a pickier eater?" They both hold up Rishi's shoe.

"Who's a better dancer?" They both hold up Gin's.

"Who spends more time staring at their phone?"

My head snaps toward Renee, who drops her phone on the table with a clatter, caught in the act again.

"Ooh, here's a good one." Asha waggles her eyebrows deviously. "Who's better at keeping secrets?"

Without a second of delay, two nude stiletto heels shoot into the air. Instead of laughter, there's a collective low-pitched "Ooooh."

Gin laughs and waves her arms like an umpire calling *safe*. "Just secret keeping in general! I'm not keeping anything juicy. No babies or anything."

My head whips back to face the bridesmaids, brows scrunched. "Did she say babies?"

"I think it's like, if she's good at keeping secrets and she's getting married, she must be pregnant," Chrissy explains.

With that, I'm officially on Renee's side: The shoe game sucks.

The questions persist, but I skip the show in favor of a virgin Bloody Mary. The bar is inside, and the bartender looks at me like I'm crazy when I place my order. I look back at him like he's . . . wait. Like he's *Waiter Boy*.

"Here's your . . . soup." Waiter Boy slides my drink across the bar top, and I giggle nervously because, unfortunately, I have seen this man naked.

"Thanks. I mean thank you . . . Hey, what's your name?"

He looks at me, if possible, like I'm crazier. "Chris?"

My gasp is, out of context, completely unwarranted. I try—unconvincingly—to hide it with a cough. "Sorry." I grip the edge of the bar, leaning in conspiratorially, but I can't look him in the eye without laughing. "Did you just say your name is Chris?"

"Yes?" He squints at me, suspicious. In fairness, I'm reacting to a top-ten generic guy name as though Waiter Boy had introduced himself as Gizmo the Clown. I slap whatever cash I have onto the bar, muttering something like "Okay, thanks" or "Wow, that's cool," and race back outside to the table.

"CHRISSY." I whisper-shout as I crash-land into my seat. "I FOUND him."

"You found him!?" Chrissy launches out of her chair like it's spring-loaded, her whole body pivoting left, then right, like she's trying to sniff him out.

"YES. He's inside. And get this—"

Before I can reveal the true identity of Waiter Boy, Chrissy takes off like someone set her on 3x speed, and the rest of the shower goes by almost as fast. Gin and Rishi open presents one at a time, everyone oohing and aahing over trivets, until one auntie squeals that she felt a raindrop. No sooner is it said than the sky opens up and the rain dumps down in buckets. Everyone scrambles to grab a present or decoration, slimy wet feather boas whipping around. Inside, we wring them out in the bathroom sinks or else slop them into trash cans while reassuring a panicked bride that this definitely won't happen on her wedding day. As if that's something any of us can control.

The I Do Crew posts up at a table by the window, and Gin chews her lip raw, watching rain pelt down in sheets. Chrissy is the only dry one among us, having been inside talking to Chris when the storm rolled in. She tries to lift Gin's spirits with a Waiter Boy name reveal (Chrissy *loves* that his name matches hers), but Gin is unmoved, her attention entirely caught up in the weather.

"Do you have a backup for the wedding?" Renee is brave enough to ask. "For if it rains?"

"We'll have a tent if we really need it," Gin says, still not looking away from the window. "It's not, like, a circus tent but a classier one. A clear one, so we can see the stars."

"That'll look so good," Chrissy assures her.

"If you even need it," I add. "Which you probably won't."

Gin perks up a little at the positivity. "Yeah! So if it rains, we'll just move the tables out of the way and have the ceremony under the tent."

"What about the dance floor?" Renee asks, and Gin's face falls again. A small breathy "Oh" slips out.

"I, uh . . . I guess we'll just . . . hope it doesn't rain."

"And what about the concert, Alice?" Renee spins her worry on me. "Is there a backup venue?"

"It's an indoor show, actually," I say. "There's this little theater in Galena, so it's a really small, intimate thing. It'll be cool."

Gin's brows pinch, but her eyes stay wide, bouncing between Renee and me in search of a shred of context. "Are you playing a concert in Galena?" she guesses.

The realization sets in as quickly as the storm. Not for lack of trying, but I never did tell Gin about the memorial show, did I?

"Right!" I cough. "I've been meaning to tell you. The Handful is playing a memorial concert for my dad."

"Oh." Gin blinks. She glances briefly at the table like she's referencing a calendar, then back to me. "When?"

"Two days before your wedding, actually. On Dad's Gone Day."

Concern moves like a rain cloud over Gin's expression. The bent umbrella of her brow can't keep the pain out of her eyes.

"I'm gonna drive back that night," I rush to assure her. "I already have it all worked out with—"

*Mom*, I don't say. A chill rolls down my spine like a marble down a track. I have *nothing* worked out with Mom. Renee shifts beside me, knowing as much. I've ignored every one of Mom's calls and texts since the Kurt incident, so that's . . . shit, it hasn't been a month already, has it?

Gin meanwhile has gone pale as a bedsheet, and I feel terrible—she must think I'm being callous with my planning, not prioritizing her wedding. I'm stammering for the right thing to say, which I'm famously horrible at; I've put my foot in my mouth so many times that my toes should be permanently pruny. Gin speaks up first, voice baked in dismay.

"I can't believe I booked my wedding two days after the anniversary of your dad's death."

My breath halts. "What? I mean . . . Gin, it's fine."

Her eyes are shiny, the tears ready to spill over.

"Seriously, Gin. Don't worry about that. It's . . . I'm just glad that I'll be able to go to both."

"Right." Her face pinches just a decimal of a fraction. "But like . . . are we invited to the concert?"

This I didn't expect at all. "Do . . . do you want to come or—"

"Of course I want to come." Her voice is wrapped in hurt.

"I'm sorry, I figured you couldn't go. You did hear me say . . . it's two days before your wedding."

"So?"

"So won't you need to be setting up and, I don't know, getting your nails done? Greeting your out-of-town guests?"

"Rishi's brother is our only out-of-town guest," Gin reminds me. "And if it's important to you, I'll be there. And I'd love to bring Rishi, too."

"Could we carpool?" Renee chimes in. "Sorry to always be that person."

Surprise bursts in Gin's eyes, and I watch her gaze track from Renee to me.

"If you're all going, then I'm going." Chrissy slings an arm around the bride and cracks a smile. "Concert with the girlies, then we get Gin married. Best weekend ever, right? How lucky are we?"

It's corny, but it really feels true. I feel so lucky to be a part of a group that would only form under one very specific set of circumstances: Virginia Bennett falling in love. But that circumstance, as it is, will be coming to a close before we know it, and I'm suddenly sad. After the vows are said and done, what will we have in common? We'll see Gin individually, I'm sure, and maybe reunite for a baby shower or a karaoke costume party down the line. It'll be fine, but it'll never be quite like this again. Not with Gin and Chrissy. Certainly not with Renee. Without the wedding in common, will we even see each other? My poor little heart soars and stings all at once, knowing all things ever do is change.

At the first break in the rain, we say our goodbyes, scattering to our respective cars and sexy waiters.

"Nicely done finding Waiter Boy." Renee buckles her seat belt, then in a lower voice adds, "Forgetting to tell the bride about the memorial show, however?"

I clack my tongue and reverse out of my parking spot, one arm thrown lazily around the passenger seat headrest. It's an honest accident that my fingertips brush through Renee's hair, but it's so impossibly soft that I have to stop myself from doing it again on purpose. Renee's softness is an infinite surprise.

She plays DJ for the whole drive home, leading with the first few tracks off The Handful's platinum record, *Songs for Alice.* My heart squeezes in my chest as she sings along, not missing so much as a word.

"Have you been studying?" I tease, and Renee shrugs and purses her lips, but she can't hide the smile in her eyes. When the chorus comes in, she lets a high note rip, and I whistle. "Damn! Ricky Pierce, who?!"

We make it through most of the record this way, both of us singing along—but Renee is *performing*, and it's a fight to keep my eyes on the road. Every song sounds that much better with her harmonies.

And then, when I least expect it, a betrayal. She switches to a song from *Rent*.

I snatch the phone out of her hand. "This truck is a no-musical-theater zone."

"Oh, come on. Just this one song," Renee pleads. "It's a duet."

"No way, Broadway." I keep one eye on the road while queuing up something listenable.

"Pleeeease. I want you to hear it," she begs. "Listen to the words. I've been thinking maybe you could sing the lower part and—"

I make a big show of flipping on my turn signal and shifting one lane closer to the shoulder. "I'm pulling over. You're walking home."

Renee only grins, her brow arching in a silent challenge. She's calling my bluff. I flip the turn signal off, trying not to feel the way her smug smile leaves me dizzy.

"What is it with you and musicals?" she asks. "What tragic theatrical backstory are you hiding?"

It's a perfect opening. "I'll tell you if you tell me what the so-called work stuff on your phone was earlier."

My eyes are fixed ahead, but I can feel Renee's energy slip in the silence, the musical theater thankfully paused. "Fine," she says, voice clipped. "It was a rejection email. From the Philharmonic." She sighs, and something withers inside me. "I really, really thought I was gonna get that job."

"Shit. I'm sorry." I'm not sure what else to say.

"It's okay," Renee says, but neither of us are convinced. "It's . . . well, it's not super okay. But I'm being optimistic. I'm waiting to hear back from that theater in the suburbs, and one of my former coworkers is on the hiring committee, so . . ." She sighs again, fully resetting as she stares down at her hands. "Okay. Sorry. Let's move on. Your turn."

I swallow hard. "You're not gonna like it."

"So? You have to. That's the deal. What's your problem with musicals?"

I clear my throat. "I, uh. I dated a girl for four years whose alarm clock was 'The Wizard and I.'"

"That's seriously it?"

"Yes."

"You hate musical theater because of Gin's alarm clock." Renee's tone demands a better explanation. But there isn't one.

"You would hate it, too, if you woke up to that song every day."

"It's a very good song," Renee says.

"Not for an alarm!" I throw a hand up, exasperated. "Not for four years! I'm traumatized! And it's not all songs from musicals. It's this one specific type of song that I really hate. It's hard to describe. It's those songs where the character is like . . ." I look longingly into the distance, eyes wide and mouth agape in the phoniest, most theatrical face I can muster. Renee reaches over and softly swats my cheek, forcing my eyes back on the road.

"I think I know what you mean," she says. "When we get that inner look at the desires of the main character. They're called 'I want' songs."

"Well, I do not want the 'I want' songs," I say plainly. "They suck."

"You heard it here first, folks. Alice Pierce hates songs about following your dreams."

"I am pro-dream and pro-song," I insist. "I am anti–corny bullshit. Like, why am I listening to this and feeling embarrassed?"

Renee doesn't answer right away, and I let my eyes wander to the passenger seat in search of evidence that I've offended her. Cautiously, she steps into a thought.

"I think chasing your dreams *is* kind of embarrassing," she says. "You have to be vulnerable enough to put yourself out there, and you're probably going to fail a lot before you get what you want. And it's embarrassing to even be the type of person who thinks they can do something or be somebody. It's embarrassing to go on auditions and get rejected, to put in all this work for nothing over and over again with the delusion that eventually it'll be something."

"Huh." I lick my lips, considering. "I disagree."

"Oh?"

"Because I think the most embarrassing thing would be to love something and not go after it."

A small sigh dies in Renee's throat. "A little easier for you to say."

"Financially? Sure. But so many people don't feel that sort of passion about anything in the first place. And then there are people like you." My gaze slices sideways, a prickle of heat in my throat.

"People who have this remarkable talent *and* a love for it and instead of pursuing it, you go and get an office job. And that's fine. It's important. It's wonderful, even—to be comfortable, and we have to survive. But if you never even tried to sing or act or perform again . . . that's the most embarrassing shit I can think of. That's a waste."

The silence cuts sharper with each passing second. As I turn down Renee's block, I pull back from the gas, buying us a little more time.

"You've got a lot to say about my talent for someone who fell asleep while I was onstage," she finally says.

"Now *that*." I slap the steering wheel and shift the truck into park. "*That* is embarrassing. Don't tell me that it's embarrassing to chase after what you want when there are people out there, people like me, who are snoring in the audience while someone is on stage actually doing what they set out to do."

The flash of surprise on Renee's face fades into something more gracious. She considers me for a moment, then lays her hand over mine on the gear shift. Electricity zips up my fingers and stalls in my chest, the best and most remarkable feeling. I'm frozen in her cool blue stare but sweating beneath the heat of her palm. Opposites. Multitudes. If I could trap this feeling in a bottle, if I could take it like a pill, I'd be hooked on Renee Roberts till the bitter end.

"Thank you," she says, her voice thick and sweet as honey. "And for what it's worth, you work really hard. You're not snoring in the audience anymore."

"Not until you're in a show again."

I wink, then immediately worry I shouldn't have, but Renee squeezes my hand, and I am one giant, beating heart beneath her touch, one breath away from closing the space between us. Renee's voice plays on a loop in my head. *I like you. A lot. You've become such a good friend.* But knowing it and feeling it are two different things entirely, and what I feel toward Renee isn't friendly. It's fierce and fiery and increasingly difficult to ignore, especially in moments like this, when it's just us and she touches me like that. In a way that likely means nothing to her. It means *everything* to me.

*Hey Dad,*

*I didn't realize it until this weekend, but it's been over a month since the K*rt incident, and I still haven't spoken to Mom. Or you! Sorry! Hi! Be proud that I've been too wrapped up in the wedding and Renee to talk to my dead dad! (NOT wrapped up in Renee like that, you sicko! Don't make it weird!)*

*Anyway, Mom has texted me a lot, but I don't know what to say. Figuring it out would mean thinking about her and Kurt, and I would rather think about almost anything else. There's so much going on that I haven't had the time to sort through my feelings anyway, but I know I'm still . . . mad. Mad at Mom. Mad at Kurt. And mad at you. Because none of this would be happening if you were still around. If you had figured out a way to feel the hard shit without liquor, then this particular hard shit never would've happened to me! So actually, this is your fault! Ha!*

*I don't want to feel angry, Dad, and I guess that's why I'm choosing to ignore it and just feel what I'm feeling with Renee instead. I've never felt this way about anyone. It's like discovering a new color. I can hardly wrap my brain around it or the fact that I went without it for so long. She said that we're friends, and maybe that's true for her, but not for me. You're the only person I've admitted that to. I've barely admitted it to myself, and I may never admit it to Renee. I'm just so happy to have friends again, no matter how temporary. I'm scared to ruin it. I'm worried I'll break it and—well, you and I both know that fixing things isn't all that simple.*

*What would you do? I wish you were here to tell me.*

*Love,*
*Your Dallas Alice*

# Eighteen

Renee does not get the job at the theater in the suburbs.

The news hits her inbox on a Friday morning at Grounds Crew, and she lets me read the email over her shoulder. It's terse and impersonal; they don't even bother to wish her the best.

She's kept a level head and a stiff upper lip since her rejection from the Philharmonic three weeks ago, but I know this one stings. We've spent dozens of hours at this very table prepping for all four rounds of interviews they put her through—ludicrous for an administrative position. She was so *sure* she'd get it. And now? A single email, and she's back to square one. Renee stares blankly down at her laptop track pad like she's praying it might move on its own and take her straight to a website with the perfect job, the perfect opportunity, the perfect next step. I can't sit and watch her sulk like this.

I close my notebook on a failed draft of a wedding speech. "Come on. We're taking a break."

Renee doesn't budge. "We haven't earned a break," she mumbles, not looking up.

"I didn't say that we earned it. I said we're taking it. We're not going to get any work done if we're in a bad mood."

"We're not going to get any work done if we stop working either." Renee lifts her gaze, but only to shoot me a look. "Not getting a job is not a great reason to take a break from applying for jobs."

"But what if we took a break and felt better and more motivated on the other side?"

"Or the break could suddenly become the rest of the day." Renee arches a brow. "Like Monday night?"

Right. Monday night, when Renee was applying for a fundraising role at a culinary institute, I swore that watching an episode of *MasterChef Junior* would help her dial in her cover letter. Maybe it did but only after we fell gracelessly into an all-night marathon. Renee lay in my lap while I played with her hair, fingertips buzzing each time they raked through her soft blond strands. I'm still struggling to convince myself it was the sort of thing Renee does with all her friends.

"That was my fault," I admit, shaking off the memory. Nevertheless, I persist in my efforts to . . . get us to stop persisting. At least for the afternoon or until some of the pain leaves her eyes. My attention wanders to the pastry case, an evergreen distraction. "Should we grab those last two chocolate croissants to go?"

Renee frowns, skeptical, but she accepts my credit card when I slide it to her. "Only because I'm hungry," she insists. "This is not an endorsement of your proposed break."

While Renee falls in line at the register, I get to work, kicking down the door of every blog and community calendar in search of alternative afternoon plans. My eyes light up on the park district website right as Renee returns with a butter-stained pastry bag. Before she can sit, I pocket my phone, shove up from the table, and duck under the strap of my messenger bag. "C'mon."

"Come on where?" Renee presses.

"My place first. After that, you'll see."

Renee grumbles in protest the whole walk back to my apartment, where I haul two camp chairs out of my storage locker, each one folded and stuffed in its nylon drawstring sack. We each sling one over our shoulders, and I check my broken internal compass against the map on my phone. "It's a bit of a walk," I warn.

"A bit of a walk to where?"

"The park."

Renee waits for more of an explanation, but I don't offer one. I just lead us off in probably the right direction.

"Why the park?" Renee presses, not willing to drop the interrogation. When I don't respond, she grinds to a halt, dropping her chair on the sidewalk with a swishy clatter. She folds her arms over her chest, one brow cocked in a challenge. Once again, she's calling my bluff.

"What if you just went with me on this?" I suggest, knowing that, for her, this is an enormous ask. "What if you didn't know all the details ahead of time? What if you trusted me?"

We stand in silence for a long moment. Renee doesn't quite smile, but her face relaxes, all the hard creases smoothing out to something softer. More willing. "Okay." She bends to pick up her camp chair. "I trust you."

Those three little words echo through me like a song in a canyon. *She trusts me.* A metallic feeling coats the entire inside of my body as we walk the rest of the way to the park, where a group of parents, siblings, and strangers have laid out a patchwork of picnic blankets. I find us a spot and set down my camp chair, freeing it from its nylon prison.

"Is this Shakespeare in the park?" Renee guesses.

"Nope. Better." I unfold my chair and motion for Renee to do the same. She obliges, and we sit down with our chocolate croissants just in time for the show to begin. Eight minutes late. I like these people already.

"Good afternoon," a woman in a floral muumuu greets us. "Welcome to the Chicago Park District Kids Theater Camp production . . ."

Renee twists to look at me, eyes wide with disbelief. "A children's theater camp production?" she whisper-shouts with the enthusiasm I'd expect had I brought her to a Broadway production.

"Please silence all cell phones and avoid talking during the show," the muumuu woman says directly to us. "These kids have worked really hard for the last six weeks, and they're excited to show you what they've learned." She swoops a hand across the stage—more of a platform, really—and steps aside to make room for three miniature pirates, each of their costumes at entirely different tiers of effort. One looks to be handsewn, another cobbled together from the best Village Thrift had to offer, and the final of the three kids wears his street clothes and an eye patch.

This proves to be a bit of a theme throughout the performance. There's a real breadth of effort and enthusiasm among the cast of whatever G-rated pirate show this is. I can't hear much of what the kids are saying, and the ones who enunciate are let down by their castmates who skip entire lines and seemingly scenes, but over the course of forty-five minutes, I watch Renee come alive. She's the first on her feet for a standing ovation, eyes welling up with tears when the cast lines up for one final bow. The pirates grab each other's tiny hands, reach them toward the sky, then all at once fold in half at the hips to the raucous applause of their parents, siblings, babysitters, and neighbors. And us.

On the walk back to my place, Renee is still buzzing as we take turns recounting our favorite parts of the show.

"I liked how the pirate with the eye patch sang all of his lines," Renee says. "That was a bold choice. He really committed."

"That was good," I agree. "But was it as good as the girl who kept accidentally slapping people with her fairy wings every time she turned around?"

"Nothing could be as good as that," Renee insists. "Actors will study her physical comedy for decades."

"And to think we may have seen some of her earliest work," I muse. "For free, nonetheless."

"Yeah, how did you find this, by the way?"

"I remembered what you said about your dad signing you up for all those theater camps at the park district, and I knew there was a park district not too far from here."

Renee's pace slows as she blinks the wonder from her eyes. They're a soft, velvety blue, almost awestruck. "I can't believe you remembered that."

"Of course I did. That was the first time you made the theater face."

"The *what*?"

"You know. Your theater face. The face you make when you talk about theater." I close my eyes, referencing the memory of her in my kitchen, swinging her legs and rambling about productions long gone. "You look . . . glowy," I say. "Confident. Like . . . like the world is made out of hope."

I open my eyes, and Renee looks back at me, raking her teeth over her plush bottom lip. "Hope, huh?"

"Yeah." I shrug. "It's the theater face. It's really cute."

The last part slips past what little filter I have, and my chest pulls tight, but Renee's smile is a perfect crescent moon, and her eyes stretch like she's trying to look at all of me at once. We long ago graduated from her icy-blue stare, the one that kept me frozen in the past, a person Renee used to know and never cared to see again. But I've been trapped in her eyes a hundred times this summer, and they've never looked quite like this. Glassy as Lake Michigan on a cool, windless morning, sparkling in the sun. Cold, yes, but not in a way that feels dangerous, not anymore. Just brisk enough to restart my nervous system, to wipe clean whatever I was thinking or feeling before and leave nothing on my mind but this moment we're in. She's not looking ahead at where we're going or behind at who I used to be. She's looking at me, right here and now, like I'm a view worth taking in.

For a moment, I'm sure she's about to say something. Instead, Renee steps forward, presses to her tiptoes, and brushes her lips against my temple in the softest, sweetest kiss. It's no stronger than the flap of a butterfly's wing, but my body swells in a feeling that can only be glory. It has to be. Anything else would be too much to hold.

"Thank you," Renee whispers, still close enough for her breath to breeze over the apples of my cheeks. It sends a lava-hot flush down my throat, and I'm nearly certain that, whatever this is between us, she's feeling it, too. She takes a slow step back and hitches the camp chair up her shoulder, and my skin still thrums where her lips barely landed, but Renee is already walking again. Soon we're back to our normal pace, neither of us saying much until we pass by the brick building plastered in Cold Sweat posters, advertising next week's show. Renee tenses and speeds up a little, steering me away, but I linger, sizing up the grayscale Solas Callaghan looming large in the center of every poster. Solas's red hair, vibrant tattoo sleeves, and deadpan green eyes have all been reduced to black and white. He's less intimidating this way. Less complicated. He's just a person, same as me, and I'm sure neither of us are who we used to be.

"Maybe we should go to that," I decide, surprising myself.

"Really?" Renee pulls back, then, doubly surprised, "We? Am I invited?"

"Only if you want to go."

There's a beat; then she hooks her pinkie into mine, and I've never been so aware of my own skin. Every breeze feels like a gust. The tiniest touch could knock me down.

"Do *you* want me to go?" Renee asks softly.

I want her to go *everywhere* with me.

# Nineteen

It rains the night of the Cold Sweat show, but the fans can't be deterred. Outside the venue, a stagnant parade of black umbrellas protects more leather and shredded denim than I've seen since . . . well, since the last Cold Sweat show I played. Now I'm just another ticket holder, huddled beneath a shared umbrella with Renee. Her clean cotton scent is washed with the smell of rain, and it's a balm for my nervous system, breathing her in, even if I can't quite relax.

"Should we run through the plan one last time?" Renee suggests, lifting a brow. I try to stick my focus there, to fix my eyes on something innocuous like her eyebrows instead of the white-hot temptation that is the rest of her. I thought I might faint when she showed up at my apartment in that thigh-skimming leather skirt and matching knee-high boots. Spiky silver studs replace her usual gold hoop earrings, and a chain belt hangs below the hem of her ribbed white tank top. When I called out the absence of her signature color, she corrected me with a swipe of deep-red lipstick that I immediately imagined staining every inch of my skin. If this is a costume, Renee Roberts is playing the star of literally all my sex dreams.

"Alice?" Renee nudges me, and given where my mind has wandered, just the bump of her elbow turns me pink. Maybe the rain isn't such a bad thing; I could use a bit of a cold shower.

"What . . . what were we talking about again?"

"The plan?" Renee looks at me expectantly, and my mouth goes dry. *Right. The plan.* We've run through this a hundred times, but right now, the only word that comes to mind is *closer.* Renee is only a breath away, but my body insists it's a breath too far.

"So we're going to go inside . . ." Renee prompts.

"Right. Okay. We're going to go inside, and we're going to try to get close to the front of the crowd so Solas and the guys can see that I'm here."

"And that will be a good thing," Renee emphasizes. "They'll be happy that you're here."

*I hope.*

"Then we'll meet them at the merch booth before the headliner goes on, and I'll say . . ." I blow a raspberry. "I'll say what I have to say."

Renee nods, and the umbrella nods with her, shaking off some of its collection of raindrops. "And what you have to say is . . . ?"

Despite a week of workshopping this exact speech, my nerves still prickle when I square my shoulders and give it one last shot.

"Solas, I want you to know how proud I am of everything Cold Sweat has accomplished. I will always be a fan of this band, and while I regret that circumstances kept me from being the reliable bassist Cold Sweat needed, I'm thrilled that you have continued to grow and make extraordinary music. I wish I could have been in the studio for your session at Gentle Giant, but I did want to tell you that I'm sober now, and I'm building a portfolio of engineering work. I would love to grab dinner and catch up when you're back in town, if you're willing."

I blow out a breath, and Renee's eyes sparkle with pride, the softest smile lifting her sinfully red lips. "You've got this," she says, squeezing my hand for half a heartbeat just as the line begins to move.

Security is a mess—all stubborn umbrellas and wet sneakers squeaking, the ticket taker hollering for us to "keep it moving!" Without a purse, I get through quickly, and Renee finds me on the other side just as the first *thump* of a bass drum hits. The crowd roars, and Renee smooths her leather skirt as an erratic guitar riff kicks in. I could play it on my heartstrings. I helped write it, after all.

"That's us," I say, tipping my chin. "Or . . . that's them. That's Cold Sweat."

We follow the sound up the stairs, bypassing the merch tables and ID checkers handing out wristbands. Renee stays just as close to me as she did when we shared the umbrella. I can't imagine being here without her. I can't imagine doing anything without her anymore. My pulse quickens, keeping time with the rattle of the hi-hat, and when I push open the double doors, it's like watching a memory on playback, but on a bigger screen. A larger stage. I don't realize that I'm frozen until Renee jostles me out of it and into a crowd that reeks of cheap beer and wet dog. It's disgusting, but damn, it's familiar. I missed it. The lights onstage flash blue to green faster than I can register either, but my brain clocks every move Solas makes. Each time he smacks the air and commands the crowd to jump, or when he reaches for a high note and the tendons strain in his neck, it tugs on the memory of an earlier version of us. Solas and I were both drunk when we met, but I still instantly knew we had our front man. I was never too worried about whether I liked him as a person; he had undeniable star power, and I liked what he could do for the band. And here he is, doing exactly that, but watching him, I don't feel jealous. It's freeing to know what I know now: that I wouldn't prefer to be up there. To like where I am—in the crowd, with Renee. Maybe it's just growing up, but there's no stage I could play that would make me half as proud as I feel when she smiles. That wide, bright smile that pushes her cheeks up over her eyes. To me, it's brighter than all the lights onstage combined.

The first song ends, and with a flip of Solas's sweaty red hair, the chug of the next song starts up. I don't know it, but the crowd does. They scream like there's a prize for the first person to tear a vocal cord. I turn to Renee, and she's looking at me, but her gaze bounces away when I catch her, the apples of her cheeks ripening to a perfect pink. She says something then, but it gets buried beneath the music.

"What?!" I lean closer, but even with Renee's breath prickling the shell of my ear, the music is too loud to make out a word she says. My face twists up in a silent apology, and Renee nods, motioning to the stage as if to say she'll tell me later. When the song ends and the crowd roars, Renee and I roar right along with them until Solas's rough chuckle comes over the mic. The sound is familiar in the worst way, and something deep inside me begins to tremble, a rockslide starting the moment I hear the words "Is that Alice Pierce?"

Every part of me freezes, except for my pulse, which charges ahead like a raging bull. This is definitely not part of the plan. I squeeze my eyes shut, then Renee's hand slips into mine, a silent reminder. *You wanted him to see you, Alice. Maybe this is okay.* When I open my eyes, a ragged smile has crept its way across Solas's mouth, and a chill rolls through me as he extends one tattooed arm, pointing into the crowd.

Pointing at me.

"We got Cold Sweat royalty in the house tonight. Can we get a spotlight on this lil lady right here?"

In my mind, I'm already running away, sprinting down the block without looking back. I'm in another city. On another planet. I am so far away from this moment that I couldn't feel it if I tried. But my actual, physical body doesn't move, and I'm swallowed by a flash of bright-white light.

"Let's hear it for Alice Pierce, the founding bassist of Cold Sweat!"

I'm frozen in the spotlight. Around me, the crowd cheers, and someone squeezes my shoulders. A nearby stranger daps me up. People pull out their phones, most of them clearly unsure why I'm important. *I'm not*, I think, but they take my photo anyway, just in case I matter.

I give Solas a weak wave, desperately trying to smile.

Solas smiles back, then sucks his teeth and yanks the mic from its stand. With a voice like he's biting down on gravel, he says, "I've got a story about Alice."

My neck goes hot. My sweat might boil on my skin.

"When we were just starting out as a band, when Cold Sweat was playing smaller shows . . . those smaller venues will give you drink tickets, right? 'Cause they can't pay you in dollars, but they can pay you in booze."

The crowd whoops. My pulse surges. *No.*

"And our entire first tour, our first time on the road, all of us." Solas motions to the rest of the band. "We all kept losing our drink tickets. Alice too. It was crazy, right?"

*No no no.*

"Come to find out, she's a little thief. She's stealing everybody's drink tickets and playing along like, *Oh no, mine are missing too!*"

The crowd laughs. Solas cracks a lopsided smile. Then Renee's hand is back in mine, and her touch is the only good thing about existing in this moment, the cool slivers of her rings the only thing about me that's not burning up.

But Solas isn't done.

"So when we were cutting demos at a studio here in Chicago, we found out that our girl Alice works there now." He's pacing the stage now, holding the mic like a stand-up comic, and I'm the unwilling subject of his roast. "So we taught the engineer a little joke the guys up here have. When you can't find your beer, we say, *All right, who's pulling an Alice?*"

I feel like I'm melting inside my own body, my soul reduced to a muddy little puddle as Solas describes someone I'd like to forget I ever was. As I realize—everything I've been worried about is true. The person I used to be is alive and well in the memories of people like Solas Callaghan. I'm *still* that person, so far as the band is concerned. My reputation is a virus; it doesn't need me as its host.

For a moment, I wish we could trade places, Solas and me. That I could be the one playing for a packed house and he was here in the crowd, having his worst self put on parade in front of a thousand fans. Maybe then he'd know how it felt to be a cautionary tale, a parable of what not to do if you wanted to make it as a musician in this city. But I know I was never cut out to be onstage, and that's why he's up there and I'm out here. Everything I practiced, everything I wanted to say, falls apart on my tongue. I won't get the chance to say it; even if I did, I know now that I wouldn't be heard.

"So this next one's for Alice Pierce." Solas plunks the microphone back in the stand. He finds my eyes in the crowd, cracks open a stage beer, and raises it high. "If you see her, maybe get that girl a drink."

The second the spotlight shuts off, I'm gone. Pushing through the crowd. Elbowing my way out. I hear the faintest shred of "Alice, wait" from Renee, but I can't look back. I have to keep pushing. I have to get out of here. I stumble down the stairs and out the door onto the rain-slick sidewalk, pulling out my phone to call a car. I don't know if it's rain or tears on my cheeks, but I have to get home.

I hear the door swing open behind me, and Renee rushes through, straight to my side. "Alice, hey." She's breathless, eyes sad and sorry. "Are we leaving?"

"*I'm* leaving. You can stay if you want." I don't really mean it. I can't bear the thought of riding home without her, trying to cry softly enough that the driver doesn't ask me what's wrong.

Renee opens her umbrella, shielding us from the rain. When I look up from my phone, she holds me in her gaze, soft and sweet and blue.

"I don't want to be anywhere that's not with you right now." Renee's voice barely hovers above a whisper, so small that it might wash away with the rain, but she stays with me. With her, I'm okay.

It's a short ride home, and neither of us says much until we're both safe and dry inside my apartment. The moment my door closes behind her, Renee announces, "Solas Callaghan is a fucking douchebag."

I sit on the floor to tug off my boots, then tip back and starfish across the hardwood, blinking up at the ceiling.

"He's not a douchebag." I sigh.

"Well, he sure had me fooled considering the stunt he just pulled."

"It wasn't a stunt," I grumble. "He was just doing crowd work."

"Crowd work? Humiliating you in front of a thousand people is crowd work?"

I don't react. I feel impossibly heavy, like I may never move again. Renee lies down beside me on the floor. She rests her head in the crook of my arm, and I fold her into me. I need her close.

"That drink-ticket thing really happened," I murmur into her hair. "And that was, like, the least of the shit I put them through."

"But that's not you anymore," Renee says.

"It doesn't matter. It's too late." My voice starts to break, the cracks in my confidence splitting me into two distinct pieces—the person I was and the one I'd like to be—while I slip through the fault in between.

Renee wriggles free of my arms and sits up enough to really see me, her cool blue eyes studying mine more closely than I'd like to be seen. "Too late? You're only twenty-nine."

"And already a legend. You heard them. They call stealing someone's drink 'pulling an Alice.'"

"So that's one person. One band."

"One band speaking in front of a thousand people. Word travels fast, and not to be like this, but I'm not nobody, you know? You think the rumor mill hasn't gone crazy with the fodder that Ricky Pierce's daughter is a drunk who can't be trusted?" Even though I'm the one who said it, my chest aches at the sound of Dad's full name. The weight of it holds me flat against the floor.

Renee trails her fingers up and down my arm, back and forth, smoothing my goose bumps. "I think you might be making a few too many assumptions."

"They're not assumptions," I tell her. "I *know*. I've been the one spreading the rumors. I've been the one drunk off her ass in the green room talking shit about other bands because it made me feel important. It made people laugh. And now I'm the joke, and that shit Solas said was only what he'd say to my face."

I feel hollow, carved out like a pumpkin. It's only when Renee wipes her thumb over my cheek that I realize I've finally begun to cry.

"You're not a joke," Renee whispers. "You weren't a joke then either. You were young and lonely and trying to cope and make friends the only way you knew how." She pauses to brush away another tear, this one off my upper lip. "What about Aidan? He doesn't think you're a joke. No matter what Solas said, you still work there, right? And those bands who have paid you to mix their albums. They don't think you're a joke."

"Yeah." I sniff. "I guess. Or they just feel bad for me because of my dad."

Renee's eyes flutter closed as she shakes her head and breathes a shaky sigh. "It's not just because of your dad. I promise."

"You don't know that."

She holds out a hand and lifts me to a seat, both of us cross-legged with our knees touching. She takes my one hand in both of hers, trapping it there like it might run away, but there's not a hair on my head that wants to be anywhere other than close to her.

"You wanna know how I know?" she says, voice thick. "Because I thought you were a real piece of shit. I thought you were a drunk, destructive person who broke my friend Virginia's heart, and even though she swore you had changed and you two were actually friends again, I didn't believe it. I figured she put you in her wedding because she felt bad about your dad. But she asked me to give you a shot, and I did. I had to actually spend time with you and get to know you, and thank God I did."

I look up at her through thick, wet lashes. I feel waterlogged with my own tears, but her smile is a lighthouse, bright and beaming and guiding me home. "Yeah?" I croak out.

"Yeah." She grabs my other hand and laces our fingers together, resting our wrists on our knees and her forehead against mine. We're in our own little bubble, our own little world where nothing and no one can hurt us. It's just her and me and the warmth of her breath as she speaks, the smell of eucalyptus in her hair and mint on her breath.

"Everything is different with you, Alice," she says. "You've changed how I see myself. You got me excited about getting up in the mornings again because I feel like I have a purpose, like I'm working on something with you instead of sitting around moping that my dream job didn't want me anymore. You've got me thinking about whether or not I even want it back." Her voice splinters, and she squeezes my hands. "With you, it's like I want to slow down for once instead of just barreling ahead into my next step. I want to sit and think and feel things with you. I want to act and sing again, even if you're my only audience. And if I could go back to that engagement dinner, I would slap myself for being so rude to you because I thought you were Gin's toxic ex with the dead rock star dad when who you actually are is the person changing my whole damn life."

I don't have to think. I barely have to move. All I have to do is lean in and let my lips catch hers, erasing the shred of air between us, and everything else slips away. I forget about Solas and Cold Sweat and this whole mess of a night. I forget that she ever said anything about us just being friends. I forget how complicated it might get if we became anything more. It's all evicted from my memory, replaced with the cool rush of Renee's gasp as she draws my breath into her lungs. We stall here for one delicate moment, our lips just barely touching. And I'm worried I've gone too far. Fear and doubt scratch inside me, and I almost pull away.

Then one soft hand lands on my cheek, holding me in place and deepening our kiss. My head swims. Slowly, Renee draws back, her lips gently sucking on my bottom lip till the last possible second, and the only thought pulsing through me is her name. Over and over, again and again, like a record skipping at my favorite part. My entire body is singing along. *Renee Renee Renee.*

"Alice." Renee hangs on to the hiss at the end of my name. Just the sound frees up something inside me that I didn't realize was caught. Her eyes flutter open just long enough to remind me of their impossible shade of blue. Everything about Renee feels so impossible, and yet here she is, brushing her thumb against my cheekbone, back and forth like a metronome.

"Was that okay?" I whisper.

"God, yes," she breathes. It's everything I've wanted despite fighting to convince myself otherwise. There's so much that I've tried not to feel toward Renee, but when she pulls me in and crushes her lips to mine, every bit of restraint inside me releases, and I'm flooded with want. I want her. As much of her as she'll give me. I kiss Renee's jaw. Her temple. The tail of her eyebrows. I brush aside her soft blond hair, tracing the shadow beneath her collarbone with my tongue. Her chest rumbles with a moan, and I do it again, losing myself in how she rumbles beneath me.

"Fuck," Renee rasps when I nip at her neck, and it's the sweetest sound. She's so reactive, a sensitive, exposed nerve of a person. My lips skid up to the shell of her ear, and she sips the air, lips pursed and head tipped back as she eases into a shuddering breath.

"Jeeeeesus, Alice." Renee cups my chin, lifting my mouth to hers again. Her hands are gentle in my rain-soaked hair, then rougher, more insistent, like a woman with a plan. Renee guides me onto my back and climbs over me, straddling me so her thighs press against my hips. I'm sure I'm stuck in a dream. Surely I'm not being straddled by Renee Roberts, her chain belt swinging against her miniskirt, the leather of her knee-high boots cool against my legs. I skate my fingers along the hem of her skirt just to confirm she's really here. I don't deserve this. I can barely resist the want pulsing through me.

"Touch me," Renee pleads, and my resistance disintegrates. I drag my palms up the soft skin of her thighs, moving slower than I thought I could, but Renee's needy, stuttering breaths are too sexy not to count how many I can get. She rocks and grinds her hips, guiding me toward where she wants me, and I can't help but tease her. I reverse my direction, sliding my palms slowly back down toward her knees. She writhes over me, a greedy whine pouring from her lips.

"*Alice*," Renee bites out; then she chases my mouth with hers, kissing and grinding and trembling over me. I know what she wants, and I know I'm going to take my time giving it to her. I want to see if she can stand it, not being in control. I squeeze Renee's butter-soft thighs, and she lifts with a gasp, blond hair tossing over her shoulders. "Fuck, Alice."

"Say please," I rasp.

"Please, Alice."

I hum and push my palms up her thighs, trying to commit every inch of her to memory.

"Please," she begs again, and the desperation in her voice sets a fire in my lungs, then another between my thighs. She looks down at me, eyes stormy and sultry and utterly irresistible. My favorite shade of blue they've ever been.

"Eyes on me," I breathe. "Just like that."

My confidence surprises me. It's been so long since I've been with anyone like this. Much longer since I've done it sober. But when it comes to Renee, I'm so entirely myself, so fully connected to what I want. I want her. All of her.

Renee bites her lip as she nods, and those blue-flame eyes don't budge from mine again. Not when I guide one hand over the wet silk between her thighs. Not when I twist the fabric out of my way. I part her with one gentle finger, and we both moan when I dip inside.

"So perfect."

Renee whimpers in reply, then again when my thumb ghosts over her clit. I go slow until she begs me not to, gentle until her hips grind and buck, demanding more and more.

The first time Renee comes undone for me, it's fitful and frenzied, and she cries out my name. I'm addicted to the sound. The second time, it's almost too easy; the release pours out of her on a honey-drenched sigh, her legs trembling even minutes after. When I go for a third, Renee flinches away, too sensitive.

"Sorry," I murmur.

Renee hums. "Are you, though?"

She smiles down at me, her tongue pressed against her teeth so little flashes of pink show through. She's so agonizingly cute. How can a single person be so cute, so hot, so striking, so everything? When she climbs up and helps me to my feet, I realize we're both still fully dressed, but that doesn't last. I shiver when Renee's hands find the curve of my waist, the button of my shorts, the waistband of my black cotton briefs. She undresses me from the waist down while walking me back into my couch until the cushions hit the backs of my bare knees. Then she sinks between them, and desire riots through me.

Her sweet blue eyes lift to mine. "Can I?"

"I'll lose my mind if you don't."

Renee hums a laugh, and a chill sparks between my shoulder blades. It spreads like a burn down the backs of my arms as she parts me with her tongue, tasting me for the first time. Heat tenses and pulses through me, months' worth of want shooting to my fingertips. My toes. The cradle of my hips, which rock into her mouth as she explores how to make me gasp and clench and sigh out her name. I lose my breath when her lips seal around my clit. She sinks into me with two fingers, and I arch and shiver, shuddering against her tongue. And then I'm gone. Unwound like a spool of silk thread until I'm nothing but a ragged breath and thumping heartbeat. My body is hot and heavy and all hers.

Renee looks up at me through her thick black lashes, blue eyes sparkling like gemstones.

"Hey, you." Her voice is a sweet, breathless rasp, and I would submerge myself in it if I could.

"Hey," I sigh out. "I . . . wow. Thank you."

She hums and kisses my left knee, then the right, then climbs up onto the couch beside me, nuzzling into my neck. Warmth fizzes at every place where she touches me: her hand on my shoulder, her cheek on my chest. I shift so I can kiss her again, and I moan when I taste myself on her tongue.

"You are way too much, you know that?" I growl, and Renee pulls back for a moment. Her eyes brim with admiration as she traces my jaw with her thumb, pressing it to my lower lip. I kiss it, and she breathes the smallest, sweetest laugh.

"You, Alice Pierce." She cups my face. "Are exactly enough."

I pull Renee's mouth back to mine, and the sweetest moan pours into me from somewhere deep in her throat. It sounds like a song I've been searching for, a melody I could set on repeat and play through the night.

And that's exactly what I plan to do.

# Twenty

For the third time this summer, I wake up already panicking.

*Where am I? Whose bed am I in? Did the tour van leave without me?*

My pulse charges against my chest, muscles braced against each racing thought before I've even opened my eyes. A train rattles past outside, and I suck in a fractured breath, placing myself back within the present. I'm at home. I'm in my own bed. And, yes, the tour van left without me. Thank *God.*

My breathing starts to even, and I open my eyes to see that, again, for the third time this summer, I'm tangled up in Renee Roberts. She's curled into me, cheek pressed just below my collarbone with her hair mussed up, blond strands falling every which way across my gray tank top. Her bare leg is hitched up, thigh pressed against the waistband of my briefs. She slept in nothing but my threadbare band T-shirt, a red one I dug out of storage, just for her. Like so many nights following a Cold Sweat show, I crawled into bed with someone, but unlike every time before, I'm sober, and she's no stranger. I know Renee Roberts better than I know myself most days. I know how to cheer her up and piss her off in equal measure. I know her favorite musicals are *Grease* and *Rent*, and I know the lyrics to my half of that stupid duet she always wants to sing. I know the taste of her tattoos, and how she moves when I trace them with my tongue.

Renee shifts the smallest bit in her sleep, the soft skin of her thigh shifting against mine. Heat pools between my hips at the memory of last night—Renee, in the kitchen, stripped down to tattoos and moonlight. How her breath wavered when I ran my hands up her thighs and pressed my thumb into the treble clef tattooed over her hip. The curve of her back as she stood, palms pressed to the quartz countertops, peering over her shoulder with a devilish grin that I kissed right off her mouth. The warmth of her moans as they spilled into my palm, how I kept her quiet with one hand and drew loud moans out of her with the other. I spun lazy circles on her clit, then faster ones, building speed and pressure and grinding my hips against her ass until she came apart, a pinched moan opening into a full, glorious sound I would've happily drowned in. I licked the taste of her off my fingers, and when I slid them back inside, the way she said my name . . . God, what was it about the way she said my name? It poured out of her like a prayer. Like a plea. Like Renee needed me.

I know I need her too.

A shard of morning sun slices through the window and over Renee's cheek, casting shadows off her eyelashes. They flutter as she stirs, curling deeper into me, so close that it's almost impossible not to kiss her. My lips skid across the crown of her head, breathing in her eucalyptus shampoo. Three months ago, I thought I might not survive sharing an Uber with Renee Roberts. Now I feel like I may not survive anything without her. It's a terrifying thought that swings into another. *I've been here before. I know how this ends.*

My memory whirls back to junior year of college, waking up in our apartment but not in my own bed. Gin, Chrissy, and I were practically magnetized by that point, an indivisible cluster of friends, and I can feel it still—that free fall of fear when I woke up nuzzled into Gin's neck. I remember thinking, *This is it. You had friends, and you ruined it.* And it wasn't true, but it would be, four years later. It was only a matter of time.

I don't want to think it. I don't want to feel it either. I want to stay here in this perfect, beautiful moment beneath this perfect, beautiful woman and pretend it will always be like this, but the deep breaths aren't cutting it. As my pulse climbs, I slip out from beneath Renee, who groans and rolls over, cocooning in my sheets. My heart squeezes tight, then stretches out, an accordion trapped in my chest. I want to keep her there. This—*us*—I've longed for this. But it certainly wasn't a part of the plan, and I know how Renee is about plans. She told me she saw me as only a friend, and then I went and kissed her anyway, and then . . . fuck. What do I say? And how do I say it without saying too much or blurting out something stupid like the truth? Like *Hey, Renee, I know it's way too soon to say this, but I think I might have feelings for you. But don't worry—it might just be that my dad died about a year ago and my emotions are treating me like one of those rage rooms where you pay to swing a sledgehammer at old TVs! I know you said you saw me as a friend, and I don't want to mess that up, but, hey, while we're talking about it, maybe we should fuck again?*

I stumble past my bedroom door and, without any conscious decision to pace, begin to stalk the width of my living room. On the wall, I lock eyes with my idols on the covers of a hundred *Rolling Stone* magazines. *What would you do?* I want to ask them, but it wouldn't make a difference if I could. If this wall could talk, this communion of sinners wouldn't know any better than me. Still, I pray to each one. To Saint Janis Joplin. To Saint Tina Turner. To anyone who could tell me how to undo this mess without fucking it all up, getting knocked back to lonely like I did when I ruined my relationship with Gin. I said all the wrong things, and where did it get me?

Like most of my early twenties, the night Gin and I broke up isn't a clear memory. It's a few random frames of a bad indie film I'm destined to summarize to therapists for the rest of my life. I remember stumbling back from a night out with Solas. I don't even think Cold Sweat had a show, but if we did, I was definitely too drunk to play. I remember walking through my front door and right into Gin's birthday party. The party I sort of planned and forgot about entirely. I was late. I was wasted. The rest of the night flickers and skips in my memory. I spilled whiskey on my Sonny Bono costume. Collected what felt like hundreds of looks of disgust and disappointment from all Gin's friends. I don't recall specifically what anyone said, but there were snide comments disguised as jokes, and I know that I tried to laugh along. After that, the flickering edge of the memory fades into the moment I stepped up for my turn at karaoke—what should've been me and Gin performing Sonny and Cher's "I Got You Babe"—but someone put the microphone in my hand, and I realized it wasn't the same karaoke machine I rented. It was a better, nicer microphone, a fancier machine that Renee must've gotten to replace the one I'd picked out. Like my machine wasn't good enough. Like Renee thought *I* wasn't good enough for Gin, and there I was, whiskey soaked and proving her right. And then, something snapped.

I'll never have a transcript of exactly what I said that night, but I remember spitting venom into that microphone. All the worst inside thoughts flew out, all at once. I was hurting. Flailing. Desperate to make myself the joker instead of the punch line, to show everyone how much better I was than this stupid party. I played stages across the country. I shared a mic with Willie Nelson. I didn't need to take shit from these losers who only held a microphone on karaoke night. I was the real thing. I was a rock star. Who gave a shit what they thought anyway? Then Renee ripped the mic from my hand. I can still hear the screech of feedback before it thudded to the ground, and Gin shouted for me to get out. That we were done. Renee shoved me out the front door, and the memory ends there. Fade to Blackout Alice. Fade to being all alone. For years, I was so devastatingly alone.

"Alice?"

*Fuck.*

At some point, I must've stopped pacing; I'm doubled over on the couch, hands fisted in my hair like I might rip it out in clumps. I'm panicking, yes, but it's more than that. It's like I've been gulped down by an enormous, ruthless feeling. I chase it through my memory, following its tracks: Turbulence. Car accidents. The giant drop ride at the fair. *Terror*—I recognize it now—it seeps into my bones.

"Are you okay?" Renee's voice is as gentle as the dab of a paintbrush, but it stings like cleaning a wound, and I wince. She takes a step toward me, and I flinch away, looking up just in time to catch the last flicker of confusion before it bolts from her eyes. All that's left behind is hurt.

"Alice, please don't do this."

"I'm fine," I say, robotic.

"You're obviously not fine."

I turn away. "I'm *fine*."

"That's bullshit, and we both know it."

"Don't tell me what I'm feeling."

"Then *look at me*, Alice," Renee begs. "Look me in the eye and talk to me instead of shutting me out if you're so completely *fine*."

My muscles clench until they vibrate, and my apartment blurs at the edges of my vision. I focus on one spot, staring down my monstera plant. A fresh green shoot has split off from one of the stems. New growth. So why am I waiting for the pot to shatter?

"Alice," Renee says. "Please." The hurt in her voice leaves me raw.

*Say something*, I think. *You're losing her*. But I'll lose her much faster if I say too much. Because that's what I do. I open my big mouth, I say the wrong thing, I make everything worse, and I end up alone.

I fist my hands, taking a drag of the air like the world is one big cigarette. It doesn't take the edge off. Right now, I am *all* edge. My heart feels stranded in the center of a tightrope. Too scared to go forward. Too far gone to turn back. *I've been here before. I know how this ends.*

I hear shuffling, and when I work up the nerve to look, I see Renee has put on a pair of sweatpants she must've swiped from my dresser, last night's clothes balled up beneath her arm. I let my gaze creep up as far as her jaw, which sets as she turns for the door.

*"Renee."* I finally blurt out, just to keep her from leaving.

She turns over her shoulder. "What, Alice?"

"Just . . . please, Renee. I don't know what to say."

From the way her jaw works, I know that alone was the wrong thing.

"And what am I supposed to do?" Renee bites out. "Stand here and wait for you to figure it out?" Her voice is clipped and cold, an icicle snapped off a gutter. "What do you want from me, Alice?"

*Everything*, I think. But I say the opposite. I say nothing. There's one last quivering silence; then the door clicks. Creaks. Slams shut. Renee is gone. A silent sob wrenches deep in my chest, but I crush it down, pulverizing the pain until it's beyond recognition. Nothing but dust. I don't want to feel, so I go numb. Like always. Classic Alice.

*Dad,*

*Figured I'd tell you I ruined things with Renee. I was feeling kinda guilty about only writing to you when things are bad, but then I remembered you'll never read this because you're dead.*

# Twenty-one

I've kept my fingers busy since Renee walked out. For the past thirty-six hours, I've been sequestered in the dark of my home studio, my favorite bass in my lap. All the time I've spent on the wedding—on Renee—has resulted in an accidental summer-long sabbatical from practicing. My calluses aren't gone by any means, but the thick armor of skin on my fingertips has gotten soft.

The skin is healing, technically, but that's not what I want. I need those calluses. Without them, the metal strings bite at my fingertips as I play, leaving behind a sharp, hot ache. Like most things at the moment, I try not to feel it. My emotions, like my phone, are tucked away and set on silent, so when I hear the buzz of an incoming call from the depths of my desk drawer, I lunge for it. Because there's only one person it could be. Only one contact I've programmed to bypass Do Not Disturb: the bride herself, Miss Virginia Bennett.

Except it's not *just* Gin. She's calling the whole group chat, and just the sight of Renee's contact photo has my heart tucking its tail. But this isn't about me or Renee or us. It's about Gin and the agonized siren of a cry that floods through the line the moment I pick up.

There's a screech of feedback that only I react to, so it could be the sound of my own brain short-circuiting. Gin alternates between sobbing and sucking in snot, wedging in a word or two in between. "I." *Sniff.* "Can't." *Gasp.* "Handle." *Sniff. Gasp. Sob.*

Renee jumps right in, no hesitation, like an emotional lifeguard who's been training for this. "Okay. It's okay. Can we breathe together?" Renee's voice is sweet and level, striking a chord on every one of my heartstrings. I breathe along to her cues, following the ins and outs of Gin's stuttering inhales and wobbly, miserable out breaths. When we've evened out enough, Renee asks, "What's going on?"

"Is it Rishi?" Chrissy guesses.

"*No . . .*"

"Your parents? Rishi's parents?" Chrissy tries again.

"It was . . . the *rain.*" Gin shudders another sob, but relief runs like coolant through my veins. *Okay. We're okay. Everyone is alive.*

I hang my bass back on its wall mount, then swivel my desk chair to face the singular window in my home studio. "The rain?" It's stopped and started like a finicky faucet all summer, but today isn't so bad. Mostly sunny, a comfortable seventy something. Not that I've left this room since yesterday.

"Yeah," Gin whimpers. "Thursday's storm, plus all the rain this summer . . . and all our hard yard work . . ." Her voice breaks like a dam, flooding the line just as Gin flips on her camera to show us a *real* flood. We're looking at the Bhats' backyard, once Gin and Rishi's ceremony site, now entirely underwater. The marsh has spilled over, stretching to the bottom of the frame, claiming the lower third of the butterfly bushes and every limestone paver.

All I can say is "Fuck."

"We. Can't. Get. Married. There!" Gin sobs.

"Not unless you want to get married in hip waders."

My joke doesn't land. Of course it doesn't. The wedding is in *seven days.*

"It's okay, Gin," Renee says. She's breathy but confident. "We can fix this."

"We *can't* fix this!" Gin fires back. "We have a *week*!"

For a minute, we just let her cry. Sometimes, that's all anyone can do. And then Rishi steps in. He helps his fiancée shut off her camera, and I can't quite hear what he's saying, but I hear *how* he says it, and every gentle, soothing murmur spaces out Gin's sobs a little more. Rishi, as always, makes everything better. When we start to brainstorm solutions and his parents weigh in with some unhelpful commentary about how this wouldn't have happened if they'd rented a hall for the wedding like they'd wanted, he handles it with grace and patience. I begin to wonder if he was specially engineered for Gin in some sort of lab. This man says all the right things.

And then, for once, so do I.

"Galena," I say with the same breath I've heard others say "Amen." It's so obvious. The perfect solution. "The backyard in Galena. You could get married there." It comes out quickly and with such authority that even I momentarily forget that the house is still not really mine to offer. But I can't stop myself. Not when Gin's sniffles subside.

I can hear the smile in Chrissy's voice when she says. "That's . . . low-key brilliant, Ali Pal."

"Do you think . . . could we?" Gin squeaks out.

"Absolutely," I say.

Given the circumstances, I can't imagine the band would say no.

And then it hits. A sharp ache like a split board in my chest. The band includes Kurt, and where there's Kurt, there's Mom.

"Okay." Gin sighs. "Okay, okay, okay. Wow." It's the steadiest her voice has been this entire call, and I refuse to say anything that could change that. I'll figure something out with the Outpost. I have to, because the crying has stopped and Gin has already begun to strategize.

"I guess it . . . it is on a hill, right? So there's probably no flooding? Could we still have a dance floor?"

We try for a while to have Gin share her screen so we can all look at the wedding spreadsheet together, but Chrissy's audio keeps cutting in and out, and the lag has us all talking over each other. There are too many details and moving pieces to reconfigure for any of us to keep it all straight over the phone, so it shouldn't surprise me when Chrissy says, "That's it. I'm clearing off the whiteboard. Who needs me to call them an Uber?"

"Me," Renee chirps, and dread drops into my chest, my gut, my shaky fingers that nearly drop my phone. I knew I'd have to see Renee again before too long, but I thought I had more time.

"I'm at the Bhats' house," Gin reminds us. "So it'll take me a little over an hour to—"

"No, no. Stay put, girlina," Chrissy cuts her off. "I'm having a bottle of chardonnay and some very powerful gummies delivered. We'll FaceTime you in. Your bridesmaids have got this."

Thus begins this summer's second Bridesmaid Summit.

As my complete lack of luck would have it, Renee and I arrive at Chrissy's place at the same time. Just the sight of her splits me down the middle, half joy, half heartache. Like two songs—one major and one minor—playing at the same time, both at full blast. To the world, she looks put together in a red tank top, denim shorts, and all her usual jewelry, but I know her. Renee would never wear her glasses outside the apartment, but there they are, perched on her nose. When she tucks her hair back, I notice she's missing some of her rings. Anyone else might mistake her for okay, but I know better.

"Hi," I squeak out, but Renee won't even give me that. She faces ahead, jaw tense, with her chin lifted as she punches in the gate code. In her other hand, she grips a brown grease-stained takeout bag, and the smell of something deep fried makes my stomach audibly rumble.

"Sorry," I mutter. "Haven't eaten much the last two days."

There's a pause. Then a barely audible "Me neither," just as the gate buzzes open.

We set up our war room in Chrissy's "office"—laptops, pens, notebooks, sticky notes; a clean slate of a whiteboard, a fresh pot of coffee; and the three largest mugs I've ever seen. Renee packed a printed-out stack of every text or email Gin has sent about the wedding for the last three months, a copy of the completed shopping list, and the crinkly brown takeout bag, revealed to contain three orders of cheese fries.

"It's giving college cram session." Chrissy giggles as she fills and distributes the enormous mugs of coffee. Even in a crisis, she's like this—bubbly and eager—but when Renee steps up to the whiteboard, Chrissy's tone turns shockingly serious. "Shouldn't Alice take the lead on this?"

I whip my head around so fast, my neck spasms. "What?"

"It's your house, Ali Pal. Or . . . your dad's band's house or whatever," Chrissy says.

"But I'm the event planner," Renee reminds us, voice stern.

"But you don't know Galena and the Outpost like Alice does," Chrissy points out. "So I think Alice should be the one to write on the whiteboard."

Renee's jaw grinds and ticks, and her eyes flash to mine for one burning second. I sizzle like a helpless ant beneath her magnifying stare. "Alice," Renee hisses, "is unreliable." She yanks her gaze away, pinning it on Chrissy. "Alice is hot and cold. She'll act like she's going to write on the whiteboard, like she really, really wants to write on the whiteboard, but then once she does, she'll shut us out and make us feel stupid for trusting her with the marker."

"You can trust me with the marker!" I blurt out. "I can write on the whiteboard! I just—" And that's when my voice fails me. Again.

"We *know* you can write on the whiteboard," Chrissy says in full sincerity, talking only about the whiteboard. Nothing else. Regardless of what this is really about, Chrissy's bright, expectant smile wears on Renee. She begrudgingly sets down the dry-erase marker and, without so much as looking at me, deflates into what used to be my seat. I take Renee's place as Chrissy slots her phone into one of her many tripods and announces, "Please hold, everyone! I'm getting Gin and Rishi on FaceTime."

It goes better than I expect, although I'm no Renee Roberts when it comes to making a plan. I have no survey to reference, no existing wedding plan from last year we might recycle for efficiency's sake. But I know the spreadsheet. I know the Outpost. And I know Gin. The rest I make up as I go. We're at it well into the night—planning, replanning, pivoting every single detail while slowly dropping like flies. Gin falls asleep first, cheek pressed directly into her in-laws' kitchen table while Rishi stays with us on FaceTime. Chrissy's snoring starts up around midnight, but she's in and out of sleep until about two o'clock.

"Stay as late as you want," she says, talking through a yawn before finally shuffling off to bed, and Rishi calls it a night shortly thereafter. He thanks us profusely, and when he ends the call, I decide not to notice that Renee and I are alone. I'm not feeling it, because that's not what's happening, so far as I'm concerned. I face the whiteboard with intense focus. There is no one behind me. Certainly no one I've been harboring a crush on all summer. Certainly no one I had mind-blowing, reality-bending sex with. Whatever I might feel in that situation—the way my heart might press against my spine, trying to work its way back to her—I'm not feeling it. Because as far as the whiteboard and I are concerned, there is nothing other than the wedding.

"So we'll cancel the tent rental but keep an eye on the weather," I mumble to myself. "We can find a rental place closer to Galena and see if they have anything available, just in case . . ."

The takeout bag crumples behind me, and it feels like my blood is flowing in Renee's direction, begging me to turn around. The writing on the whiteboard blurs and drips the longer I stare at it, but I brace my core and reset my focus. *The wedding. Only the wedding right now.*

"The Mediterranean restaurant won't deliver outside of a twenty-five-mile radius, so we'll need to find another catering option."

*I don't want to find another catering option,* my thoughts butt in.

*I want Renee.* I have this urge to spill my heart like a jar of loose change, but I'm afraid of what all will come out. I need time to sort through it all first. If I say something now, it'll surely be the wrong thing, and I'll make things worse than they already are. With the wedding in crisis and only a week away, now is not the time, even if I did know what to say.

I review the remainder of my chicken scratch notes, checking the last few mental boxes of our brand-new plan. "I think all we're missing is . . ."

"Permission to use the Outpost," Renee finishes behind me in a cold, unfeeling voice.

My heart rams full force into the brick wall of my chest. *Right.* The single most integral piece of this puzzle, the piece everything else depends on, is a bit of logistics only I can do. I need to talk to my mother. I need to talk to Renee. But the wedding relies on only one of those conversations. I'm not ready for either.

I scratch my thumbnail over the stiff skin on my fingertips. *This is what it takes,* I think. It has to hurt at first. That's how you build up the callus.

"I'll talk to Mom tomorrow," I say.

# Twenty-two

In lieu of talking to my mother, I do literally anything else. I clean my oven. I steam my bridesmaid dress. I check my tire pressure and get legitimately upset when not one tire needs to be refilled. I toss my tire pressure gauge back into the glove compartment, where it will remain until the next difficult conversation that needs to be postponed. Every minute of stalling is one minute closer to Gin and Rishi's big day, the likes of which is riding on my ability to have an honest, vulnerable conversation with my mother. The type of conversation I know needs to happen in person. I need to go back to the house.

Luckily, there are many more extremely important and time-sensitive things to do this Sunday morning. I tweeze my eyebrows. I make the chicken thing from *The New York Times.* After lunch, I carefully vet every item of clothing in my closet, trying to determine the right uniform for apologizing. I decide on a sleeveless jumpsuit, the only bit of red in my wardrobe, like I'm borrowing a bit of Renee's confidence. Had this gone down just a few days sooner, Renee likely would've come with me today. I can picture her beside me, pinkie looped into mine, but I crumple the image and tuck it away. *Focus, Alice. One thing at a time.*

The maps app says it's twenty-five minutes to Home Avenue, and even with my sudden devotion to speed limits, I pull into the driveway just twenty-eight minutes later. Much like my last visit, mine isn't the only car in Mom's driveway: Kurt's silver Lexus still sits right where it was. My stomach somersaults. I should've known I'd be running that risk, showing up unannounced, but too late now.

When I step up to the front door, I feel a little like I'm preparing to enter my own court hearing rather than my childhood home. My finger hovers over the doorbell, but I can't make myself press it. Turns out, I don't have to. The door creaks open before I can work up the courage.

"Hi." Mom's voice is short, but her thick, silver hair is longer than I've ever seen it. It must've been pulled up last time, or else I was too caught up in Kurt to notice.

"Hi, Mom."

"You're . . . here."

"I am." I give her a watery smile. There's a screen door between us, a sieve that our conversation filters through.

"That's . . . a surprise." Mom's thin brows leap up to her hairline, digging four distinct grooves in her forehead like well-planned rows of a garden.

"Well." I splay my arms out in a pose that's usually accompanied by a *ta-da.* Mom doesn't look impressed. "Do you, uh . . . can I come in?"

Mom doesn't say anything, but she does push open the screen door, and once I'm inside, I feel a little more welcome. I haven't been cut out of any of the family photos on the wall or anything, and if the cops are on their way to arrest me for crimes against my mother's well-being, she doesn't let on. Instead, Mom digs back into the cupboard for my favorite mug—the yellow one that we stole from a coffee shop in Michigan when she and I road-tripped up to see Dad play a festival. She doesn't ask, just fills it most of the way with coffee and then dresses it up exactly right: a splash of oat milk and two packets of sweetener. My heart stings like a scraped knee. It's been so long, but Mom still knows me so well.

She makes herself a mug of tea, and we walk to the living room—she in a slow, deliberate march, I with a tentative shuffle. Mom sits on one end of the couch, and I opt for an armchair, leaving a coffee table's width of distance between us. I'm not sure what to say, so I start again with "Hi."

"Hi." Mom doesn't look unhappy, per se, but there's a visible discomfort in how she's situated on the couch, shrinking into the armrest like she's hoping to slip between it and the cushion.

In my kindest, most even-tempered voice, I ask. "Where's Kurt?"

"Upstairs."

"He can come down, if he wants."

Silence. Mom frowns and dunks her tea bag. "I wasn't sure he'd be invited."

"It's not my house," I remind her. "I don't choose the guest list." After a beat, I add, "How's he doing?"

"He's great. The band is excited about the show." Mom dips her chin. "They're hoping you're still going to attend."

"Of course I'm coming." I'm offended she'd ever think otherwise.

"Well, we hadn't heard from you, so we weren't sure."

"I wouldn't miss it," I insist, but it stings to realize she has no reason to believe me. How many times have I told her I would show up only to cancel at the last minute? There's a lump in my throat that the coffee can't wash down, and I abruptly change the topic. "I love what you've done with the living room."

Mom's frown pulls her whole face toward the floor, but her eyes stay firmly on me. "I haven't done anything to the living room."

"Really? Didn't there used to be something in the back corner? A plant or something?"

"Yeah," Mom says flatly. "The Christmas tree."

*Right.*

After Dad's funeral, I stayed with Mom for three weeks. I don't remember whether we discussed it, but it just didn't seem right for either of us to be alone. Once I moved back home to my apartment, I still had built-in reasons to come back every month for a while—Mom's birthday, then Dad's, then Thanksgiving, all spent crying and reminiscing at Mom's kitchen table. Christmas was for fielding weepy phone calls from distant relatives while eating my weight in peppermint bark. It was exhausting. Then it was New Year's, and the world rang in a fresh year that Dad would never see, but it also was no longer the year my dad died, and it never would be again. Mom wanted to keep up with the crying and reminiscing, but I didn't. It hurt too much. I had to look forward. I had to focus on myself. But I'd left her there in the hurt, all by herself.

"I'm sorry." I barely recognize the tender, shaky voice as my own. It feels silly to tell her that I don't want to feel this—who would? But I know that I don't have a choice. I'm still learning how to feel, how to sit with a pain that I'm certain will kill me if I don't run from it or numb it or pack it away. All I can choke out is "It's so *hard*, Mom."

"I know." Mom's eyes are glossy with tears. "It's hard for me, too. To live here without your dad."

I drop her gaze and fall right into a wave of nausea. *Right.* I got to walk away from the place where Dad died. Mom still has to wake up here every morning, to find a way to move through her day-to-day without him.

I choke out a question I don't really want the answer to. "So does Kurt . . . live here now?"

Mom shakes her head no. "Kurt and I . . ." She steeples her fingers and rests them against her lower lip, and when her eyes flutter closed, she looks like she's praying, asking God for the right thing to say. She draws in a deep breath through her nose and says, "When you stopped by and surprised us . . . that's not how we wanted you to find out."

"Of course not," I say, although that does raise the question of how they *did* want me to find out, if they had concocted some kind of plan that would've made it feel cool and normal that my mother was dating her dead husband's drummer. Any method would've been less destructive, I'm sure, than the one I accidentally chose for myself, but none would've been painless. I look down at my hands. "Can you just confirm something for me?"

"Of course."

My eyes ricochet between Mom and the staircase. "This is all just . . . this is just the past few months right? Nothing like . . . before?"

"Oh heavens, I would never." Mom leaps on her answer with reflexes I didn't know she had. She doesn't sound offended so much as it seems like this might be the first time the thought has occurred to her. "I wouldn't . . . oh, Alice, no. It's not like that at all." Her eyes crinkle with a sad smile as she shakes her head. "I'm lonely, Alice. I miss your father. I miss him so, so much." Her voice frays, and a prickle inches up my throat. This is part of it. The reason I haven't been home in so long. I hate seeing my mother cry, and I'm sick of crying myself. Mom starts again. "Kurt misses him, too. He lost one of his best friends. He understands what I'm going through because he's going through it, too. Something very similar at least. And it's . . . it's good for us to have each other. Does that make sense?"

"Yeah." I blot the tears with the side of my hand. "I'm glad you have that. I'm glad you're not alone."

"You need to understand—I'd been losing your father for a very, very long time," Mom goes on. "Long before he was actually gone. I did everything I could to support him. I was with him until the bitter end. But, God, was it bitter."

"I know," I remind her. "I was there, too."

"You were, I know you were. But there was plenty we didn't let you see, Alice."

I frown. What does *that* mean?

Her gaze drops into her tea. "That summer we sent you to band camp instead of bringing you to the Outpost? Remember?" She looks up. I nod. "We tried to have an intervention. The whole band had agreed to make it a sober house for the summer, but it . . . he wasn't willing."

My heart boomerangs, my voice low and thin. "Why didn't you tell me?"

"Because I didn't want you to see your father that way."

"So . . . you lied?" Something withers in my chest.

"No, honey, no." Mom's voice is thick with a hurt I haven't

heard since last year. Likely because I haven't been *around* to hear it. "I knew I'd tell you someday, but you were so young then. We wanted to protect you. But, of course, in the end . . ." She shakes her head with a sputtering sigh. "There was no preventing you from seeing him like that." She closes her eyes. "Oh, Alice. You don't know. You don't know the nights I spent calling ambulances or staying up wondering if he was going to make it home safe."

The world sways and tilts around me, my reality warping in real time. "I had no idea."

"I didn't want you to," Mom says. "But it's just . . . it's been so lonely for so long. And if not for Kurt these last few months . . . I couldn't do this alone."

I break like an egg, the tears coming all at once. I peel myself out of the armchair, and Mom throws out her arms. She's crying now, too, and I bury my face in Mom's long silver hair. I let myself just be her daughter.

"I'm sorry," I squeak out. "For all of it. I don't want you to be alone."

"I'm sorry, too," Mom says. "And I'm not alone, sweetie, I'm not alone. I'm so glad you're here. I love you."

"I love you."

We stay like this for a good long while, taking turns crying and apologizing. I'm sorry that I blew off rescheduling dinner, but she knows it was an accident. She's sorry that she wasn't clear about needing to talk to me about something in person, but I know she was trying to keep from driving me further away. She wanted me home, and now I am, even if just for the evening. And it *is* still home, even after all these months. Even if Dad isn't here.

I'm not sure how much time passes before a long, drawn-out

creak echoes from the staircase, the sound of one hesitant step. It's the sound a question mark would make if it could speak.

"Kurt, honey?" Mom sits up, dabbing at her nose with her sleeve. I do the same with mine, composing myself enough to be perceived.

"You can come down," I call out, and Mom looks at me with so much gratitude. More than I deserve, considering the question I have yet to ask. A few more creaks of the stairs later, I summon enough courage to say "I actually need to talk to both of you. I kind of have a favor to ask."

Mom grunts a laugh and rolls her eyes. "So that's why you're here. I should've known."

My pulse charges ahead. "It's not just—"

"I'm kidding, I'm kidding." Mom lays a hand on my knee with a smile that doubles as an apology. Kurt appears just behind her, looking cautious but hopeful. "What do you need?" Mom asks.

I pinch one red button on the front of my jumpsuit. "It's not really for me," I admit. "It's for the bride."

# Twenty-three

I haven't been back to Galena in years, but I could still make the drive to the Outpost with my eyes closed. It's perhaps the only trip I can make without a GPS, actually—seven or so years later, every landmark and speed trap is still mapped in my memory. Once we're past the city traffic, it's three hours of mostly farmland, all lush and green from the rain. As many times as I've done this drive, it's my first time leading a convoy—Rishi trails behind me with Gin and his parents, and Mom and Kurt bring up the rear. Beside me, Chrissy is riding shotgun in the truck, humming along to country songs she definitely doesn't actually know. Renee is in the back, so quiet I can almost forget she's even there.

*Almost.*

"How far out are we?" Chrissy asks—the first words out of her in some time. She hasn't been as chatty as usual, at least not with me. She's been tapping out texts to Chris the Waiter this whole drive.

"We've probably got about twenty minutes to go," I estimate.

Chrissy whines in response. "Can we stop?"

"No. We've already stopped twice." Renee's voice slices through the air like the cold edge of a blade. It reminds me of how she spoke to me at the start of the summer, but this time, it's directed at Chrissy instead of me. But that's only because Renee and I aren't speaking at the moment. Not really, unless it's about the wedding. I'm no closer to knowing what to say or how to handle things with her; there hasn't been time. Emotionally, I'm worn thin, and going back to Galena is sure to wear me even thinner. I'm not sure if I'm ready, but it doesn't matter. We're almost there.

We peel off the highway and cross the bridge into town, and my heavy heart leaps with a weightlessness I forgot existed. I've never lived in Galena for longer than a summer, but driving back into the antique play-set town still feels like a homecoming. The road curls like a ribbon between rows of brick buildings at mismatched heights—boutiques and breweries and knickknack shops begging you to get lost within them. The sidewalks swarm with a crowd not entirely unlike the people of Palm Springs. Wine moms, girls' trip goers, elderly couples on group vacations—it's all so familiar, the same old drive down the same old route to the house where I've been going all my life.

The truck bumps up the hill, and at the first crunch of gravel beneath the tires, I finally feel the shift. It's like we've crossed into a different time zone, and all the clocks are instantly wrong. It's all wrong. Everything. Because things aren't the same at all. My chest winds so tight, I can feel my pulse beneath my tongue. I'm here and Dad's not, and he never will be again. As much as I'm trying not to feel right now, I can't override the grief. It's here, as real and tender as a bruise.

At least there's some relief, seeing that the house looks more or less how I remember it, the color of fresh gingerbread with grayish-blue shutters that read almost periwinkle in the midday sun. Dad was usually the one to mow the lawn, but it's only a little overgrown, so someone else must be tending to it. My heart rips in two, half grateful someone has taken care of this place, half livid it couldn't be the person it should have been. I didn't know a heart could ache this way, just from looking at a building, but I can feel it, sore, deep in my chest.

I park the truck at the top of the driveway, and Chrissy hops out first. Then there's a gentle pressure on my shoulder, so quick that I almost think I've imagined it—but that one touch from Renee, the cool brush of her rings against my skin, will ripple through me for the rest of the day. I know it might not mean much—even at her coldest, Renee always showed compassion regarding Dad's death. But still, she touched me. Despite how I hurt her. It feels like it means something. I need it to.

I don't get out of the truck right away. I'm not sure how long I sit there, actually, staring at the house but too anxious to go in. I hear the gentle rap of a knuckle on the driver's side window. Gin gives a timid smile and a wave, and I sigh, then step out of the truck. For her. I can do this for her.

"Hey. You doin' okay?" Gin asks. "Do you need a minute?"

I shake my head. I wish I knew what I needed, but when I try to guess, all I can scrape out is a sigh.

"I'm here," she reminds me. "Anything you need, I'm here."

We congregate on the front porch: Gin and Rishi, Mom and Kurt, Mr. and Mrs. Bhat, Chrissy, and Renee, who lingers near the porch swing, putting an uncomfortable amount of distance between us.

"It's as gorgeous as I remember," Gin says, blinking up at the gabled roof with a wistful sigh.

"Thank you," Mom and Kurt reply in unison, and I consider whether I should speak on behalf of the house, too. It's not mine, but it belongs to me the same way The Handful does—crucially, but not in a way that would hold up in court. I'm pleased to see that my sole contribution to home renovation has stood the test of time: Above the door, the house number I stenciled in fluorescent paint as a teenager still stands—404 Fairbanks Avenue. *Error 404! House not found!* Dad and I used to joke when visitors had a hard time finding the place.

"So . . . you're thinking the ceremony would be in the backyard?" Rishi probably thinks he's smiling the same way a four-year-old thinks he's smiling on picture day. It's more of a wince, the face of a man trying to convert his anxiety into enthusiasm.

"The backyard definitely has the most space, although we can keep the living room as a backup in case it rains." I turn to Kurt for input, and he holds up his palms as if to say *This is all you.* My throat double knots over my hammering heart as I slip my silver key into the lock and twist, unsealing the smell of pine and old paper. It's like cracking open a time capsule; the ache comes back, deep in my chest. Grief shape-shifts quicker than I can catch it.

Kurt must sense the shift in my energy or else he's feeling a version of this, too; either way, he steps in as grand marshal to lead the group to the backyard while Mom and I fall back to inspect our memory of this place. I trail my fingers through the thick coat of dust along the banister and watch the particles scatter in the caramel light. Just the whine of the back door sounds so paralyzingly familiar that I briefly lose my grasp on time—it's every summer, all at once—and then the door slaps shut, and we're here again. Now. I catch Mom's glassy gaze from across the living room—the first time I've really looked her in the eye since we arrived. Instantly, we break. Of course we do. Both of us, just like yesterday and so many nights this year. I think we might just break like this forever, over and over. It may never be enough, but someday, it won't hurt so much. I have to think so, at least. I have to believe that grief, like staying sober, will get a little easier even if it's never quite easy. Right now, Mom and I just hold each other. I'm so glad I'm not alone.

"Oh, sweetie," Mom croaks. That's all there is to say. We cry until we've soaked each other's sleeves with an unholy mixture of snot and tears. Our sniffles grow further and further apart, and then Mom disappears into the bathroom for tissues and returns with a roll of toilet paper, still crying. She unspools an outrageous amount of toilet paper, way more sheets than I could possibly need, rips them off, and holds the wad up like it's a fish and she's a guy on a dating app. I laugh. And then she laughs. Then we're both cackling. A lot. Mom smacks a hand over her mouth, bracing herself against the wall like the laughter might knock her over. I don't know what comes over me, but it happens fast. I snatch up the toilet paper and wind it around the banister like a party streamer. Mom howls. She scuttles off to the bathroom and comes back with three more rolls, tossing one over a chandelier. Long, billowing strips of white shoot like jet trails overhead as we throw roll after roll, again and again, until we've made weeping willows out of every light fixture and I can't tell if the tears are from laughter or grief.

"Is this normal?" I cry as we collapse on the floor beneath our artwork. Mom tosses her hands and swipes at her tears.

"I don't know, honey. Whatever it takes to get through," she says, and when I fashion myself a toilet paper bow tie, I recognize my own smile in the crooked hook of Mom's lips. Maybe Dad's not the only one I take after.

Rishi's parents are rightfully perturbed by the impromptu toilet paper decorations, and regrettably, I'm not sure I could explain if I tried. Luckily, I don't have to—Chrissy is the last to walk in, but when she busts out her biggest laugh, Asha takes the cue and does it, too. Then Kurt joins, then Gin, and soon, it's all of us—nine unique laughs layered into one extended chord. The house swells with a rich, textured harmony, and I can hear Renee rise above the rest, her tambourine rattle of a laugh just as sweet as ever. There are always just as many reasons to laugh as there are to cry.

"Shall we continue the tour?" I dab my tears with one hand, motioning to Kurt with the other. He shares a brief look with Mom, then back to me.

"Courtney and I are going to stay downstairs." He loops an arm around Mom's waist. "Old house. Narrow halls. Lotta people." He bounces a glance off the staircase and with a crinkled smile, asks, "Alice? Would you mind?"

My chest tightens just as the air-conditioning kicks on, grunting and humming to life and blowing up from the floor vents. Overhead, the toilet paper garland flutters and flaps. A few white strips whip loose and swirl to the ground, and my laugh dislodges the lump from my throat. If I believed in signs, I'd say that one was from Dad.

Mom and Kurt step aside, and I lead the group up the creaky stairs and single file down the corridor. As we go room to room, the conversation ducks in and out of wedding logistics and spring break stories. For once, I'm the one trying to get Gin to focus, but she and Chrissy ricochet from the trundle bed to the crimped lampshades, activating new memories with everything they touch. Renee lingers on the outskirts, smiling when someone is watching, but otherwise, she keeps her gaze low. I drag my eyes away from her again and again, and if she looked back, I'm not sure what she'd see. If my eyes are even a tenth as expressive as hers, I'm sure they're screaming an indecipherable mess of mixed messages. *Yes. No. Maybe. I want. I need. I can't.*

We conclude the tour and convene in the living room to lay out a plan for the week: Mom and I still need time to go through Dad's things—and Kurt will be joining us, I guess. The rest of the group will return to help clean and start setting up on Wednesday.

"Work permitting, of course." Gin looks intentionally at Chrissy, then Renee. "I'm not sure if you guys took any time off or . . ."

"Oh, I'm technically working right now," Chrissy says, batting her wrist. "No biggie."

Renee is less confident. Her gaze drops to the side. "I've been meaning to talk to you about work, actually."

A prickle of interest climbs up my arms. Is this it? After an entire summer of keeping her job at the Blomquist under wraps, is this what unravels the lie? I chance a look toward Renee, and she's looking back at me, eyes the color of worn denim. A pulse, then she pulls away.

"Gin, could we drive back to the city together?" Renee asks. "I think we should talk."

Something leaps inside me. She's really going to do it, isn't she? And then, as always seems to be the case lately, the conversation shifts back toward a plan. Who is driving which car, and who do I trust to take the truck? Logistics. It always circles back to logistics, and while I may have run the whiteboard, I yield all ringleading to Renee now that we're here.

"Our professional event planner in residence!" Chrissy sings out. "Awfully nice of the Blomquist to lend you out for the week."

And I know that Renee and I aren't really talking right now. I know that I should bite my tongue and not risk another glance in her direction. But I remember that quick, gentle pressure on my shoulder before she climbed out of the truck. How long did she think that over, I wonder? Was it an accident? Was it an impulse? If she could go back, would she do it again? My brain whirs away from me, but as we rotate through our group goodbyes, I do what feels right. I return the favor—one gentle squeeze of Renee's shoulder just before she walks out the door.

# Twenty-four

Mom's hair and relationship status aren't the only major changes in the last eight months. In the morning, I slink downstairs just in time to catch her mid–quad stretch, warming up for her morning run. I'm partially asleep, but I try to make a face that's encouraging instead of completely shocked. The array of vitamins lined up on the counter are a second surprise. Losing Dad seems to have inspired some healthy changes in both of us.

Unfortunately, those changes don't inspire much in the way of breakfast. The fridge looks like it was stocked by a distracted wellness influencer—I don't mind that it's healthy and protein packed; it's just that it doesn't make sense. We have a bag of baby carrots, a block of tofu, lean ground turkey, two apples, organic ketchup, an avocado, low-fat cream cheese, and two flavors of high-fiber bagels. I pop a blueberry bagel into the toaster and put on a pot of coffee, then sit down to eat. A floorboard whines upstairs, then the thud of shuffling footfalls just before Kurt ambles in with a sleepy wave. He scratches his belly through a paint-splattered T-shirt, yawning and assessing the contents of the fridge. "Shit, was I high when I went grocery shopping last night?"

"I don't know." I quirk one brow. "Were you?"

Kurt's laugh is like a barstool dragged across a dive bar. It sounds to me like a summer bedtime—Mom tricking me into brushing my teeth while I could still hear the band having fun downstairs without me.

"I wasn't high," Kurt assures me. His voice suddenly turns serious. "I'm about a year sober, actually."

I set down my bagel, clapping the crumbs off my hands. "Like, completely sober?"

"No weed, no pills, no booze." He pops one of each type of bagel in the four-slot toaster. "It's been good. I feel ten years younger. Which, you know . . ." He coughs. "Makes me seventeen."

I'm not sure of Kurt's exact age, but he can't have more than a year or two on Dad. His beard is indisputably gray, but the silver strands on his head are mixed in with chestnut-brown ones. One prominent wrinkle runs across the middle of his forehead, an inevitable side effect of his concentrated drumming face.

"Were those things a problem for you before?" I ask. "Weed, pills, booze?"

Kurt adjusts his glasses, eyes clouding over with a stormy memory. "I never saw a musician without some type of problem with something."

My chin dips, skeptical. "C'mon. Really? Not even one?"

Kurt slowly shakes his head and looks around like he's watching the room fill with ghosts. "We've all got vices. I've seen a lot of shit." He grunts and scratches his head, lips tilted up.

The toaster pops, and I stop myself just shy of telling Kurt where to find the plates. He knows this place as well or better than I do. For a while, the only sound between us is the scratch of the butter knife against a toasted bagel face.

Then Kurt pulls out a chair and sits down next to me. "Your

mom said you've been sober about three times as long as I have." He bites into a bagel, and his bushy gray-black eyebrows lift, offering me the floor.

"No weed, no pills, no booze," I echo.

He nods, impressed. "And you're how old? Twenty-eight?"

"Twenty-nine," I correct him.

"Well, congrats." Kurt tips an invisible hat. "You're twenty years ahead of every other musician I know."

"Yeah, I guess."

"I'm not guessing." Kurt's expression is serious again. It's not quite the concentrated drumming face, but there's an intensity in his eyes that I can't turn away from, a pinch of worry hanging in the dents between his wiry brows. "I don't wanna get preachy with you, kid," he says. "But I've been in this business for thirty-some years, played shows with a thousand different people, and not one of 'em was as talented or as good of a man as Ricky Pierce."

My throat constricts. *He was a good man, wasn't he?*

"But," Kurt goes on, "he sure had his demons, and those get tougher to evict if you let 'em stick around. I guess what I'm saying is . . . you're a lot like your dad, kiddo, but you're smart like your mom. Keep using that brain she gave you. It'll getcha quite a bit further than your dad got to go."

We don't say much for the rest of breakfast. I feel like I've just received a prophecy, like Kurt read my palm. But this isn't woo-woo. It's genetics.

Mom returns from her run and fixes herself a bagel with a side of enough vitamins to constitute a trail mix.

"Should we make a plan for the day?" I suggest, trying not to wince at how much I sound like Renee.

Mom hums. She and Kurt exchange a quick, pinched glance. *Suspicious.* "Actually, we'd like to talk to you first."

"You're engaged."

Mom lets out a long sigh. "No, Alice."

"Oh." I'm more relieved than perhaps I should be. "Then what?"

"We have some updates about the house. This house."

My heart hits the gas. "You're selling it."

*"Alice."*

"Sorry, sorry." I sit on my hands as if they were the ones causing trouble. Mom looks to Kurt again, and Kurt takes the cue, excusing himself for a moment. He returns with a manila folder stuffed to its limits. On the white tab are the words *Outpost—Important?* My heart gives a little spasm; they're written in Dad's messy handwriting.

Kurt licks his thumb and flips open the folder. "Do you know how we got this house?" He's looking at me.

"The band bought it shortly after I was born," I recite. Dad told the story in all sorts of interviews.

"The band bought it," Kurt agrees, nodding as he thumbs through paperwork. "It was owned by that separate LLC for a number of years . . . and then *Songs for Alice* went platinum."

I flinch. *Songs for Alice* was released the year I turned two. It didn't go platinum until I hit middle school.

Kurt folds his hands. He peers at me over his glasses. "At that point, your dad bought us out of our shares."

I stare at Kurt, waiting for the next sentence. It doesn't come. "Okay?"

Kurt spins the folder and pushes it across the tables. He looks to Mom for her approval, and she nods, urging him on. "The reason he did this," Kurt says, "is because you were the only kid any of us planned to have, and if not for you, we wouldn't have this album. And that was around the time Ricky's drinking was getting real bad. We all agreed it made good sense that Ricky owned the place so if anything happened, if the band broke up or, well, y'know." Kurt's throat bobs with a swallow. "He could leave it to you."

I blink at him. At Mom. My brain feels like an overstuffed manila envelope.

"He left it . . . to me?"

My eyes take a lap toward the living room. There's dust on the fireplace, the warm butter-yellow glow of the lamplight diffused through antique shades. *My dust on my fireplace*, I think. *My lamplight through my antique shade.*

"Why didn't you tell me?"

"At first, we didn't think you were ready." Mom rests one hand on Kurt's thigh, a silent reminder of who *we* is. "Then—well, we've been trying to tell you for a while now. It's just not the type of conversation to have over text or a phone call. We wanted to make sure you got out here to see the house first before you made any decisions."

"Decisions," I parrot. "Like . . . what? Sorry, I'm just . . ."

"You're doing great, kiddo," Kurt says. "You let me know if we need to slow down, but essentially, there are two big options." He dips his chin, and his glasses slip down his nose at least an inch. "You can keep the house. Mortgage is paid off. Just taxes and maintenance on this place, which . . . it ain't free."

"Or?"

"Or we'll buy it from you." Kurt pauses, then adds, "And by *we*, I mean the band."

"You'd buy back your own house?"

"It's not our house," he reminds me. "But it's set up for us, and with all the new music we have to record, we sure could use it. And we've already gotten it appraised and can pay cash for what the place is worth."

He sorts through his papers, then passes me the documents from the appraisal. It's like peeling back the film on the last year of my life. My underwhelming inheritance, the one I assumed Dad had blown on booze, was only that small because I'm sitting inside the walls of the rest of it. I could buy a place in the city and still have plenty of money left. It's not retire-at-thirty money, but it's a rock-solid foundation to do anything I want to do.

"Of course, if you do choose to keep the house, the band would love to work out terms to use the studio, if you're willing. It could be a pretty bit of recurring income for you, if that's the route you take."

My brain whirs like an old, overheated computer. This is way more data than I'm built to process. I rest my head in my hands, a little woozy.

"I know it's a lot," Mom says. "Which is why we wanted to tell you now instead of waiting until the end of the week. That was always our plan, to tell you once we had been here a day or two, but then of course the wedding threw a big wrench in that. But we knew there'd be questions about the house once you were here again, and . . . we just didn't want to keep it from you any longer."

"Right," I say. But my voice doesn't sound like me. I'm still processing. "Yeah, that . . . that makes sense."

"And you can talk to us about it as much or as little as you want," Mom goes on. "There's not a right or wrong decision, okay? Just take your time. No rush."

The words clang in my ears—*no rush.* They feel so out of place. We'll be rushing all week to get the house in wedding shape. *One thing at a time,* I think, but when Mom and I head up to clear out Dad's closet, I can't squash the anxious flutter of a time crunch. It's hard to hold both at once, to move with drive and purpose as we sort through clothes and crates of Dad's records, to make snap decisions about what stays and what goes knowing every small choice is building up to the final boss, the biggest keep or toss at hand. What do I want with a house in Galena, so far away from anywhere and anyone I want to be close to? But if Dad left it for me, did he want me to have it? To keep it? To do something with it?

At times like this, I wish I believed in signs. Angel numbers on the clock. A cardinal landing nearby. Whatever it takes to move through the grief, I support it, but it doesn't work for me. I don't believe in it, but I understand it—that desperate search for something that will make it okay. When I'm sorting through Dad's record crates, I dip my hand into every record sleeve, hoping for a hidden note or some kind of clue from Dad that will tell me what to do with the Outpost. But there's nothing—just records and dust.

*Hey Dad,*

*Surprise! I'm a homeowner! But you knew that already. Why didn't you tell me I'd be inheriting the Outpost? A heads up would've been nice, but maybe you wanted it to be a surprise? Or maybe you planned to tell me—I dunno, some other time? But then why didn't you try to stick around to do it? I hate that I'll never really know.*

*But let me backtrack here for a second and say this: Thank you, Dad. What a gift. I'm so sorry for assuming you blew all that money on booze. I feel like an asshole for that, but I hope you can forgive me. I'm working on forgiving you, too. It's easy to feel like you gave up on living, but I'll never know what it was like to be you. Maybe someday I'll understand how it feels to decide that I've had my turn and it's time to pass the dice.*

*Until then, it's good to be back at the Outpost. I feel close to you here. I sort of wish I came back sooner, but there's no point in wishing that, is there? What's done is done. You're gone, and I'm here, and I miss you all the time. I love you, Dad. Whatever I do with this place, I'll be doing it to make us both proud.*

*Love,*
*Your Dallas Alice*

# Twenty-five

I was naive to think we could ever scrape thirty years of Ricky Pierce out of the Outpost. Mom, Kurt, and I spend two days hauling dozens of trash bags' worth of junk from the house, plus seemingly infinite trunkfuls of donations. It's exhausting work, and I spend nearly every minute of it thinking about Renee, wondering how that ride home went and if she came clean about her job after all. I've heard nothing from her—or anyone else—except in the group chat, and those texts are pure wedding logistics. Still, every time I stumble across some funny knickknack, anything of Dad's that sparks a memory, I have to resist the urge to text Renee about it. If things were smoothed out between us, I would want her here. Everything is better with Renee.

We hold on to a few small things that matter. Kurt rescues Dad's leather jacket. Mom and I each fill a box with his T-shirts and keepsakes, but even when we've cleared out all Dad's belongings, he isn't gone. Ricky Pierce has seeped into the foundation of this house. Each creaky floorboard sounds like the first chord of a song he never finished. I suppose I'm meant to finish it for him, to carry on my father's legacy, but I'm no closer to knowing what that looks like than I was two days ago. *No rush*, I remind myself.

Back before I graduated with my music degree, I asked Dad if he thought I should give it a shot—start a band, be like him. It was spring break, that one infamous night Gin, Chrissy, and I overlapped with The Handful. Dad and I sat shivering on the porch swing, and I remember the haze in his eyes as he sipped his whiskey. He told me that so long as The Handful was relevant, Ricky Pierce's kid had opportunities as a musician. But that wouldn't last forever. The band's tour and album sales had dipped, and my last name was likely a depreciating asset. *Not every door stays open*, Dad said. *You better walk through 'em while you still got the chance.*

I can still hear him now in the low whine of the porch swing as I sip my coffee, watching for my truck—*Dad's* truck—to pull up. After this weekend, Renee and I won't have the wedding in common, no organic reason to interact. I'm running out of chances to have this conversation. The door is closing, but I'm no closer to walking through it.

What I would give for a template, a friend of a friend with an excellent spreadsheet for a situation just like this. I'm beginning to understand Renee's love for a well-organized plan. It must feel nice to fool yourself into thinking you're in control.

Rishi's parents are the first to arrive, then Chrissy and Chris with a baffling number of suitcases. Mom and I help them lug it all upstairs, where we begin to negotiate the bedroom situation, but then I hear it—a faint but irritatingly familiar melody building in the distance. My eye twitches, and I stomp down and out to the porch just in time to witness my personal nightmare: My own truck crunches up the driveway, every window rolled down, blaring "You're the One That I Want" from *Grease.*

Gin seems to be the culprit. She's smiling in the driver's seat, shamelessly turning up the volume. Beside her, Rishi puts up his hands either in surrender or just to show he's not controlling the playlist. All I can see of Renee are a few golden strands of hair billowing out the back window, but just knowing she's here makes the air feel thick, harder to breathe.

Gin jogs up the steps to return my keys, and I put on my *I'm not mad, I'm just disappointed* face. "You know better than to play show tunes in the truck."

"But I'm the bride!" Gin reminds me. As if any of us could forget. She says something else, too, but I don't hear it. My attention is locked on the long tan legs draped out the side of the truck. Renee hip checks the door shut, pushes her sunglasses into her hair, then looks directly at me, her gaze unflinching. I'm not prepared; I have to steady myself against the banister. It hasn't even been that long since I've seen her, but I *missed* her.

"Alice?" Gin's voice is a playful warning. I can feel her watching me, but I can't tear my gaze from the slow swing of Renee's hips as she breaks our eye contact, rounds the truck, and lets down the tailgate. Gin jogs down the steps to help unload all manner of wedding supplies but not before casting one last baited line over her shoulder. "Don't blame me for the show tunes," she says. "Renee is the one who had to *practice*."

My thoughts zigzag. "Practice?" But I don't get an explanation, because just then, Kurt calls for me from the living room. I sigh, then turn inside, where Kurt is slouched on one of the couches, flicking a pen against a notepad.

"This should all be down there in the studio, butcha might have to do some digging." Kurt tears the perforated page from the notebook and hands it off to me. It's a list of audio equipment for the wedding.

"Would you mind . . . lending a hand?"

"Would if I could." Kurt pats his thigh through his cargo shorts. "I'm no spring chicken, kid, and all that house-clearing took it outta me. I gotta keep the stairs to a minimum." As if to prove his point, he slowly extends one leg, and his knee crunches like a bag of potato chips.

"Yuck," I say, accidentally out loud, and he laughs, then looks past me, one wiry brow arched.

"I bet she'll help ya out."

Even before he says it, I know.

"It's . . . Renee, right? Wouldja mind giving Alice a hand?"

I haven't yet been down to the studio this week, and with Renee at my heels, my nerves feel stripped raw. A single bulb lights the gray slatted basement steps that used to trip me up on drunken nights, but even stone-cold sober, I stumble on my way down. A muted red Persian rug hides all but the corners of the concrete floor. Any wall that isn't covered in spongy gray-black sound paneling boasts dozens of pedals, basses, and guitars. Dad's Gibson hangs among them, a cherry-red electric guitar with its own gravitational pull. Renee runs her fingers over the fretted neck, and I feel it in the arches of my feet.

"Wow." Her whisper ripples through me.

"Yeah. Wow is right." Hundreds of thousands of dollars of equipment wait here at our fingertips, all state of the art and hidden beneath a blanket of dust.

I walk a slow lap around the studio, switching on one lamp after another. Not a single bulb has burned out, and the resulting glow is so warm and sweet, I would sip it from a mug if I could. Every breath tastes like whiskey and amber with a heavy pour of fabric softener, an expensive cologne spritzed on a dive-bar napkin.

Renee's eyes drift throughout the room—from the deep wood of the *Songs for Alice* platinum-album plaque to the enormous mixing board below it, dappled with knickknacks and tour souvenirs. My mind latches on to one of so many futures for this place—this could be my recording studio, forever. *My* mixing board. *My* tour souvenirs. I could run it as my own studio or just lock myself away to make whatever music I want until the money runs out. But I'd be leaving behind my life in Chicago—Gin. Gentle Giant. Renee, if she's even mine to leave.

It would be lonely, but I've been lonely before.

I picture the alternative—selling the Outpost back to the band. It makes the most sense. Take the money and run. What business do I have with a five-bedroom house when I could use that money to build a studio anywhere else? But it's hard to stomach the thought of letting go of this place.

Renee turns back to me, and I'm sure she's about to say something, but the thought splinters when her eyes catch on mine. My skin hums to life, like every cell in my body is competing to be seen by her, to spend just a second pinned beneath that soft blue stare. Her lips part on a breath, but she turns away.

"What?"

"Nothing."

"Not nothing. You were going to say something."

Her eyes come back to mine, but they've steeled over again. "Nothing," Renee says. "Just tell me what to carry."

Tucked beside the laundry room, the storage closet is beyond well stocked. I'm steeped in that same golden ticket feeling I get at Gentle Giant. But this is different. This is mine. I'm Charlie Bucket with an entire chocolate factory dropped in my lap, and my biggest problem is what to do with it. I didn't ask or work for it. Not like Renee worked for her master's degree and every role on her impressively stacked résumé, and still she can't find a job. I want to tell her about the house. I want to tell her about everything, but even if we were on speaking terms, I can't imagine the guilt of flaunting my champagne problems while she's still skimming the bottom shelf. Though there is one practical question that begs to be asked, if only for Renee's sake. Even in the safety of a soundproof studio, I keep my voice low.

"Hey, Renee? Am I still keeping your job situation a secret?"

She chews her lip, eyes cast low. Silence. I turn to dig out a cable, and then—

"I told them," she says. "Gin and Chrissy. I didn't want to make up another lie as to why I'm so available to help this week."

"Oh."

"Yeah." She clears her throat. "Anyway. No need to be secretive about it. Thanks for checking."

A dampened silence spills out between us.

"Okay," I finally say, and I should leave it at that, but the next thought barges out anyway. "I'm proud of you."

More silence, and Renee still won't look at me. I can't blame her. I'm the one who ruined this thing between us. She picks up a coiled cable, and with a pointed sigh—"The things we do for the wedding, right?"

I try to smile, but it doesn't really work. I feel pliable, like a cheap wire hanger that can't take the weight of all the unknowns. *One thing at a time*, I think. One mic stand. One cable.

Kurt's equipment list was solid, but I take a few liberties. Upstairs, I walk him through my vision for the live sound setup, and surprise fades to pride in his eyes. He isn't Dad, and he's not a Grammy-winning engineer like Aidan, but Kurt's approval still means something. It's a zap of energy, one I wish I could distribute throughout the house because, damn, the group is fading fast. Chrissy and Chris are draped like matching throw blankets over the couches. At the kitchen table, Rishi's parents sleepily fold napkins like it's a punishment.

"Coffee run?" Gin suggests. The mere mention of it gets the whole house's attention, and Renee sets off collecting orders. Gin requests that I tag along. Renee will need a second set of hands to carry coffees, Gin insists, and there's no use arguing with the bride.

As I'm sliding on my sneakers, Kurt stops us by the door, holding out a thick metal credit card like a sideways cigarette. "Coffee's on the band," he grunts.

"Thanks, Kurt." I pluck the card and grin. "Chocolate croissants are on the band, too."

We're nearly halfway down the hill when Renee finally cracks the silence. "It seems like you and Kurt are on decent terms."

"Decent," I allow. Then with a sigh, "He's a good guy for my mom."

"And how are things with your mom?"

"Better. Not perfect, but better."

"Glad to hear it," Renee says, and even in the silence that follows, there's a warm, swirling reassurance, knowing she still cares.

It's a sun-soaked afternoon in downtown Galena, the whole town like a living postcard photo. Tourists mill about clutching coffees and shopping bags. A bespectacled shopkeeper in a checkered apron sweeps the sidewalk like a character in a play about a charming small town. Galena is a menagerie of darling details, and Renee's eyes leap from one to the next. Watching her see Main Street is a view of its own.

"Have you been here before?" I ask.

"Once or twice. We're only about an hour from where I grew up."

"In Iowa, right? And your parents are still there?"

Another nod, then she fixes her eyes straight ahead. It's not much, but it's nice, these tiny doses of conversation. It's better. And probably about as good as it can be right now.

Past the popcorn, fudge, and ice cream shops, the playhouse is a big brick castle of a building, much grander than it stands in my memory. Renee slips a brochure from the box on the door, a little reading material for the surprisingly long coffee shop line. Just glancing at the brochure, I'd guess that the Galena Playhouse does not employ a graphic designer. I've never seen a Canva template go so horribly wrong, but the venue photography is stunning, a showcase of a gloriously restored historic theater with steep auditorium-style seats.

"Capacity of 520," Renee reads aloud. "That seems *really* small for The Handful."

"I think that's the idea. Since it's a memorial show, I think they wanted to keep it intimate."

*Intimate. Intimate. Intimate.* I couldn't have chosen a different word?

At the counter, Renee sets the brochure down, and I pick it up, mostly as an excuse to move closer to her than I should. She either doesn't notice or doesn't mind, and I wish I knew which. If I could brush back that soft blond hair and peer into her thoughts, maybe I'd know exactly how to play this. Am I too late? Is she done with me? When I figure out what to say, will she still be around to hear it? I'm paging blindly through the rest of the brochure, sorting out my own messy head, when my eyes land on something that makes every other thought skid to a stop. The playhouse is putting up two musicals this year: *Rent* and *Grease.* It feels like a sign. I'm just not sure what of.

# Twenty-six

After a long day of manual labor, there are no words more beautiful to me than *homemade chicken biryani.* The Bhats are certainly showing off; the chicken tikka falls right off the skewers, and the saffron rice is fluffy and divine. We're ravenous, all of us gathered around the dining room table, shoveling up heaping bites at the speed of a time-lapse video.

"Hershel is the chef between us," Asha brags on her husband's behalf, although Mr. Bhat insists the opposite, giving his wife all the credit for the meal. Asha tuts and gives Gin a small, knowing smile. "You know our Bhat men. So humble."

Maybe it's the Chrissy-fication of Asha, or else all the time they spent together getting the backyard in wedding shape brought them closer together. Whatever the explanation, Gin seems fully herself around the Bhats. She swipes a napkin over her lips and asks, "Have you thought about teaching your son to cook like this?"

Mr. Bhat lifts his brows along with a forkful of biryani. "Perhaps we can arrange cooking lessons after the move."

It's a passing comment, one I might've missed if not for Mr. Bhat's reaction—it's the most expressive I've ever seen him, the face of a man who doesn't often misspeak.

Naturally, Chrissy's the one to say something. "Did you say . . . *the move*?"

The exchange that follows between Gin, Rishi, and Rishi's parents consists only of blinks and head tilts. Finally, Gin sighs and swipes open her phone.

"We were going to save it till after the wedding," she says, "but I guess it's about time we shared the news."

*The move. The news.*

My phone rumbles in my pocket, and Chrissy and Renee reach for theirs, too. Gin has texted a link to the group chat. A listing. A house.

My stomach free-falls, but Gin and Rishi are smiling, so I try to stay calm.

"We weren't really looking for a house," Gin admits, "but after all the time we spent in the northern suburbs working on the yard for the wedding . . . it started to make sense."

I hold my breath and press my thumb to the link. A redbrick ranch with deep-green shutters and a wraparound porch. I swipe through the gallery, touring the living room, the kitchen, all three beds, and two baths. It's bright and inviting, full of natural light and dark hardwood floors. The listing is marked in red: *pending*.

"It'll be closer to family—and to Rishi's work," Gin goes on. Rishi's holding her hand now, their smiles the same amount of proud. "We drove past this for sale sign so many times, so we swung by the open house just for fun. And then . . . well . . . but it wasn't just for fun after all!"

And there's that old familiar feeling. Joy and grief, all at once. I'm happy for Gin and Rishi, but I also feel like I'm halfway through a board game, and just when I'm finally starting to understand the rules, someone has flipped the board. The pieces have gone flying, and I'm frozen in fear at the thought of starting again. It's all happening so fast. This is now. This is *pending*.

After dinner, I slip out to the porch for a breath. This week has been madness, one curveball after another, and tomorrow will bring a new brand of chaos, a fresh blend of all the best and worst feelings when The Handful takes the stage without Dad. I watch the sun tuck itself beneath the horizon knowing that, the next time it rises, Dad will have been gone one full year. Will I make it to midnight? I'm barely awake now. The slow back and forth of the porch swing rocks me to the verge of sleep; then the chains jangle with the weight of someone sitting down beside me. Gin.

What she says is "Mind if I sit with you for a sec?" But her tone says *This is your wellness check*. I must not have kept the poker face I thought before slipping away.

"I'm okay. Just a lot happening at once."

"I know. That's why I came to check in."

Gin Bennett, as always, is a better friend than I could dream of being.

I hum a sigh in the back of my throat, and somewhere in the dark, a bullfrog croaks back. We laugh—a sound that plays on the soundtrack to all my best memories. So many are set here at this house. *My* house, although I'm not sure it'll stay that way. I could buy a house anyplace if I sold this one. Even . . .

"So the suburbs, huh?"

"The suburbs," Gin echoes. "Cue the minivan and the two-point-five kids. Isn't that crazy?"

"It feels crazy," I admit, "but I know it's not. It makes sense." But it still feels like the end of something I'm not ready to leave behind.

"And we don't want kids right away," Gin clarifies. "Rishi's dad is planning to retire in the next two to three years, so . . . we'll probably start trying around then."

Her words stick like pushpins into the spongy cork of my brain. *Trying. Two or three years.* There's a *plan.* It sounds so impossible—hypothetical, at best—but I remember what Gin said at the start of summer, how excited she was to be a Bhat instead of a Bennett, to start a new chapter with a new last name. A new family all her own.

"You're gonna have . . . the coolest kids," I decide, "and I am going to buy them a drum set and ruin your life."

Gin winces. "All the more reason to wait a few years."

"And then someday, they'll come here to ski over spring break, and they'll be all bummed that their cool lesbian aunt won't buy them booze."

At this, she laughs. "Aw, I want to go skiing here again." She leans back and lifts her feet, gripping her imaginary ski poles as the porch swing transforms into a chairlift. We're nineteen years old again, riding to the top of the only ski hill in Galena; then there's no stopping till we hit the bottom. One good run of a life blurring by. Even the bumps don't slow us down much.

Gin breathes out a long, nostalgic sigh. "We've had some good times here, huh?"

"Some bad ones, too," I joke. "Back when I sucked."

I wait for her laugh, but instead, it's crickets. Literally. Their scratchy chirping underscores the rattle of the wind in the catalpa trees.

"You didn't suck," Gin finally says. "Be nice to my friend Alice."

"She wasn't very nice to you."

"That's not true." Her voice is sharp, and I jolt. It's as though Gin has smacked my words right out of the air. "Sometimes you act like our whole relationship was bad. And our friendship before it. I know you don't remember very much, but . . ." Three cricket chirps, then she looks at me sideways. "It wasn't, you know. Bad."

I give a weak smile. "I'm not sure I believe that."

"Well, I *know* it," she says. "I loved having you in my life, Alice. It got hard at the end, yeah. You were mean when you were drunk, and you were drunk a lot the last couple of years, but you weren't a bad person. You were just . . . young."

"And an alcoholic." I don't use the word often, and even now my throat closes around it, trying to trap the truth. The running joke around Dunlap College was that you weren't an alcoholic until after you graduated, but it wasn't so funny once I became the punch line.

"You had some issues to work out," Gin agrees, "and I didn't really understand that back then. But you're not defined by your worst moments, Alice. None of us are. Being drunk and unreliable . . . I think a lot of people go through that on some level in their twenties."

"You didn't."

Her laugh is one long *pffft.* "That is *not* true. Remember? Chrissy told you in Palm Springs. I had quite the ho phase after we broke up."

I bite back a smile. "I wasn't sure how much you remembered from that night."

"Oh, you mean this night?" Gin tugs her bangs, and I snort a laugh. "This haircut won't let me forget." Carefully, she kicks off from the porch, setting the swing into gentle motion. When she speaks again, her voice is just as gentle. "There were bad times, Alice. But there were good times, too." Then her tone shifts, like the soft protective barrier has been stripped away. Beneath it, her voice is almost breakable. "What hurt the most was how you disappeared after we broke up."

My chest feels tender, like pressing on a bruise. Am I remembering this wrong?

"You threw me out, Gin," I remind her.

"Of the apartment." Her tone sharpens—not angry but direct. "I didn't throw you out of my life, Alice. You were my best friend before we started dating, and I needed space when we broke up, but I didn't want you gone forever. But you never reached out, and when I tried, you had already blocked me on everything. Then I heard you quit Cold Sweat, and I kept waiting to hear from you, but it really took your dad dying for you to finally call." Her voice fractures, but she threads it back together, not quite finished. "Then I read that *Rolling Stone* article and found out he'd been dying for a full two years . . . that broke my heart, Alice. I could've been there for you. I felt like such an asshole that this was happening and I didn't even know."

"No one knew," I choke out. I'm beginning to think that's the problem, the way I can only exist in extremes. I'm sober or blacked out. I say everything or nothing at all. Maybe I should have told someone about Dad's health instead of gritting my teeth and carrying it alone, but it was so much, and I didn't think anyone gave a shit. After the way I'd been, I didn't see why anyone would.

"You can talk to me about anything, you know," Gin says. "Anything, anytime."

"I know."

"Do you?" Her eyes slit, two slivers of mossy tree bark. "I feel like everyone's been keeping secrets from me this summer."

"You literally just revealed that you bought a house without telling anyone," I point out, and Gin's mouth twists to the side.

"Okay, valid. But still. The memorial concert, Renee's job . . . I mean, Kurt and your mom? Why didn't you tell me about that?"

I swallow a few too-honest versions of the truth before landing on "You've been pretty wrapped up in the wedding."

"Fair." Gin blows a sigh up into her bangs. "But you're allowed to make me listen, you know. You're allowed to tell me you need me. How else am I supposed to know? This is all so . . . *big*."

Bigger than she knows. I need time to sort through the story well enough to tell it—how I tried to surprise Mom and Kurt surprised me instead, how I wound up outside Tweedy's, where Renee saved me from myself.

"It is big," I agree. "And . . . complicated. And with the wedding and everything, I just kind of . . . I don't know, set it on the back burner. Like I could ignore it for a while and work through it on my own time without having to talk about it."

"Has anyone ever worked through something without talking about it?" Gin challenges.

I bite my cheek. She has a point. "Maybe I could've been the first?"

"I'm serious, Alice. You can talk about something without having it all figured out. That's the *point* of talking it through."

"I just never want to say too much," I admit. "Or the wrong thing."

"But what if there is no wrong thing?" Gin presses. "There's never an exact right thing to say or the perfect time to say it. And don't get me wrong. It's impressive, the way you've slowed down and . . . I don't know, installed a filter between your brain and your mouth? But you don't have to filter *everything* out. It's not all or nothing. You can just be honest and hope for the best."

Something like a tectonic plate shifts inside me. Maybe I'm reading too much into the glint in Gin's eyes, but I'm not so sure we're talking about Mom and Kurt anymore.

"I don't know. I'm just . . . bad at this kind of stuff." I look down at my feet, and Gin nudges my leg.

"You're not as bad at it as you think you are," she says. "Give yourself a little grace."

"I've already gotten more grace than I deserve."

"It wouldn't be grace if you deserved it. It's not something you earn. You just give it out to the people you love and hope you get a little bit back." Gin clears her throat, eyes bouncing away into the dark. "Like . . . when your in-laws' backyard floods and your bridesmaids have to rescue your entire wedding in a week?"

A laugh fires out of me like a shot from a cannon. It is a little ludicrous—not just the mayhem of this past week but all the wild left turns along the way. The stain on the engagement-party dress. The smell of Gin's hair as it went up in flames. The slithery wet snake pit of rain-soaked feather boas. What a gift, to have topped off all our old memories with some fresh new ones—some good, some bad, most a swirling blend of both. *Tomorrow,* I think, *will be the worst and best of all.* But that's tomorrow. Tonight, it's just Gin and me, together on the same porch swing like so many times before. Chrissy's not around to capture the moment, so I squeeze my eyes shut, snapping a mental picture I'm sure to revisit again and again, year after year. No matter where we live or how things change.

Only after the Bhats have gone to bed do we remember that the bedroom situation remains unresolved. There are five of them, and we have four couples, plus me, and of course—

"Renee and Alice, would you mind sharing a room?"

I don't know who asks, but before I can even catch my breath—

"I'll take the couch," Renee says.

*Dad,*

*'Twas the night before Gone Day, and all through the Outpost, not a creature was awake enough to finish this joke.*

*I'm not going to make it to midnight tonight. I'm fading just writing this while brushing my teeth, but I don't think I need to stay up. I don't need to prove to myself that I can face a hard day. I've done 364 hard days, and this is just one more.*

*Anyway. I'm going to bed. I just wanted to drop you a quick note to say I love you, Dad.*

*Love,*
*Your Dallas Alice*

# Twenty-seven

One year ago, I got the call.

It was a Wednesday at the end of August, the kind of night for throwing open the windows to let in the last summer breezes of the year. I was at home, curled up on the couch watching *The Princess Diaries.* It was my first time watching it in at least a decade, and I remember thinking that Mia Thermopolis was out of her mind. Who would ever second-guess inheriting the kingdom of Genovia? Who wouldn't want to be a princess, given the chance? I ignored Mom's first call, too engrossed in the movie, but then she called again. A third time, and something hard and terrible settled over me. I knew.

One year ago, Dad was finally gone.

It's a specific kind of pain to lose someone who is actively opting out of the fight to live. This was the ending we knew to expect, but that didn't make it hurt any less. You can't drink poison and be shocked when it poisons you, but that doesn't dull the pain when it does.

Now, I wake up while the sky is still a black sheet outside my window, but I can't fall back asleep. I just sit in bed and soak up the quiet, and when the birds sing up the sun, my heart wrings out like a sponge. The sun is up, and Dad is gone. That's just the way it is.

I try to picture how Dad might commemorate the occasion. Probably with a beer, or a whiskey, or both, but that's no different from how he treated every day. I guess it is just a day, and a year is just a bunch of days, but I have made it through my first one without Dad. There's only the rest of my life to go.

I get my tears out in the shower, then slip on the outfit I've had picked out for weeks: black denim shorts and a vintage heather-gray The Handful T-shirt from the *Songs for Alice* tour. I haven't worn it all year, and when I look in the mirror, there he is—Ricky Pierce, clear as day in my smile, my eyes, the way my eyebrows don't thin out on the ends. I'm so proud of the ways I take after him, but I'm even prouder of the ways we're not the same. I have his passion. I have his vices. But I can take what he gave me and do better with it than he could.

Downstairs, Mom sits on one of the matching olive couches, bent like a question mark over a book in her lap. She has every right to be a complete and utter ghost today, but when her attention lifts to me, she looks as good as—or better than—ever. Her silver hair has been smoothed into submission, and her skin is warm and rosy against a stark white cotton dress. No black for the mourning widow. Just a clean slate of a look, like a wearable fresh start.

"Morning," I greet her, intentionally leaving off the *good*. "Where is everyone?"

"Rishi's folks left to pick up his brother from the airport."

"And everyone else?"

"Stepped out." Mom turns a page in her book—it's a scrapbook,

I realize. Dangerous territory on a day like this one. I nestle beside her and rest my head on her shoulder, and she stacks her head on mine, both of us trying on a touchy-feelyness that wouldn't ordinarily suit us. So far, it's the biggest difference between today and every other day of this year.

On the pages of the scrapbook, Mom and Dad are baby-faced and smoking cigarettes outside a neon-lit venue. They're asleep in the back of a tour bus or backstage with the band, everyone pointing to Mom's pregnant belly. There are dozens of pictures of Dad onstage. Mom in the crowd. Both of them holding their new baby girl.

"You were so tiny," Mom whispers, running her finger over baby Alice's little bald head. "And you looked exactly like your father from the start. Isn't that unfair? I carried you for nine months, and you came out looking like him."

"Sorry." I lift my head to get a better look at Mom in profile: the sharp slope of her nose, the crinkle around her eyes when she smiles. Her hair is silver now, but it doesn't feel like so long ago we were matching shades of brunette. "I think we look more alike now, though," I say.

She turns to me with the start of a smile, assessing my features against her memory of her own. "I guess we do," she admits. "That feels nice."

Mom turns the page again, taking us through our first few summers at the Outpost, the years too far back for me to remember. The pictures are all I have, but they're fantastic. I'm a chubby-cheeked one-year-old wearing custom merch—a onesie that says *Little Handful.* Turn the page and I'm a toddler, tracking mud onto the carpet in my light up tennis shoes. There are a few photos of Mom deserving of a brow raise, including one where she's straddling a motorcycle, which makes me do a double take.

Mom laughs and lays a hand over mine, linking our fingers. Filling in the gaps. "God, the stories I could tell."

"Yeah?" I smile up at her. "We've got time."

In the kitchen, Kurt has put together a very disorienting Gone Day brunch: grapes, tortilla chips, and a tofu scramble with sugar-free pudding for dessert. A mismatched meal for a mismatched family. I'm loading up my plate when I hear the front door click open. Renee stands silhouetted in the doorway holding a full drink carrier from the coffee shop in town. My heart squeezes. For a moment, she looks at me, eyes soft and hesitant, but there's something else. Like I'm the finish line in the distance, but she still has miles left to run. She distributes coffees to Kurt and my mother, then to me. Just the brush of her fingertips against mine has me reeling, but one sip and I'm flooded with warmth. It's not the temperature of the coffee; it's that Renee got it exactly right. A splash of oat milk, two packets of sweetener.

"Just like your dad, minus the bourbon," she whispers, and this feeling—I can't name it, but I can track it through my memory. My first session at Gentle Giant. The first time I held a bass guitar. I'm not even sure where in my body it sits. Everywhere? I'm coated in the feeling, dipped like an ice cream cone into chocolate. I don't know what it's called, but I know what it sounds like. It sounds like *I know.*

"Thank you," I whisper, and Renee's lips part with a breath. There's some urgency to it, like she's on the verge of saying something I need to hear, but it's buried beneath the trumpet of Chrissy's voice yelling, "Where's our girl!?"

*Our girl,* it turns out, is me, and the remaining members of the I Do Crew strut in with their plus-ones. My jaw hangs open. They're wearing matching black shirts decorated with puffy paint, like high schoolers on their way to a homecoming game. My eyes bounce from one shirt to the next—Rishi's says *I HEART THE HANDFUL.* Gin's says *I AM THE HANDFUL.* Chrissy's shirt says *I'LL GIVE YOU A HANDFUL.* And Chris—yes, even Chris—is wearing a shirt that reads *RIP ALICE'S DAD.*

I laugh like I just learned how. Relentlessly. With my entire body. I pitch over with it, slapping the table like I missed the memo that today isn't supposed to be funny. Maybe that isn't true. Maybe today is supposed to be whatever we need. Tears spring to my eyes as I go down the line hugging each of my friends, plus this one waiter I kind of know. I can hardly believe this is my same life from a year ago, when Dad died and I had no one to call but my ex-girlfriend. I have *friends.* I don't know what will happen after the wedding, if a moment like this will ever happen again. Right now, it doesn't matter. Today, Dad is gone, and I am not alone.

"The shirts were Rishi's idea." Gin is googly eyed, both hands hanging tight to the arm of her soon-to-be husband. "Isn't he the best?"

"Better than the best," I say, and Rishi and I trade smiles.

"And Renee has one, too," Gin says, "but it's still drying, 'cause she insisted on doing the front *and* the back."

Renee swigs her coffee, brows bouncing once behind her cup, and my first thought is *Always doing the most.* My second is that I wouldn't want her any other way.

We spend the bulk of the day reminiscing, passing scrapbooks back and forth between the couches that just barely fit all of us, thigh to thigh. Maybe it's intentional that Renee sits beside me, or maybe it's just the luck of the draw. Either way, my concentration splits between the pictures and the few smooth inches of Renee's thigh touching mine. I'm certain my leg has a heart of its own, the way all the blood rushes there, spilling heat throughout my body on its way. Gin's voice rings clear in my memory. *You can just be honest and hope for the best.*

Every photo tweezes out a long-buried memory. The summer of the notorious prank war, then the following summer of peace as a *result* of the prank war that we swore never to speak of again. In fifth grade, when I insisted upon a talent show and the band made up a dance to ABBA's "Gimme! Gimme! Gimme!" I still don't have a clue where four grown men found tutus on such short notice. Growing up at the Outpost was like being raised at the kids' table, but all the kids were adults, making records and memories, and Mom carefully scrapbooked every summer but one. The summer I spent at band camp. There's no evidence on the page of the failed intervention. Mom only documented the good times, but we can't erase the rest, so she still tells the story, even though her voice shakes. The mistakes and the missteps, the trying and failing, are all a part of what got us here.

Somewhere between revisiting my middle and high school years, Renee presses her leg a little harder into mine. When I turn, our noses are just inches apart, so close that I have to squash an impulse that scratches in my chest.

"Do you remember how you said I have a theater face?" Renee murmurs.

It takes a second for my brain to make the multiple leaps to catch up with hers, but I do remember. I picture her dancing in my living room and prattling on about *Grease.* The look on her face was the same then as after the park district show, when she kissed my temple and I floated the whole way home. I could live a hundred lives and never forget that look. *Glowy. Confident. Like the world is made out of hope.*

"I remember."

"Good." Renee nudges my leg a little harder, and the goose bumps fly. "Because I think you have an Outpost face."

The implication shakes every branch of my nerves, but as she often is, Renee might be right. This place is written in my DNA. It's what music has always been about for me—creating something honest with the people I care about. My heart soars toward an idea, a future I could build for the Outpost that's not so different from its past. If I only get one life, I don't want to spend it working with the Solas Callaghans of the world, regardless of what Aidan thinks it could do for my career. It's *my* career, and I admire Aidan, but I want to build something that matters to *me.*

It's a liquid-gold feeling, but it shrinks away at the sound of Chrissy's cackle, then disappears entirely when she plunks one manicured finger on a scrapbook page, pointing to something I can't see. "That," she says, "that right there is Classic Alice."

Shame spills through me as Chrissy passes the scrapbook. Gin laughs, and so does Rishi, and I'm almost too afraid to look. I brace for the worst, but when the scrapbook lands in my lap, my mind erases like a whiteboard, leaving only one giant question mark behind.

I haven't seen this picture in years, but it's one of my favorites: I'm thirteen years old, tucked behind my upright bass at my last middle school orchestra concert. I'm wearing the same pressed red polo and black dress pants as everyone else, but my slacks are tucked into a pair of glittery teal cowgirl boots. It is, I would argue, Classic Alice, but not the way Chrissy has used it in the past, so I have to ask.

"What . . . what do you mean by that, Chrissy? When you say something is . . . Classic Alice?" The words turn to ash on my tongue, but Chrissy doesn't hesitate.

"Oh! You just do your own thing, y'know? You're a rule breaker. A rock star. I mean, I know you're not a *rock star* rock star anymore, but it's still in you, ya know?" With a wink, she adds, "Maybe it's genetic."

My brain stalls. My breath freezes. I feel like I've been staring at an optical illusion for an entire summer and have only now been told this rabbit is actually a duck. I turn to Gin, waiting for her to disagree. Instead, a smile creases the corners of her lips, and something unfolds inside me. A map smoothed flat. An answer key to my own secret code. All this time I assumed Classic Alice and Blackout Alice were the same, but I was wrong, and maybe Gin was right. I'm not defined by my worst moments. None of us are. When I pass the scrapbook to Renee, my eyes skate across the tattoo on her wrist. The moon is meant to change, and so are we.

For dinner, we polish off what's left of yesterday's biryani, then it's off to the concert, a swarm of us descending from the house on the hill. Renee, I realize, has changed into her puffy-paint T-shirt, and I jog ahead to see what it says. When I'm close enough to read it, I stumble. My heart just might roll down the hill without me and leave me in the dust, because Renee has covered her shirt, front and back, in her favorite lyrics off *Songs for Alice.*

*I know. I know. I know.*

Mom and I peel off to join the band backstage in a greenroom a fraction of the size they're used to. We all suffer through shots of zero-proof whiskey in Dad's honor, then Nathan—the rhythm guitarist—is the first to pull me in for a hug. "We miss him like hell, kid." He thumps me on the back. "And we've missed you, too."

My heart is a guitar string wound too tight, and my voice comes out accordingly taut and high pitched. "I know" is all I manage to squeak out before I'm biting back tears. Karl, the bass player, squeezes my shoulder before roughing my hair. Kurt folds me into a hug. And last but not least, the new lead singer steps up to shake my hand.

Julie must be ten or twenty years younger than the rest of the band. Her denim coveralls stack over a pair of turquoise cowboy boots, and beneath a vintage The Handful trucker hat, her shaggy brown hair is cut a lot like mine.

"It's an honor to meet you," Julie says brightly. "Your dad was a legend."

"I know," I tell her. "He always will be."

Mom hangs back with Kurt and the rest of the band, but I'm ready to find my place in the crowd. The theater is packed beyond capacity—even the overflow seating spills over, averaging two people to each metal folding chair. Eight or nine rows up, I spot the neon puffy paint on Rishi's black T-shirt—he waves his arms overhead, and I take the steps two at a time. They've saved a seat for me next to Gin, and when I arrive, Chrissy cheers loud enough to momentarily confuse the audience into thinking the show has started.

"Sorry! False alarm!" Chrissy alerts anyone within earshot—which, for her, may well be the entire county. Not a split second later, she's yelling again. "Oh my God, Renee, would you get off your damn phone?" She swings her handbag into Renee's gut.

"Sorry, sorry," Renee grumbles, eyes still locked on her screen. "Work stuff."

"But you don't have a job!" Chrissy whines. "Wait, sorry, is that okay to say?"

"Yes, Chrissy. That's true. It's fine." Renee drops her phone into her purse, but before the screen dips to black, I swear I see a flash of a familiar picture. I reach for my own phone and confirm it. The Galena Playhouse website, the same photos from the brochure. My mind whirs like a coffee grinder. It could be nothing. Or it could be *work stuff.* My thoughts criss and cross, but I set the tangled knot aside when the house lights fade and this little theater puts on its stadium voice.

The band takes the stage with humble waves, and it's all so familiar—I'm every age at once. And then Julie struts out, and it could only be now.

"We're The Handful," she growls, "and we're gonna play loud enough that Ricky Pierce hears every note."

What follows is nothing shy of a baptism. Songs I've heard a thousand times sound brand new with Julie's vocals, but the words still fall off my lips like they've been waiting there all year. Julie doesn't try to sound like Dad; her warm, round tone is nothing like Dad's gritty, broken tenor, but it *works.* At least once every song, she holds the mic out to the crowd and lets us take the vocals. It feels less like Dad has been replaced and more like we're all stepping into the space he left behind.

When The Handful kicks off the title track from *Songs for Alice,* I'm soaring, ascending to the rafters while my feet stay firmly planted on the ground. The chorus comes around, and even a few seats away, I can hear Renee singing along, her voice cutting through the noise like a comet through the sky. She catches me watching, but I surprise myself. I don't look away, and neither does she. The rest of the crowd falls away, and for those last few bars, there's only us, and Renee is singing just to me. I let myself feel it—this golden moment I'll never be able to replicate. This woman I am absolutely certain about. *I know. I know. I know.* I may not know if it's possible, this thing with us. I don't know if she feels the same, but the way she looks at me, I don't feel like I'm holding on to hope; it feels like hope is holding on to me.

*Dad,*

*Well, it's 12:01 a.m., meaning I have officially made it through the first anniversary of your Gone Day. I've survived one full year of firsts without you, and I'm still here, and you're still gone.*

*Did you catch tonight's concert from wherever you are? The band sounded great, and Julie is a showstopper. It's funny how things can be exactly the same in a brand-new way.*

*That's how I feel about the Outpost, too. I love it here, Dad. It's the same as it's always been, but I'm starting to see what it might become next. Renee says I make the same face talking about this place as she does when she talks about theater, and I . . . well, I think she's right. I don't think I can sell it back to the band. I'd be ignoring my own advice—if I'm passionate about this place, it'd be a waste to walk away.*

*But it'd be a waste to walk away from the person I'm passionate about, too. I feel more certain about Renee than I feel about much of anything right now, but I'm not sure that she feels the same, even if she did before. I wouldn't blame her if she didn't want to get involved, but I would blame myself if I never gave it a shot.*

*So you're the first one I'm telling, Dad. I'm keeping the house, and tomorrow, I will talk to Renee. Hold me to both of those, would you?*

*Love,*
*Your Dallas Alice*

# Twenty-eight

It's jarring to jump from Gone Day back to wedding mode, but that's how it is these days: a sequence of heartbreaks and celebrations, strung together like beads on a friendship bracelet. It's always *and*, never *or*. Grief *and* joy. Light *and* dark. Multitudes, all playing out at once. Somehow, I move through it, and this morning, I'm moving *fast*. We all are; the house is buzzing, a hive of worker bees flitting about like they'll fall asleep on their feet if they dare slow down.

If it's possible to iron tablecloths *intensely*, that's what Mom's up to in the living room. At the kitchen table, Chris and Chrissy have a system for stuffing welcome bags, and while it's not one that makes any sense to me, the job is getting done. Out front, Rishi and his brother wave in a giant beeping truck of wedding rentals. But no Renee. I swear my heart has arms, the way it reaches for evidence of her. There's only the bed pillows stacked beside a neatly folded Pendleton blanket on the couch where she must have slept.

"Have you seen Renee?" I ask anyone within earshot. Mom shakes her head. Chrissy and Chris are just as unhelpful. In the kitchen, still no Renee, but the fridge is freshly stocked, replete with caffeine options: cans of nitro cold brew, Diet Coke, and the same energy drinks Aidan likes. I can smell it—that inedible combination of peaches and batteries, wafting from behind me. Gin hovers by the window, her short red hair slicked back with sweat into the tiniest nub of a ponytail. There's an energy drink in her hand.

"Since when do you drink those?"

"Since somebody left a case of them in the teacher's lounge last year." Gin's face twists into a shameful wince. "I know, I know. It's bad."

"There are worse vices."

"No, Alice. I mean it's *bad*." Gin smacks her tongue against the roof of her mouth. "These things taste like cat pee. But the *energy*." Her pupils dilate. "I feel like I could fight God."

I laugh as I snap open a can of cold brew and join her at the window, scanning the backyard for signs of Renee. There's only Rishi's parents, assembling a four-posted arbor of sorts.

"That's the mandap." Gin lifts her chin to the half-assembled structure. "It's the altar, essentially. It'll get draped in tulle."

"Do we have tulle?"

"Renee is picking it up right now."

My head jerks toward her. I'm like a dog who just heard the word *treat*. "Do you know when she'll be back?" I ask. A little too eagerly, it seems, because Gin sputters a laugh.

"So are you going to tell me what's happening there or what?"

"What's happening . . . where, exactly?"

"Between you and *Renee*." She traces a heart in the air. "I should have known I'd have to drag it out of you."

Something inside me stops and starts at least twice. "So you know about that."

"Of course I know about that," she says flippantly. "I *did* that."

"I . . . you what?"

Gin's smile is somehow both regal and villainous. An evil pageant queen, claiming her crown. "You two think you're so slick, keeping all sorts of secrets, like I haven't been trying to set you up all summer."

Whatever gears have to turn to keep my brain functioning grind to a screeching halt.

"I really thought you'd figure it out in Palm Springs," Gin goes on. "You know, when I wanted to room with Chrissy?" She drains what's left of her energy drink, winces, and adds, "You *know* that girl snores even louder than she laughs."

For a moment, all I can do is stare at her. Then my mind rewinds. The hotel room. The request that Renee and I really *try* to get along. Her excitement that we *were*. "I . . . you . . . but . . . the room . . ." I'm trying to form a thought, but I've been reduced to slinging single syllables.

"Just admit it." Gin lifts her chin in pride. "I'm a genius."

"An *evil* genius," I amend, and she claws her hands, tips her head back, and does her very best supervillain cackle. There's no one here to witness, but I'm still secondhand embarrassed.

"I sometimes forget you used to do theater," I grumble, accidentally out loud.

"I'm pretty sure that's a compliment, coming from you. Although . . ." Gin pokes my bicep and smiles smugly. "Word on the street is that a certain someone can really nail the harmonies on the *Rent* soundtrack."

My entire body flushes, and a long line of questions marches to the tip of my tongue. *Renee told you about that? What else did she tell you? Do you know how she feels about me? About us?* I don't get to ask a single one because here comes Kurt with a fist full of cables, requesting my help with setting up sound. Time is ticking down, and ready or not, there's a wedding tomorrow. I refuse to let "or not" be an option.

For the rest of the day, Renee and I are like planets, orbiting each other but never colliding. She returns with the tulle just as I'm leaving to pick up an extra extension cord. Then I'm back, and it's time to test the ceremony mics, but Renee is suddenly needed inside. It's amazing, really, the way we were stuck together all the times we didn't want to be, but now that I'm desperate to get her alone, we're parallel lines, our paths never crossing. Not even at the rehearsal dinner downtown, where we're seated on opposite ends of an extra-long table. I hardly have an appetite. The only thing I want is to talk to Renee.

Back at the Outpost, we break out the mehndi kits, and Asha paints swirling florals and detailed mandalas on the bridesmaids' hands in henna. It's hard to sit still and even harder not to scratch my itchy hands while the henna dries, but it's nothing compared to the itch I can't scratch. The conversation I need to have, if only I could get Renee alone. Every time her blue eyes flash to mine from across the living room, I hear that same, steady cadence. *I know, I know, I know.*

The right time never presents itself. It hardly ever does. Once the house has all gone to bed, I slip back downstairs, where Renee lounges in the golden lamplight, cozied beneath the Pendleton blanket. She's wearing her neon-pink bachelorette party T-shirt, and for a moment, I worry she may be asleep, but then her eyes lift to mine, tired and blue.

Our gazes hold in one long silent question, but when a twitch of a smile tugs at her mouth, all the worry and nerves melt away.

What was I so scared of? I have been honest with Renee all summer. I can be honest with her now.

"Can we talk?" I finally ask out loud.

Renee looks at me—*really* looks at me—before she nods, just barely, then shifts to a seat, clearing space for me beside her on the couch. She lays the blanket over both our laps, our own little woven cocoon. Finally, it's just us, and I don't want to overthink this. So I start where it makes sense. With the person who brought us together in the first place.

"So I talked to Gin."

"Did you?"

"And it seems like you . . . talked to her too? About . . . us?"

Renee stares at her hands. She twists the thin gold band on her middle finger back and forth. Left, then right. Every second of silence between us carries its own electric charge.

"I did," she finally admits. Her throat bobs with a swallow, and her voice is steadier when she speaks again. "I'm sorry if I shouldn't have said anything. I just needed a gut check with people who have known you longer than I have."

"People? Plural?"

"Chrissy, too."

I want to comment on how impressive it is that Chrissy's kept her mouth shut about that, but I'm keeping mine shut too, waiting for Renee finish her thought.

"We talked about it on that drive home when I told them about losing my job," she goes on. "And . . . well, *this*." She draws a line in the air, connecting her heart to mine. "According to Gin, *this* was all *her* doing."

I bite down on a smile. "Yeah. She told me that, too."

We both roll our eyes.

"Pretty funny, huh?" Renee says.

"I think it's funny she thought we'd be good together, honestly."

At this, Renee flinches, but she doesn't disagree. Even before we met, we knew we were opposites, destined to butt heads. "We don't have much in common," she admits. "And yet . . . here we are."

*And there's nowhere else I'd rather be.*

It's quiet for a moment while I search for what to say next, then Renee draws in a shaky breath, and I think she's about to say something. She doesn't. Instead, she lays a hand over my knee. Heat, instantly, down my neck and the arches of my feet, and it's instinctual, the way I tangle my fingers into hers. The right thing to *say* may evade me, but this—holding Renee's hand—feels like the right thing to *do*. I've missed her touch, and every second that she doesn't let go feels like the new best second of my life.

*I know. I know. I know.*

What I *don't* know is what I'm going to say, but I start to say it anyway, reading whatever script my heart offers up.

"I'm so sorry, Renee. I'm sorry I panicked."

That's as far as I get before my tongue turns to sandpaper. I swallow hard and start again.

"I care about you. A lot. And I've been so afraid of saying the wrong thing and fucking this up. Because that's what I do, you know? Or . . . it's what I've done. So I'm trying to just say whatever I'm feeling right now, and I'm sorry if it's messy. You're my best friend, Renee. Maybe that sounds stupid because we've only—"

"It's not stupid," she interrupts.

"But I'm not like you," I cut back in. "I'm not everybody's bridesmaid, and the last time I got romantically involved with a friend, that was Gin. And we all know how that went. I'm only now getting my friends back, and I can't do that again." Tears needle behind my eyes, but I bite them back. "I didn't shut you out on purpose. I just thought I might've fucked things up again."

"You didn't." Renee's broken whisper coils through me like smoke. "That morning . . . I didn't get it. I was angry. I know it's been a really horrible few years for you, but I wasn't thinking about that. I just woke up and saw this person I . . ." Her eyes glisten as she swallows a word and starts again. "I care about you, Alice. But you shut me out in this really vulnerable moment. I was hurt."

"Of course you were." I squeeze her hand a little tighter. "I'm sorry I hurt you. I just didn't know how to talk about this, and I didn't want to lose you." I hear my voice begin to crumble. "No matter what, Renee, I just don't want to lose you."

"I don't want to lose you, either, Alice," she says. "I want this. I want us."

She sounds so certain, and for one shimmering moment, it's perfect.

And then Renee sighs and says, "But."

That one little word, and my hope disintegrates. I feel like I'm shrinking, shriveling inside myself. *I should have known. I should have known. I should have known.* I loosen my grip on her hand to pull away, but she holds tight. Doesn't let go.

"I have to be honest with you," Renee says. "I don't think it's fair to have this conversation without telling you that I'm leaving Chicago."

I feel my entire body go slack.

"It's probably not a forever thing," Renee cuts back in. "But since I haven't found a job, I'm moving back in with my parents for a while. I'll be in Iowa, about an hour from here, and I'll save a little money, figure out what's next, and . . ." Her gaze lifts to mine, and despite the sadness in her voice, her eyes sparkle when she says, "I'm going to focus on auditions for a while."

"You're . . . are you serious?"

She nods, and I shift beneath the blanket, one leg bent while the other hangs off the couch. Renee does the same, and we're inches apart. A bright, burning feeling lights up inside me, an emotion too big to be contained. It's like my heart can't choose between leaping out of my mouth or slamming right through my chest, so it's trying to do both. The slightest bit of sadness hangs on to Renee's eyes, but there's hope there, too, as she does what she does best. She begins to verbalize a plan.

"I know it's not ideal, and I completely understand if you don't want to do the distance thing and you just want to be friends. I can handle that, if that's what you need. Or if you just want to take things as they come and see where we—"

I close the space between us, a thousand things I could say flashing through my mind, but none of them feel as right as when I kiss her. I'm still kissing her as she starts to rumble with laughter.

I only pull back to say "I'm so proud of you."

Renee takes my cheeks in her hands and pulls me close again, her mouth opening to mine. She tastes like wintergreen, and when my tongue dips between her lips, the softest moan catches in her throat. It's dizzying. My mind spins away to the life I'm already imagining with her. Just us. I picture her pink nosed on the ski hill in the winter, raking red-and-gold piles of leaves in the fall. When I look ahead, she's there, in every version of my future.

And it destroys me to break our kiss again, but I have to tell her.

"Guess what?" I whisper. "I'm leaving Chicago, too."

Renee's hands drop from my face, but I catch them, twining her fingers with mine.

"It's okay. It's good. I'm moving here. This is *my* house." It feels as true and right as my own name. It's the best I've felt all summer. All year.

I tell Renee everything, legal jargon and all. I tell her about my vision for this place, and her smile widens with every detail, most of all the part about how I'll be just an hour away. That is, if she doesn't want to move in here with me instead.

"I don't mean to interfere with your plans to live with your parents, but—"

Her mouth drops onto mine mid-thought, and whatever I meant to say dissolves into sweet, staticky bliss. We kiss until our lips are tender and swollen, testing how much of each other we can taste and touch without making a sound. People are sleeping upstairs. There's a wedding tomorrow. But the only thought rattling inside my head is her name, over and over, again and again. *Renee Renee Renee.* It's all I want, maybe for the rest of my life.

*Dad,*

*I don't want to get ahead of myself, but I think I met my wife.*

*Love,*
*Your Dallas Alice*

# Twenty-nine

I have decided to believe in miracles. It's the only way to make sense of a day like today. After a frantic, panicked week spent shifting an entire wedding 150 miles west, Saturday arrives with a blue sky, a gentle breeze, and not a single percent chance of rain. Last week, we thought we'd be washed away in the flood; today, all we're missing is the rainbow.

In all the commotion of getting ready, I don't see the backyard in its final form until I'm floating down the aisle to Pachelbel's Canon. Sunlight refracts through the pale-green tulle softening the corners of the mandap. Lush green garlands frame the top like a halo hovering over the lawn. Beneath it, Rishi looks cool and collected until the moment Gin steps into view. She's a flame lighting the aisle—her auburn hair almost glows in the sun beneath her sheer red veil, perfectly matched to the same cherry-colored bridal lehenga Asha wore on her wedding day. Thirty years haven't dulled its shine in the slightest. The gold details on the full skirt match the copper swirls of henna vining up Gin's hands and forearms, although her mehndi barely shows beneath the bouquet of ferns and dahlias in her grip. She walks alone. No parents or stand-ins to usher her down the aisle. Just Gin, stepping boldly into the life and the family she is creating for herself. It feels a little like crossing a finish line when they're pronounced man and wife, but it's only their beginning.

After the ceremony, we take endless pictures—one round in our traditional North Indian attire before we change into our Western looks and go again. I'm the first out of my sari and ready in my bridesmaid dress, and given the frustrated grumbles coming from Gin's room, I suspect she needs a hand.

"Knock knock?" I nudge the door open an inch. "Need some help?"

Gin tugs the door open the rest of the way. Sweat beads on the tip of her nose, and her eyeliner has smudged a teeny bit at the corners, but she still looks like she's wearing a filter in real life.

It takes some finessing to free the vintage zippers on the lehenga, but her wedding dress zips up like a dream. Gin is a vision. The long, sparkly straps hold up the weight of a full, flowy skirt, and the detailing on the bodice looks remarkably similar to the gold patterns on the lehenga, a cohesion that feels meant to be.

Gin twirls like a ballerina in a music box, her dress billowing around her ankles like the edges of a wave. In my mind's eye, every version of her twirls right beside her. She's eighteen, with all her summer freckles, in the freshman dorms. There she is, twenty-one and pale as a Midwest March, shutting down the karaoke bars with "You Oughta Know." She's dressed in black in the back of Dad's funeral or all in white beneath the neon lights of a Palm Springs bar. What a privilege to have known and loved so many iterations of Virginia Bennett, exactly the same but entirely different.

"All right, bitches!" Chrissy kicks open the door. She hoists high her makeup bag in one hand and a fifth of tequila in the other. "Who needs a touch-up, and who needs a shot?"

Just behind her, Renee steps into view, and the head rush is a higher proof than I've ever known. She is all contrast. A thin gold chain rests over her collarbone, with silver hoops climbing the cartilage of her ears. Bright fuchsia fabric flows over one of her shoulders beneath hair so blond it's almost white. Her expression is sharp and serious, then full of wide-eyed wonder when her eyes find mine. Renee bites down on an impossibly adorable smile, and the breath leaves my lungs.

"You're stunning," I tell her.

"Not as stunning as you."

Chrissy rolls not just her eyes but her entire head. "*Finally.* I was so over you guys pretending *that* wasn't happening."

"I'll drink to that," Gin says, then takes a swig of tequila straight from the bottle, but perhaps not as large of a pull as she might have taken at the start of the summer. "I'm cutting back." She twists the cap back on. "You know. Since I've been *burned* before."

When Gin laughs, it's permission for us all to laugh along.

"All right!" The bride claps her hands once. "Are we ready? Just one more round of pictures, then it's dinner, drinks, and *speeches*!" She flashes me a smile, and I smile back like there isn't an avalanche happening inside me, everything crumbling down to pure, jagged panic.

*The speech. How the hell did I forget about the speech?*

I'm in my head for the rest of photos and cocktail hour, cutting and splicing scraps of speeches I drafted this summer, but none of them feel right. I'm still scrambling when we're directed to our tables, and Rishi's brother kicks things off with a best man speech cataloging their most memorable trips to Taco Bell. Brilliant. Hilarious. Absolutely impossible to follow, and considering how things went the last time I took the mic around Gin and her friends, running away sounds like a viable option. Still, when I'm announced as up next, I step up and take the mic, holding on with both hands for dear life.

"Hi, I'm Alice." *So far so good.* "If you don't know me, maybe you know my house!"

I fling an arm toward the Outpost, and soft laughter hums through the crowd.

"Thank you so much for making the trip out to Galena. We decided it was a better option than putting the bride and groom in scuba gear."

This time, a rumble of laughter. I straighten, relaxing my white-knuckle grip.

"This house has been important to my family for a long time, and it's been important to my friends, too. Gin and I met in college, and we came here every year for spring break. We lived in the same building our freshman year and went on to share an apartment, and . . . I guess this is where people might say *We've been inseparable ever since,* but that's not true. Gin and I didn't speak for a number of years, and it was my fault." I look right at Gin; she's smiling at me, steady. "But we found each other again.

"Anyway. I wrote so many versions of this speech this summer, but none of them felt good enough. Because . . . it's Gin. She deserves the best of everything, and I'm notoriously pretty bad with words. And I . . . I really shouldn't say this, but with the chaos of essentially replanning this wedding in seven days, I never did finish a final draft of this speech. I was doing *this.*" I gesture left, right, all around. "And I forgot. I'm sorry."

Despite my confession, Gin's smile hasn't budged an inch.

"I'm not proud of that," I admit. "I can be forgetful, and I say the wrong thing sometimes. Gin knows that. She knows me better than . . . almost anyone. Recently, Gin said something that really stuck with me. She said there's usually no one right thing to say, and sometimes, the best thing to do is just be honest. So let me be honest and say that this past week has been . . . really hard. Moving the wedding out here was a lot of work—plus I lost my dad last year, and the anniversary was just two days ago. So I . . . oh God, I'm making this about me, sorry."

"You're fine!" Gin shouts through cupped hands. "Keep going!"

"What I mean to say is that Gin has never been afraid of doing hard things. She shows up for people when they need it and loves them exactly how they are. I bet a lot of us have benefitted from Gin going the extra mile once or twice."

The crowd nods like a life-size bobblehead collection.

"So you get it then, right? You understand why I wanted to give the best possible speech today? I wanted to say the exact right thing to explain how I feel, and I was so in my head and terrified of screwing it up . . ."

A lump the size of a clementine forms in my throat. I chance a look at Renee—her eyes are like blue silk, almost liquid in the sunlight, and when her lips lift, it's undeniable. That's *the look.* It's how Gin looks at Rishi. How Kurt looks at Mom. It's how I want to look at Renee for the rest of time, as long as she'll let me.

"It's hard." I clear my throat. "To be honest sometimes, but the things most worth doing usually aren't the easiest. They take a lot of work. A little planning. A little improvising. Like this wedding. Like . . . love." I lift my water glass high. "So cheers to love, even when it's hard. And to Gin and Rishi, who make it look easy."

A tide of champagne flutes rises, and I find Gin's glassy, golden-green eyes again. She mouths a single word: *Perfect.*

It really is perfect. Every detail. I can barely believe this wasn't the plan all along. We spin beneath strands of fairy lights to a playlist perfectly curated by our bride—Pitbull songs that turn Chrissy into a human pogo stick and Indian pop hits that pull Rishi's parents onto the dance floor. The song from *Dirty Dancing* plays, and Chris demonstrates that he can do the signature lift. Not with Chrissy, though—with Rishi's brother, who soars like an angel in the steady arms of a man once known only as Waiter Boy.

Gin doesn't touch her Palm Springs level of drunk, but when she's tipsy enough to put on "Defying Gravity," I rip a sheet of green tulle from the mandap and tie it around her neck like a cape.

"Classic Alice!" Chrissy shouts over the music, and my cheeks will ache from smiling until Gin and Rishi's first anniversary.

The bride's lips get looser with every song and every seltzer; we're nearing the end of the night when she corners me by the cooler of water bottles, a look of fierce determination in her eyes.

"Hello? Why aren't you making out with Renee yet?"

I cough out a laugh, but Gin doesn't look like she's kidding.

"I . . . here? In the middle of . . ." I gesture broadly. "It's your wedding, Gin."

"It sure is." Her eyes glint with mischief. "And you wouldn't want to let down the bride."

Whether it's the order of Gin's playlist or just an act of fate, the final chorus of "Pink Pony Club" fades into the bright, open twang of a guitar. My heart forms a fist around the melody I know so well, the one that's existed in me since the day I was born.

"Willin'" by Little Feat.

I step cautiously into the firefly darkness, scanning the yard for Renee, and when our eyes lock, the divot between her brows smooths, and I'm certain she was searching for me, too. I think I've been searching for her all my life.

Slow, certain strides bring us together beneath the glow of twinkle lights. Renee's full lips tick up; then her brow lifts. A question. An offer. I accept.

As the first verse comes in, Renee guides me close to her by the small of my back. Through the fabric of our matching dresses, my hips brush the tops of her thighs. I rest my chin in the curve of her neck, breathing her in. Cotton and eucalyptus and . . . something else. Is that . . . cherry blossom?

I pull back just an inch. "Are you wearing . . . ?"

"It's Chrissy's perfume." She doesn't roll her eyes so much as bounce them off the stars. "It's called—"

"Love Spell," we say in perfect unison, and Renee's nose scrunches when she laughs. If it were possible to tattoo a sound on my body, I'd cover every inch of my skin with that laugh. The sound of knowing and being known. Our gazes hold until the joy in my chest feels so enormous it might burst through and fill the entire sky. I could stay in her eyes forever, but when she lifts my chin and seals her soft mouth to mine, forever doesn't feel like long enough. My heart is on fire. My hands are in her hair. If anyone is watching, they'll know what I know: I am in love with Renee Roberts.

# Epilogue

*Three years later*

We decided to stick to calling it the Outpost. No other name really stuck. We tried on "the Artist's Loft" and briefly "Ricky's Place," but we kept slipping up and defaulting to the original name. The gingerbread-colored house on the hill lives on as what it has always been: a place to gather and create. Not just music, although that's certainly at the forefront. We host touring acts passing through on their way to or from Chicago, plus sober songwriting retreats every fall. Mostly, we're a full-service recording studio with sliding-scale rates and scholarships available for sober acts. Dad gave me the privilege of chasing a dream, a gift I'm passing along in fractions eleven months a year, all except August. That month is reserved for the band that started it all.

This really is Ricky's place, regardless of the name. He's in the creak of the floorboards, the whine of the back door, the jangle of the porch-swing chains. All the ordinary music of this place reminds me that he's still here. That I'm never alone.

And I rarely am anyway. I hardly leave Renee's side. My best friend. The love of my life. The only woman for whom I would willingly attend all twelve performances of a production of *Grease.* She is, by far, the hottest of the Pink Ladies. And the cutest. And the smartest. She is the best person I have ever known.

But I haven't been honest with her. Not about everything. Next month, when Gin turns thirty-two, Renee thinks we'll be singing a track off *Songs for Alice* at her karaoke costume party. And we will, that's true—but that's only the start of my plan. I can't control how it plays out, but I can create the environment that allows the moment to happen. I'll hang the twinkle lights. I'll dress as Danny Zuko. I'll somehow cram a ring box into the pocket of my leather pants. When the song ends, the next one will begin: that damn duet from *Rent.* I, Alice Pierce, will publicly perform a show tune, loud and proud, taking all the harmonies. It might be embarrassing, but not nearly as much as not going after what you love.

When I drop to one knee, I'm praying she'll know exactly what to say.

# Acknowledgments

Writing *For the Bride* was a transformative process that broke me and built me up again. Everyone who helped shape this book deserves much more than a mention in the acknowledgments, but it's certainly a place to start, so let's begin, shall we?

Infinite thanks to the entire team at Viking Penguin. Specifically, thank you to Colin Weber and Katie Smith for another gorgeous cover; to Alicia Lea, Nicole Celli, Marinda Valenti, and Chelsea Cohen for catching my mistakes; and to Chantal Canales, Ivy Cheng, and Paige Touse for getting this book out into the world.

To my editor, Nidhi Pugalia, you were this book's maid of honor. Thank you for your clarity, your encouragement, your patience, and your trust in me. If I found a genie, I'd use all three wishes to work with you again.

Thanks also to Dana Murphy, without whom my life would be entirely different and wholly worse. I am the luckiest girl in the world.

The work of this book was the work of facing my own demons, mental health battles, and grief. Thank you to my therapist and psychiatrist for seeing me through the challenging assignment of being alive. Thanks also to those who have trusted me with the stories of their grief. Mandy Allender, who is the genius behind "Gone Day." Rory Kai's mom is a true ray of light. Sarah Proctor, I love you so much, and I know Diane would've loved this book. And Laura, I wish I could've met Mary. I would have told her that her daughter is a remarkable writer, but an even better person.

Thank you to Joe Shadid, Nathan Graham, and Aidan Gavura for allowing me to mine your knowledge of the music and recording industry. Thanks to Meaghan and Hershel for throwing a wedding so incredible that Team India became a part of this book. Sonia, your parents are so cool. Thanks also to Chrissie Capobianco for simply existing. I had no choice but to put you in a book. And, of course, thank you to Danny, Logan, B, and Luxianna for sitting with me through the final stages of this book. Special thanks to Danny and Logan's couch, where so much of the revision magic happened.

To every bookseller and reader who sang the praises of *I'll Get Back to You*, you have my entire heart and all my gratitude. It seems like we ought to throw a parade in honor of all the independent bookstores that stock queer books like mine. A second parade will be thrown for my parents, followed by an enormous fireworks show for John, who is the entire point of my life.

Finally, thank you to my bridesmaids and to every bride I've had the honor of standing beside on their wedding day, except for the one with the homophobic husband. I'd like to dedicate the gay sex in this book to him.

## ALSO AVAILABLE

# I'll Get Back to You

## A Novel

Murphy is stuck in a hellish suburban holding pattern—until she meets Ellie, a former classmate who's way cuter and not *nearly* as straight as Murphy remembers. She's *also* stuck—but if they plot together, they might both get the freedom they want. Full of humor and heart, this is a giddy love letter to anyone in need of a bit of bravery to step up to the plate.